ULTIMATE ISSUE

D0767256

Also by George Markstein and available from New English Library

TRAITOR FOR A CAUSE

George Markstein

ULTIMATE ISSUE

NEW ENGLISH LIBRARY

For Jacqui because she first sounded the alert
and then kept it going.

First published in Great Britain in 1981 by New English Library

First NEL Paperback Edition 1982

NEL Books are published by
New English Library,
Barnard's Inn, Holborn,
London EC1N 2JR, a division of Hodder and Stoughton Ltd.

Printed and bound in Great Britain by
©ollins, Glasgow

0 450 05381 4

It is a political error to practise deceit,
if deceit is carried too far.

Frederick the Great, 1740

I have a rendezvous with Death
At some disputed barricade.

Alan Seeger, 1888-1916

LIKE a buzzing hornet, the olive green painted Mi-1 helicopter with the colours of the German Democratic Republic whirred its way over the suburbs of East Berlin.

The journey to the enclave would have taken him only half an hour by road, driving at high speed in the bullet-proof Zis limousine with a Volksarmee escort, but Walter Ulbricht preferred travelling this way. A thousand feet up in the air. It was safer.

The helicopter was a present from the Kremlin, for his personal use. He appreciated the gesture. And the fact that it made him a more difficult target.

Below him he could see the Tetlow canal and the S-bahn, and the network of roads that led to Bernau and the east. He watched a Russian army convoy, looking like a collection of toy tanks. There would be many more convoys soon. Moving westwards . . .

Walter Ulbricht, the most powerful man in East Germany, First Secretary of the party, had plenty on his mind. He was a short tempered man, and he hated wasting time. Now that the decision had been made, he wanted to get things going. Of course he understood that the complicated preparations would take time, and he had agreed to Moscow's schedule.

But the August deadline still remained eleven weeks away.

He resented the hiatus the delay would cause. The quicker the plan was implemented, the better. Each week of inaction was costing the Democratic Republic dearly, as he had pointed out.

Through the glare-proof plastic of the observation window, he could see, far away on the horizon, three MIG fighters in the clear early June sky. They would keep well away, of course. Air control at Schoenefeld had given the helicopter a VIP air corridor all to itself. No aircraft were allowed within ten miles of the chopper.

He heard his personal pilot talking to ground control, and as the Mi-1 started to descend he saw the enclave spread out below him. The two road blocks that guarded the approaches. The six-foot wall that surrounded the enclosure. Floodlit at night, it was steel reinforced so that even a tank would have difficulty breaching it. And along the top ran a fine wire guaranteed to electrocute anyone climbing over.

Slowly the helicopter lost altitude and then, gently, it touched down on the landing strip inside the VIP compound. Steel-helmeted, jackbooted Volksarmee soldiers, drawn up in a rigid rank, sprang to attention.

Ulbricht's aide, a captain, jumped from the helicopter first, and stood ready to help him alight. Ulbricht, who prided himself on his Spartan fitness, ignored him.

The captain handed him the slim, locked briefcase, and the soldiers gave Ulbricht the state salute, the sun glinting on their bayonets. The men of the Wachtregiment, his personal bodyguard, 150 dedicated volunteers, were the elite of the entire People's Army. Ulbricht had personally approved each man. He had followed a good example for the unit, Adolf Hitler's Leibstandarte.

Ulbricht gave a curt nod, and entered the shiny black limousine, flying his own personal standard, which had drawn up by the landing strip. Although his villa was closeby, he avoided walking.

The car drove past the tennis courts, the swimming pool, the private cinema, the kindergarten school, the concern hall, and finally reached the most exclusive part of the compound. The residences of the state leaders.

Smoothly, the limousine halted in front of Ulbricht's custom-built villa. The Volksarmee captain who sat in front beside the NCO chauffeur jumped out and opened the door for Ulbricht.

The two sentries in front of the villa presented arms. Again Ulbricht just nodded, then walked into his residence. He was carrying the locked briefcase.

In it was a sealed folder which contained a document with the highest security classification existing behind the Iron Curtain.

On the folder there was just one word:

'Berlin'.

She typed slowly and very carefully. The major from security sat by her desk, watching her as she transcribed her shorthand notes.

'How much longer?' he asked.

'I'm almost finished,' she replied. The memorandum of agreement was a short one. Only half a dozen paragraphs. But there was no carbon copy.

Ulbricht himself dictated it to her on his return from the three-day summit meeting at Pankow. It had been a very secret meeting, and throughout the doors were guarded by Volksarmee men, fingers on the triggers of their submachine guns.

The conference had been held in an ornate room with glass chandeliers hanging from the ceiling, and thick carpets on the floor. In deference to Ulbricht, nobody smoked though ash-trays had been courteously provided. So had bottles of mineral water.

Not often had Pankow seen such a high-powered delegation from Moscow. Marshal Rodion Malinovsky, defence minister of the Soviet Union, had led it, and with him he had brought the top brass, including Marshal Andrei Grecho, commander in chief of the Warsaw Pact forces. The East German contingent comprised Grotewohl and Willie Stoph, the sinister one, as well as Ulbricht himself.

They had sat facing each other across a big polished table,

each man with a notepad and pencils laid out ready for him. After every session, the military aides made sure no incriminating notes had been left on the pads.

They had talked about Berlin, and several times they had looked at huge, large-scale maps of the city spread out before them.

As soon as he'd returned to his villa, Ulbricht called her into his private office and dictated the aide memoire.

'Type it on one page,' he instructed. 'No copy, you understand.'

After that, the major never left her side, walking along the corridor with her and not taking his eyes off her as she removed the cover from her typewriter, inserted the sheet of paper, and started typing.

Helga's face did not betray any emotion when she saw what they had agreed.

'Right,' she said finally, and stopped typing. She took the sheet of paper out of the machine and put it in a folder.

'I'll have that,' said the major.

'But . . . it's most secret,' she protested. 'It must not be seen by anyone . . . '

'Exactly,' said the major, who was Ulbricht's most trusted staff officer.

Then he leant over, and ripped the page of shorthand out of her notebook.

'I don't have to remind you that divulging a state secret is high treason,' he said pleasantly, 'Do I, Fraulein Braunschweig?'

She shook her head, and watched him leave.

But she remembered what she had typed. She remembered it very well.

She looked at the calendar on her desk. It was less than eleven weeks away.

She didn't have much time.

ON June 3rd, 1961, President John F. Kennedy arrived in Vienna to meet with USSR Premier Nikita Khruschev.

The following day, they issued a joint communique reaffirming support for the neutrality of Laos and stating they had discussed disarmament, a nuclear test ban and the German question.

Later, in the afternoon, President Kennedy flew to London.

Hours before his arrival, the crowds started gathering on the streets. They stood patiently, lining the pavements, waiting for the Presidential cavalcade to pass. All along the route from Heathrow, enthusiastic Londoners greeted their arrival.

The President and his entourage drove straight into central London.

That night, while the Kennedys stayed privately at Princess Lee Radziwill's small town house, across the street from Buckingham Palace, the Soviets issued a memorandum urging the demilitarization of Berlin.

At the American Embassy in Grosvenor Square and in the Foreign Office in Whitehall, the lights burnt late.

The next morning, a top Anglo-US meeting was scheduled for 10.30 a.m. to discuss the Khruschev talks. But something went wrong. The summit was suddenly cancelled.

Instead the President and Prime Minister Harold Macmillan unexpectedly met alone for two and a half hours behind closed doors. There were no witnesses, and whatever they said was off the record. To this day their discussion remains secret.

That was on Monday, June 5th, 1961.

Wednesday, June 7, 1961 – MANNHEIM

Verago was sweating. It was a warm, beautiful summer's day, and the weather wasn't the reason he felt sticky, uncomfortable. Private First Class Benjamin L. King was the reason. Verago wasn't looking forward to their meeting.

He hated stockades, especially the one at Mannheim. He suspected the army encouraged the reputation the place had. A spell inside Mannheim was calculated to teach an errant soldier the folly of his way.

The tall guard towers dominated the square complex. At night, the surrounding spiked brick walls were brightly lit. The MPs who moved around the penal barracks were unarmed, so that if they were overpowered, the prisoners couldn't seize any firearms. Mutinies were not unknown at Mannheim. But the perimeter guards had guns, and anyone foolish enough to make a break for it would quickly find out they were loaded.

Inside, the place smelt of carbolic. The provost lieutenant who escorted Verago to King's cell block smelt of it too.

He was aware how much the lieutenant disapproved of him. The man was scrubbed and spruce like the floors and walls of the barracks. To him, Verago looked like a civilian in uniform. Too portly. Needing a haircut. Uniform unpressed. Unpolished shoes. The lieutenant's shoes shone like a mirror, his creases were razor sharp, his figure athletic.

'Is he your only client here, Captain?' asked the lieutenant.

'At the moment,' grunted Verago. But he was no stranger to Mannheim. In his tour of duty as an Army lawyer in Germany, he had had many occasions to visit GIs in custody here. Too many occasions.

'I guess he'll be moved on soon,' remarked the lieutenant.

8

'I imagine so,' agreed Verago.

'He hasn't given us any trouble. Not so far anyway.'

God help the poor bastard who does, thought Verago.

A helmeted face peered at them through the grille of a steel door, and then the door was unlocked and they entered another corridor. It was lined by cages, and in the cages were men. One of them was King.

'Open up,' ordered the lieutenant, and the MP unlocked the cage door. King was sitting on his bed, in fatigues. He didn't stand up when he saw Verago.

'Get up, soldier,' ordered the lieutenant.

King stared at them, then slowly got to his feet. The movement was a study in dumb insolence to rank.

'Goddamn it, stand straight,' shouted the lieutenant.

'It's alright,' said Verago. 'You leave me with him.'

'Yes sir,' said the lieutenant. He gave King a last angry look, and slammed the door as he left.

The cage was made of fine wire mesh. The floor was spotless. On top of the locker, King's toilet things were symmetrically laid out, like a parade. Toothbrush, toothpaste, soap, rigid at attention. The razor was missing. There was a bible.

'Smoke?' suggested Verago, offering the soldier his pack.

King shook his head.

He didn't look the part of a GI caught trying to rape a fraulein in the back of a car, thought Verago yet again. A cleancut, lanky young man, studious, aloof. Not the type to spend his time in a Kaiserlautern off-limits joint. But after two years with the Army in Germany, nothing surprised Verago anymore.

'Sit down,' said Verago, lighting his cigarette. He pulled the single stool over and sat down. King perched on the edge of the bed.

'How they treating you, Ben?'

King shrugged. 'OK.'

'Chow alright?'

'OK.' The same flat tone.

'I got some good news,' said Verago. All night he'd been bothered just how he was going to tell him. Because he knew

9

what the reaction would be. 'They've cut your sentence.' He didn't wait for King to say anything. 'By a third.'

That sounded better, at least.

'Eight years?' asked King.

Verago nodded. 'It's been reduced to eight years.'

'Well, Captain, I am very grateful to you. Yes, sir.'

The way it was said Verago winced.

'Eight years on Leavenworth, that isn't too bad, is it?' went on King sarcastically. 'I'd say you've done a mighty good job.'

Verago stubbed out his cigarette.

'You should've considered the consequences before you messed with her. You should have thought of it then.'

King looked at him gravely.

'She wanted it.'

'Oh sure,' snarled Verago. He was angry. 'That's what every guy who tries to rape a woman says. Afterwards. She asked for it. She wanted it. She liked it. Bullshit.'

'But I wasn't trying to. It got out of hand.'

Verago sighed. 'We've been all over that. You hit her, you tore her bra off, you . . . hell, you know what the MPs saw when they found you two.'

'She called me a black ape.'

'You told me,' said Verago, more gently.

'She said I was a black . . .'

'Yes?'

'Forget it,' said King. 'Just forget it.'

'That's mitigation, maybe, but no defence,' said Verago patiently. 'A deal was our best way out. Under the circumstances. And we haven't finished yet. It's still going through channels. I'll do my best, Ben.'

King smiled coldly. 'Don't you worry about me, Captain. I'll survive.'

Verago had a growing sense of claustrophobia. The wire of the cage was so finely meshed that he couldn't see anything out of it. He felt trapped. He could hear the prisoners in the other cells, coughing, shuffling about; he felt their presence, but he couldn't see them.

'Is there anything you need?' asked Verago. He felt the trickle of perspiration under his left armpit.

'Yeah,' said King. 'A woman.'

Momentarily, Verago didn't know what to say.

'Sorry, that's against regulations,' he finally joked, weakly.

King looked at him unamused.

'When are they shipping me out?'

'I don't know. When the reviewing authority has finished with your case.'

'I know it wasn't your fault, Captain,' he said unexpectedly. 'I know you tried your best. Trouble is, you made one hell of a big mistake.'

'What was that?'

'You trusted them. You thought you had a deal. You really believed that. I got a piece of advice for you too, sir.'

Verago waited.

'Go fuck yourself, Captain.'

It was said quite mildly, almost respectfully.

Verago got up, the stool scraping on the floor. He was pale. He wasn't a man who liked to control his temper.

'I'm sorry that's the way you feel, soldier,' he said at last.

He turned and rattled the gate of the cage. It was unlocked from the outside.

'You all through, sir?' asked the MP.

'Yes,' said Verago, 'I'm all through.'

Friday, June 9, 1961 – WEST BERLIN

They were just carrying the stretcher into the ambulance when Pech arrived.

He was driving himself, and parked his official black Mercedes between a Kripo car with its blue light still flashing, and the police surgeon's Porsche. He slid into the gap neatly.

11

Pech was an excellent driver.

He got out of the car and walked to the ambulance. A Schupo barred his way.

'Verfassungsschutz,' said Pech crisply, and flashed his ID card. The cop was vastly impressed. The Office for the Protection of the Constitution did not usually turn up within ten minutes of a shooting.

A doctor was bending over the body of a man in a green suit. The blood from two bullet wounds was spreading across the man's chest.

'Is he dead?' asked Pech.

'Nearly,' replied the doctor.

'Let me see,' said Pech, almost brutally, and the doctor reluctantly gave way to enable Pech to lean over the stretcher.

The dying man's eyes were closed.

'Can you hear me?' asked Pech.

The eyes stayed shut.

'Martin, can you talk?'

The doctor intervened.

'There's no time for that. He's got to get to hospital now,' he protested angrily.

'I believe,' said Pech, straightening up, 'that he just died.'

The doctor grabbed the man's wrist and felt his pulse.

'Right,' he said, with finality, 'take him away.'

Pech stood in front of the block of flats and lit a cheroot.

'Excuse me, sir,' said a Kripo officer respectfully, 'do you know anything about the dead man?'

'Maybe,' said Pech.

The detective was holding a wallet.

'According to his papers, he's from the other side.'

'Other side?' echoed Pech, amused.

'The East.'

'Really?' remarked Pech.

'If you could tell me anything about him . . . ' The detective found Pech's cold eyes disconcerting. 'To help my report . . . '

'I don't think it will really matter what your report says,' said Pech.

He started to walk to his Mercedes with the official plates.

The Kripo man always felt uneasy with the people from security.

'But the investigation . . . ' he started to say rather lamely.

'I imagine you'll find that the case is closed,' said Pech.

'The formalities . . . '

'Don't worry about them,' said Pech. 'My department will look after it.'

He got into the Mercedes, smoothly reversed it and drove into the Berlin night.

Monday, June 12, 1961 – LONDON

The moment the jury returned to the court room, Daventry knew that he had won. It was a kind of sixth sense he had acquired, and it seldom let him down.

Up on his dais, Mr Justice Rodman sat hunched, his fingers drumming impatiently.

'Members of the jury,' said the clerk, 'will your foreman please stand.'

The bald man in the brown suit rose. Daventry suspected it was *the* suit, reserved for the few special occasions in his life.

'Mr Foreman,' sang out the clerk, 'are you all agreed upon the verdict?'

The bald man was nervous, but he tried hard not to show it. At that moment, every eye in the Old Bailey court room was on him, and to be the centre of attention was a unique experience for him.

'We are.'

'Do you find Michael Connor guilty or not guilty?'

'Not guilty.'

Mr Justice Rodman stopped tapping his fingers. He frowned.

'Do you find Kevin Connor guilty or not guilty?'

13

'Not guilty.'

Mr Justice Rodman pursed his lips. His normally thin face looked even more pinched. He was angry. His summing up had been clear and to the point.

In the dock, the two Connors broke into wide smiles. They turned to each other, and shook hands. Then one of them winked at Daventry. He ignored it.

'They are discharged,' said the judge, and his tone left no one in doubt of his disapproval. He gave the jury a look of cold reproof.

From the bench behind, Rippon, Daventry's instructing solicitor, tapped him on the shoulder.

'Costs,' he mouthed, 'ask for costs.'

Daventry shook his head curtly. It would only give the judge an opportunity to savage the verdict. Anyway, the Connors could well afford paying for their freedom.

Mr Justice Rodman stood up, and everybody in the court room rose. The judge gave a cursory nod and swept out.

'Splendid work, Mr Daventry,' said Rippon. He looked remarkably respectable for a solicitor who was on a retainer to a dozen of London's most undesirable citizens. 'Absolutely splendid.'

'Thank you, Mr Rippon,' replied Daventry diplomatically. Rippon, after all, provided some very lucrative briefs.

In the well of the court, Chief Superintendent Lock and his CID men were having a quick conference. He glanced over and saw Daventry looking at him.

'Well, sir, are you pleased?' he asked, not even attempting to hide his bitterness. The verdict had destroyed three years of work, trying to break up one of Soho's nastiest vice kingdoms.

'That's hardly the question, is it, Superintendent?' said Daventry coldly.

'I only hope your clients are duly grateful,' retorted Lock. And he turned his back.

Daventry gathered his papers together and put them in his monogrammed leather attaché case. He knew they loathed him at Scotland Yard. He got too many villains off for their liking. And they knew he didn't lose a night's sleep over it.

14

The younger Connor brother pushed his way towards him.

'You were fantastic, Mr Daventry,' said Kevin. 'Me and my brother, we're tickled pink. You had that jury eating out of your hand.'

'Not really, Mr Connor.' He started to move away. 'Now, if you'll excuse me.'

He went out of the swing doors of No. 1 Court, into the big main hall on the first floor of the Old Bailey.

Over on one of the benches, Mary Donovan, the Crown's chief witness, sat pale faced. Two of Lock's detectives hovered around her protectively. From the moment the jury had brought in their verdict, she was a marked woman.

She sat, her mascara smudged, tightly clutching her handbag, nervously smoking a cigarette. She knew what was in store. The Connors would pay her back. Giving evidence for the prosecution was the supreme betrayal; they had to show the other girls that it wasn't worth it.

In the robing room, Daventry removed his wig. He was an unsentimental man, but the yellowing horsehair meant a lot to him. It was his father's old wig, and the judge had given it to him when he was called to the bar in 1949. For twelve years, Daventry had worn it at every court appearance, and it had almost become a talisman. It was nonsense of course, but it had brought him a lot of good luck.

Without the wig, he seemed younger than 38. He was a tall, thin man, with finely chiselled features, aristocratic looking. The eighteenth-century barrister's costume suited him.

He took off the black serge gown. Underneath was the daily uniform, a Savile Row tailored clerical suit. Daventry was an elegant man, in clothes and manners, and studiously careful about his appearance.

He frowned. He wished he could stop thinking about Mary Donovan. She wasn't attractive, and her fingers were tobacco stained. She had eleven convictions for soliciting, and, in the medieval language of the law, she was listed as a 'common prostitute'.

But it had given him no pleasure to reduce her to tears in the witness box, and to ensure the Connors' acquittal by cutting

15

her evidence against them to shreds.

Thornley the Crown Prosecutor came into the robing room.

'Ah, Gerald,' the prosecutor said. 'Congratulations, another good day's work, eh?'

The sneer was implicit. Congratulations for getting a bunch of pimps off the hook. Full marks for making an ass of the law. I hope the fee was worth it.

'I'm just leaving, Harold,' said Daventry.

Thornley slipped out of his gown.

'Give my regards to your father if you see him,' said Thornley.

'Of course.'

Daventry looked at himself in the mirror. He was used to Thornley's dislike. It was one of the prices of success.

He didn't have any qualms that a lot of villains owed their liberty to him. Daventry had often reflected about it, but he was always honest with himself, and the truth was that he rather enjoyed the reputation he had acquired of being one of the best advocates in England to get a guilty man off against all the odds.

Maybe that was why he liked defending so much better than appearing for the prosecution.

It also paid rather well.

Tuesday, June 13, 1961 – THE NORTH SEA

They knew the man was a spook. He boarded the nuclear submarine, his face partially hidden by the fur lined hood of his parka, carrying a briefcase.

All the 112 crew members were aware that something out of the ordinary was happening when they had received a signal to rendezvous with a US destroyer eighty miles off the Danish coast.

16

At that time, the *USS Sharkfin* wasn't due to surface for another nine weeks and anything that commanded the 3,000 ton submarine to the top during one of the classified patrols was highly unusual.

Down below the man took off his jacket. Under it, he wore a white roll-top sweater, and slacks. He had curiously piercing eyes.

'Welcome aboard,' said Commander Douglas, the *Sharkfin*'s skipper, uneasily. He disliked unexpected complications. The spook's arrival was one.

'My orders,' said Clyde Unterberg, handing the commander a sealed manila envelope. Douglas tore it open, and read the contents.

They confirmed his disquiet.

'They're aware that the Baltic is a Soviet sea?' he asked.

'I don't think they're under any illusions, Commander,' said Unterberg.

'And that the part we're suppposed to search is like crossing Red Square?'

'Correct.'

Commander Douglas shrugged resignedly, and gave orders to set the new course.

Later, when it was night, and the control room illumination had switched to red, Douglas decided he was entitled to know a little more.

'What exactly was this plane?' he asked.

'An RB 47H,' said Unterberg, surprisingly readily.

'And what the hell was it doing over the Baltic?'

'Ferreting.'

'Eh?'

'Testing their radar defences. I guess that might describe it.'

'When did it go down?'

'It didn't go down, Commander,' said Unterberg. 'They shot it down.'

'Jesus.'

Douglas felt cold suddenly. It had got to this.

'That's going to take some explaining.'

'Not at all,' said Unterberg smoothly. 'The official version is that a plane is missing on a training flight. Over the North Sea. Accidents will happen.'

On the chart table before them lay the map, with the search area marked out.

'What precisely are we looking for, Mr Unterberg?' Douglas asked.

'Anything. A rubber dinghy. Wreckage. Maybe a body. We'd like to recover anything we can.'

'If there's anything, the Russians will have picked it up.'

'Maybe they missed something,' said Unterberg. 'It had six men on board.'

'*Six?*'

'Three extra men. In a pressurised compartment in the bomb bay.'

Douglas was about to say something, but Unterberg cut him short.

'Electronic specialists,' he said briefly. His tone was final. Explanations would now cease.

On the *Sharkfin*, the crew had been on war alert since they entered the Baltic. The search periscope swept the surface, the sonar and sensor operators watching, probing, listening. They could detect the sound of waves breaking on a beach 100 miles away.

They also knew the Russians were listening too.

Thursday, June 15, 1961 – SWITZERLAND

The two men met at the secluded villa overlooking Lake Geneva at noon. They arrived within four minutes of each other in cars not even displaying diplomatic plates.

The Russian looked like the chairman of a successful business corporation, in a smartly cut suit, and a snow-white shirt. His tie, like himself, was immensely discreet.

The American had rimless glasses, and was rather more casually dressed. But his clothes were expensive. Had he been sitting in the Polo Bar of the Beverly Hills Hotel he could have been taken for a successful film producer.

The villa was neutral ground. It belonged to a Swiss millionaire who enjoyed playing a back-room role in the intrigues of the super powers.

'We have two of the bodies,' said the Russian, after the polite preliminaries. The two men were sitting facing each other alone. On the polished table between them was a bottle of Vichy water and two glasses.

'Only two?' The American frowned.

'The other crew members . . . ' The Russian paused briefly. 'I am sorry. There wasn't much to pick up. It was a nasty accident.'

The American's face remained bland. It wouldn't be playing the game to point out that the Air Force had been monitoring the Soviet MIG19 that blasted the RB47H out of the sky at 41,000 feet.

Instead, he said quietly:

'We would like the bodies.'

The Russian nodded understandingly.

'Of course. They will be handed over. I suggest at sea.'

Circumspection was the order of the day. Neither side wanted prying eyes to see what would happen.

'Very well,' agreed the American.

'Good.'

The Russian opened a silver cigarette case. It had been given to him by Gromyko during a session of the UN in New York. He had been rather useful to Gromyko.

'Do you mind if I smoke?' he asked courteously. He didn't offer a cigarette to the American; he knew he didn't use them. They were well acquainted with each other's idiosyncracies.

'Perhaps your submarine could take the bodies aboard,' he said lighting his cigarette.

'Submarine?' echoed the American, apparently startled.

'The one you have in the Baltic.' The Russian shook his head regretfully. 'It was really a very rash thing to send her.'

'I haven't been briefed about this,' lied the American.

'It doesn't matter,' said the Russian tolerantly. 'I suppose she was ordered on a search mission. To see if she could find anything left of your unfortunate plane. Military people have such crazy ideas, don't they?'

'As I say, it's news to me.' The American looked him straight in the eye.

'Our navy has had her pinpointed for the last twenty-four hours. At this moment she is surrounded by our ships. They are poised to . . . deal with her. You know how neurotic our admirals get about any of your nuclear submarines in Baltic waters. But don't worry. Our governments hardly want a naval confrontation on the high seas, do they?'

'You have my assurance,' said the American, as he had been instructed to say when the matter was raised.

'Of course they don't,' said the Russian. 'Well, that's settled then. You get your people to send a signal, ordering her to surface, and a launch will bring over the bodies from one of our ships.'

'And then?'

The Russian smiled benignly. 'We will escort your submarine out of the Baltic.' He saw the American's expression. 'Oh relax, she can submerge. Her dignity will not be bruised. We will escort her on the surface.'

'Is that really necessary?' asked the American.

'We want to make sure she gets home safely, don't we?' purred the Russian. 'I am told that the Baltic can be quite treacherous. We will see to it that she does not meet with an accident.'

'Okay,' the American agreed. 'I'll tell Washington.'

'Excellent,' said the Russian. 'Isn't it marvellous how we can cooperate? Have you ever thought how easy it is to reach agreement if only we are left to ourselves? Look how quickly we've been able to resolve this little problem.'

He reached over for the Vichy bottle, and looked at it in disgust.

'Our Swiss host is very prim. I would like to toast the successful outcome of our meeting, but this stuff . . . '

He pulled a face.

'You guarantee secrecy?' asked the American. 'No cameras at the exchange of bodies, no announcements?'

The Russian laughed. 'Of course not. Who needs to know?'

'Well . . . ,' said the American. 'We haven't got it made like you. It's not easy for us to keep things under wraps.'

The Russian stood up.

'You're doing alright, my friend,' he said jovially. 'I remember your communiqué. "An Air Force plane is missing over the North Sea on a training flight"! Very good, very good indeed. It wasn't the North Sea, and it wasn't a training flight, but you didn't tell them that. Very wise. You're learning.'

His eyes twinkled.

'You're learning from us.'

Within half an hour, 'Eyes Only' code messages reached certain desks in Washington and Moscow, and shortly afterwards a Navy signal was sent to the *Sharkfin*.

The submarine surfaced at the prearranged rendezvous sixty miles off the Lithuanian coast, where the Soviet missile cruiser *Kinda* was already waiting with an escort of four destroyers.

A naval cutter came across carrying two metal caskets in which the Russians had thoughtfully packed the bodies of two Americans in dried ice.

The *Sharkfin* loaded them aboard, and submerged again. It set course for the British Isles.

Three days later, the widows of the two dead crew members were officially notified that the bodies of their husbands had been recovered from the North Sea not far from the British coast.

In all, the wing commander, Brigadier-General Croxford, wrote six letters of condolence by hand. He paid warm tribute to the lost officers, and regretted their accidental deaths.

The dead men's replacements arrived at the plane's base at Laconbury, England, thirty-six hours later.

Monday, June 19, 1961 – FRANKFURT

Colonel Ochs, VI Corps staff judge advocate, preferred things neat and tidy. It was one of the reasons he didn't like Captain Verago. Things had a habit of getting fouled up when Verago was involved.

'Sit down, Tony,' he invited cautiously. He had asked Verago to his office, and it was not a meeting he particularly relished.

'Thank you, sir,' said Verago politely.

The colonel's desk was totally bare except for three things: his name plate, complete with silver eagle, the mandatory photo of Mrs Ochs, and a folder.

The two telephones were on a side table, at the colonel's right hand.

'Well, how are things?' enquired the colonel.

Verago eyed him moodily. He was still feeling the after effects of a long session in the bar of the Casino officer's club the previous evening.

'Alright,' he said warily. The folder on the desk worried him. It spelt trouble.

'Remember the King trial?' asked Ochs.

'Indeed I do.'

'I'm getting flak over it,' said the colonel reproachfully.

'Oh?'

'Strictly unofficial, mind you, but I don't like complaints about my officers.'

'Who's making them?' demanded Verago. He wished his tongue didn't feel so thick.

'Dan Worden. He says you behaved in an uncalled for manner after the trial. You apparently abused him and used

22

highly improper language.'

Ochs regarded Verago severely.

'It won't do, Tony.'

'Captain Worden is a son of a bitch,' said Verago.

The colonel sighed.

'Look Tony, I'm trying to do this as painlessly as I can. You can't go round calling a fellow officer the kind of things you did.'

'You know what *he* did, sir.'

Ochs shook his head. 'I read your report. And your pleas to the reviewing authority. I do not think you have any cause for complaint. Captain Worden made no promise, gave no undertaking.'

'Yes he did, Colonel.'

'Not as far as I am concerned. Anyway, your man's sentence got reduced, so there's no point arguing.'

Verago glowered at him, silent.

'Try to remember that we Army lawyers over here are a tight little group, and we got to stick together. It's tough enough administering military justice without getting in each other's hair.'

The colonel leant forward in his chair.

'You see that, don't you, Tony?'

'I see it, sir, but I don't agree.'

The colonel tightened his lips.

'What don't you agree, Captain Verago?'

Verago took a deep breath. 'Your priorities. Depends which comes first. The military, or the law. Being an officer, or a lawyer. Are we here to see justice done, or uphold regulations?'

Ochs flushed. 'Both.'

There was a knock at the door, and a WAC put her head in.

'Excuse me, sir, would you and Captain Verago like some coffee?'

Ochs looked at Verago questioningly.

'Please,' said Verago. 'Make it black and strong.'

She closed the door.

'Is that why you wanted to see me, sir? To have a little debate about the conflicts between the Uniform Code and

23

individual rights?'

'No,' snapped Ochs. 'Not at all.'

Verago knew he was right. The reason was in the folder.

'I think you could do with a change, Tony,' said the colonel.

The WAC came back. She put a coffee mug in front of Ochs. It had 'Ochs' and a colonel's eagle painted on it. It would have, thought Verago.

She handed him his mug.

'Hope it's strong enough, sir,' she smiled.

'I'm sure it is,' said Verago, 'thanks.'

She closed the door, and Verago drank deep. The hot coffee flooded into him comfortingly. The hangover was passing.

'What kind of change, sir?' he asked.

'Well,' said the colonel, 'it so happens that your services have been requested. As individual counsel for the defence at an Air Force court martial.'

Verago sat up. 'Air Force?'

'Yes, don't ask me why,' said the colonel. His tone indicated that anyone who asks for you is crazy. 'But as you know, it's perfectly legal for an accused to request counsel from another service.'

Verago put his coffee mug down on the colonel's desk. Ochs winced. It might leave a mark on the polished surface.

'What's the charge?' asked Verago.

'Article 134.'

It was an old friend. The catch-all. Prejudice to good order and discipline. Conduct of a nature to bring discredit upon the armed forces.

'And the offence?'

Colonel Ochs sniffed. 'Adultery.'

Suddenly Verago no longer had a hangover.

'You're kidding.'

'It *is* an offence, Tony,' said Ochs primly.

'Colonel, in that case they ought to try half the Army.'

Ochs was outraged. 'That is not in good taste, Captain,' he grated.

But Verago's mind was already on other things.

'Who's the guy?'

24

'The accused is an Air Force captain,' said Ochs stiffly.

'Why does he want me?'

'I suppose,' said Colonel Ochs meanly, 'your reputation has spread to the other services. Maybe somebody heard of your enthusiasm for tackling lost causes.'

Verago felt his temper rising. 'Who says it's a lost cause?'

'I think you can take it for granted the military doesn't charge an officer with adultery unless it has all the facts.'

'Well, I'll have to see what I can do,' said Verago.

'Good,' said the colonel. He opened the folder. 'The request has been formally approved. Your orders are being cut now. I don't envy you, Tony.'

'Sir?'

'An Army lawyer at an Air Force court, surrounded by blue suits. I imagine you'll encounter a certain degree of, er, hostility.'

Ochs had difficulty in concealing his pleasure at the thought.

'I'll feel at home,' said Verago. 'What's the outfit?'

'Oh, didn't I mention it?' Ochs opened the folder and peered at its contents. 'You're going to England.'

'England?' He was surprised.

'Yes. The accused is at an air base called Laconbury.'

He shut the folder.

'I guess it'll be a new experience for you.'

He appeared to relish that idea too.

Tuesday, June 20, 1961 – FRANKFURT

Four days after being lifted off the deck of the submarine *Sharkfin* by a Navy helicopter, Clyde Unterberg entered an office building in the centre of Frankfurt, off the Hauptwache.

He went to the second-floor office of Euram Marketing Inc, a business company incorporated in Wilmington, Delaware.

It was a comparatively shabby office, with a worn green carpet in the entrance hall, flat white lighting, and an anaemic plant in a pot on the desk of the girl who doubled as receptionist, switchboard operator and copy typist. Euram Marketing gave a distinct impression of watching the pennies.

Herr Weber, the caretaker downstairs, would tell callers who had time for a little gossip that Euram Marketing was pretty shaky financially. He believed it was a business venture started by a couple of Americans who had settled in Frankfurt with big ambitions but few resources. The company was so broke, he confided, that the staff even had to do the window cleaning.

And if anybody asked him what Euram actually marketed, he was rather vague.

'I think they're in the import busines,' he'd say. 'Or is it export? Something like that. I don't think they make a lot of money. There's only a handful of people working up there.'

Some shrewder characters suggested that Euram was probably the offshoot of a much bigger firm, and really a cleverly manipulated tax loss.

They were partly right. Euram Marketing Inc was established in 1951, under a top-secret directive 10-2 of the National Security Council. It authorised the setting up of 'special operations, always provided they are secret, and sufficiently diminutive in size as to be plausibly denied by the government.'

The girl with the plant pot smiled at Unterberg as he entered.

'Hi, Clyde,' she greeted him informally. 'Good to see you again.'

She came from Arizona and was the wife of an officer stationed across town in the IG Farben Building. Her security clearance was formidable.

'You look great, Jeannie,' said Unterberg. 'Is he in?'

'Waiting for you.'

He opened the door marked 'Private' without knocking.

The only furniture in the room were three armchairs, and a round coffee table. There was another undernourished plant in a similar pot to the one outside. A TWA calendar hung on the wall.

'Make yourself at home,' invited the man already sitting in

one of the armchairs. He wore rimless glasses. He had recently returned from Switzerland.

Unterberg, a big 6-foot, 2-inch 240 pounder, eased himself into one of the other armchairs.

'Boy, you must have been cramped in that sub,' the man sympathised.

Unterberg shook his head.

'Plenty of space. You'd be surprised how roomy those tin cans are.'

'Rather you than me, friend,' said the man. 'Stuck down there, it's one hell of a way not to see the world.'

'I sent the report to Washington,' said Unterberg. 'Including the autopsy findings on the two bodies.'

The man was interested. 'Which were?'

'The Navy says they didn't find out much. The poor bastards had burns, and exposure.'

'You think they were dead when the Russians fished them out?'

'It looks that way.'

'I hope so,' said the man. 'I'd hate to think the Russkies got hold of anything.'

He might have been talking about chess pieces. It didn't surprise Unterberg. He knew the man well, even before they joined the company. They were both alumni of Stanford University, and had been in the same fraternities, Phi Beta Kappa and Sigma XI.

Then their ways parted until they crossed one another's paths in OPC, the covert, highly classified Office of Policy Coordination. A beautifully meaningless title. The man had reached OPC's higher command level; Unterberg worked in the field.

'How was Geneva?' asked Unterberg.

'We reached an – arrangement of convenience,' said the man. 'I'm sure the French got a word for it, but I can't think what. Got you out of a hole, didn't it?'

'It wasn't my idea to go fishing in their back yard,' snorted Unterberg. 'The Navy swore they could do it undetected.'

The man stretched himself. 'Sometimes I worry about the

military. The Air Force think they can get away with flying their fucking bombers over Russia, the Navy thinks it can go for pleasure cruises in their waters and they're surprised if people build bomb shelters.'

The end of one of his shoelaces was hanging loose and he started retying it. While he was concentrating on his shoe he said, without looking up:

'Got any plans?'

Unterberg became wary. 'I got thirty days leave, if that's what you mean. Starting on Monday.'

'No you haven't,' said the man. 'Sorry, Clyde.'

'The company's suddenly short of staff?' said Unterberg sarcastically.

'Very.' The man was not smiling.

Unterberg knew the signals.

'Let me guess. Turkey. No, some real asshole of a place. Libya, Iran? No thanks.'

'England,' said the man.

Unterberg was surprised. 'That's where I was going. London.'

'Good,' said the man. 'Any particular reason?'

'She's none of your business.'

A briefcase leant against the man's armchair. He picked it up, opened it and took out an envelope.

Unterberg took the sealed envelope.

'Exactly where?'

'Laconbury,' said the man. He indicated the envelope. 'It's all in there. Keep the travel orders. Burn the rest.'

'Now wait a moment.' He took a deep breath. 'I don't like that. I don't like off the record assignments. The last guy who was told to burn his documentation was Brooke. And he never came back.'

'Well,' said the man, 'you'd just better make sure nothing unpleasant like that happens to you, don't you think?'

The man's smile was famous. If piranha fish smiled, thought Unterberg, they'd look just like that.

28

Wednesday, June 21, 1961 – LONDON

It was one of those paragraphs *The Times* publishes as if it was trying to hide it because it was trivial and hardly worth the record.

But the six lines had a big effect on Daventry.

'What's the matter?' asked his wife, across the breakfast table.

Alex Daventry was an attractive woman, even first thing in the morning. She was also very ambitious for her husband, practical and deeply loyal. Her life revolved round Daventry and she showed this in her thinking, her helpfulness and her total consideration of him.

Without a word, Daventry passed the paper over to her, indicating the story, tucked away insignificantly.

'Paddington Murder' read the tiny heading.

'Miss Mary Donovan, aged twenty-six, received fatal stab wounds when she was attacked by an unknown assailant outside her basement flat in St Stephen's Gardens, W. She was recently a witness at an Old Bailey trial.'

Alex gave the paper back to him.

'One of yours?' she asked.

'She gave evidence for the prosecution in the Connors case.' His mind's eye replayed the sight of the girl after the verdict had come in, fear struck, scared of what lay in store for her. 'She turned informer.'

'Well, couldn't the police look after her?' demanded Alex.

'Apparently not.' He read the story again.

'You're not blaming yourself, are you?'

'Of course not,' said Daventry.

'Well then . . .'

'But if those bastards hadn't got off, she might still be around. They couldn't wait to pay her back once they had the chance.'

'You can't help that,' said Alex firmly.

'I put them back in circulation.'

She was getting annoyed.

'For God's sake, don't talk rubbish. It's your job, isn't it? You've always said you'd rather get people off than send them to prison. And listen . . .'

He looked up at her.

'I'd rather be married to a man who wants to help people no matter what they've done than some sort of avenging prig.'

The grandfather clock in the entrance hall struck nine, its sonorous tones echoing.

'I'd better get going,' said Daventry. He took a hasty sip of tea, and got up.

Alex rose too and came over to his side of the table.

'Promise me?' she said.

'What?'

'Promise you're not going to go around blaming yourself for what happened to that girl?'

'I'll try,' he said.

She kissed him lightly.

'What would your father say?' she smiled.

Ah, yes. The old judge. Daventry knew perfectly well what he'd say. He would peer at him over his half-moon glasses, snort and growl:

'Twaddle. Absolute twaddle. I've hanged eleven men, and never lost a night's sleep. Can't afford this kind of rubbish, damn self-indulgence. Forget about it, and get on with the next case.'

'Have a good day, darling,' said Alex at the door of their house, just off the King's road.

At his chambers, when his clerk, Pettifer, put a bundle of red-tape-tied documents on his desk, Daventry said to him:

'Have you read about the Donovan girl?'

'Indeed,' sniffed Pettifer. Few things escaped him. 'Sad case. But then, she was no better than she should be, was she, sir?'

30

He shut the door, and Daventry wished he had never heard of Mary Donovan and what had happened to her.

But what really annoyed him was that he felt sorry for the girl. Mr Justice Rodman would wildly disapprove.

He reached over for one of the briefs, and slowly started to untie the red tape. It was perfectly true. There was nothing he could do about it. No one could help her anymore.

Pettifer knocked and came in diffidently.

'I had Mr Rippon on the phone, sir,' he said. 'He wondered if you would care to have lunch with him next Friday? At the Wig and Pen perhaps?'

His tone indicated that it was advisable to accept. Rippon channelled a continuous stream of cases to Daventry's chambers. Like the Connors.

'Tell him I'm busy,' said Daventry curtly.

'Perhaps I can suggest a convenient date?' offered Pettifer hopefully.

'Not at the moment, I'm afraid,' said Daventry.

He had other things on his mind.

Thursday, June 22, 1961 – NORTHOLT

There were only two passengers on the Air Force shuttle plane from Lindsey base at Wiesbaden to Northolt. One was an armed Air Force courier, the other Verago.

The courier was a captain who was paying for a weekend in London by carrying some classified documents for the Air Force which could only be transported in the custody of an officer. To protect them he had a holstered .45 strapped round his waist.

The courier eyed the crossed sword and pen insignia on Verago's lapel. Army lawyers were unusual passengers on Air

31

Force planes.

'Going on leave, Captain?' asked the courier.

'No,' said Verago. He had been wondering what kind of man he was going to defend. And something nagged him; Colonel Ochs and his warning about the hostility he would encounter.

'You going over for a trial?' enquired the courier.

Verago didn't feel like small talk. He had a lot to think about.

'Yes,' he said curtly.

The courier looked surprised. 'Didn't know we had any Army courts in the UK.'

'It's not an Army trial,' said Verago. He reached for the copy of *Stars and Stripes* he had picked up at Lindsey.

'What kind of court is it?'

'One of yours,' grunted Verago. 'Air Force.'

It left the courier even more puzzled.

'Kind of unusual, isn't it, Army lawyers at an Air Force trial?'

Verago shrugged, and turned to the comics page. He was a keen follower of Terry and the Pirates.

The courier gave up.

Verago finished the comics. He wished there was a crossword. He couldn't understand why *Stripes* didn't carry one. Maybe the Army doesn't approve of crosswords, he thought to himself sarcastically. Maybe there's some general who considers they undermine discipline.

Verago gazed out of the window. He was looking forward to England. It would make a change. And it would give him some satisfaction to defend a man stuck with an adultery charge. All he knew was that the man who had asked for him was a Captain John Tower. He didn't even know his outfit, other than he was stationed at Laconbury. And he had never heard of Laconbury.

It was about two hours from London, Colonel Ochs had told him. A staff car would meet him at Northolt and drive him straight there.

Verago considered it an abomination that in 1961 a man could still face a criminal charge because he had slept with a woman who was not his wife. He had looked up the penalty. Dishonourable discharge and confinement at hard labour for 12 months.

'Here we are,' said the courier.

They were touching down. Compared to some of the airfields he had seen in Germany, Northolt was quite small. As the plane slid to a halt on the runway, Verago caught a glimpse of a Battle of Britain memorial, an old Spitfire.

In the arrival hall, an Air Force sergeant looked at Verago's travel orders.

'I'm going straight on to Laconbury,' explained Verago. 'There's a staff car meeting me.'

The sergeant looked at a clip board.

'Captain Verago?' he said. He sounded bewildered.

'What's the problem, Sergeant?' asked Verago. The courier had already passed through. Nobody questioned his orders.

'Just a moment, sir,' said the sergeant. He went over to a lieutenant standing by a door, and spoke to him.

The lieutenant looked across at Verago, and then came to the counter.

'Did you say you were being met here, Captain?' he asked.

'I told the sergeant. There's a staff car from Laconbury for me. I'm going straight there.'

'No, sir,' said the lieutenant. 'There's no car for you.'

Verago took a deep breath.

'Well, Lieutenant, you'd better start calling somebody,' he said. 'I need transportation.'

'I'm sorry, sir,' said the lieutenant.

Verago knew the familiar feeling. He was starting to get mad. 'What does that mean?' he asked very quietly.

'Well, sir, I guess it means that there's no transportation.'

'Who's in charge?' said Verago.

'I am, Captain,' smiled the lieutenant. It was a self-assured, confident smile. 'And I guess you're all on your own.'

But Verago had already got the message. They knew damn well he was coming, and that was why there was no car for him.

LONDON

Feliks Petrov, staff officer of the Glavnoye Razvedyvatelnoye Upravleniye at the Soviet Embassy in Kensington Palace Gardens, was pleased with himself.

He was one of the six GRU men in London under Deriabin, the head of the detachment. Deriabin insisted that his GRU outfit kept its distance from the vastly larger KGB section at the London Embassy. The GRU's job was strictly espionage, collecting military intelligence. He was happy to leave the dirty stuff to the KGB, with whom he worked closely, even sitting in on their staff meetings. Deriabin also had the ambassador's ear, and was privy to the most secret activities in the rambling Victorian houses adjoining Kensington Gardens.

Petrov's speciality was the American services in England, especially the Air Force units. In his safe, he now had files with data on all the bases, Sculthrope, Wethersfield, Bentwaters, Mildenhall, Woodbridge, Brize Norton, Greenham Common, and the others.

He had also started a little archive on other American installations, from which no planes flew, but whose activities were of equal interest.

Petrov, a charming, pleasant man, found his sources of information all over the place. He avidly read the local papers from the districts where the bases lay. He kept himself abreast of the activities of the CND, the nuclear disarmers, whose demonstrations and sit downs at military installations provided him with a marvellous cover for studying them more closely. And he had his private informants.

On his way to Deriabin's office, Petrov bumped into Ivanov, one of the naval attachés. The two men liked each other. They both enjoyed London, lived in apartments near each other in Bayswater, had even joined forces taking out current girl friends. Ivanov knew a man who laid on parties attended by gorgeous women, and sometimes took Petrov along.

Ivanov was also grateful to him for providing a contact who was now happily supplying useful information from Holy Loch about the newly arrived American nuclear submarines.

'You look happy, my friend,' remarked Ivanov.

Petrov smiled. 'Life could be worse,' he said.

'Have a good day,' said Ivanov, giving an excellent imitation of the Americans, and they both laughed.

Deriabin, who had the rank of a full colonel but was listed as an economic attaché, listened to Petrov's morning report without comment. A couple of times he made a cursory note on his pad, but that was his only reaction.

'Good,' he commented finally. 'Proceed as usual.'

'I have one other thing,' Petrov added. He knew this one would please his boss. 'About the base at Laconbury.'

'Yes?'

Laconbury was high on the list of American installations they had special interest in. It was after all the major aerial spy base in the UK, and they monitored it as best they could.

'A little piece of gossip, but interesting,' said Petrov. 'Indicative perhaps of the state of morale at the base.'

'Get on with it, Feliks.'

'Apparently there's going to be some sort of court martial because – you'll never believe – an officer has been sleeping with his girl friend.'

To his surprise, Deriabin suddenly became tense.

'What else do you know?' he demanded, sharply.

'That is really all, Comrade Colonel, but amusing, don't you think? Apparently it is a crime in the American Air Force to make love to somebody other than your wife.'

Deriabin sat stony faced.

'What is the source of your information?'

'A contact in Cambridge. He was in a pub, and an American airman was drinking too much. My contact encouraged it, and the airman let it slip. He is a clerk and heard about the court martial being set up.'

'Did you find out the officer's name? Anything about him?' asked Deriabin sharply.

Petrov was puzzled. Instead of enjoying the little delicacy, Deriabin was almost reacting as if he disapproved.

'No,' said Petrov, 'but I can try and pursue the matter . . . '

'Don't, Captain,' said Deriabin.

Petrov stared at him.

'I do not wish this followed up or any attempt made to get involved. Is that clear?'

'Yes, but . . . ' Petrov stared at his chief, astonished.

'I am now giving you a formal order,' said Deriabin. 'Do not concern yourself in this matter. Leave it alone, do you understand?'

'Naturally, if that is your instruction,' said Petrov. Greatly daring, he asked: 'But may I enquire why . . . '

'There is no need for you to know,' said Deriabin roughly, and Petrov had never known him to be so severe. 'It is a matter of official policy. You are to forget about this officer, about the court martial. You are not to record the information, or file it, you will keep it to yourself. Is that clear?'

Petrov nodded.

'And do not probe any further,' added Deriabin. 'If your contact or any other source wishes to dig deeper, discourage them. Order them to drop it.'

'Very good,' said Petrov. 'But I must confess I am a little mystified why . . . '

'Yours is not to question, Captain. I will tell you only one thing, and that is most secret, you understand?'

'Of course.'

'We are well aware of what is going on,' said Deriabin. 'As a matter of fact, we know everything about it.'

Petrov stared at him.

The colonel hesitated a moment. Then he added:

'It is very important that this court martial takes place. More I cannot say. But it must take place.'

After Petrov had gone, the colonel dictated a secret memo ordering that Petrov was to be immediately transferred back to

Moscow for reassignment.

As he explained to the ambassador later in the day, the man unfortunately knew too much for his health.

SOUTH RUISLIP

Verago pushed open the door marked 'Colonel Raymond Kincaid, Staff Judge Advocate' and dropped his holdall on the floor with a thump.

A girl was typing in the outer office. She looked up, startled at his unexpected entry. Army uniforms were a rare sight in the headquarters of the Third Air Force.

'Anything I can do for you, Captain?' asked the girl. She had short dark hair, and Verago found her almond shaped eyes disconcerting. They were violet eyes, he thought. He couldn't be sure, but he knew one thing: he hadn't seen eyes like that before.

'I want to see Colonel Kincaid,' said Verago.

'He's tied up right now,' said the girl.

'Now. I want to see him now,' insisted Verago.

'You are . . . ' She left the question in the air, but her eyebrows were slightly raised.

'Captain Verago.'

She nodded, as if a missing piece in the jigsaw had turned up.

'Please sit down, Captain,' she said going to the door opposite her desk. She knocked. Verago heard a voice, and then she went inside. She shut the door.

He looked around the office. So far he wasn't impressed by Third Air Force.

He had finally got a cab at Northolt, and arrived quarter of an hour later at the headquarters complex in South Ruislip. It wasn't very imposing, more like a used car lot than a military nerve centre.

He had shown the white-capped APs his Army ID, and asked for the SJA's office.

'Building 3,' said the AP. He was chewing gum, and didn't even call him 'sir'. In the back of the guard shack, two of his buddies were playing cards.

It was a great start.

The door of the colonel's office opened, and she came out.

'Go in, Captain,' she said. He caught a whiff of her as he came past. It was a nice scent.

He entered the office. Colonel Kincaid was in his shirtsleeves, tiny silver eagles pinned to his collar. He was surprisingly young for a full bird, thought Verago.

'How are you, Captain?' welcomed Kincaid, holding out his hand. He was smiling, a frank, boyish smile. 'Make yourself at home.'

'I didn't intend coming here, sir,' said Verago. 'But my arrangements seemed snafued. I guess the lines got crossed?'

The colonel looked concerned.

'What's wrong, Captain?' he asked.

'I'm on TDY, sir. Just arrived. I'm Captain Tower's counsel.'

'Oh, of course,' said the colonel, as if a great mystery had suddenly been explained.

'My transportation doesn't appear to have materialised,' said Verago, choosing his words carefully.

'I don't understand, Captain.'

'A staff car was due to meet me, and take me straight to Laconbury. There was no car. Nobody's heard of me. Every call I make is a dead end. So here I am. I want to know what's going on.'

The colonel seemed amazed.

'Did your office tell us you were coming?' he asked.

'They sent a TWX,' said Verago. 'Twenty-four hours ago. It was acknowledged.'

'But nobody showed up?' The colonel frowned. 'Have you got your orders, Captain?'

Verago handed him the envelope. He took out the papers,

read them.

'Well, they're okay,' he agreed, 'I don't get it. Excuse me.'

He got up, and opened the door.

'Laurie, can you get us some coffee,' he sang out. He sat down behind his desk again.

'I'm sorry about this,' he apologised. 'You must think we got a hate on the Army.'

'Not at all, Colonel,' Verago was being diplomatic.

'Of course, the whole thing may be a wasted journey for you anyway.' Kincaid was almost casual.

'Sir?'

'What I'm trying to say, Captain, is that, speaking off the record, bringing you over here is sort of superfluous. Captain Tower is already represented by a perfectly competent counsel. I personally appointed him. He is a very able man.'

Verago took a deep breath. 'Colonel, Captain Tower is entitled to individual counsel, and to request the services of any legal officer he wants.'

The colonel's eyes glazed over.

'You don't have to tell me the regulations, Captain,' he said, the boyish charm evaporating a little. 'I'm sure the Army has a lot of work for you, and I simply thought I'd caution you that it could be an . . . an unnecessary trip for you.'

The girl came in, with two mugs of coffee. She put one in front of Verago, and as she bent down, she looked him straight in the eyes. It disturbed him.

'Thank you, Laurie,' said the colonel. He took a sip of his coffee, staring at Verago across the rim of his mug.

'Anyway,' he said. 'What is it you want?'

'I'd appreciate you cutting some red tape, authorising transport for me, and quarters.'

'Of course.'

'Thank you, Colonel,' said Verago. 'By the way, when is the Article 32 set for?'

'The Article 32?' repeated Colonel Kincaid.

'The pre-trial hearing,' said Verago patiently. 'I'd like to know if there's a date yet.'

'It's already taken place,' said the colonel.

Verago was staggered.

'You've had the Article 32 investigation without a defence counsel?'

'Certainly not,' replied the colonel indignantly. 'I told you, Captain Tower already has a counsel. His rights were well protected.'

Verago controlled himself.

'I want the record of the proceedings.'

'Sure,' said the colonel. 'Trouble is, I haven't got a copy of the transcript here. I imagine you'll get it at the base.'

'And I'd like to talk to the officer who carried out the Article 32 hearing.'

Colonel Kincaid sighed. 'I knew you'd say that, but the problem is he's been transferred out of England. I think he's in Turkey. Or is it Libya? He's out of this command.'

He looked out of the window.

'You're certainly lucky with the weather. I hope it keeps fine for you.'

'Colonel,' said Verago. 'I'd like to get to Laconbury as quickly as possible.'

The colonel nodded. 'We'll check the motor pool. But we're kind of short of staff cars these days.' He saw Verago's face. 'Don't worry, Captain, we'll get you there.'

He called out: 'Laurie.'

She came in. She had put on some fresh lipstick, decided Verago.

'Ah, Laurie,' said the colonel, 'see if you can fix up Captain Verago with some transportation. He can't wait to get to Laconbury.'

'Right away,' she said, and closed the door.

'You like the theatre, Captain?' enquired Kincaid. 'London's a great town for plays. You ought to take in a couple of shows while you're here.'

'If I have time,' said Verago.

The colonel smiled drily. Then a thought seemed to strike him.

'You've got a full security clearance of course?'

'To go to the theatre!'

Kincaid did not seem amused. 'How far are you cleared? Top Secret? Cosmic?'

'They trust me,' said Verago. The whole thing didn't add up.

'I have to ask,' said the colonel. 'We haven't got your 201 file over here, but I have to insist that you are cleared for classified information all the way.'

Verago's unease grew. 'Colonel, this is an adultery case. The guy's charged with sleeping with the wrong woman, not trying to steal the H bomb.'

'Laconbury is a tight base,' said the colonel. 'They're pretty security conscious.' He switched on his boyish man-to-man smile. 'I know it's a pain, but they're mighty careful about the people they let in there. Even the cooks are cleared right up to . . .'

'Cosmic?' interrupted Verago sarcastically.

'Well, maybe not that far, but certainly top secret.'

'I look forward to eating their classified corned beef hash,' retorted Verago. His anger was growing.

'Better take it seriously, Captain. They do.'

'Well, you can tell them I got a total clearance. Cosmic and all.'

'Excellent,' said the colonel. But he had difficulty hiding his disappointment. 'I'd have hated it to be a problem.'

Verago stood up.

'Thank you for your help, Colonel,' he said, straight faced.

Colonel Kincaid also rose.

'Tony,' he said, and Verago tried not to smile at the sudden cordiality. 'Feel free to contact me at any time. We're all lawyers, and we have to help each other. You run into any trouble areas just come to this office. That's what I'm here for. We'll do all we can to make things easy.'

I bet you will, thought Verago.

'Thank you, sir,' he said again, and saluted.

Kincaid acknowledged it. The last thing he did was to flash an encouraging smile at Verago.

In the outer office, the girl was just putting down the phone.

'Oh, Captain Verago,' she said, 'I'm sorry. There's no transportation to Laconbury today.'

He wasn't even surprised.

'Why not?' he asked curtly.

'They're clean out of staff cars. Everything's booked.'

'I'll hire a car,' said Verago.

'Your per diem won't cover that,' she pointed out. 'But we can get you there tomorrow. Another day won't matter, will it?'

The violet eyes were studying him.

'You're a good secretary, Laurie,' drawled Verago. 'Colonel Kincaid is a lucky man.'

There wasn't a flicker of resentment.

'Thank you, Captain,' she said innocently.

'Just one thing.' He wondered why she intrigued him. 'Where the hell do I stay tonight?'

'That's all settled, Captain,' she said. 'I've made a reservation for you at the Columbia Club. Down town. You can get a bus from the base here.'

'Well, you've certainly taken care of things,' said Verago.

'My pleasure.'

He picked up his holdall.

'I hope you like it,' she said. 'London can be a lot of fun at night.'

Momentarily, the almond-shaped eyes regarded him challengingly. They were alert, questioning eyes.

He nodded to her, and left the office.

As he walked along the corridor of Building 3, he was wondering who she slept with.

LONDON

'There's a Miss Howard to see you,' announced Pettifer, making no attempt to hide his disapproval.

Pettifer didn't appreciate unexpected callers. He ruled Daventry's professional life; organised the briefs, negotiated the

42

fees, arranged the time tables, booked the hotels, filled in the diary, set up the appointments.

He was a precise man, pedantic to a point. He always caught the same train from Orpington in the morning, and daily had the same lunch, a glass of white wine and a sausage roll, in the saloon bar of the George, across from the Law Courts.

And as clerk of Daventry's chambers Pettifer did not take kindly to surprise visitors, especially when their names meant nothing to him.

Daventry took off his reading glasses.

'Miss Howard?' he said puzzled.

Pettifer sniffed. 'The lady says you and your wife know her. She wonders if you could spare her a few minutes.'

Daventry was trying to recall where he had met her. The name was familiar, yet . . .

'Shall I tell her you are busy, sir?' suggested Pettifer hopefully. It would bring the situation back onto its orderly rails.

'Did she say what it's about?'

'No sir.' He looked over Daventry's shoulder. 'I gather it's personal.'

The rebuke was implicit.

Then Daventry remembered. The Howard girl. Of course. She had been introduced to Alex and himself at a Sunningdale garden party. Her father was something at the Foreign Office. They had made small talk for a few minutes. What on earth did she want?

'Alright, I'll see her for a minute,' said Daventry.

'I can easily get rid of her, sir.' Pettifer was making his last stand.

'Ask her in,' said Daventry coldly. The way Pettifer exercised his proprietory rights over him sometimes got on his nerves.

She came in nervously. She was blonde, and wore little make up. She seemed very tense. Last time he had seen her it had been strawberries and cream time in the lovely Sunningdale grounds.

Daventry rose. 'This is an unexpected surprise,' he said.

She gave a little tight smile.

'I know this is unforgivable,' she said. 'It's very kind of you

43

to see me, Mr Daventry. You don't know . . . how much I appreciate it.'

'Sit down, Miss Howard.'

He tried to recall what her father did at the Foreign Office. Something quite high up. One of the Under Secretaries? He made a mental note to ask Alex, she always remembered such things.

She perched on the edge of the chair.

'I . . . ' She stopped. She was trying to pluck up courage to say something.

'Yes?' prompted Daventry.

'I feel so silly,' she blurted out. Her eyes were troubled. There were dark circles under them from lack of sleep.

'I'll get us some tea,' said Daventry, and picked up the old-fashioned house phone. The instrument had been installed in the '30s, but few things got modernised in the chambers. Pettifer didn't believe in change.

'Two cups of tea, please,' instructed Daventry.

It had given her a chance to compose herself. She took the plunge.

'I need some advice, Mr Daventry,' she said.

Daventry sighed.

'Look here, Miss Howard – '

'Please, Serena.'

He cleared his throat. He knew this was going to be awkward.

'If you want legal advice, I must tell you straight away that you shouldn't even be here. I am not allowed –'

There was a tap on the door and Pettifer came in, balancing two cups of tea on a tray. Normally Judy, the typist, would do it, but Daventry knew Pettifer couldn't resist the chance of intruding.

He put down the cups. There was a single digestive biscuit in each saucer.

'Thank you, Charles,' said Daventry.

Pettifer removed himself, but not before he had given the girl a hard look.

'As I was saying,' continued Daventry. 'I can't possibly discuss anything professional with you. We have very strict

44

rules. If you need a barrister, you must go through a solicitor.'

'I know that,' she said, in a low voice.

He frowned. 'In that case, you will realise that .we can't discuss whatever it is any further.'

She was silent.

'How is your father?' asked Daventry, changing the subject as quickly as possible.

'He's fine,' she said in a dull voice. 'He's in Washington at the moment. But he'll be back soon.'

She was pale.

'Mr Daventry.'

'What is it?'

'Please help me. Please.'

Her eyes were pleading too. She looked helpless, almost trapped.

'The best thing you can do is to go to your solicitor,' he told her. 'Whatever it is, he'll help you, tell him everything, and leave it to him. It's his job.'

He smiled at her encouragingly.

'I can't,' she said.

'Nonsense,' said Daventry, 'a solicitor is like a father confessor.'

She bit her lip. 'I haven't got a solicitor.'

'Your father must have one. Go to him.'

'That's not possible.'

'Well . . . ' He paused. 'I suppose I could give you the name of somebody. Unofficially, of course.'

She was holding herself upright, and trying to stop herself from crying.

'I'm so sorry,' she whispered. She reached for her handbag, pulled out a handkerchief and started dabbing her eyes. Then she blew her nose.

'I do apologise,' she said. She was embarrassed, but she also trembled a little. 'I'm not really a cry baby.'

'That's alright,' he said gently.

'I was thinking desperately who I could turn to. There's nobody. Then I remembered meeting you. At the party. Somebody said you're a fantastic lawyer. And . . . '

He waited, silent.

She blew her nose again.

'And, well, I thought I could trust you.'

Daventry always felt cosily insulated from his clients. He never saw them alone. Etiquette was a very useful barrier. The fact that a solicitor was always present at meetings ensured his aloofness.

Serena Howard was having an effect on him. Sitting there, trembling, begging him to help, the tears she was trying to hold back, looking lonely, vulnerable, afraid. He felt sorry for her. He wanted to help. As Pettifer would have said, it was very unprofessional.

'What *is* the trouble?' Daventry said gently, and the moment he said it, he knew he had gone too far.

'You won't tell my parents?'

'Of course not. Now, what's this all about?'

She licked her dry lips.

'I've been having an affair,' she said.

Suddenly he felt enormous relief. So that's all it was! He had imagined something awful had happened. She had committed some crime, stolen something, run somebody down in her car, got caught up in narcotics and drugs.

He tried hard not to smile. Poor, frightened Serena Howard, so secluded in her safe, conformist suburban world that when she has an affair she thinks it's the end of the world.

'That's not so terrible,' said Daventry.

She's become pregnant, of course, he decided. She doesn't know how to tell her old-fashioned parents. Silly girl, she doesn't need a lawyer. She wants a doctor.

She looked at him.

'He's American,' she said. 'An officer, in the Air Force.'

'Lots of English girls have fallen in love with American servicemen,' said Daventry encouragingly.

She still had that ashen look.

'He's going to be court-martialled.'

'I see,' he said quietly. 'What for?'

She swallowed. 'Adultery.'

'That's the charge? Adultery?'

46

She nodded. 'It's a crime,' she said. 'In the American forces.'

'Good god!'

She paused. 'He committed adultery with me.'

'That's why I need help,' she added.

She leant back in the chair, waiting for his reaction. She was half afraid, half defiant.

'But you're in no trouble, Serena,' he assured her. 'I mean, they can't drag you into it.'

'Oh yes, Mr Daventry. They can.'

'Who told you that?'

He was fascinated by the ring she was wearing. It was silver, a mask, leering. It was most unusual. He wondered if it was some sort of engagement ring.

'An American officer came to see me. He said that John was going to be tried, and that the prosecution might ask me to give evidence. I said I wouldn't, and he hinted they could make me.'

It was ridiculous. 'Nonsense,' said Daventry. 'You're a British citizen, on British soil, adultery is not a crime and no foreign court martial here has jurisdiction over a British national. They can't force you.'

'That's not what he said.' She swallowed.

'They're trying to bluff you,' said Daventry firmly.

'No,' she insisted quietly. 'I don't think so. I think they mean it.'

He began to have nagging doubts. She was so positive. He pulled a pad towards him.

'What's his name?'

'John?'

He nodded, gold pencil poised.

'Captain John Tower.'

'Where's he stationed?'

'In East Anglia. The base is called Laconbury.'

He made a note.

'This officer who came to see you. You know who he was?'

She shook her head. 'I don't remember, I was in such a state. He may have told me his name, but I've forgotten.'

'Didn't Captain Tower tell you he was in trouble?'

She took a deep breath. 'It all happened so quickly. He was

due to come to London that weekend. He said he had something important to tell me, but not over the phone. He never came. Instead, this officer turned up and said he was going to be court-martialled. For adultery.' She lowered her voice. 'With me.'

'That must have been quite a shock,' said Daventry. 'I'm sorry. But really, I'm sure you don't have anything to worry about.'

He smiled.

'Tell you what, would you like to have lunch with me tomorrow?'

She stared at him.

'You *are* going to help me?' she asked optimistically.

'Not at all,' he said stiffly. 'I want to check up on the law, and set your mind at rest. I think it's better if we meet informally. That's all.'

'Thank you,' she breathed.

'One o'clock,' he said, writing it down in his leather desk diary. 'The Isola Bella, in Frith Street. You know it?'

'Don't worry,' she said eagerly. 'I'll find it.'

He walked her to the door. She stopped.

'My parents . . . ' she began, and faltered.

'They don't know about you and Captain Tower, correct?'

'Please,' she said. 'I don't want them to find out about this business.'

'It might be better if you told them,' he suggested.

'No,' she said fiercely.

He regarded her gravely. 'You sure?'

'Quite sure,' she said firmly.

She held out her hand.

'Tomorrow. One o'clock.'

Then she was gone.

He returned to his desk. He sat down and looked at the entry in his diary.

He knew one thing. He had made a big mistake.

LONDON

They're all alike, thought Verago, sitting at his table in the corner. The Columbia Club was like the Casino Club in Frankfurt, and the Von Steuben in Wiesbaden, and all the rest of them. And the people were the same. Well scrubbed, cast out of the same mould, talking the same talk, eating identical food.

When he first came to Europe, in '59, he couldn't understand what a major had meant when he'd said that if you stayed within the confines of the US military complexes it didn't matter what country you were stationed in. France, England, Germany, Italy, they all looked identical from inside the fence.

You could get born in the base hospital, be educated at the base school, meet a girl in the club or at the base movies, marry her in the base chapel, break the law and get tried on the post, serve your time in the stockade, die and have the autopsy done on your body in the base mortuary. You didn't have to leave to cash cheques, or go shopping, play bowls, go dancing, change your religion, have an affair, or commit suicide.

There was only one time you did have to leave that base. When you died they didn't bury you. For that, you got shipped into the outside world.

The major had been right, Verago thought as glanced round the room. Although Hyde Park was outside the window, they could all be having dinner in Heidelberg or Frankfurt.

He finished his chopped steak and house salad with roquefort dressing.

'Was everything alright?' asked the waiter in the red monkey jacket. Verago was a new face in the officer's open mess, and might be a good tipper. One never knew. It was worth investing a little special attention.

'Fine,' said Verago.

'You care for some dessert?'

'Just coffee.'

There were a lot of civilians around. At least, they wore civilian clothes. English-type blazers with brass buttons, club ties, and tweed coats. They spelt 'headquarters' in great big letters. Verago had to grin.

The waiter put the cup and saucer in front of him, ready to pour coffee, but Verago stood up.

'I've changed my mind,' he said. 'I think I'll go to the bar.'

It was crowded. People were sitting in little groups. A two-star admiral was holding court, surrounded by a fawning group of naval officers dutifully smiling at his jokes.

Verago managed to find a niche at the bar. 'Scotch,' he ordered. 'Make it a double.'

He felt restless. It had been a frustrating day.

He wondered what sort of man Captain Tower would turn out to be. Not popular, he was sure of that. Nobody gets charged with adultery whose face fits. Maybe the guy had fallen foul of somebody. Maybe he had screwed the colonel's wife. A sardonic smile crossed Verago's face at the thought.

They were in a hurry to get him tried, that was obvious. They had rushed through the Article 32 hearing, so that the court martial could be set up as quickly as possible.

'Give me another,' Verago told the barman.

He had an etiquette problem on his hands too. The counsel Third Air Force had appointed would hardly welcome his arrival. Tower was fully within his rights to ask for his own counsel, and an Army lawyer at that! The other fellow was bound to resent it.

Verago had already decided to play it softly. He didn't want to antagonise the man. He hoped they could work together; it wouldn't do Tower any good to have his defence team feuding.

He picked up his glass, and then stopped, his hand frozen half way. At a table by the wall sat the girl with the violet, almond-shaped eyes. Kincaid's secretary.

She was smiling at something the man sitting opposite her was saying. He was a big, heavily built man, and Verago disliked

50

him instantly. He didn't know why; maybe because he was with her.

Since Verago had seen her that afternoon, she had changed. She had more mascara on, and she wore an eye-catching black and white dress, which looked expensive. Verago studied her. She had small breasts, a slim waist, and long attractive legs. What you should do, an inner voice told him, is to go up to your room on the third floor, go to bed, read up the law on adultery, and have an early night.

'One more,' ordered Verago.

The barman only started taking notice of his customers when an officer had three or more double scotches. An Officer of the Day roamed round the Columbia Club, and it tended to be the barman who got blamed if there was trouble.

'Yes, sir,' he said, his eyes signalling caution.

The big man at her table whispered something to her, and got up. He walked out of the bar. She sat, still with a drink, smoking a cigarette.

The bastard's coming back, thought Verago. Probably just gone to the men's room, but he'll be back. So what.

Verago slid off his stool, glass in hand, and moved between the groups to her table.

'Hello,' he said.

The violet eyes looked up at him and she gave a smile. Maybe it was the scotch, but it seemed to him to be a welcoming smile.

'Why, Captain Verago . . . '

He looked at the empty chair.

'Do sit down,' she invited.

'I don't want to intrude,' he lied. 'I know you're with somebody.'

'That's alright,' she said. She offered no other explanation.

'Well, in that case . . . '

He sat down on the other man's chair, feeling a little awkward.

'Can I get you a drink?' he volunteered.

'Tequila sunrise,' she said.

He signalled a waiter and gave the order.

'And a double scotch for me,' he added.

'How's the room?' she asked.

'The room?' Then he realised. 'Oh, here? The room's fine.'

'Good. That's the least we can do for you. And I've ordered the car for tomorrow.'

'Thanks, Laurie.' He added a little apologetically, 'I don't know your name . . . '

'Czeslaw,' she said.

'Czeslaw?'

'It's Polish. My folks were Polish.'

'Laurie's very American.'

She stiffened. 'I'm American, Captain.'

'Pardon me,' he said. 'And listen, my name's Tony, OK?'

'Hi, Tony,' she smiled, and he felt warm. He didn't think it was just the whisky.

He followed the sudden direction of her eyes, and saw the burly man making his way towards their table.

Shit, thought Verago.

'Clyde,' she said, as Verago reluctantly stood up. 'This is Captain Verago. He's over from Germany.'

The man offered his hand.

'Clyde Unterberg,' he said.

Verago took it. The man had a firm grip.

'Glad to meet you,' said Verago. He was doing a lot of lying. 'I'm sorry, I've taken your chair . . . '

'Don't worry about it,' said Unterberg. He reached over and pulled a chair across from the next table, braving the hostile look of a naval commander.

'Captain Verago is here to attend a court martial,' said Laurie.

'Is that so? Not yours I hope?' And Unterberg laughed.

'I'm defending,' said Verago unsmiling. 'A man who's accused of a ridiculous charge.'

Laurie put out her cigarette.

'Oh? What's that?' asked Unterberg.

'Adultery.'

'You think adultery is ridiculous, Captain?'

'I think to try a man for it and send him to jail is ridiculous.'

'Well,' said Unterberg, 'maybe with you defending him,

he won't go to jail.'

Verago sniffed. 'Where the hell are our drinks?' he demanded. He gestured to the waiter. 'What's yours, Clyde?'

'I like the same as you. Scotch.'

Verago was surprised that Unterberg knew what he drank.

'Where is this trial going to take place?' enquired Unterberg.

'Laconbury,' said Verago.

'That's Air Force.' Unterberg shook his head. 'What's an Army lawyer doing at an Air Force trial?'

'Tony's been specially requested by the accused,' intervened Laurie.

'You must have some reputation,' said Unterberg. 'All the way from Germany! Or do you know the man?'

'Never met him, never even heard of him,' said Verago.

'But you like fighting lost causes, don't you?' smiled Unterberg.

Again, Verago had a moment of unease.

'Are you in the service?' he asked.

'Clyde's a civilian,' said Laurie, as the drinks came.

'Technician?'

'Sort of,' said Laurie.

'Lockheed?'

Instead of answering, Unterberg lifted his glass.

'Success,' he toasted. 'How long are you planning to stay?'

'As long as it takes,' said Verago.

'Well, good luck.' He finished his drink and pushed back his chair. 'You'll have to excuse me. I've got to drive to High Wycombe tonight. I'll give you a call, Laurie.' He pecked her cheek. Then he nodded to Verago. 'Nice to have met you, Tony.'

Something doesn't fit, thought Verago, as Unterberg made his exit. It doesn't seem right. Had he really planned to leave her on her own and take off. What if he hadn't shown up? Would Unterberg still have left her high and dry? Why the hell was he leaving the stage clear for somebody else?

'You're not very talkative, Tony,' said Laurie. It seemed to him her eyes were slightly mocking. 'Something on your mind?'

'What does he really do?' asked Verago.

53

'Clyde?'

He nodded.

'He's a spook,' she said quietly.

Suddenly he looked at her in a new light.

'That's what I thought,' he said. 'Thanks.'

'What for?'

'For playing it straight.'

'Playing what straight?' she asked, surprised. 'Telling you he's a spook? Well, he is, isn't he?'

'Who for? Who with?'

'Come on, Tony,' she said, and again she was slightly mocking. 'Would I know?' she smiled. 'He's not with the Russians, if that's what you mean,' she laughed.

The idea really amused her.

'CIA? OSI?' he pressed. 'Some outfit like that?' He frowned. 'How do you know him?'

'Captain Verago,' she said, sham serious, 'this is not a court room, I'm not on the stand, and you're off duty. Agreed?'

Damn it, she's attractive, he thought. She's not beautiful, she's got more than that going for her.

He wished the chair was closer to her.

'Remember what you said today?' he asked.

She shook her head. 'What?'

'You said "London can be a lot of fun at night".'

'You want to go sightseeing right now?' she teased him. 'The pubs will be closed.'

'I didn't have pubs in mind.'

The almond-shaped eyes flickered.

'What do you have in mind?'

'I leave that to you,' said Verago.

LONDON

As Alex handed Daventry his drink he suddenly asked her: 'You

54

remember the Howards? I met their daughter today.

'Oh?' said Alex, 'and how is Serena?' She had a fantastic memory for names. She had trained it. She noted every address and phone number and kept a special book with dozens of people's birthdays in it.

'Fine,' he replied casually. It seemed to him his tone was almost too casual.

'What's she doing now?'

'She didn't say.'

'Wasn't she doing some modelling? At Fortnum's?'

'I don't know.'

'She's got a very nice figure.' She took some crisps then offered Daventry the glass dish. 'Which I won't have if I go on nibbling these. Do you want one?'

He shook his head as he studied her. 'You don't have to worry, Alex,' he said, kissing her on the forehead. She worked hard at keeping slim, because she knew he disliked fat women.

'They're nice people, the Howards.' Her U-turn back to the subject slightly startled him.

'Yes,' he said, rather flatly.

'Don't say it,' smiled Alex. 'Too cocktail partyish for you. They bore you.'

'Alex, I don't even know them well enough for that.'

'I'd have thought Serena would have been married by now,' she remarked, almost to herself.

He was curious. 'Why?'

'Well,' said Alex. 'She's very attractive, isn't she? I shouldn't imagine she'd have any difficulty finding somebody. Don't you agree?'

'Yes, I suppose so. If she wants to.'

'She didn't strike me as being the career girl type.'

It was the end of Serena as a topic of conversation. Alex changed the subject with an announcement she had been saving up.

'By the way, I got the tickets. For the Kirov.'

Her voice was triumphant.

The Kirov season at Covent Garden was the big sensation. There were all night queues at the box office, and getting seats

55

was a major achievement.

'How did you manage that?' asked Daventry.

'Ah.' Alex enjoyed playing it mysteriously. 'I've got hidden talents.'

'When are we going?' he enquired.

'Next Tuesday. Put it in your book now. Kolpakov is dancing Giselle. I think you'll enjoy it,' she said encouragingly. 'They've got a dancer called Nureyev, and he's supposed to be fantastic. If only we had somebody like that over here. I think I'll try for Sleeping Beauty as well,' continued Alex's voice, as if from a distance. 'We might as well make the most of it while the Kirov's in London, don't you think?'

'Yes, why not,' he muttered, but he hardly heard her. His mind was on his lunch date the following day. He wished he knew how to get out of it.

The trouble was that Gerald Daventry was a coward.

LONDON

Laurie lived in a furnished apartment in a smart block of flats in Sloane Avenue. It was an oppressively small place, almost cramped, but she had given it some personal touches. Plants by the window, a couple of modernistic prints, a ceramic figure of a jester. They helped, but it was still an anonymous, lonely habitation.

'I'll fix you a drink,' she said, and disappeared into the tiny kitchen.

On top of a book case was the framed photograph of a lieutenant in the Marine Corps.

'That's my brother,' she said, coming in with a tray, a bottle of scotch, an ice bucket, and two glasses on it. 'He won the Bronze Star in Korea.'

'Where is he now?' he asked.

'Naples,' she said, pouring the drinks. The ice clinked.

'Your only brother?'

She nodded. 'I have a sister, but she's a bitch.'

He wanted to know more, but her tone was uninviting.

Verago tasted the whisky with relish. It was good, well matured, at least twelve years old. He appreciated it. The effects of the drinks earlier had worn off in the cab ride to her place.

'Where's your home, Laurie?'

'Chicago,' she said. 'What about you?'

'New York.' He didn't amplify. 'So tell me, what brought you over here?'

'You are nosey, Captain Verago,' she said. 'They sent me here. I'm a GS8, right. I work for the Department of the Air Force, I go where I'm sent. Satisfied?'

She got up, went over to a drawer in the sideboard and brought out a box of cigars. She held it out to him.

'You like Upmans?'

He took one, incised the end with his nail, and lit it. So, she kept cigars in her apartment. All the home comforts for a man. What man? The spook? Her boss?

She put the box of cigars back in the drawer.

'You won't like Laconbury,' she said unexpectedly. She had kicked off her shoes.

'Oh? What's wrong with it?'

'You'll find out.'

That annoyed him. 'I don't go for riddles, Laurie. What's wrong with Laconbury?'

'You ever heard of Detachment 7?'

'No.'

She leant across and poured him another slug of whisky.

'How do you defend a man charged with adultery, Tony?' she asked.

'Detachment 7,' he insisted. 'What about it? What is it?'

'Oh, I just wondered what you had heard of it,' she said dismissively. She raised her glass. 'Salut.'

They both drank. Then she repeated the question: 'You still haven't told me. How do you set about defending a man

57

accused of adultery?'

'Why do you want to know?'

'I'm curious. We don't get many adultery cases in the office.'

'Well,' said Verago slowly. 'There's only one defence. That he didn't do it. If you can prove that he didn't sleep with the other woman, or that if he did, he wasn't married, and so he didn't commit adultery.'

'And if that doesn't work?'

'You put your money on mitigation. You plead an unhappy marriage, you say it's all washed up anyway, the affair hasn't harmed anybody, we're all men of the world, and isn't it kind of inhuman to send a guy to jail for trying to find a little happiness with somebody else.'

She pulled a face. 'You make my heart break,' she said.

'I know. It rarely works,' he admitted ruefully.

The phone rang. It startled him. He looked at his watch. It was 1 a.m.

'Excuse me,' she said, uncurled herself from the armchair, and went to the coffee table by the window where the phone was and picked it up.

'Hello,' she said, and listened.

He wondered who would ring her at this time. Mr Unterberg maybe? To tell her he'd arrived at High Wycombe and was cosily tucked in?

'No, I haven't forgotten,' she said.

She glanced at Verago as she spoke. Then she turned her back.

'No, I appreciate that,' he heard her say. 'Don't worry, I'll take care of it,' she said, and hung up.

'That was your favourite man,' she announced, settling herself back into the armchair.

'Eh?'

'Colonel Kincaid.'

'Really?'

She laughed. 'Oh come on, Tony, you're dying to know why my boss should call me at home at . . . ' she glanced at her wristlet watch, 'at one o'clock in the morning.'

'It's none of my business, Laurie,' he said stiffly. 'Anyway, I think I ought to go.'

'It was about you,' she said.

He sat very still. 'Me?'

'He asked me to make sure that as soon as I get to the office in the morning I send a priority TWX to USAREUR. He wants your personnel file.'

'What the hell for?'

'He didn't say, but I guess the colonel wants to know all about you.'

The violet eyes stared straight at him.

'I guess so do I,' she added.

'It's very late,' he muttered, thickly.

'Why don't you stay here tonight?'

'Here?' he repeated stupidly.

'You can be back at the club for breakfast,' she assured him.

Jesus, he thought, we haven't even touched each other. We haven't even kissed. We haven't . . . and here she is inviting me into the sack with her.

'I'd like that very much, Laurie,' said Verago, and meant it.

'I know,' she said. She got up and opened the door to the other room. The bedroom.

There were twin beds in it. But only one was used that night.

Friday, June 23, 1961 – LONDON

Laurie woke him up with a cup of instant coffee. They looked at one another, and smiled. It had been a good night.

Then she nearly spoilt it all.

'Here,' she said, and handed him a razor and a half-used tube of shaving cream.

In the small bathroom, he scowled at the mirror as he shaved. He didn't know which aggravated him more; that she had a man's shaving things in her apartment, or she didn't care if he knew.

He realised that what he felt was a pang of raw, primitive jealousy, and that annoyed him too. It was an emotion he detested.

You stupid bastard, said his inner voice. You sleep with a woman you haven't known for more than twenty-four hours, and you get screwed up because another guy's stayed in her apartment.

But all the misgivings were swept aside when he was ready to go.

'You think you'll get back to London soon?' she asked.

'Of course. The base is only a couple of hours away, isn't it?' The robe she wore seemed to accentuate her naked body underneath. The dormant desire for her was beginning again. 'Try stopping me,' he added, his voice husky.

'That's good,' she said simply.

'I'll call you,' he promised.

Suddenly, unexpectedly, she pressed her body to his, and kissed him hard on the mouth.

'See you,' she said, a little breathlessly, pushing him out of the front door.

'Sure thing, Laurie.'

She stood in the doorway, watching him go to the lift. He turned and she gave him a little wave before shutting the door.

He rode down from the third floor, and reflected how little he knew about her. Sure he knew her body, the way she made love, her laugh, those curious eyes, that she had a Polish surname, came from Chicago, and was an Air Force employee. But that was all.

Yet he didn't care. He wanted to see her again, he wanted to hold her once more.

'You're making a big deal out of a one-night stand, cautioned his inner voice coldly.

'Shut up,' said Verago aloud.

Outside, the early June morning smelt good. A cab cruised towards him, its 'For Hire' sign illuminated. Verago flagged it down.

'Columbia Club,' he instructed.

The cab drove off.

The two men in a black Chrysler parked opposite the block of flats didn't follow. One of them merely made an entry in a note book:

'06.20 hrs: Left the apartment.'

LONDON

'Here you are, sir,' said Pettifer acidly.

He put a copy of the Visiting Forces Act 1952 in front of Daventry.

'Is there anything else you require?'

'Not at the moment, thank you,' said Daventry.

Pettifer sniffed and went out of the study leaving Daventry surrounded by Orders in Council, and Crown Statutes, volumes of International Law and now the Visiting Forces Act for which he had asked urgently.

No case that Pettifer had on his list for Daventry required those legal authorities. He was evidently reading up on something Pettifer did not know about, which meant that he was putting in valuable time . . . to do somebody a favour? And being wily and shrewd he immediately suspected it had something to do with that curious visit Daventry had received from the Howard girl.

She had preyed on Pettifer's mind. It wasn't social, he was sure. And it couldn't have been business because he didn't know about it. There had been no preliminaries, no solicitors. And yet . . .

He had spent agonising hours wondering whether he should challenge Daventry about it outright. As clerk of the chambers, he was not only entitled to know what was going on, it was his duty. Daventry's time was valuable. A morning's devilling on a case was worth a handsome fee.

Not that Pettifer believed Daventry had taken on a case without his knowledge. Accepting a brief direct was the ultimate professional crime. It would mean disbarment and disgrace. It would be suicide and he knew Daventry would never do that.

Pettifer sighed. He was indeed a worried man and only hoped that Daventry knew what he was doing.

In his study, Daventry read through the thin 1952 Act a second time. He glanced at the notes he had made.

It was bad news. Very bad news.

ESSEX

The airman first class who drove the staff car to Laconbury was not talkative. Verago sat in the back watching the flat, monotonous East Anglian countryside roll past, wondering why he had a growing sense of foreboding.

Kincaid's curious interest in his security clearance, for instance. It had never happened to Verago before. All because he was to defend a guy who had cheated on his wife.

'Are you stationed at Laconbury?' Verago asked the driver.

The airman turned his head slightly. 'Yes, sir.'

'What's it like?'

The airman didn't take his eyes off the country road.

'Alright, I guess.'

'What do they fly there? Bombers? Fighters?'

'Sir?'

'I'm Army,' explained Verago hastily. 'We know nothing about you people over here.'

'Yes, sir,' said the airman, and left it at that.

It was like questioning a piece of wood. Yet the airman was

intelligent, alert.

Verago decided to try again.

'You know a Captain Tower?' he asked.

He saw the airman's back visibly stiffen.

'Sir?' The same damn reaction.

'I just wondered if you'd heard of him.'

The airman kept his eyes straight in front. 'I wouldn't know, sir.'

Verago sighed.

'What's your name?'

'Flynn, sir.'

'Your first name?'

The airman frowned. Was this visiting fireman going to make trouble? 'Teddy, sir.'

'Well, Teddy, what does a fellow do for fun around here?' Maybe, thought Verago, that's the way to break the ice.

'Not much, sir. Most of the guys go to London. Or Cambridge. That's about it.'

His tone was final.

They drove through some small villages, followed a bumpy minor road, then past acres of farm land. They had left London two hours previously.

Suddenly a sharp-nosed jet streaked past over a wood.

'We're nearly there, sir,' said the airman. It was the only time he had volunteered anything. They passed a tiny hamlet, and a twelfth-century, ivy-covered church.

'There's the base, sir,' said Teddy.

Verago didn't know what he had expected, but it wasn't this. Just hedgerows. A long line of them, blocking the view of what lay beyond them. He saw, in the distance, a couple of tall radio masts, and a high wire fence.

'Welcome to Laconbury,' proclaimed a notice board at the entrance to the base. It had an emblem, the head of a Cyclops, with one huge staring eye in the middle of the forehead. And there was a motto underneath: 'Ever Vigilant.'

The car slid to a halt at the guardhouse. The APs were smart, really smart. They had razor creases, and their white laced boots shone like mirrors. Their cap covers were snow white, like the

63

lanyards of their pistols.

They waved down the car. One AP came over, the other two stood watching.

Teddy handed the AP a slip of paper. The guard peered at Verago, and gave him a copy-book salute. Verago had rolled down the window, and awkwardly saluted back.

'You will proceed to headquarters, sir,' said the AP respectfully, very correctly, and yet giving a firm order.

The car entered the base, and Verago saw a lot of anonymous buildings. And several of those radio masts. The only sign of it being an air base were a couple of men in flying suits. The flight lines, the hangars, the planes, the runways, Verago guessed were at the other end, out of sight.

In front of the headquarters building were two flag poles. One flew the Stars and Stripes, the other had an RAF ensign on its lanyard. A lieutenant was already waiting in front of the building and when the car stopped, he came forward, and stood watching while Teddy got out of the driver's seat, and opened the door for Verago.

'Thank you,' said Verago.

'Good morning, sir,' said the lieutenant. 'This way please. The general is waiting for you.'

'The general?' repeated Verago.

'General Croxford, sir,' said the lieutenant. 'Our commander.'

He made it sound like their privilege. He was *their* commander, nobody else's. He belonged to them.

An airman walked behind them, carrying Verago's holdall.

They turned into a carpeted corridor, to an outer office. The lighting was soft, subdued. Here there was air conditioning and silence. The airman placed Verago's bag near a desk, then left.

The lieutenant knocked on a door.

'Yes,' came a voice.

The lieutenant went inside, came out after a moment and said:
'Please go in, Captain Verago.'

Brigadier-General Croxford did not get up. He sat behind his desk in his smart, tailor-made blue uniform, the single silver star gleaming on his shoulder. He had four rows of medal ribbons, under the command pilot's wings.

Behind him on the wall was a giant replica of the Cyclops crest, and the lone eye seemed to be staring straight at Verago. The flags were there, standing by the desk, a Stars and Stripes and a blue and yellow Air Force flag.

The only pictures on the wall were black-framed photographs. One of President Kennedy. Another of a B29, and it was only later that Verago found out it was a picture of the plane that dropped the atom bomb on Hiroshima.

The general had three aircraft models on his desk. One was a silver RB47, another an RB66. Verago didn't know what kind the third was, a needle-like, sharp-pointed plane with curious wings that looked out of proportion.

'Sit down, Captain,' invited the general. He was soft spoken, and had dark brown eyes. His complexion had a pasty pallor, as if he spent a long time indoors, or underground. He looked like a man who could do with a good vacation in the sun.

'Thank you, sir.'

'I'm sorry about this affair,' said the general, without preliminaries. 'I hope we can get it over as quickly as possible.'

Verago felt it wise to stay silent.

'You will of course be given every facility to defend this officer, and we'll try to make your stay comfortable.'

'Thank you, sir.'

The general contemplated Verago for a moment. His brown eyes were quite unashamed in their curiosity.

'I believe you don't know Captain Tower, is that right?'

'No, sir. Not yet.'

Verago tried to recall if he had ever heard of an air base commanded by a general. He didn't know much about the Air Force, but this place seemed heavy on top brass.

'It's an unpleasant business,' went on the general. 'I dislike this kind of case in my command.'

Verago led with his chin.

'I am not sure we should discuss the case, sir,' he said.

'I see.'

The general was poker faced.

'In that case, Captain, we won't discuss it.'

Verago waited.

'But I think I ought to tell you that this installation has a classified mission.'

'I understand, sir.'

'This is a tactical reconnaissance wing, and we don't talk about our activities, is that clear?'

'Yes, sir,' said Verago. The old unease started up again.

'Good. So neither of us will discuss certain sensitive areas. Agreed?'

The general allowed himself a cold smile.

'Very well, General.'

'You'll find Lieutenant Jensen has done an excellent job.'

'Who is Lieutenant Jensen, sir?' asked Verago.

'I thought you knew. Captain Tower's defence counsel of course. The one we appointed.' The hint of impatience was not disguised. 'He's done all the ground work. A good lawyer. I guess you won't find much to do around here.'

Was it a hint? Or a warning?

'I look forward to working with him,' said Verago, carefully. 'But first I'm going to see Captain Tower. I think it's about time I met my client.'

'Sure thing,' agreed Croxford. He shifted the model of the RB47. It had not been in straight alignment with the other two planes. 'As soon as we can fix it.'

'What's the difficulty?' asked Verago, very quietly.

'Captain Tower isn't available right now.'

Of course. He should have expected something like this.

'I don't get it, General,' said Verago. He sat up very straight. 'What's the problem?'

General Croxford frowned. He was not used to being cross-examined.

'Your client is in the base hospital. I believe he's had some kind of nervous breakdown.' The general shook his head. 'I'm sorry, but the doctors have given orders he's not to see anybody.'

He paused, but Verago just stared at him.

'Obviously, we mustn't allow anything to happen that could harm him. Like pressurising him. I'm sure you concur with

66

that, Captain.'

The ear-splitting roar of a jet plane flying low shook the office. The noise made Verago wince, but General Croxford tilted his head, and listened to it like a conductor appraising his orchestra.

'You'll get used to that, Captain,' he said when the sound faded. 'Leastways, I hope so.'

He brushed an invisible spot off his immaculate uniform.

'Hell, we don't want you to have a nervous breakdown too.'

Verago wasn't smiling. 'I don't think that's likely, General. But I'd appreciate knowing how long he'll be in there.'

'Captain, I'm no psychiatrist. How do I know?'

'What about the trial?'

'That's for you to sort out. Anything else?'

'Not now, General.'

Croxford gave him a sharp look.

He leant forward. His voice was softer.

'Say, Verago, what's your handicap?'

'Sir?' Verago was baffled.

'Don't you play golf?'

'No, sir.'

The general leant back in his chair. 'Pity,' he said coldly. 'That's great pity. Well, if you'll excuse me now.'

Verago stood up and saluted.

The general saluted back, but he had pulled a file in front of him, and he was no longer looking at Verago.

Only the baleful eye of the Cyclops on the wall glowered at him. It was a cold cruel eye.

LONDON

The Isola Bella was buzzing with lunch-time conversation, and

Daventry was glad, because they could talk without being overheard.

Serena looked fresher, less strained than the day before. She wore a bright patterned dress, the top three buttons undone. A tiny gold chain circled her slim neck.

'Any news?' he asked over the melon con prosciutto.

'No. I haven't heard a thing from John.'

'Can't you call him?'

She shook her head. 'He once said never to phone him at the base. I haven't even got the number.'

'Well,' said Daventry weakly, 'no news is good news. At least, so they tell me.'

Why was he doing this, he asked himself. Why was he getting involved in her problems?

Could it be that for once he wanted to help someone not because they paid him, not because it was his job, not even because he knew them, but to make amends to the likes of Mary Donovan?

But why put his professional ethics on the line first, he asked himself.

'How about you?' Her question interrupted his thoughts.

'Well,' he said reluctantly, 'I've looked up a few things. Not that that means anything.'

'No. Tell me.'

'As far as I can see . . . ' He stopped.

The waiter brought the pollo alla Sophia Loren. They were both having the same thing. She ignored the food.

'Please. I want to know.'

'It seems they can call you to give evidence at the court martial. It appears that the general and specific privileges applicable to the Crown have been extended to visiting forces in the United Kingdom . . . '

He was talking like a lawyer. It annoyed him. She must think him very pompous.

'In simple terms, Serena, it means they can subpoena you.'

Her face drained.

'Your food's getting cold,' he pointed out. She picked up her knife and fork like a robot.

They ate silently for a few minutes.

'What does that mean?' she asked at last.

'Well, a subpoena is an order to a person to attend court and give evidence.'

'And if I don't?'

He took a deep breath.

'You're in trouble. Disobeying an order of the court is contempt. They could even say you're deliberately obstructing the course of justice by refusing to testify. That's contempt too. You go to jail for it.'

She looked incredulous. 'You mean the Americans can send me to prison? Here, in England?'

'Not the Americans. We can. Under the act, the subpoena would be issued by an English judge at the request of the Americans. And he would deal with you if you disobeyed him.'

'My god.'

She pushed her plate away. 'I'm sorry,' she apologised. 'I'm not very hungry.'

She fiddled with the wine glass.

'How long is the prison sentence?'

He raised his eyebrows. She sounded very determined.

'People stay locked up until they've purged their contempt – or done what they were ordered to do. Actually, there's no time limit.'

'It's medieval,' she said.

'I agree. So is putting a man on trial for – ' He was going to say adultery, but he changed it. '– for having a relationship.'

She raised her head, almost defiantly.

'So,' she said, with a thin smile. 'I've had it.'

'No of course not,' protested Daventry. 'I've just told you what the law is. They may never ask for you to be subpoenaed.'

'They will,' she said quietly.

'Well, they haven't so far.' Her fatalistic acceptance of the situation aggravated him. 'And even if they serve you with a witness summons, they have to give you at least fourteen days before you appear in court. A lot of things can happen in fourteen days.'

'Finished?' asked the waiter, looking reproachfully at the

69

half full plates.

'Yes,' said Daventry. 'Very nice, thank you.'

He sipped some wine.

'May I ask you something . . . rather personal, Serena?'

She nodded.

'This American friend of yours. Captain Tower. You've known him some time?' He felt awkward. 'I mean this relationship?'

She was not embarrassed. 'You want to know whether we're serious or if it's just a passing thing? A casual affair? Is that it?'

He shifted in his chair. 'Well . . .'

'I got fond of John, and I tell you one thing. Never will I give evidence that can send him to jail. Never. No matter what they do with me.'

If he had been in a court room, his next question would have been: 'You say you are fond of him, Miss Howard. But do you love him?'

Here, in the restaurant, it remained unasked.

Instead she took the wind out of his sails.

'I might as well tell you. I am engaged.'

'To him?'

'Oh no. My fiancé is in the diplomatic service. He is a junior attaché at the British Embassy in Tokyo. Tokyo is a long way away . . .'

Daventry put down the wine glass. She's nice looking, he thought, but she doesn't seem the sort to be engaged to one chap and behind his back have an affair with another one. She looks so correct, so prim, so proper.

'I know what you're thinking. I'm not a very nice girl . . .'

'Not at all,' interrupted Daventry. 'If I have learned one thing, it's not to make moral judgements.'

He meant it well, but it came out sounding patronising, priggish. Momentarily he felt terribly old-fashioned. It must be the influence of his father, the judge.

'I don't blame you,' said Serena. 'Things sometimes get fouled up, as John would say. I met him last autumn . . . and it just happened. Philip's been abroad for almost a year so he doesn't know a thing about it. He's not due back until

November, and then . . . well, anyway. That's the position.'

'And that's why your parents mustn't know either?'

She hesitated. 'It's one of the reasons. They adore Philip. Oh, it's very complicated.'

'Are you planning to marry Captain Tower eventually?' asked Daventry.

'Mr Daventry, he's married, remember.' She shrugged. 'Isn't that what this bloody business is all about?'

She stared at the tablecloth. 'I suppose I should have been more honest. Written to Philip about it. Told my parents. It's so easy to say that, believe me, but to do it . . . '

'I know,' sympathised Daventry. 'Try to forget about it for now. Keep in touch. Nothing may happen. But if you do hear something, let me know. And Serena . . . '

She looked at him slightly watery eyed.

'Chin up.' Daventry could be very Eton and Harrow at times.

'Thank you for being so understanding,' she whispered.

He paid the bill, and then left the restaurant with her.

Unterberg made no attempt to follow them. He had enjoyed his meal, and although he had not been able to hear any of their conversation, he had watched them with interest.

Now he also paid. And as he walked out, he stopped by the head waiter.

'The couple who sat at that table,' he said. 'I think I know the man, but for the life of me I can't remember his name.'

'Table nine, signor?' the Maitre d' looked at the reservations book. 'That was Mr Daventry.'

'Oh,' said Unterberg, 'of course. How stupid of me.'

He slipped the man a pound note.

LACONBURY

The hospital stood on the other side of the base, sandwiched between the gym and the large, supermarket-style commissary.

It had an antiseptic smell and the first thing Verago saw when he entered was a line of women in various stages of pregnancy sitting on a row of chairs. Baby producing was a side industry of Laconbury, and the ante-natal clinic was never short of customers.

'I'd like to see Captain Tower,' said Verago to the nurse at the main reception desk.

'Visiting hours . . . ' she began, but Verago was ready for that.

'I'm over from Germany specially,' he said. 'I'd sure appreciate it . . . '

She consulted a revolving index and found the slotted card.

'He's in . . . ' she stopped. 'Oh, I'm sorry, Captain, he's not allowed any visitors.'

'Is he that bad?' enquired Verago, sounding very concerned. He had talent.

'I wouldn't know,' said the nurse. 'I'm sorry. You want to talk to somebody?'

'No, that's alright,' said Verago vaguely. He gave the impression of a man collecting his thoughts. But he knew already what he was going to do.

He ambled over to the lift. The nurse was already busy with somebody else. He pressed the button for the second floor.

He hadn't been able to read everything on the card when he'd peered over the nurse's shoulder, but he had seen a large number '12'.

There wouldn't be twelve wards in the hospital he figured. It wasn't that big after all. But room twelve. That was a possibility.

He got out of the lift, and walked purposefully along the corridor. There were wards on either side of it, and no one took any notice of him. He came to some doors. 'X-ray room' said one sign. 'Therapy' read another. There were also some numbered doors, but none above eight.

Verago took the lift to the next floor. It was quieter there. A nurse with first lieutenant's silver bars passed him, but he walked on unhesitatingly, as if he knew his way and she

72

ignored him.

The fifth door he came to had the number 12. Also a little sign hanging from the handle: 'No Visitors'.

Verago slowly opened the door. He didn't know quite what to expect.

It was a pleasant, airy room. The bed was made, but it was empty. A captain's uniform jacket lay on it. In a chair, by the window, sat a man in shirtsleeves.

The man was reading, and he looked up.

'Captain Tower?' enquired Verago.

The man put down the book. He had a scar under his left eye. He was in his thirties, and the touch of grey in his hair suited him well.

'Who are you?' he asked.

Verago shut the door.

'I'm Verago,' he said. 'You sent for me.'

The man frowned.

'Can I see your ID, Captain,' he asked.

Verago pulled out the AGO card with his photograph and handed it to the man. He studied it, then glanced up at Verago as if to compare the face with the photo.

He gave it back.

'I'm sorry, Captain,' he apologised, 'I just don't know who's who anymore. I want to be sure who I talk to.'

The way he said it did not sound irrational.

'You're satisfied?' asked Verago.

'Sure,' said the man. 'Thanks for coming. I didn't think you'd make it. What I mean is, I didn't think they'd let you make it.'

Verago sat down on the bed.

'Why are you in here, Captain?' he asked.

Tower smiled derisively.

'Haven't they told you? I'm supposed to be having a nervous breakdown. I'm supposed to be in bad shape.'

'Why no visitors?'

'You don't know anything, do you, Captain?' said Tower. 'What this is all about?'

'I'm trying to find out,' said Verago. 'Why don't you

73

fill me in?'

'First you tell me. Do you think I've cracked up? Look at me. Do I look like a guy having a breakdown?'

'I don't think so,' said Verago slowly. 'I'd say no.'

'Thank Christ for that.' A look of relief crossed his face. 'How come they let you see me?'

'They didn't,' said Verago. 'I sneaked in here.'

'Well, we'd better talk quick. When they find you here, they'll throw you out. You'll get your ass kicked, believe me, Captain, and I'll probably get a guard on the door.'

'Listen, I'm your counsel. I've got every right to talk to you. Nobody can come between lawyer and client.'

'Oh no?' He looked hard at Verago. Then he reached over to his jacket, and pulled out a packet of King Edwards. He unwrapped one and lit it with a silver lighter. Verago hadn't seen a model like that.

'That's unusual,' he said.

'It's Russian,' said Tower. 'Oh, I'm sorry, do you want one?' He offered the pack of cigars.

Verago shook his head.

'I want to get some things straight,' he said. 'They've had the Article 32, I understand.'

'That's right.'

'And Lieutenant Jensen has been handling your defence?'

'Jensen!' It was a snort of contempt. 'Have you met him?'

'Not yet,' said Verago. 'I'm going to read the record, of course, but what kind of evidence have they got?'

'Plenty.' Tower curled his lips. 'As much as they need.'

'Why did they put you in here?'

'It's a nice way of keeping me out of circulation until the trial. It might also help.'

'Help what?' asked Verago.

'To discredit me. No smoke without fire, that kind of thing.'

'Just because you've been having an affair?'

It was hard to take, and yet Verago believed the man. But he had to ask.

They could hear voices outside, and Tower tensed.

Suddenly the door burst open. A man in a white coat stood

74

staring at them. On his uniform collar were the oak leaves of a major.

'Who are you, sir?' he demanded.

Verago stood up.

'Captain Verago, judge advocate's department. I am this officer's counsel.'

'Didn't you read the notice?' asked the major. 'This man is not allowed visitors.'

Behind the doctor, a flustered nurse appeared.

'I'm sorry, doctor. I had no idea . . . ' she gasped.

'He seems alright to me,' said Verago. 'As a matter of fact, I want to talk to you, doctor. I want to know why you're keeping him like this.'

The doctor avoided Verago's eyes.

'This is not the place to discuss it, Captain,' he said.

Verago turned to his client.

'I'll be back, John. We'll get all this sorted out. I'll see you soon.'

He tried to sound reassuring.

Outside, in the corridor, Verago turned on the doctor.

'I don't know what the hell is going on here, doctor, but that officer is perfectly normal. Who authorised that he can't see anyone?'

The doctor bit his lip.

'It's in his own interest,' he said, awkwardly.

'Bullshit,' snapped Verago. 'I'm looking after his interests and I want him out of here. I want to know who gave the orders . . . '

'Well,' said the doctor uneasily. 'We're only trying to be helpful. We were asked to keep him, well, away from people. As I said, in his own interest.'

'And who asked you?' demanded Verago dangerously. 'Who wanted him locked away?'

'His lawyer,' said the doctor. 'I mean, his other lawyer. Lieutenant Jensen.'

LACONBURY

First Lieutenant Cyrus Jensen was an unfortunate man. He was short, baby faced, with thick bulbous lips which somehow made him look sullen. As if to make up for his appearance he was also aggressive, except to his superiors.

'I'm glad to have you on this case, counsellor,' he said briskly when Verago walked into his room at the base legal office.

'That so?' It surprised Verago. He had already convinced himself Jensen would resent his very presence.

'Yeah. Maybe you can make this idiot see some sense.'

'How's that?'

'He's wasting everybody's time. The case is open and shut.'

They were words Verago loathed. Every prosecutor he came across in the military trumpeted he had an 'open and shut' case. Only this man was supposed to be defending the accused.

'It's solid, Captain,' added Jensen, and pushed a file across to Verago. 'You just read the Article 32.'

'You were there?'

'Of course,' said Jensen indignantly. 'I did my best, but Jesus, you can't fight a brick wall.'

That was better. Jensen was living up to expectation after all.

'So what do you suggest?'

'We got no choice,' declared Jensen, not unhappily. 'He's got to plead guilty, and hope for the best. Unless of course . . . '

Verago's eyes narrowed. 'Unless what?'

'Unless we can get him boarded out. Discharged for "the good of the service". Something like that.'

Verago's dislike of the man grew by the minute.

'That finishes him.'

Jensen laughed. 'Well, he won't become a United States senator, that's for sure, but he'll be able to sling hash or clean windows. Better than Leavenworth any day. Who wants a guy like that in the service anyway?'

'I see,' said Verago.

'By the way, there's a second charge now. Violation of Article 133 . . . '

'But he's already charged with prejudicial conduct . . . ' interrupted Verago. 'What the hell are they trying to do?'

'Counsellor, this is conduct unbecoming an officer and a gentleman. It's quite different,' said Jensen piously.

'You mean they want to hang him twice.' He took a deep breath. 'And what's the specification this time?'

'The same. Having sexual relations with a female not his wife.' Jensen evidently liked the sound of it.

Verago leant back.

'Have you had many of these, Lieutenant?'

'I don't get you.'

'Have a lot of men on this base been accused of adultery?'

The thick lips pouted.

'Er . . . no . . . I guess not.'

'And how many men are stationed here?'

'That's classified,' said Jensen hastily.

'Bullshit. Anyway, it doesn't matter. Say three thousand? Four thousand?'

'Well?' Jensen's annoyance was growing.

'So, Lieutenant, here are hundreds, maybe thousands of married men stuck in the middle of nowhere, in a foreign country, for three years at a time, and not one of them apparently has got himself involved with a woman. It's a great outfit you got here.'

'This isn't Germany, Captain, and we're not in the Army.'

'And you don't fuck?'

Jensen's babyish face reddened.

'That's uncalled for, sir. I heard about your reputation, Captain, now I believe it.'

Verago smiled benignly. 'No kidding? And who told you about me?'

For the first time, Jensen seemed embarrassed.

'I can't remember, but I guess somebody must have said

77

something when they heard you were coming. You know how it is.'

'I do indeed.'

'But I'm sure we can co-operate and look after Tower's interests,' Jensen added, suddenly conciliatory. 'Let's show them, right?'

'Fine,' said Verago. 'And as a start you can get our man out of the hospital. What the hell is he doing there, anyway?'

'The doctors . . .'

'The doctors nothing, Jensen.' Verago stood up. 'You had him put in there. Either you or somebody who told you to do it. Well, get him out. Right away.'

His anger was still controlled, but Jensen sagged.

'It's . . . it's for the best, counsellor. He's been under a strain, and I thought it would help to keep him out of the way . . .'

'Sure,' said Verago. 'And it wouldn't do any harm to plant the suggestion the guy is a psycho, right? Needs mental care. Isn't reasonable. What a great way to have a man booted out of the service.'

'There's no suggestion . . .' objected Jensen.

'OK. Just get him out. And listen, Lieutenant, if you don't . . .'

He stopped. From the outer office came the clatter of typewriters, and in the distance the sound of jet engines warming up. But Jensen was transfixed by the man facing him.

'If you don't, I'm going to fly in civilian psychiatrists, the top men, people the military can't fix. And they're going to look over Tower, and then tear your medics apart, and God knows what else.' He paused again. 'Capito?'

He picked up the Article 32 folder.

'I'll see to it, Captain,' said Jensen. Verago wasn't sure, but momentarily those thick lips seemed to tremble.

'Good.' Verago stopped at the door. 'You've fixed quarters for me?'

'Well,' began Jensen and looked away. 'We got a small problem.' He saw Verago's look, and hastily added: 'Oh don't worry, we got you a place.'

'So what's the snag?'

Jensen cleared his throat. 'Fact is, we got no room at the base. There's a squadron in from Edwards on TDY and all the BOQs are full. They got priority, you understand. Being operational.' He laughed weakly. 'I guess we legal eagles don't rate high on the list.'

'Where am I staying?' repeated Verago, very quietly.

Jensen again avoided his look. 'We were lucky.' He was nervous. 'We booked you into the George and Dragon. It's a nice pub. Seventeenth century. Oliver Cromwell stayed there. You'll like it.'

'I'd prefer to stay on the base,' said Verago. 'I like to be in the middle of things. It's more handy.'

'Couldn't agree more, counsellor,' toadied Jensen. 'But we can't make space where there isn't any. Can we? Anyway, the Air Force pays. And it's only four miles away.'

Four miles! With no car. The idea of a four-mile hike to and from the installation every day did not appeal to Verago.

'I'll need transport,' he announced.

'Leave it to me,' promised Jensen. 'And listen, if there's anything you require this office is at your disposal. While you're over here, you're one of us.'

Heaven forbid, an inner voice said to him, but Verago curbed his tongue.

'And when you've read the Article 32, maybe we could have a little strategy meeting, and get it all sorted out. I don't imagine this case will keep you here long.'

Jensen gave what he firmly believed to be an encouraging smile.

Somebody must love you, thought Verago. Your mother. A woman maybe. God knows why.

'You'll be seeing me,' he said.

And he meant it.

As soon as he had gone, Jensen went back to his desk, and sat scowling.

Then he slammed down his fist on the desk, rattling his empty coffee cup in its saucer.

'Son of a bitch,' he snarled to himself, and though it was an impotent gesture, he felt better.

He left the office, slamming his door, and walked a few hundred yards to a little concrete building with windows barred by steel grilles.

He entered and came to another door which had a sign on it reading:

'Office of Special Investigations. Restricted Area. Authorized Personnel Only.'

Jensen pressed a buzzer, and a partition in the door slid aside. A face peered out at him.

'Come in,' said the face's owner.

The door opened electronically, and Jensen was admitted in a tiny hallway.

'Is Duval free?' he asked.

'Go right in, Lieutenant,' said the man at the door.

Jensen was familiar with this place. He knew exactly which was the office he wanted. He knocked and entered.

'Hi,' said Duval. He wore a herring-bone sports jacket and well-cut flannel trousers from Simpson's. He was a handsome man, with dark wavy hair. 'Take the load off your feet, Cy,' he invited.

'Boy, have they picked the wrong guy.'

'We didn't pick him,' Duval pointed out gently. He had a pleasant, resonant voice, and could have been a radio announcer. 'Our friend picked him. And that's his right.'

'I know, I know,' said Jensen irritably. 'But the guy's a real pain.'

Duval settled back in his chair comfortably.

'OK,' he said, 'tell me all about Captain Verago.'

VICTOR ALERT

The planes were clustered at the end of a long concrete runway, more than a mile from the main buildings of the base.

Nearby were a couple of reconnaissance bombers, Boeing RB47Hs, but these were different. For one thing, they seemed lopsided, their wings longer than their fuselage.

They had no insignia. No Air Force markings, no crests, no emblems. They were painted black all over. They sat on the ground, brooding, like sinister birds who had intruded in a nest.

Verago stood at the far end of the flight line, and he remembered where he had first seen that strange shape. On General Croxford's desk. One of the models looked like that.

Verago screwed up his eyes. He wished he could get a closer look. He could see some figures bustling around, but from this distance he couldn't make out what they were doing.

He didn't notice the approaching jeep until it pulled up behind him with a screech of tyres. Three airmen were in it, wearing combat kit. Two of them had carbines. The third man, a master sergeant, had a pistol holster. It was unbuttoned.

The sergeant got out of the jeep.

'Sir,' he said, 'what are you doing here?'

'Looking around.'

'Your ID please,' requested the sergeant.

Verago showed it to him. The two men in the jeep waited, tensely. Their carbines pointed, almost nonchalantly, in Verago's direction.

The sergeant did not return the plastic-covered card. Instead, he asked:

'What are you doing on this base, Captain?'

'Is that any of your business?' snapped Verago. What was the matter with this damn place?

'Everything is our business, sir,' replied the sergeant unsmiling.

He went back to the jeep. Its tall radio antenna was waving in the breeze. The sergeant picked up the radio phone and started talking quietly.

Verago couldn't hear what he said, but the man read the details on his ID card out aloud, looking at Verago as he talked. Then he replaced the radio phone, and walked over to Verago.

'Here you are, Captain,' he said, and handed back the ID card.

'Are you satisfied, Sergeant?' asked Verago, and he hoped it sounded sarcastic.

'Sir,' said the sergeant, 'you are in a restricted area.'

Verago looked around.

'What area? There's nothing here. They're a mile away, at least.' He nodded at the planes.

'This whole section of the base is restricted to outsiders, sir,' said the sergeant.

He made outsiders sound dirty.

'What's your outfit,' asked Verago.

'Air Police, sir.' The face was impassive.

'Well, you tell your commander that I'm here on official business, and Sergeant . . . '

'Sir?'

'You tell him I'm a United States officer, and I may not be Air Force but I'm certainly not an outsider on an American military installation.'

'Yes, sir.' The man was utterly unmoved. 'But if you want to enter this area, you'll need special clearance. Otherwise we got strict orders. From the general.'

'What orders?'

'If we find unauthorised persons trespassing in certain parts of the installation, we can, if necessary, shoot.' He waited for the effect, then he added: 'If they fail to identify themselves, or attempt to elude us. And this is one of those parts of the base.'

He saluted, and climbed back into the jeep. But it didn't drive off. The three airmen sat silent, watching Verago. Slowly he began to walk away, towards the main part of the installation.

It was only later he recalled what those black planes were. A year earlier, Gary Powers had been shot down near Sverdlovsk in one.

They were U2s.

He needed a drink. A strong one.

In the officer's club, he ordered a scotch. It was noisy, crowded, and he decided he wouldn't stay long. Another thing annoyed him: over the bar was a replica of the wing crest, the one-eyed Cyclops. Like a constant, nagging reminder.

'Another one, sir?' asked the barman.

'Why not?'

Verago hadn't even been aware how quickly he had gulped down his first drink. Inwardly he knew the necessity for caution. He needed a clear head. And this was certainly not the place to tie one on. One more, and that would be the lot.

He wished he could get rid of the psychosis that he was being watched the whole time. Especially since nobody in the chattering, laughing knots of people around him even seemed to spare the lone Army officer standing by himself a second look.

'I'm imagining things,' he said to himself.

But he knew he wasn't.

Saturday, June 24, 1961 – LACONBURY

It wasn't a cell, but it had the spartan austerity of a confinement facility. Iron bedstead, a hard-backed chair, a wardrobe, a wash basin, a toilet. For light relief, there was a small radio, and a poster on the wall listing 'You Are An American Fighting Man'.

It sternly declared that rank, name and service number was all that a man in enemy hands could honourably tell an enemy about himself, that to aid, co-operate, give comfort and above all betray information, was akin to treason. They had first started appearing on military bases after Korea, and Tower hadn't seen one for a long time.

The worst thing about the room was the heat. It was next to some boilers, which not only made a curious kind of rumbling noise, but turned it into a mini oven.

'I guess it's not as comfortable as the hospital, but you can thank Captain Verago for that,' sniffed Jensen. 'He insisted you get moved out.'

'What's happened to my quarters?' asked Tower.

'They got assigned to somebody else. I'm sorry about that,

John, but you know how crowded we get here. Anyway, this is only temporary.'

'Until when?' But Tower already knew the answer, and Jensen only confirmed it.

'Until after the trial.'

He left the rest unsaid.

Tower sat on the bed. It had a wafer-thin mattress.

'You want anything from the PX?' offered Jensen. Cigarettes? Candy? Booze?'

'That's OK, Lieutenant. I can get it myself.'

Jensen shook his head. 'I guess I didn't explain, John. You're restricted to your quarters.'

Tower stood up, and advanced on him. Jensen retreated a step. He was reassured by the presence of an AP at the door.

'I'm sorry. General Croxford's orders,' he added hastily. 'The general feels that pending disposition of the charges you should stay in your quarters.'

To Jensen's relief, Tower sank back on the bed.

'Of course.' he said quietly.

'If you want to go for a walk or something, just call the escort.'

Tower nodded silently.

'Here,' said Jensen and handed him a *Stars and Stripes*. 'Maybe you'd like to catch up on the funnies. I find my day isn't complete without Lil Abner.'

'I'd like to see Captain Verago,' said Tower.

'Guess that'll have to wait, John,' replied Jensen carefully. 'He isn't around right now.'

'Get hold of him. Please.'

'No can do.' Jensen was enjoying it. 'He didn't tell me where he was going.'

But he was curious.

'Anything I can do?'

Tower started unwrapping a cigar.

'No,' he said, 'I think you've done quite enough already, Lieutenant.'

They didn't lock the door, but that was only for appearances' sake.

Sunday, June 25, 1961 – HUNTINGDON

Oliver Cromwell may have stayed at the George and Dragon, but Verago had never known a more depressing hotel room.

The ceiling had a big brown stain, where it had been flooded from upstairs. The wallpaper, a faded green, was torn in two places, the bed creaked and the chintz-covered armchair had a lump in it.

There were two prints to decorate the ghastly walls, both Pickwickian hunting scenes. One showed a red-coated huntsman falling off his horse at a jump, with the inane caption underneath: 'Oops what a spill'.

But even more dispiriting was the Article 32 file. Verago read the record of the pre-trial investigation twice, and there was no doubt. Captain John Tower had had it. They had got him to rights.

They seemed to know everything. Every time he met the English girl they had known about it. Every time they went out to dinner, or a movie. Every time they slept together.

It was almost like reading an itemised itinerary.

'20:01   Both arrived at Kettners restaurant, Romilly Street. Had dinner, left in a cab.

22:51   Both returned to her apartment on Charlotte Street.

23:22   Both seen to embrace.'

They must have been watching from the outside, thought Verago with distaste. Somebody must have stood in the street below and seeing through the window the outline of their bodies as they had kissed, reached for his notebook.

'23:46   Lights out in the apartment.

06:15   Capt. Tower departed.'

And so on, after every tryst, noting the exact minute when they held hands, when the curtains were drawn, when the light was switched off, when they were seen to kiss.

And that wasn't all.

The OSI had produced a detailed record of their trips together. A weekend on the English channel coast at Brighton, with exact times of arrival, and departure, hotel room number, the names under which they registered (Captain and Mrs Harry Brown). Who did they expect to fool, poor idiots, thought Verago.

There was sworn testimony by OSI agents about the later visits, a trip to Stratford on Avon. They had noted when Tower went into a florist in Berkeley Square, and ordered flowers for her.

They had been there when the girl and Tower met in Cambridge, and the pub outside Ipswich where they spent a Saturday night.

There were copies of prosecution exhibits attached to the file.

Photostats of the hotel bills where they had stayed together, and of the hotel registry entries. There were copies of statements by chamber maids, waiters, cab drivers, identifying the couple as being together.

Christ, the OSI had worked hard at it. Verago was almost impressed by the thoroughness. There was even a photostat of Tower's pocket diary, with the pages on which he'd noted a date with Serena.

And then there were the photographs. Pictures of Tower and the girl laughing together, swimming in a lido, leaving a hotel carrying suitcases; enlarged photographs, taken from a distance, of them kissing, even shopping in Selfridges.

Verago contemplated Serena's photo. This particular one showed the sun on her face, it was in her eyes, and she was making a grimace, but it caught her freshness, her good looks.

'Poor kid,' thought Verago.

He stretched out his legs, and rested his socked feet on the bed. The maid – who wafted garlic, and had the makings of a moustache on her upper lip – had turned back the covers, but Verago wasn't tired yet.

The only thing they needed to hammer the final nail in was an admission from Serena herself that she had indeed slept with Tower. They had everything else they needed, all the circumstantial evidence, witness statements, documentary proof. But to lock the door finally she'd be useful to them.

Well, baby, said Verago to himself, I hope they don't get you. But whether they got hold of the girl or not the evidence was absolute. He would hardly be able to argue that on all those nights alone together in hotels and her flat, all they did was play chess.

Almost irresistibly, he was drawn back to the file. The Article 32 officers, whom they had so conveniently shifted elsewhere, had of course, recommended court martial proceedings. Brigadier-General Croxford confirmed and approved and Third Air Force ratified. It had all been done very quickly, very neatly.

He rubbed his chin. It had been a long day and his face felt bristly. He wasn't even aware of it at that moment though, because the obvious suddenly struck him.

God damn it, it was all too neat. Why go to all the trouble? Why mobilise an army of Air Force spooks to do nothing but keep on the tail of a cheating husband? What the hell did it matter that Captain Tower was screwing somebody?

The file gave Mrs Tower's address as New York City; she wasn't even in Europe with her husband. She wasn't even living with him here. So she wasn't running around raising hell.

They were all so damn keen to hang Captain Tower it seemed a shame to cheat the hangman, grinned Verago savagely. But cheat the son of a bitch he was going to.

LONDON

All weekend he'd wondered whether he should tell Alexandra.

Perhaps he ought to keep it to himself, but then again, the mere fact that he wondered about it really made it necessary to tell her. He didn't like having secrets from his wife, and turning Serena Howard into one would be absurd.

'Alex,' he said, when the moment came, 'I think I'd like a little advice.'

She was reading *The Tatler* but she put it down, and looked up at him, a little astonished. They shared confidences, and occasionally he used her as a kind of sounding board, noting her reaction, but seldom indicating whether he would take heed of it. This approach she had not known before.

'Yes?' she said and waited.

'It's the Howards' daughter.' He paused. 'She's got herself into a pickle.'

'And she wants you to help?'

He was grateful to her for making it easier.

'Yes,' he said. 'That's the snag. I mean, you know the position . . .'

'Professional etiquette?'

She was absolutely matter of fact.

'In a way, yes. I don't know quite what to do. She asked me not to tell anybody. She's desperately anxious that her family doesn't find out. It's really a bit awkward.'

'Don't tell me if you don't want to,' said Alex.

'No, I'd like to know what you think. She's been having an affair with an American officer. He's married, and they're going to court-martial him for committing adultery.'

'I don't believe it,' she gasped.

'I know, but it's their law. Bloody medieval. The point is she's afraid they're going to subpoena her and make her give evidence before the court martial. Make her tell how it all took place.'

She was appalled. 'That's barbaric. Why should she?'

'That's why she's asked me to help her,' said Daventry.

Alex frowned. 'Can they make her?'

'They can, take it from me. I checked on it.'

'Well,' said Alex. 'I think you should try and help her as much as possible.'

He waited a moment.

'You sure?' he asked finally, very quietly.

'Of course,' said Alex firmly. 'You can't stand by and watch the girl being hounded.'

'It's a little irregular. I've checked with Boulton and the other authorities. I'm on thin ice, but the rules say I can give advice, up to a point, to a friend.'

'Then do it,' said Alex. 'Do what you can. But be careful.'

'I don't think she's got any money,' added Daventry. Not that he cared, but his legal mind insisted he raised it.

'I think you can afford to give a little charity,' smiled Alex. 'We won't starve.'

'Pettifer disapproves wildly.'

'Be very nice to him and he'll get over it.'

She stood up. 'I'm going to put on some coffee,' she said.

He embraced her. The kiss left her a little breathless.

'Wow,' she gasped, and her pleasure was evident.

'I think, Alex, you're a very wonderful woman,' said Daventry.

'I'm obliged, your honour,' she laughed.

Later, in bed, he lay staring into the darkness. He was still nervous about the whole business. He still had the uneasy feeling that he was getting himself into something that held many unknown hazards for him.

And perhaps the biggest one was Serena.

But his gratitude to Alexandra for understanding that he had to go through with this was overwhelming. She felt his sense of outrage at what they were doing. Maybe she sensed the risks as much as he, but she had given him the strength to do what he had to do.

He turned towards her in the bed, and she was waiting for him, warm, sensual, and very abandoned.

Alex Daventry was a very shrewd woman.

Pech's superior in Department B1 had given him strict instructions.

'This cheese shop is in Jermyn Street, Helmut, Picton's or Paxon's, something like that. Marvellous cheeses. Bring me back a Stilton, a little Cheddar, some Wensleydale, a little collection of English cheeses. You'll have time to do that, won't you?'

'Of course, Herr Unruh,' Pech replied respectfully.

But he had only a day in London, and cheese shopping was not the primary object of his mission. In the morning, after he landed from Tempelhof, he made a courtesy call to the West German Embassy, then took a cab to an anonymous building behind Artillery Mansions in Victoria where he spent half an hour talking to a tweed-clad man who until recently had been head of the Foreign Office's intelligence section in West Berlin.

He and Pech had worked together, at Marienfelde, and elsewhere in Berlin, and had established an easy professional relationship. Pech felt that the man, for an English blimp, was a useful ally, and the man had to admit that Pech, considering he was a German, was a decent enough cove.

The only reason Pech went to call on him was that if the man found out that B1 had had somebody in London, however briefly, without getting in touch, he would have resented it. It was the man's personal pride that while in Berlin, he had sewn up B1 and that they wouldn't make a move without telling him, or keeping in touch.

Pech was not about to disillusion him.

The man invited him to lunch at his club, but that was reserved for the real purpose of the trip. To see Unterberg.

By unspoken agreement, the German and the American had decided it would have to be a very English restaurant. Pech wanted a change from rouladen, rostbraten and ragouts.

'How's Berlin?' asked Unterberg after they had settled themselves into Stone's, and waited for the roast beef trolley.

'Beautiful, in the sunshine,' beamed Pech. He was enjoying

his day in London.

'That's not what I meant,' said Unterberg.

'Oh *that*.' Pech shrugged. He was a thin man, with bony shoulders. 'Status quo. I think that describes it.'

The carver arrived, pushing his trolley.

'The mutton's excellent today,' he promised, sliding back the big lid.

'We ordered roast beef,' said Unterberg.

The carver was quite put out. 'I'm sorry, sir,' he apologised. 'I'll get the beef over.'

'Typical, is it not?' commented Pech, who did not like the British. 'You ask for beef, and you get mutton.'

'It's not the end of the world,' said Unterberg. He broke his bread roll. And he decided now was as good a moment as any.

'What's brought you over, Helmut?' he asked cautiously. The classified TWX had not explained anything.

'To see you of course, my friend,' said Pech. 'And to buy some cheese for my boss.'

Unterberg's chair creaked as he shifted his big frame in it.

'The real reason,' he pressed.

'Well,' said Pech slowly. 'You know how it is when one is separated. Face to face, nothing is a problem. One discusses everything, one reads each other's minds. But from a distance . . . I think you could say, B1 needs a little reassurance.'

Unterberg frowned. 'What's wrong?'

The roast beef trolley arrived, and Unterberg tipped the carver.

'But he is not the waiter.' Pech was quite startled.

'It's a tradition,' said Unterberg, and felt pleasantly smug.

'Excellent,' said Pech munching his food.

'You still haven't told me what's bugging you people.'

'Nothing at all, Clyde,' said Pech. 'We only want to know from your side that the Tower business is fully under control.' He picked something out of his tooth. 'A reassurance, as I say.'

'You got it,' said Unterberg.

'Good,' nodded Pech. 'Not that I had any doubts. But you know what Karlsruhe is like.'

His organisation, the Federal Republic's Office for the

Protection of the Constitution, as Bonn liked to call its counter-intelligence service, operated from there. B1 was one of its classified departments.

'Anything special worrying them?' enquired Unterberg.

'My friend, they always worry. It's their nature. And this business especially.'

Unterberg piled the horseradish on a piece of meat. He was wondering if the rumours about B1 were true. East German propaganda said it was a nest of ex-Nazis. That even some of the secretaries had worked for Goering and Himmler. The CIA kept out of it; they hinted quietly, in highly classified reports, that some of it might be true, but they had no proof.

He respected Pech as a professional. A damn efficient guy. Aged about, he guessed, fifty, so he'd have been in his mid-twenties in the war. Interesting. There had been Gestapo field officers in their twenties.

'Tell them to relax, old buddy. We got a tight rein on things here, believe me.'

He poured Pech some Châteauneuf-du-Pape. The wine waiter hadn't been watching the glasses.

'Helmut, how's the girl?'

'Helga?'

'Who else?'

Pech was still having trouble with the piece of meat in his teeth. 'Difficult,' he said. 'A very difficult girl. She is so suspicious.'

'Do you blame her?' asked Unterberg dryly.

'She should trust us more. Doesn't she understand that we are all on the same side?'

'Yeah,' said Unterberg. 'But, maybe she can't work out which side that is.'

Pech blinked.

'I'm only kidding,' said Unterberg hastily.

'She is making life very difficult for everybody.' Pech sniffed disapprovingly. 'How about your man? Is he behaving?'

'Captain Tower is well taken care of,' said Unterberg. He hoped he was right. 'You want dessert?'

Pech looked at his watch.

'I think I'd better not,' he replied. He patted his stomach. It was flat like an athlete's. He was in good shape but he liked to make out he had a weight problem. 'Must watch it.'

'Me too.' Unterberg was still trying to work out if that was the only reason Pech had come over. To ask him for a 'reassurance'.

'Things still tight in Berlin?' he enquired gently. It was only the second time Berlin had been mentioned. Yet that was the thing uppermost in both their minds.

Pech lowered his voice. 'It's getting worse, between you and me, Clyde. We're bursting at the seams. The office is drowning. You should see the paper work.'

He finished his wine.

'I must go.'

Unterberg paid the bill. Outside, in Panton Street, as they waited for a cab, Pech explained:

'I have to go and buy cheese. That is very important. My plane leaves at five so I have very little time. I'm sorry I can't stay longer.'

'So am I,' lied Unterberg. Hoping it sounded utterly disinterested, he casually added: 'Anything else you have to do before you leave?'

'Only the cheese,' said Pech, and stared him straight in the eye.

'Well, I hope the trip's been worth it.'

'To make contact with you, my dear colleague, is always worth it,' said Pech.

And he actually meant it, even if it wasn't for the reason Unterberg thought.

Wednesday, June 28, 1961 – MOLESWORTH

John Tower faced the two men in the barely furnished room

to which he had been escorted.

'Who's he?' he growled.

Lieutenant Jensen indicated the bald Air Force officer with the captain's bars.

'This is Captain Perriton,' he announced.

The bald man smiled amiably.

'What does he want?' demanded Tower. He looked a little more careworn than when Jensen had last seen him.

'Sit down, John,' said Captain Perriton.

There was a table in the middle of the room, and three chairs, two on one side and the third facing them. He indicated the third chair.

Perriton and Jensen took their places opposite Tower. On the table lay a briefcase. Perriton opened it, and took out a pack of cards. They were much bigger than playing cards.

'What's the idea, Jensen?' asked Tower.

The small lawyer creased his thick lips into a semblance of a smile.

'It's a little test,' he said reassuringly. 'It might be useful at the trial.'

'Test?'

'Captain Perriton is from Burderop Park,' explained Jensen. 'He's come up specially.'

Tower's eyes narrowed. He had heard about Burderop Park.

'Are you a doctor?' he asked Perriton.

'Sort of. But that isn't important, John.' He laid the stack of cards face downwards. From his briefcase he also produced a clip board. 'You just relax, and enjoy it.'

'Where is Verago?' demanded Tower.

'We don't need him for this,' said Jensen soothingly.

'I want to see Captain Verago. Right away.'

'Not right now,' said Jensen.

'It's alright,' interrupted the bald man. 'It's perfectly understandable. But we're doing this in your interest, John. Lieutenant Jensen feels that it will help your case. It'll give Captain Verago more ammunition.'

He pushed the pile of cards forward.

'Just look at each card. You'll see a funny shape on it. A kind of ink spot. You'll simply tell me what it reminds you of.'

'I know about the Rorschach test,' said Tower curtly. 'You're a psychiatrist, aren't you?'

'Does that worry you?' asked Perriton. He had the Korea ribbon on his uniform. Tower suddenly wondered if he had been on the brainwashing commission for the Pentagon.

Tower stood up.

'That's all, gentlemen,' he said.

They stared, owlishly. Jensen's baby face had darkened.

'Now just a moment, John . . . ' he began angrily, but Perriton silenced him with a little gesture.

'You got it all wrong,' he smiled at Tower. 'The Air Force has been using this test for years. That's how combat air crews were assessed in the war. It's perfectly routine.'

'Not for me,' said Tower.

'Before you say no, you might consider one thing,' said Perriton almost silkily. 'It won't help you if the court got to hear you'd refused to go along with us.'

They were the enemy, of course. He knew that. Jensen, in the guise of defence counsel, and the bald man as the ever-helpful psychiatrist. They had picked a time and place when Verago wasn't around to entangle him deeper still.

Tower smiled. It was a dangerous smile. He sat down.

'OK,' he said, 'let's play cards.'

Jensen looked relieved.

'Now,' said Perriton. 'Study each card. Tell me what image it suggests to you. If you see more than one shape, don't worry. Give me all the pictures you see in your mind.'

He turned up the first card.

'Mickey Mouse,' said Tower without hesitation.

Perriton made a note on the clip board, then turned up the next ink blot.

'Donald Duck,' said Tower.

Perriton raised an eyebrow.

'Is that all? Nothing else?'

Tower leant forward, and studied the card again gravely.

'Yes,' he said. 'Positively Donald Duck.'

The third card was exposed.

95

'Ah,' said Tower. 'Now that could be a flat lettuce leaf. Or maybe just an ink blot.'

Perriton was annoyed.

'If you're not prepared to do this seriously . . . '

'Oh, but I am. I really am,' said Tower.

Jensen gave him a furious look.

'Alright,' said Perriton. 'Try this one.'

He turned up another card.

'That's interesting,' said Tower. 'It's General Croxford, upside down.'

'Right,' said Perriton. He grabbed the pile of cards and put them back in the briefcase. 'I don't think there's any point in going on with this.'

'Neither do I,' agreed Tower mildly.

Jensen was biting his lip nervously, but Perriton resignedly put his clip board away.

'Just what are you afraid of, Captain Tower?' he asked.

'Bats and butterflies,' said Tower.

'What's that?'

'It'd make you happy, wouldn't it? If I played the game and came up with fire-spouting dragons, and twisted faces, and poisonous insects, then you could deduce that I hated my father, never knew my mother, and fell downstairs when I was six.' He paused. 'Or better still that I was mentally unstable, an advanced hysteric, obviously unreliable. Wouldn't that make everybody happy?'

'You got a problem, John,' said Perriton.

'So who are you going to testify for, the defence or the prosecution?'

Jensen went to the door. Two white-capped APs, both armed, were outside.

'Sergeant,' he said, 'escort Captain Tower back.'

Perriton stood up and held out his hand.

'Anyway, glad to have met you, Captain,' he said. 'Anytime you feel you need any advice, don't hesitate to let me know.'

'Sure,' said Tower. 'You got a permanent vacancy for me in Ward 10.'

He didn't take Perriton's hand.

After he had gone, they were still trying to work out how he knew that Ward 10 at Burderop Park was always kept locked, day and night, because it was reserved for very special cases.

Thursday, June 29, 1961 – LONDON

That day at 5.10 p.m., Daventry received a phone call at his chambers from Serena Howard.

'Can you come over?' Her voice was a little breathless.

'Now?' He sounded somewhat irritable.

'I wouldn't ask if it wasn't important,' she said.

'Won't it keep?' he asked.

'Something's happened,' she said. 'I need to see you.'

He frowned. It was awkward.

'Look here, Serena, it's late. I'm sure it will keep. Perhaps we could meet briefly . . . '

He hesitated. Tomorrow was Friday. He had a busy day ahead. Then the weekend. That was impossible.

'How about Monday?'

'Mr Daventry, I'm frightened.'

'What on earth for?' Really, she was a curious girl. She sounded very apprehensive.

'Couldn't you just come for ten minutes? *Please.* It's only Charlotte Street. You've got the number, haven't you?'

He looked at his watch. He was about to go anyway. He might as well . . .

In the cab, Daventry sighed. When Pettifer arranged his life, everything was always so uncomplicated. He missed his good offices.

Her flat was on the first floor above a shop displaying a huge photograph of Mao and giving its window over to the writings of Marx, Engels and various Spanish-sounding gentlemen

Daventry had never heard of.

There was a Turkish restaurant opposite, and parked in front of it was a black Chrysler. The two men in it stared at him as he paid off the cab.

Upstairs he rang the door bell. Serena had on a sloppy wool sweater, and slacks. Her face was drawn.

'Thank you for coming,' she said.

She led him inside.

'I've got some coffee on,' she said, as he sat down. The floor was covered by multi-coloured rugs with weird patterns. On the wall hung three primitive, garishly hued masks. She seemed to have a penchant for Mexican art. At least, Daventry thought it was Mexican. He wasn't sure.

'I can only stay a few minutes,' said Daventry. 'Now what's all this about? What's happened?'

'Look,' she said, going over to the window. She stood a little to one side, so that the curtain concealed her from the street.

He got up, and looked out of the window.

'What is it?'

'I'm being followed,' said Serena. 'You see that car. The men in it. They've been following me.'

'Yes. I saw them when I arrived,' he said. 'They don't look very suspicious to me.'

'They're watching me,' insisted Serena.

'How do you know?' asked Daventry.

She poured him some coffee from a small cona bowl.

'I know,' she said, as if that was final proof. 'Milk? Sugar?'

'Just a drop. One lump. Why should they be following you?'

'They're there, keeping an eye on this flat. Seeing who goes in and out. Taking pictures.'

'What?'

'They're photographing me with a telephoto lens.'

He stirred the coffee slowly. 'I see. And they tail you?'

'Not exactly trail me . . .' She brushed an errant blonde hair away from her brow.

'You said they followed you?' repeated Daventry, as if he was questioning an uncertain witness who kept changing her facts.

98

'They turn up where I happen to be. Sometimes. It's horrible.'

He sipped the coffe, and leant back in the wicker chair.

'Have you told the police?'

'Yes.'

'And?'

'They said thank you.'

'That's all?'

'They hinted I was seeing things. That it didn't matter. They weren't very interested.'

'Of course their presence may not have anything to do with you at all, Serena,' he said, putting down the cup.

'I don't understand.'

'Well, you seem to have a rather, er, radical establishment downstairs . . . '

Her eyes opened wide. 'You mean Ron? The Maoists? Oh, they're absolute sweeties.'

Daventry put his fingertips together.

'I don't doubt they're very nice people, Serena, but the authorities do keep an eye on extremists and radicals. I mean, it's quite possible that, well, perhaps the Special Branch is watching these premises. And you simply happen to live on the first floor.'

'And that's why they take my picture? Or suddenly show up in Petty France when I renew my passport? Or lurk out there right now?'

Daventry liked commonplace explanations for uncommon happenings.

'What do you suggest it's all about?'

'It's to do with John,' she said, firmly. 'I know it is. It's something to do with the court martial. I'm convinced of it.'

Daventry got up.

'There's not much more you can do about it. You've told the police. If they continue to annoy you, tell them again. Make an official complaint. Personally, I can't see how it's got anything to do with the other business.'

She came closer to him. 'Can't you find out? It's terribly worrying. I feel . . . it makes me so . . . uneasy.'

99

'I'd just try to forget about it. Take no notice. I think it's your friend below they're interested in.' He did his best to sound reassuring. 'By the way, have you heard anything more?'

She shook her head.

'Nothing from . . . Captain Tower?'

'No,' she said. 'And that's worrying me too.'

On the TV set stood a framed photo of a man in US Air Force uniform. There was the faintest trace of scar under his left eye. She followed Daventry's look.

'That's John,' she said.

'He's not a pilot then?' asked Daventry.

'How do you know?' She looked surprised.

'No wings on his uniform.'

'I never noticed,' she said.

At the door she turned to him.

'I really am most grateful to you for coming over,' she said.

'That's alright, Serena, but there really wasn't any need for panic. You mustn't start imagining things. It'll all get sorted out.'

It was as much for his own sake that he wanted to put her mind at rest.

'Gerald,' she said.

He froze. For some reason he was taken aback at her using his first name.

'You will stand by me, won't you? You will help me if they come for me?'

Her eyes were wide, pleading.

'If you have any legal problems, well, phone me,' he said, and fled.

'Thank you again,' she called after him, as he went down the stairs. In the hallway he became aware for the first time of a strong aroma of curry. Ron must be having a cook up, he thought.

He stood in the street, troubled. Whatever he was getting involved in, it did not fit the nice, regular, predestined pattern of his life. Personally, or professionally.

He also wondered why, if she had a photo of the American, he hadn't seen a single picture of her diplomatic fiancé. Or perhaps she kept that in the more intimate surroundings of her bedroom.

Daventry hurried down to the junction of Mortimer Street to get a cab, never noticing that one of the men in the black Chrysler had photographed him several times with a long-lensed camera.

'He was only up there fifteen minutes,' remarked the man who had taken the pictures. 'You think he fucked her?' He unscrewed the telephoto lens and put it in its case. It was an expensive piece of government property.

Unterberg didn't particularly like the OSI photographer.

But all he said was: 'I don't think Mr Daventry works that fast, Alvin.'

Saturday, July 1, 1961 – LONDON

'Were you followed?' was the first thing Laurie asked.

'No.' Verago frowned. 'I mean, I don't know. I didn't look. Who should be following me?'

'I thought you might know by now,' she replied.

She was tense, almost nervous.

He took the glass she offered him. 'Know exactly what?'

Her beautiful antique whisky still tasted superb, and she looked as good as ever, but over her shoulder, on the shelf, the ceramic jester intruded. Last time he had just been an ornament, now he jarred. His hunched back, his big nose, the lewd grin, there was something obscene about him.

She saw his reaction. 'You don't like Smiley?'

'Not my favourite.'

'He's very special,' she said.

Verago raised his tumbler, 'Skol. I'd rather look at you. You're prettier than General Croxford, and you got much better legs than Lieutenant Jensen. Even when you're being all mysterious.' The second swallow was even more warming 'What are you trying to tell me?'

She sat in the armchair opposite him, so near and yet so far.

'Tony,' she said gravely, 'you got any idea what you're into?'

'You fill me in.'

She hesitated. She tapped her cigarette nervously on the ashtray that rested by her arm. Then she stubbed it out. She seemed to have reached a decision.

'I've found out something. About you. You're under surveillance, Tony. Every where you go. Everything you do. Everybody you see. You're on the list.'

If she expected him to be shaken, she was wrong.

'I see,' was all he said.

'A blue file came into the colonel's office. Blue for top secret. The OSI's marked your card.'

He still sat impassive.

'You watch yourself,' she added.

'Maybe you ought to,' said Verago.

She raised her eyebrows.

'You tell me I'm being shadowed. That they know everything I do, everywhere I go. So you let me come here, right to your apartment.' His lip curled. 'What's the matter, you tired of your job?' She flinched, and he went on: 'You know you can't get away with it. They'll know you saw me. Maybe they've even bugged this place. Maybe *he's* recording every damn word!'

He scowled at Smiley.

'They don't need to listen.' She paused. 'You see, I tell them everything.'

He picked up his whisky glass, and took a hasty sip. It still tasted nice, but he felt he had had enough.

'Everything,' she repeated.

'You tell the OSI?' he croaked.

'I report everything.' She got up, and without asking, refilled his glass. 'Like the other night when you stayed here. And I'll report tomorrow that you came around. And that we slept together afterwards.'

She had that mocking smile again.

102

'Because isn't that what we're going to do?'

'I . . . ' he began, and stopped, confused.

It amused her.

'You should see yourself, Tony,' she exclaimed. 'Mouth open, as if the ceiling's fallen in on you. Relax.'

She bent down and kissed him. Her lipstick tasted nice.

'I'm only saving the government money,' she added. 'They'd know all about us anyway, so I got in first. I like to help them keep the files up to date.'

She lit a fresh cigarette and exhaled a cloud of smoke.

'Maybe with any luck they'll ask me to spy on you.'

'And will you?' he asked, coldly.

'Of course,' she smiled. 'Every little inch.'

She settled back in the armchair, and stretched like a cat. It accentuated the contours of her breasts under the tightness of her silk shirt.

'Shocked are you, Tony?'

'It's a little hard to take. You forget I'm just a simple country lawyer.'

'Oh yeah,' she remarked sardonically.

'Anyway, just how much do you feed back?'

'Exactly what I want,' she replied. 'OK?'

He got up and walked over to the window. Nobody seemed to be watching the apartment block as far as he could see. Nobody was loitering in a doorway, no car stood with two occupants never taking their eyes off the building.

'I told you,' called Laurie. 'They probably followed you here, but as soon as they saw where you were going, they called it off because they knew I'd be a good girl.'

She was standing up too. He wanted her, badly. He walked towards her, and kissed her, long and hard.

'I hope you can stay tonight,' she whispered in his ear.

'I . . . I ought to get back to the base,' he murmured, and he knew that was true, but he also knew he didn't care at that moment. 'I've got lots to do.'

'Stay,' she urged. 'They'll be pretty disappointed if you don't, I suspect.'

She pressed him to her body.

'So will I,' she added.

'Well,' said Verago, and started unbuttoning her silk shirt, 'I hate disappointing people.'

Sunday, July 2, 1961 – PROBE

The ugly misshapen plane, with its curious outgrowth on top of its fuselage, flew 26,000 feet above Czechoslovakia, the 30-strong double crew at action stations.

Inside the aircraft, a transformed Super Constellation few unauthorised people ever got close to, seven and a half tons of special, most secret electronic equipment was listening, watching, recording, supervised by the men in flight suits.

Some were Air Force personnel, others civilian technicians. None of them ever talked about their job, but they had a cover story. They were 'meteorologists'. They chased the weather. All they were interested in, they said, were cloud formations, high-pressure zones, depressions, wind and rain.

The WV-2E was doing a dangerous job. The only guns she carried were the side arms some of the aircrew wore. She had no defence against attack, other than some electronic gadgets to confuse and mislead enemy radar.

And it didn't fool the thirty men crouched at their posts. They knew that, thousands of feet below, invisible eyes were following them. That on radar consoles and flight-plotting screens, they were being trailed. That was the mission. To test reaction.

This night, July 2, 1961, O for Oboe's mission was another move in a mutual chess game in the skies over Europe. For high above the British Isles, a Tupolev TU-16 was being tracked by NATO's silent defences.

The Badger, cruising at 31,000 feet, had had a busy night,

scouting across East Anglia, making electronic recordings of the US bases dotted about the flat countryside, and was now swinging north-west for a quick peep at Holy Lock, and a few other interesting locations on the way.

The twin-engined, Turbo prop TU-44's crew of ten had made the flight before. To them, like the men of the WV-2E, it was almost routine.

Lately, of course, there had been a certain unease among some of the flyers on the illicit long-distance ferret missions.

Like spies on the ground, the game had a set protocol. CIA men did not, on the whole, kill KGB men in Paris or Rome or London. Nor did the KGB, its rival professional colleagues. That kind of viciousness only led to reprisals and cost both sides valuable operatives. It was messy, and in the long run, unproductive.

By the same token, ferrets on both sides were generally allowed to do their snooping unhindered, providing the ground rules were obeyed.

A couple of U2s had overstepped them, and never returned home. So not long afterwards a Myasishchev M-4 Molot strategic radar plane disappeared somewhere over the Atlantic. The message was mutually understood.

For months now, the game had been played strictly by the rules. But then came the RB47H. She must have done something that annoyed the Russians to get shot down over the Baltic.

It worried some of the men on Oboe as they watched the blips and indicators and radar sweeps on their equipment. They had no idea what the other plane's mission had been, but its loss served to remind them that game though it was, the pawns died if somebody made the wrong move.

It was usually just a gesture, but that didn't make the thought of being blown apart by a missile, or torn to pieces by 23mm cannon shells any more attractive.

There was another reason why the lost RB47H was in their minds.

It had been based at Laconbury. And that was Oboe's home too.

LACONBURY

The unhurried, cathedral-like calm of the operations room wasn't disturbed by the arrival of Brigadier-General Croxford.

Thirty feet below the base of Laconbury, nuclear war proof, this nerve centre was manned twenty-four hours a day. And to the Cyclops wing it was the focal point of the universe.

As if to prove it, the clocks on the wall gave the simultaneous times in Omaha, New York, Los Angeles, Tokyo, Sydney, London, Berlin and Moscow.

Omaha time was specially important. A bright yellow phone linked them directly with the heart of a mountain in that state. And in that mountain was the voice that could start World War Three.

High in his chair, the duty controller, a lieutenant-colonel, surveyed his silent cohorts. In front of him was the status board, showing at a glance the instant readiness of the units that would begin that war.

There was a huge electronic map of Europe, little lights blinking on it from time to time, and another large board which had black curtains drawn across it. Every man in the room was cleared to see that board, but, like a holy shrine that must only be uncovered on special occasions, the curtains remained closed.

Behind them, on the board, were the targets. The places on the map which would evaporate in a few minutes after Omaha had given the word.

There were other wall displays. They indicated weather conditions, the status of missions in progress, expected arrivals at the base from others abroad, the names of squadron and flight commanders on stand by at that moment.

106

And there were phones. Batteries of them. Apart from the yellow one, a whole array, in different colours. Duty officers sat at curved consoles, each with a panel of switches and knobs and buttons in front of him, and his own private allocation of phones.

Most of the people in the room were in shirtsleeves. All of them had plastic badges hanging from a button; ordinary ID cards did not gain entry here.

Occasionally a low voice spoke softly into a phone. A computer screen glowed. In one corner, teletypes periodically coughed out short messages. Nothing was rushed. Nobody raised their voice. The carpet on the floor was dark blue, the lighting pleasantly subdued, the air, carefully filtered, clear, the temperature just right.

The general quietly walked over to the controller. The lieutenant-colonel handed him a situation clip board. Croxford glanced at it.

'Good,' he nodded. He gave it back.

'How long was the Badger overhead?' he asked.

'Just passed by, General. They got him tracked over the Irish Sea right now.'

'Hmm.'

Croxford looked at the controller's log.

'What's the status of Oboe?'

The controller leant forward, and tapped a keyboard. Some electronic letters flashed across a screen in front of him.

'Over Austria, sir.'

'No problems?'

'None we know about, General.'

'Who's the commander?'

'Colonel Mason, sir.'

The controller was puzzled. Croxford usually knew that kind of detail. He was famous for remembering names, knowing every man's job, even the squadron nicknames of individual pilots. The general must have something on his mind.

'You ever sat on a court martial, Bob?' asked Croxford.

It took the controller completely by surprise.

'Sir?'

'I asked if you had ever sat on a court.'

'I was on a couple of Specials. In the States.'

'We're going to have a general soon,' said Croxford.

'Is that so? I heard something mentioned . . .'

'What did you hear?' demanded Croxford sharply.

One of the duty officers looked up from his console. He couldn't make out what the old man was saying, but the general didn't often indulge in chats in the command post. He wished he was closer.

'Just scuttlebutt, General,' said the controller hastily. 'Bar talk.'

Croxford grunted.

'I don't want any gossip about it. Is that clear?'

'Understood, sir.'

Croxford prepared to go, then paused.

'I want a good board,' he said. 'A smart court. You get me?'

'Yes, sir.'

Croxford nodded.

'Keep me posted on Oboe. I'll be in my quarters.'

The blue phone buzzed softly. The controller picked it up, listened. He handed it to Croxford.

'For you, sir.'

The general took the phone. They usually didn't bother him when he was down in the command post. Unless it was very urgent.

'Croxford,' he said.

'General, it's Duval.'

'Well?'

'There's no sign of Tower, sir.'

'What the hell do you mean?'

'I guess he's gone, sir.'

The controller had no idea what it was about, but the last time the general had such a look on his face was when Gary Powers failed to take the death pill and allowed himself to be captured by the Russians.

LACONBURY

Tower stood in the shadow of the warehouse, watching the AP jeeps race past. They were racing all over the base like angry ants. The white hats waved down cars driven by the wives, held up supply trucks, checked the family housing area, searched the bowling alley, and swarmed all over the barracks and the mess halls.

The gates to the base were double manned and any vehicles that left were searched. And they had the dogs out.

The dogs were out looking for him. Tower feared the dogs. The AP squadron prided itself on its canine unit. Sergeant McKluskey, the man in charge, had a special technique. Everybody hit the dogs, except their handlers. His men would walk down the lines of kennels, and when a Doberman stuck out his head, he'd be whacked across the nose with a gauntlet.

So they hated every human being. Their handlers they just about tolerated, because they fed them and were the only people who didn't hurt them. Every other person was an enemy.

That was the way McKluskey wanted it.

The dogs roamed loose in certain parts of the high-security zone, where no one was supposed to enter. McKluskey sometimes wished somebody would try a little sabotage in the maximum security compounds. It would give his pets some exercise.

Tonight was the big event for the dog section. Tower was their quarry.

Getting out of the cell-like room by the boiler house had been no problem. He had carefully picked his moment, and simply walked out.

He wore uniform, and the airmen he passed gave him cursory

109

salutes, but no second look. He walked along Texas Street, the thoroughfare in the middle of the dependent housing area, and made his way to the car park alongside the NCO club.

His only plan was to get out. To reach London. And there . . .

But London, right now, was on another planet. He had to get off this sprawling, huge triangular complex, surrounded by hedges, and behind them ten-feet high wire fences.

Whatever he did, he knew he had to avoid the operational area of the base. They were always tightly guarded and tonight the sentries would really be on their toes. They'd enjoy it too. Guard duty was monotonous; at last there was something to watch for.

He had a vague idea to steal a car, and somehow drive off the base. Bluff his way past the guardhouse. Try to pull rank on the APs. Crash his way through. Anything.

But when he got to the car park, he found the APs were already there. Shining flash lights into every car, standing in a group. He heard walky talkies chattering. Hastily, he turned the other way.

He tried to recall, in his mind, the layout of the base. The flight lines and runways stretched to the east. The administrative areas were ahead of him, the big sprawling family complex at his back.

To the south alongside Laconbury, was the highway to London. A busy route, with constant traffic. Private cars. Trucks. If he could reach it, he could hitch a ride. They'd be surprised to see an American air force officer thumbing a lift, every Yank was believed to have his own huge limousine, but they'd certainly pick him up.

He had to get to that main road.

Tower began to walk, hugging all the buildings along the way, staying in the shadows as much as he could. The part of the airfield he was making for was open country and grass land. Just the occasional store house. There was nothing sensitive, no special guard posts.

He was on open ground now, but if he was lucky nobody would see him in the dark. He started running towards the wire fence a mile away.

Suddenly he heard barking behind him, and when he looked around, two shapes were streaking towards him. He ran faster. He wasn't just running to get to the fence, he was running to escape the dogs.

He was afraid. Recently fear had been a familiar companion. It was almost as if he was re-enacting a movie. Fleeing for his life, the dogs behind him, and the men behind them.

It had been a wood in Germany last time, not an airfield in rural England, and the uniforms had belonged to a different country. But the fear tasted the same. His throat tightened with panic as the dogs came nearer, and started to catch up on him.

His face was a grimace of pain as he put all he had into escaping, his heart pounding so hard that he knew soon, any moment, it would explode. Christ, those dogs. They were gaining on him. Closer. Closer . . .

Reality and nightmare, the present and the past were madly somersaulting round his mind. The scar on his face, the panic, the desperation to get away, to escape.

They had to get him, to stop him. But they . . . who were 'they' this time? Had it all happened before or was it the same moment, over and over again?

A stack of empty oil drums, shaped like a pyramid, loomed in front of him. Last time it had been trees, the wood . . . or was it back streets, and dark alleys.

Oh God, he had no strength left. He knew it was useless. Now the dogs were snapping at his heels. He stumbled, like a crazy drunken man, and fell against the drums, just as the whistle shrilled.

There had been a whistle last time. But this one sounded different.

The dogs froze, their eyes red, crazed with fury, shining brightly in the dark, saliva dripping from their jaws, panting with eagerness to tear his flesh.

But they obeyed the whistle. McKluskey had trained them well. They stood over Tower, waiting, hoping he would move, so that they'd have their excuse.

For a fleeting moment, Sergeant McKluskey had the insane idea of giving them their reward. He allowed himself the

111

pleasure of savouring the sight of the exhausted, cowering fugitive, mesmerised by the Dobermans. He relished the idea of giving them a taste of the real thing, instead of the man-sized dummies they usually savaged in training.

But, like the dogs, McKluskey was well disciplined.

He gave another whistle, a different note, and they stood back.

'Well done, you beautiful bastards,' crowed McKluskey. 'Now sit.'

He lifted the walky talky.

'Post 11,' he said. 'We got your man.'

Monday, July 3, 1961 – LACONBURY

The cab he had taken from the station dropped Verago at the gates of the base next morning at 8:40 a.m.

The AP checked his ID again, but then, instead of waving him through, said:

'You'd better get out, Captain.'

And he opened the door of the cab for him.

'Hey,' said Verago.

'Pay the man, sir,' ordered the AP.

Verago stared at him in disbelief.

'Who the hell do you think you're talking to . . . ' he began.

'Five pounds,' said the cab driver. He didn't know what the fuss was all about, but he wanted to be out of it. He made a good living overcharging Laconbury Yanks who had no cars. If he had trouble with the APs, he'd lose out badly.

Verago paid him, and the cab reversed out of the gate, and drove off.

'Step this way, please,' said the AP.

In the guardhouse, the staff sergeant behind the desk got up slowly as they entered. He sauntered over to the counter, eyeing Verago with some curiosity.

Maybe I'd better start teaching these bastards a little military courtesy, thought Verago. He wasn't a spit and polish fanatic at the best of times, but this studied insolence was too much even for him.

'Sergeant,' he snapped.

'Yes, sir?'

'You know who I am?'

'You're Captain Verago,' replied the sergeant nonchalantly.

'And don't you forget it,' whiplashed Verago. It was unusual for him to browbeat an enlisted man but when he did his victim seldom forgot it.

But not this time.

'Wait here, Captain,' instructed the sergeant.

'What for?'

The sergeant was dialling an extension on the phone. He turned his back. He said something into the phone, hung up and sat down.

'Do you always sit down when an officer is standing?' grated Verago.

The sergeant got to his feet.

'Sorry, sir,' he mumbled. 'They'll be here in a moment.'

The other AP still stood by the door, gazing into space.

Verago turned to go, but the AP moved so that Verago couldn't pass him.

'Give me the phone,' said Verago tersely.

'I'm sorry about this, sir,' said the sergeant, 'but we got orders.'

'Just give me that phone,' demanded Verago.

The sergeant swallowed. He saw Verago's expression, and whatever the guy had done, he had those captain's tracks on his shoulders. You could never win an argument with an officer.

The car saved him.

It pulled up outside the guardhouse with a squeal of brakes and they all heard a door slam.

Duval came in.

'Come with me, please,' he said to Verago.

'Who are you?'

'Duval. OSI.'

'Well, Mr Duval, you'd better tell me what's going on here,' said Verago.

'Let's go to my place,' said Duval, as if he'd issued a dinner invitation.

They got into the car, and the driver started the engine.

'Did you give them orders to detain me at the gate?'

'The APs were told to report the moment you stepped on the base, Captain,' replied Duval.

'Why?'

But the car had already arrived at its destination inside the base, the concrete building with the barred window.

'Come into the office, please,' said Duval, pressing the buzzer. The door swung open.

'Sit down, Captain.' Duval placed himself opposite Verago. 'We've been very anxious to talk to you, but we didn't know where you were.'

You fucking liar, thought Verago. You know I've been in bed all night with Laurie Czeslaw in London.

'This is not formal, Captain,' said Duval. 'Nothing's being written down. Not a word recorded.' He held up his empty hands like a conjurer at the beginning of his act. 'You can walk out any time you want.'

Somewhere close by a teleprinter was stuttering, and a phone rang briefly. But Verago's mind was on other things.

'When outfits like the OSI say something's off the record, I shut up on principle,' he said. 'Nothing personal, Mr Duval. But you'd better tell me quick what's going on before I – '

'I understand your indignation,' intervened Duval. 'At the same time, you'll appreciate what a sensitive installation this is, and when something like this happens . . . '

'Like what?'

Duval regarded him in disbelief.

'Oh come on, Captain. You don't know, I suppose, that your client tried to go absent during the night?'

Verago sat very still.

'Go on.'

114

'He broke restriction. He tried to get away, and almost made it. The APs just caught him. Near the perimeter fence. We think . . . ' Duval stopped, and then added slowly: 'We think a car was waiting for him.'

'And you're suggesting?'

Duval was chilly. 'I'm suggesting nothing. Our job is security. And, well, let's say you didn't exactly go by the book when you smuggled yourself into his room at the hospital. You've gotten yourself a reputation for – well, playing it by your own rules . . . '

'Unlike you fellows, of course.'

Suddenly Duval grinned. 'Listen, I don't hold it against you.' The grin vanished. 'But I got a lot of unanswered questions.'

Verago looked at his watch.

'I'd like to see Captain Tower,' he said.

The noise of an aircraft stopped Duval answering right away. Then he said:

'I'm sorry. Right now he's in close confinement.'

'Duval, you don't seem to get it,' grated Verago. 'I'm his attorney. You can't stop me seeing him.'

'No?' enquired Duval.

'I'll take it to the top.'

'Your privilege,' said Duval coolly.

They stood face to face like two antagonists about to come to the confrontation they had both expected.

'Alright,' said Verago, 'you asked for it, friend . . . ' He reached for the phone.

Suddenly a siren started shrieking. Somewhere, simultaneously, a bell rang stridently.

'What the hell is that?' demanded Verago.

'That,' said Duval, 'is the war alert.'

And in the distance, they could hear the planes starting to take off.

115

RED ALERT

At 1005 hours, Laconbury air base was completely destroyed by a multi-megaton weapon dropped from a Soviet bomber which was subsequently listed as probably shot down by an F-100 from Bentwaters.

But although Brigadier General Croxford and his command ceased to exist, on paper, in what would be one sudden, fiery bright flash, the exercise was rated a big success.

All Laconbury's serviceable aircraft had been airborne within six minutes of the alert, allowing them to disperse all over the map, as laid down in the contingency plans.

It was a very good performance, as they told the general on the hot line, after he had been informed he and his outfit were dead.

By 1600 hours, the alert was over. The Air Force children in the dependent school no longer had to lie flat on the classroom floors, the commissariat was open for business again, outgoing calls were allowed once more, and servicemen could enter and leave the base.

Captain Verago would have died a split second earlier than some other people on the base, because the focal point of the bomb's explosion was the spot where the OSI building stood.

It was an academic point, since the effect of the blast would also have destroyed a substantial part of Cambridge, Huntingdon, Peterborough, St Ives, Ely, and other towns in the East Anglia area.

Verago never knew any of this, because the report on the alert had the highest security classification.

Captain Verago spent a good part of the seven hours of the alert in the officers' club and, by the time he was technically reduced to cinders, was already pleasantly drunk.

His greatest achievement, he felt, was being able to somehow persuade the barman to keep serving him drinks during the alert. He congratulated himself for having entered into the spirit of the event. If it ever happened for real, that's the way he wanted to go.

Wednesday, July 5, 1961 – LACONBURY

They had cut Tower off from the outside world, no doubt about it.

The place, outwardly, wasn't as forbidding as other stockades Verago had known, but then he had never been in a lock-up on an air base. At first glance, Laconbury's confinement facility merely consisted of a couple of brick buildings adjoining the dog kennels, standing in an open space, surrounded by an innocuous looking wire fence.

But they were taking no chances. The fence had a little sign fastened to it, with two red lightning flashes and the word 'Danger'. And two armed APs with walky talkies hovered around.

Verago had protested at Tower being locked up, but the AP commander shrugged it off.

'What do you expect? He broke restriction. The book says we've to ensure the presence of the accused at his trial. That's all we're doing. Ensuring. Don't worry, he's pretty comfortable. And he gets the same chow as everybody.'

At least they didn't search Verago when he came to see him. After his run-in with Duval, nothing would have surprised him.

Tower was lying on his bunk when Verago was let in.

'Well,' he said. 'I didn't expect to see you again.'

Slowly he rose from the bunk.

'Make yourself at home, counsellor. It isn't the Ritz, but they keep it clean.' He stretched himself.

'You're a dumb son of a bitch, you know that?' said Verago irritably. 'What was the idea of trying a stunt like that?'

The sun shone brightly through the barred window, and in the light, the man suddenly looked different to him. The mouth was weak, the eyes shifty. Or was he just sick of the guy?

117

'I got fed up. OK?'

'Oh great. A real smart thing to do. Just calculated to help your case.'

By the pillow on the bunk lay a packet of cheap PX cigars. Tower took one, and lit it with his lighter. It was Russian, Verago remembered.

'I don't want to talk about it,' said Tower.

Verago stopped half way in the act of opening his briefcase.

'Mister, I'm your attorney, remember? You're supposed to confide in me.' Verago allowed himself a wry smile. 'To trust me.'

'I don't trust anybody. Not any more. Nothing personal.' Tower's statement was matter of fact, without heat.

Verago snapped shut his briefcase.

'I guess that's it,' he said. He started to go towards the door.

'What's that for?' demanded Tower.

'You just fired me.'

'Oh for Chrissake, don't start acting the big lawyer. Just get on with the case. Do your best. With what you've got.'

Verago snorted. 'Which isn't much.' He opened the briefcase again, slowly. He pulled out a yellow legal pad. It was covered with notes. He had been doing a lot of work, and he didn't have good news.

'I've studied the Article 32 hearing and the exhibits and all the rest of the evidence they've piled up, and their case is solid. You committed adultery.'

'I never denied it.' Tower blew out a cloud of smoke.

Verago took a deep breath. He felt like throwing his pad in the man's face. He hated clients who played games.

'So our best line of defence is that you have committed a purely technical offence. You and your wife have lived apart for so long now that this is not a case of flagrant adultery, but the natural behaviour of a man who is virtually married in name only.' He paused. 'You go along with that?'

Tower shrugged. 'Does it matter?'

'Well, you're not helping that's for sure.' snarled Verago. He controlled himself. 'So I'll try to make my big pitch when it comes to mitigation. I don't think we can stop you being

118

convicted, but maybe I can save your career.'

Tower laughed in his face.

'What's so funny?' asked Verago, angry.

'Save my career. I love that. You're a great trier, Captain.'

The walls started to shake as the thunder of jet planes taxiing on a runway reverberated across the base. The sound grew, until it swept over the buildings like a thunderclap, making it impossible for them to talk.

Tower sat, puffing, avoiding Verago's eyes.

Then, as the roar receded, and the planes were airborne, Verago added:

'That way Miss Howard shouldn't have a tough time on the stand. We'll concede that . . . that you two had a relationship. It should be over pretty quick for her.'

'Good,' was all Tower said. Verago shot a hard glance to him. Didn't he care more than that?

'Of course, you're being optimistic,' added Tower. 'Mighty optimistic.'

'What about?' He was getting under Verago's skin. In his anger, he broke the point of his pencil. 'Shit.'

'I'm going to get put inside, you want to take a bet?'

'Thanks for the vote of confidence,' said Verago.

'I'm sorry.' He leant over and offered Verago one of his cheap cigars, as if to make amends. 'Here.'

'Thanks,' growled Verago, as Tower lit it. Then he asked: 'Can I see that?'

Verago turned the lighter over in his hand.

'Russian, you said?'

Tower nodded.

'How did you get it?'

'A present,' said Tower. 'Not much to look at, but it's pretty tough. Never lets me down.'

'Souvenir?'

Tower had a curious smile.

'Yes,' he said slowly, 'I guess you could call it that.'

He took the lighter back, and looked at it.

'Yes,' he nodded, 'a souvenir. Not worth a damn.'

Except to you, thought Verago.

LACONBURY

Verago came out of the Class VI store clutching his 40 oz bottle of duty-free whisky which would console his night, when Jensen pounced on him.

'Ah, counsellor,' he said, his thick lips curled into a sluggish smile. He eyed the brown paper bag Verago was carrying; its contents were not concealed.

That's right, Verago felt like saying to him, I'm a solitary drinker, a lush, I keep the stuff in the lampshade and the drawer and under the bed, bottles all over the place, and the idiot would believe every word.

'I hear you've had a session with our client,' Jensen continued, falling into step with him. 'Don't you think both counsel should be present?'

Maybe Verago was mistaken, but Jensen's lips were greasy. As if he had been eating something, and then forgotten to wipe his mouth. In such a hurry, perhaps, to catch up with him.

'We were talking about cigarette lighters,' said Verago.

'Is that all?' The sarcasm was heavy.

'Oh, and a few routine matters. Nothing special.'

'And?'

'What else did you expect, Cy?' enquired Verago amiably.

'Well,' said Jensen, a little nervously, 'I think we ought to work very closely together on this case. A team. You and me.'

'But I thought we were already,' smiled Verago.

'Of course, of course.' He was wary of Verago.

He cleared his throat.

'I had a run in with the OSI about you,' he announced.

'Really?'

'Yes. After our client tried to go AWOL. They started asking

120

me questions. About you.'

'You're kidding.' Verago made a good job of sounding astonished.

'Yes,' said Jensen with mock indignation. 'And I gave them a real blast. I'm not going to be interrogated about a colleague.'

'Good for you,' said Verago approvingly. He was keeping his face very straight. 'And what did they want to know about me?'

'They were working on some crazy theory that Tower had a car waiting for him outside the base, and the whole thing was some kind of . . . well, I don't know what . . . '

'And how did I figure in that?' asked Verago innocently.

'Well, they wondered if you were around, and if you could know something . . . '

He was perspiring a little.

'And you said?'

'I told them to go jump in a lake,' said Jensen virtuously, 'and that in any case, they had the wrong guy, because you weren't around here at all, you were in London . . . '

'That was a swell thing to do.' Verago could have fooled a lot of people.

'We got to stick together, haven't we?' said Jensen.

It was a good try, thought Verago, after the man had gone. Trouble was the OSI hadn't worked out the script with Jensen too well.

Because at no time had he told them about being in London.

NEW YORK CITY

The two men, wearing grey suits, button-down-collar shirts, and sober ties, looked almost like identical twins. They had neatly cut short hair, and both smelt of aftershave.

121

They entered the brownstone block on West 30th Street, near the junction with Fifth Avenue, and took the lift to the sixth floor. Neither spoke as they slowly rode upwards.

When they got out, they walked along the corridor, past several doors, until they got to apartment 6d. They pressed the door bell.

From inside, the chamber music ceased abruptly. Then the door opened to the maximum possible on a safety chain. A woman peered out through the gap.

'Mrs Tower?' enquired one of the men politely.

'Yes,' she said warily. She kept the door on the chain.

'FBI,' said the man. He and his companion produced wallets and held up their identification at her eye level.

'What do you want?' she asked.

'We'd like to come in,' said the man courteously. 'It's about your husband.'

Momentarily, she hesitated. Then the chain was slipped, and the door opened wider.

The two men stepped inside the entrance hall of the small apartment. A cat quickly scuttled out of their way.

'Is he alright? Has anything happened,' asked the woman a little nervously. She must once have been very good looking, but she had put on weight, her eyes were puffy, and her chin was now too fleshy.

'There's nothing to worry about, Mrs Tower,' said the FBI man. 'I'm Special Agent Sullivan, and this is Agent Mattingly. We have a few questions we'd like to ask you. It won't take long,' he added like a dentist before a tooth extraction.

'You'd better sit down,' she said indicating the living room. It was untidy, a newspaper on the floor, a shopping bag on the table, a coat flung over the back of a chair.

'I'm sorry, it's not . . . ' she began, but didn't finish. She appeared tense. 'I wasn't expecting anyone. I only just got in from work.'

'Don't worry about it,' said Sullivan. 'May I?'

She nodded and he sat down in one of the armchairs. Mattingly sat on the couch.

Mrs Tower perched on the edge of a chair by the dining table.

'You're FBI?' she repeated, as if she had only just realised who they were. 'What does the FBI want with me?'

Mattingly took out a notebook, and a ballpoint pen. He sat at the ready, like a stenographer about to take dictation.

'It's routine,' said Sullivan crisply. Everything about him was crisp.

'You're Mrs Marion Louisa Tower, and you're married to Captain John Herman Tower?'

'Yes,' she said puzzled. Then she thought. 'At least . . . '

She stopped.

'Yes?'

'My husband and I, we . . . well, we've been separated since '57.'

'But you are still married to him?' asked Sullivan sharply.

'We're not divorced,' she said. 'Not yet.'

'You are married?' he repeated insistently.

'I told you.' She was getting annoyed. 'What's this about? Why these questions?'

'And are you receiving a marriage allotment from the Air Force?'

'Of course.'

Mattingly was making careful notes. He wrote shorthand.

'No children?'

'No,' she said curtly.

The cat crept into the room, and eyed the two strangers suspiciously.

'How often do you hear from your husband?' asked Sullivan.

'Why do you want to know?'

'I'm sorry,' said Sullivan. 'It would help if you just answered the questions. I don't have many.'

'John is stationed in England. He goes where he is sent. Germany, France, what do I know?'

'But you keep in touch?'

She raised her head, and there was anger in her look.

'Sometimes,' she said, in a low voice. 'Not often. Like I've said, we are separated.'

'He writes to you?'

She nodded. 'Now and then.'

'When did you last hear from him?'

'Oh, months ago. I don't know. March. April, I don't know. Just a short letter.'

'Have you still got it?'

She stared at him, uncomprehending.

'What's it got to do with the FBI?' she demanded.

'Captain Tower is currently facing court martial proceedings. The Air Force has asked us to make some routine enquiries.'

She sat frozen.

'Court martial? I don't understand. For what?'

Sullivan glanced at Mattingly. He was getting it all down.

'Adultery,' he said at last.

'No, it can't be,' she cried. 'It's crazy. We've split up. We lead our own lives.'

'Mrs Tower, he is married to you.'

She was flushed with indignation.

'Don't you understand?' she almost shouted. 'We've split up. We . . . reached an arrangement. I do my thing, he does his.'

'But you *are* married,' insisted Sullivan.

'Whose goddam business is it?' Her fists clenched. 'It's private between him and me.'

'You are not divorced,' said Sullivan, almost accusingly. Mattingly made the note.

'That's our business.' She stood up. 'I think you ought to leave.'

He remained seated.

'I'm going to raise hell about this,' she added. 'What's our relationship got to do with the Air Force; with Washington, with the FBI? Who brought the charges? Why is he being tried?'

'It is an offence for an officer who is legally married to commit adultery with another woman,' said Sullivan. 'That's the law, ma'am.'

'And the FBI gets involved?' She was breathing heavily. 'I want to know why. After all, if I don't care what he does, why should anybody else?'

'You don't seem very surprised he's been committing

adultery,' said Sullivan. 'Or did you know about it?'

'Go to hell,' she said, and her lips were trembling.

Now he got to his feet.

'We need the letter he wrote to you. And any other correspondence you've had with him.'

'Too bad,' she said.

'You've still got the letters?'

'I'm not answering another question.'

Sullivan pulled a folded paper out of his inner breast pocket.

'Mrs Tower, this is a search warrant. We have authority to search this apartment and everthing in it, and to take whatever is material evidence. Now, will you co-operate, or do we have to take the place apart?'

She gaped at him.

'Please,' he offered. 'Read it yourself.' He held the paper out to her. She took it, and unfolded it, and scanned it with almost unseeing eyes.

'Why?' she asked. 'Why?'

'That's what the Air Force asked for.'

'Who in the Air Force?'

'The Office of Special Investigations. The OSI. We're only doing a job for them. We're not involved. Now, Mrs Tower, let's see the letters.'

She walked slowly to a door leading to her bedroom. It stood open, and they saw her go to the dressing table and open a drawer. She took out three letters.

'Here,' she said, when she came back. 'I hope you think they're worth it.'

She sank down on the chair, and buried her face in her hands.

'They're only three letters here,' said Sullivan, looking at the envelopes. 'February 1961. December 1960. May 1960.'

'That's all I've got,' came her muffled voice. 'Look for yourself if you think I'm lying.'

'No, that's alright, Mrs Tower,' said Sullivan. 'These will do.'

Out of one of the envelopes dropped a small snapshot. It was a picture of a man in civilian clothes.

'Is this your husband?' asked Sullivan.

She didn't even look up. 'Yes.'

'Where was it taken?'

'Berlin, I think,' she said.

'Thank you, Mrs Tower,' said Sullivan, and he paused. 'We appreciate your co-operation.'

Mattingly stood up, and folded his notebook.

'Don't disturb yourself, please,' added Sullivan. 'We'll let ourselves out.'

Even after she heard the door slam, she sat there for a long time.

At last she got up. She went over to a cupboard and took out a bottle and a glass. Slowly, deliberately she filled two thirds of the glass with vodka. Then she drank it, in big gulps.

She held up the glass against the light, and stared into it, like a fortune teller into a crystal ball.

Then she hurled the glass right across the room, and it smashed against the wall.

MARIENFELDE

On the edge of the Soviet sector, the camp sprawled over an acre of West Berlin territory.

'Warning!' cautioned the big sign inside the entrance, 'Beware of Spying and Abduction!'

Pech drove his Mercedes past the main gate of Marienfelde reception centre, and briefly showed his pass to the guard. The man nodded, and waved him on.

Department B1 had its own office in the camp, tucked away between the administrative buildings, the dormitory area, the medical division, and the big central dining hall, where meals were served in shifts.

Marienfelde was bulging with 3,000 refugees from the East

sector, but Pech was concerned with one girl.

They had her in custody, and she wasn't permitted to go anywhere unless accompanied by a plainclothes man from B1.

Chaperoned, she was allowed to stroll in the fresh air, and she was given five marks a week pocket money. Sometimes her escort bought her a Coca Cola from the little stand in the camp. She liked coke; it was a forbidden drink where she came from.

Pech parked the car in his own reserved space in front of the B1 building. He got out, and walked towards a hut.

'Attention,' called out the camp loudspeakers. 'Will the following please report to administration: 2690, 6498, 7125, 8843.'

No names were allowed inside Marienfelde. Everyone was a number, because names betrayed identities, and those became secret once inside the gates.

Helga was 6221. And she was very special.

Most of those who got across the border stayed in Marienfelde for two or three weeks only, while they were vetted, interrogated, debriefed and assigned to other locations inside West Germany. The average investigation lasted twelve days, while stories were checked, relatives in the West contacted, and clearances given.

But there were some who didn't move on.

Like Helga.

The hut which was her home in Marienfelde stood in a little enclosure surrounded by a wire fence, and the gate was guarded. There too they knew Pech.

She looked up when he entered. She was pale with sunken eyes, her straight hair tied in a bun, wearing a reefer jacket and shapeless trousers. On the table in front of her stood a mug of cold coffee, a tin plate, with a piece of garlic sausage, two thick slices of bread, and a pat of butter.

'You haven't touched your breakfast,' observed Pech reproachfully.

'Any news?' she asked. 'Is there any news?'

She twisted her fingers nervously.

Pech sat down on a stool.

'Not yet,' he said. 'You have to be patient, Helga.'

'How much longer?'

'These things take time, my dear,' said Pech. 'We're trying to process you. We have to be careful. It takes time. We can't just go across over there and ask them about you. We have to check things by other means. And you're not helping us by refusing to co-operate.'

Outside they could hear the PA system calling for more numbers to report immediately.

'I want to see Captain Tower,' she demanded.

'Well you can't,' he replied curtly.

'Where is he?'

'In England,' said Pech.

'Tell him I want to see him. He'll understand.'

'I regret that's impossible,' sighed Pech. 'How often do I have to explain to you that the Americans have officially handed you over to us. Forget about them. You are our responsibility.'

He smiled at her encouragingly.

'Why don't you tell us the whole story? Why don't you tell us what you told Captain Tower?'

'Do you know where we are?' she asked unexpectedly.

For a moment, he looked puzzled.

'What do you mean?'

'This camp? Marienfelde. This reception centre. Where is it?'

'I don't understand you,' said Pech baffled. 'This is Berlin. The Western sector. What do you mean?'

'The other side of the camp,' she said. 'Where is that?'

'Helga, I don't follow.'

'It's five metres from East German territory,' she said slowly. 'That's why I won't talk to you.'

Pech smiled again.

'I assure you, you are perfectly safe. They can't touch you here. You are under official care. You have the department's assurance.'

For the first time, Helga smiled too. A wry, cynical smile.

Pech found it quite disconcerting.

Hans Jurgen Kohl, alias 9684, leant against the wall of one of the twenty-five residential blocks, and watched Pech leave the wired enclosure.

Kohl knew who Pech was, and who he had been to see in the guarded hut.

That was the reason Kohl was in Marienfelde. His orders were explicit and they only concerned the girl whose number was 6221.

Kohl, freckle faced, and slightly built, was regarded by the SSD, the East German security service, as one of its up and coming young men. He had the rank of lieutenant, and he specialised in cross-sector operations.

It had been no problem for him to pose as an East zone fugitive, and get into Marienfelde for processing.

He had been very well briefed. He knew about Pech, where B1 had its office, and the location of the security compound. In fact, curiously enough, the whole sprawling camp, with its teeming mass of refugees, held little mystery for him.

Kohl had a good story ready for anyone who wanted to know what made a young man like him commit the heinous sin of Republikflucht (desertion). He was about to be called up for Volksarmee, and no way, he explained, was he going to become one of Ulbricht's goose-stepping soldiers.

He was admirably convincing, and people were quite sure that he'd make a good living for himself once he settled in West Germany. They didn't know, of course, that he was in no hurry to leave Marienfelde.

'Attention,' blared the loudspeaker. 'Will 9684 report to Room 9, Building 77, immediately.'

He heard the announcement, and then he froze. 9684! That was him.

Building 77 was an administration block, so what did they want? He had already been debriefed, had his medical, and received his money allowance . . .

He walked along the corridor, and found room 9. It gave no clue to its occupant.

He knocked on the door.

'Come in,' answered a voice.

Kohl entered, and stopped. There was only one man in the

office, sitting behind a trestle table on which lay a single file.

'I said come in,' repeated Pech. 'Come in and sit down.'

Warily Kohl pulled a wooden chair forward and sat down facing the desk.

'You know who I am,' said Pech. 'And I know who you are, Lieutenant.'

Kohl's mouth felt dry.

'Lieutenant?' he echoed. 'I am a civilian. Somebody has made a mistake.'

'No mistake,' said Pech. He was quite cheerful. 'It is all here.' He tapped the unopened file. 'You are an Officer of the Staats Sicherheits Dienst of the DDR.'

Kohl decided to stay silent.

'And people like you are not welcome to Marienfelde.'

Maybe it was a test, thought Kohl desperately. Maybe they're trying it on.

'This is nonsense,' he said. 'I have no idea what you are talking about. I fled to avoid conscription. I would like to go to Bavaria. Anywhere far away from the DDR.'

'I'm sorry, Kohl,' said Pech. 'You've been rumbled. It was a nice try, but it didn't work. I know this will be a blot on your excellent record sheet, but that can't be helped.'

The sarcastic bastard, thought Kohl.

'I am not the only SSD man in Marienfelde,' he said maliciously.

'But you're the one who's been spotted.'

Kohl scowled.

'So what happens now?'

'Back you go to Herr Ulbricht,' said Pech jovially. 'I'll even get a driver to drop you at zonal boundary.'

'That's all?'

Pech's eyes gleamed. 'What do you want me to do? Have you shot? That's not the way the game is played, Hans. If we all started shooting each other . . . well, I ask you!'

Kohl sniffed.

'Just for the record,' added Pech, 'would you formally like to tell me who you were sent to spy on in here?'

'I think you know the answer I'll give you,' replied Kohl drily.

Pech shrugged. 'I had to ask you, of course, it's routine.'

'I hope your boss is pleased,' said Kohl, with a touch of bitterness.

'Well,' said Pech, 'I try to keep him happy.'

Half an hour later, Kohl was on his way to SSD headquarters in East Berlin.

And Pech called his boss in Karlsruhe, and reported on events.

Unruh congratulated him. It proved that B1 was very alert.

'What about the girl?' he asked.

'Ah, the girl,' reflected Pech. 'She is still a problem, I'm afraid.'

'Damn.'

'She seems to be afraid something might happen to her. But I reassured her.'

'You did?'

'Yes sir,' said Pech, 'I promised her that she was quite safe.'

LONDON

The Bryanston Mews party was in full swing when he came up to her.

'Are you the remarkable American girl everybody's been telling me about?' he asked.

'Remarkable?' she echoed, eyebrows raised.

He was very tall, but good looking, with tousled dark hair, and laugh lines round his mouth. He wore a turtle-neck sweater, and his Rolex watch was twenty-one carat gold.

'A girl of many talents, they say.'

'You can only be Gene,' said Laurie, and she couldn't help smiling at the unabashed cheek of his approach.

'We obviously have mutual friends,' said the man, in his curious accent, a mixture of American and central European.

'I was looking out for you,' he added, gently steering her to the punchbowl on the big table at the side of the room.

'Really?' said Laurie.

He ladled some of the liquid into a glass for her.

'I think they've put everything including aftershave into this,' he cautioned, 'but it doesn't matter anymore. Two sips and you don't care.'

There were about twenty people in the room, chatting and laughing to a background of records. Nina and Frederick's latest was fighting a losing battle amid the hubbub.

He filled his own glass, and raised it.

'This is my third,' he confided. 'It makes the world look beautiful.'

He took her arm, and guided her into a corner.

'Tell me,' he said, 'what have you heard about me, Laurie?'

Her almond-shaped eyes twinkled.

'You really want to know?'

He held up one hand. 'No, I will tell you. This man, Ivanov, don't trust him an inch. He is a lecher. He chases women. He adores pretty girls. They're not safe with him.' He became mock serious. 'They're quite right.'

'You have a high opinion of yourself, Gene,' remarked Laurie.

'Can I help it if I am so attractive to them?' he grinned. He saw her raised eyebrows.

'Don't worry, I never force myself on a lady.' He paused. 'Except maybe in the line of duty.'

Laurie put her glass on top of a cabinet containing a collection of Chinese figurines.

'Are you on duty now?' she asked.

'No more than you, Miss Czeslaw,' he said genially. He finished his drink. 'Excuse me,' he said. 'I must get another. Would you like a refill?'

She shook her head, and watched him make his way through the crowd to the punchbowl. So this was Yevgenni Ivanov, Captain 2nd Rank, Soviet Navy, assistant naval attaché,

Russian Embassy, London. Man about town, official playboy, assigned special duty.

Very special duty.

Ivanov came back to her. His face was slightly flushed. He likes drinking, she noted.

'Stephen gives good parties, don't you think?' he commented, looking round the room. 'He has this knack of always inviting the most unexpected people.'

'Like you,' said Laurie.

'Or you,' said Ivanov. 'Maybe we should both be grateful to him.'

He took a drink from his glass. 'I think they've added some deodorant,' he said, pulling a face.

'So why do you drink it?'

He lowered his voice, confidentially. 'Because, my beautiful Laurie, Stephen is too mean to serve decent drinks. That is his one great failing. I have never seen a drop of champagne at one of his do's. One is left with this.'

'You come quite often?' she asked.

He shrugged. 'It passes the time,' he said airily.

Near them a girl suddenly raised her voice in protest. 'Look what you have done,' she cried, accusingly, holding out her skirt, soaked with the drink a man had spilt over her.

'I'm ever so sorry, darling,' mumbled the man, swaying slightly. He was in shirtsleeves, his eyes slightly glassy. 'Buy you a new one. Ever so sorry.'

He took a handkerchief, and started to dab her skirt.

'Oh, go away,' snapped the girl irritably.

'You see that man?' said Ivanov sarcastically. 'Pillar of Fleet Street. Peter Dawkins. Always good for a scoop if you can pour it into him.'

'For a navy man, you're well informed about journalists,' remarked Laurie.

He smiled. 'No more than you I imagine. Tell me something. Your name, Czeslaw. Interesting. Eastern European.'

'American,' she said shortly.

'But originally . . . My grandfather was a Tsarist grand duke,' he went on. 'He loved good restaurants, parties, the ballet, the

133

good life. He adored the ladies. He took to luxury like a duck to water.' He winked. 'Just like me. It's in the blood.'

'Even though you're a good communist.'

'Of course. Not only good. A trusted one. You understand?'

The atmosphere was getting smokier, the noise louder, the music shriller.

'I think,' said Laurie, 'it's time for me to go.'

'So soon?' he protested.

'I have an early start in the morning . . . '

He was charming about it. 'I understand. There'll be plenty of other times. I'll call you at your flat.'

'You have the number?' she asked, surprised.

'Of course.' The smiling eyes stared straight into hers. 'And I look forward to seeing quite a lot of you, Miss Czeslaw.'

At the door, she glanced back, and saw him watching her across the room. He raised his hand, blew her an extravagant, continental kiss. He was still smiling.

Yes, decided Laurie, it had all gone like clockwork.

Thursday, July 6, 1961 – LONDON

Serena Howard lay back in the bath tub, luxuriating in the warm, perfumed water.

She stretched her long legs, and relaxed. She was a girl who enjoyed pleasant physical sensations. Like silk against her skin. A man's hands exploring her body.

And here, immersed in the scented bath, she felt secure, safe.

She always took her time over her bath. It had become a ritual, and part of the pleasure was that she could linger as long as she liked.

Sometimes she indulged herself by having a cup of coffee in the tub, or even reading the paper. Often she smoked a

134

cigarette. But mostly she just lazed.

The door buzzer sounded.

She lay rigid for a moment. Living alone, it was the thing she loathed most – that the phone should ring, or somebody come to the door while she was having her bath.

She had taken off her watch, but she had got up late, and she knew it must be around 10:30. In the sitting room, the radio was playing softly. She wasn't expecting anyone.

Again the buzzer sounded.

'Go away,' said Serena to herself. If was too late for the postman, she had paid the milk last week. She was suspicious of these unexpected callers anyway. Like a couple of Sundays back when she'd been roused from a deep sleep, by a man and woman with toothy smiles offering to 'discuss a Bible message'.

She'd slammed the door in their faces rather more forcefully than was necessary, and swore next time she simply wouldn't answer.

Stick it out, ignore them, and they'll finally give up, she assured herself.

But not today. This time the buzzer was pushed impatiently, three times in succession.

'Shut up,' shouted Serena, but she knew that she couldn't be heard by anyone outside the front door.

Then the knocking began. A couple of sharp raps, finally a peremptory thumping.

'God almighty,' she swore, raising herself and stepping out of the bath, her naked body dripping. She had a slim, boyish figure, a tiny waist, small, firm breasts, and very good legs. But she didn't even look at herself in the long bathroom mirror. She briskly towelled herself dry.

'Yes, damn it, I'm coming,' she called out furiously as the banging continued. She wrapped a bath robe round herself, and went to the front door.

'You don't have to knock the house down,' she said angrily.

A shabbily dressed man in a grubby raincoat smiled at her nervously. Incongruously, he had a bowler hat on.

'I'm sorry, miss,' he apologised, 'but I knew you was in, and I thought maybe you hadn't heard.'

135

She caught a whiff of his stale breath.

'What do you want?' demanded Serena, pulling the robe closer around her.

'Miss Serena Ann Margaret Howard?' he enquired, rattling off the string of names on her birth certificate.

'Yes,' she confirmed nervously.

'Here you are, miss,' he said, and handed her an envelope. It was buff, and it had OHMS on it. Before she could even look at it, he held a book and pencil in front of her.

'Sign here, miss.'

Despite his shabby looks and bad breath, his tone had become authoritative.

'It's just a receipt,' he added, and, hardly thinking, she scrawled her name.

'Thank you,' said the man. He raised his bowler hat politely. 'Sorry to trouble you.'

'What is this?' she asked as he started to go.

'Just a witnesss summons,' he said. 'Nothing to worry about. Good day.'

She closed the door and stared at the envelope in her hand.

OHMS. On Her Majesty's Service. And in the bottom left hand corner, 'Lord Chancellor's Office'.

Suddenly, the feeling of wellbeing that she always had after a bath disappeared. Her stomach was tightening into a knot.

She ripped open the envelope. The paper was a printed sheet and only some particulars had been typed in.

It ordered her to appear in person at RAF Station Laconbury on Tuesday, July 25th, at 9 a.m. to attend in the matter of the United States v Tower, and to give and render such particulars as may be required of her.

She put the paper down, and went over to her handbag. She took out a small pocket diary. Today was the sixth. Her hand trembled slightly as she counted the days. They had given her just under three weeks.

She sat down and tried to think rationally. Nineteen days. Two weeks and five days. Oh yes, that was right. Daventry had said they had to give at least fourteen days notice in a subpoena. They had been very generous.

Serena looked in her diary again. She found the number she wanted, and she reached over and put the phone on the floor next to her. She dialled the number, and held on while it rang.

Finally it answered.

'Mr Daventry, please,' she said.

The voice at the other end asked something.

'It's Miss Howard,' she said, rather formally. Then she added.

'Tell him it's very urgent.'

Two miles away, in a tall building in Holborn, a red light flashed on a control panel in a room which, at first glance, looked a little like a recording studio.

A spool began to revolve slowly. This was one conversation which was going to be transcribed in full as soon as it had been recorded.

SOUTH RUISLIP

In her office, Laurie's phone rang.

'Colonel Kincaid's office, Miss Czeslaw speaking,' she announced.

'Hi, Laurie,' came the familiar voice. 'Listen, you free Saturday?'

'I can be,' she said.

'Let's meet at our little French restaurant. Or you got any better ideas?'

'No, that sounds fine,' she said. 'I look forward to it.'

'Eight o'clock then. I got a few things to talk about.'

He hung up.

She had been expecting Clyde Unterberg to call.

In fact, if he hadn't she would have called him. She too had a few things to talk about.

BURDEROP PARK

Duval was enjoying his day out to Wiltshire driving an unmarked OSI car from the motor pool. He relished the green English countryside in the bright July sun.

Outside Swindon he got lost, but the policeman he stopped to ask the way to Burderop Park USAF Hospital gave him excellent directions, and he arrived only half an hour later than he had arranged.

He parked the car by the administrative building, and walked up the path, lined on either side by neatly trimmed six-inch-high hedges. They and the closely cropped lawn gave an impression of almost fastidious tidiness.

Duval wondered, idly, who kept it all so orderly. Some of the patients, maybe, but certainly not inmates of Ward 10.

He found Captain Perriton waiting in his office a little impatiently.

'Sorry I'm late, doc,' apologised Duval. It was the most familiar he had been so far with Perriton and he registered an immediate resentment. He made a mental note always to call Perriton doctor, or by his rank. Funny people these psychiatrists.

'Let's go and eat,' said Perriton. His bald head gleamed. Almost as if it had been polished.

'I passed a cute little pub on the way here. Looks two hundred years old. Why don't we take my car and have a beer there?' suggested Duval.

He had decided during the drive, that it would be much better to have his discussion with the captain off base. It somehow made it less official.

'I got a lot of patients to see this afternoon,' grumbled

Perriton unhelpfully.

'That's OK. It's only ten minutes from here.'

The pub was the ideal place for a private little chat. It had a quiet lawn at the back, with benches set far apart.

'What will you have?' asked Duval.

'A shandy.'

'A what?' Duval had never heard of it.

'Lemonade and beer . . . It's sort of peculiarly English,' explained Perriton. He also liked buttered scones, crumpets, and little pork pies because he prided himself on getting to know a country's way of life.

'Sounds it,' said Duval doubtfully. He walked into the saloon bar, ordered a scotch and soda and a shandy.

'With ice,' he added.

Although Duval was in civilian dress, he might as well have worn a uniform. His suit was American, like his shirt, his tie, and his shoes. In the village bar, he stood out.

The fat girl behind the counter carefully dropped one lump of ice in each glass. Duval still couldn't believe it. He had been in many pubs and bars since arriving in England, and the English reluctance to serve anything iced always amazed him.

'Give me a little more ice.'

If his clothes and his accent hadn't branded him, this would have been it.

He carried the drinks out to the garden.

'Cheers,' said Perriton, to underline his acclimatisation.

'Nice part of the country you got here,' remarked Duval. He wanted to play it gently.

'Mr Duval,' said Perriton, 'you haven't come all this way to talk about the scenery.'

'No,' said Duval. 'It's about Captain Tower.'

'Of course.'

Duval shot him a quick sideways look. Just how much did this trick cyclist know.

'I'm sorry he was so uncooperative at the test,' said Duval. 'He wasted everybody's time.'

'You haven't come just to tell me that either.' said Perriton testily.

139

Damn, thought Duval, he got out of the wrong side of bed today.

'No.'

'Well?'

'Doctor, this is absolutely unofficial,' said Duval.

'Aha.'

'And absolutely off the record.'

'So?'

'We're very concerned about Captain Tower.' Duval juggled his glass, but the ice had melted and there wasn't the clinking sound he usually enjoyed. 'He's in a lot of trouble. And we hate to see a good man in trouble.'

'What are you trying to say?'

'Well,' said Duval. 'He goes on trial soon, as you know, and he looks like going straight into the hoosegaw. Hell of a shame. I'd hate to see my worst enemy in Leavenworth.'

'I didn't know the OSI cared so much,' commented Perriton.

'Sure we do. We look after our own. Now, I appreciate the test you made was inconclusive. But we think Captain Tower has problems. So I want to have your advice.'

The bald man stared at him.

'It wouldn't be too difficult to set up a board, would it?'

'A board?'

'Section 121. If certain observations of a man's behaviour are reported through channels, regulations provide an enquiry into his mental condition may be appropriate. It only needs two medical officers. One of them should be a psychiatrist. You follow, doctor?'

'For what purpose?' asked Perriton. His look was cold.

'Well, procedure lays down that the accused can be placed under observation, examined, and further investigated. Right here, for example. At Burderop.'

'So?'

'Supposing,' said Duval, looking into the distance, 'supposing you find an accused may have, er, difficulty to intelligently co-operate in his defence. I'm quoting the book, of course. "Intelligently co-operate in his defence." '

'I know the book,' said Perriton.

'If that were the case, it would not be fair to subject such a man to a court martial. I'm sure you agree, doctor.'

'Guess so,' said Perriton slowly. He had worked with the OSI before.

'So, if the poor guy needs help, the right thing is to ship him out of here, and confine him in a place until you people can shape him up again, wouldn't you say?'

It was restful on the lawn. Birds sang, and a man lay on the grass, his eyes closed. Two benches away, a young couple had their heads together, and were laughing, oblivious of their surroundings.

'Have you got evidence that there is something wrong mentally with Captain Tower?'

Duval stared straight at Perriton.

'You saw him. Donald Duck! Mickey Mouse! The guy was irrational. Wouldn't co-operate. You said so yourself. And Lieutenant Jensen agrees. He's trying to help the man, but he just won't listen. Wants to plead not guilty against the best advice.'

He leant closer.

'Look doctor, what I'm saying is, we want to help him. He's done great work. I can't talk about it, but he's risked his neck. He's been under terrific strain. Never knew when he'd get a bullet in his back.'

Perriton raised his eyebrows.

'You got no idea what Captain Tower's been through. The pressure on him . . . Jesus, I'd crack, that's for sure. I can't tell you more. It's highly classified. You can guess how secret. But the least we owe him is to try and help him.'

'So why try him at all?'

'He broke the law,' sighed Duval. 'Crazy guy. Gets involved with this English girl, shacks up with her. The whole thing leaves a bad taste, but we got to enforce the law. If every married guy in the service thought he could get away with adultery . . . '

'A lot do and nothing happens,' interrupted Perriton. His smile was chilly.

'Poor Tower got caught. But we want him off the hook.'

The bald man looked at his watch.

'What exactly are you asking me?'

'All I'm trying to find out, strictly unofficially, is if you'd co-operate . . . ?'

'To find him mentally unstable?'

'To take appropriate action so that we get him out of trouble.'

'I don't know . . . '

'It would also protect national security,' added Duval softly.

Perriton looked up. 'How is that?'

'I can't tell you any more, doctor. But believe me, it might be very much in the interests of the United States.'

Perriton stood up.

'I've got to get back,' he said. 'Anyway, I can't answer hypothetical questions. If a request for a board comes through channels, I'll consider it. That's all I can say.'

'That's all I wanted to know, sir,' said Duval.

He drove the psychiatrist back to the hospital. He nearly asked if he could have a look at Ward 10, but he realised they wouldn't want visitors there at any time. What happened behind its locked doors was not discussed outside Burderop Park.

He was pleased with himself on the return drive to Laconbury. After all, it was a basic military principle to have a contingency plan. You never knew when you might need it.

Although he knew that the file he never saw also had other proposals about how to deal with Captain John Tower.

He was almost relieved that he didn't have to know about them.

LONDON

It was 12:40 when Arthur Rippon got out of the cab. Not only the invitation, but the venue puzzled him. Curzon Street was not lawyer's locale, and the Mirabelle certainly not their stamping ground.

Daventry was already sitting in the lounge when Mr Rippon entered, and welcomed him with a charming smile.

'I hope the traffic wasn't too bad,' he greeted him. 'Do sit down. What would you like?'

Mr Rippon blinked. Daventry was always polite, correct to him, if somewhat distant. This friendliness was something quite new.

'Gin and dry ginger,' said Mr Rippon.

Daventry did not even wince.

'Well, this is a pleasure, Mr Daventry,' said the solicitor. 'Especially,' he added pointedly, 'as you're always so busy.'

'Yes, I'm sorry we haven't managed to do it before,' nodded Daventry. He was very much at ease.

The menus came, and Mr Rippon opened his. He was impressed.

Daventry was an attentive host, chatting urbanely about all kinds of insignificant topics. As Mr Rippon toyed with his Dover sole, and he ate almond trout, Daventry spiced the conversation with a few gossipy bits about legal figures and court gaffes which both amused Mr Rippon, and gave him a growing sense of equality with the barrister.

'A little Armagnac perhaps? Or a Napoleon?' suggested Daventry over coffee.

'I have to work this afternoon,' said Mr Rippon. But he quickly added: 'Yes, please. I'd find Napoleon brandy very agreeable.'

It was a double in the big balloon glass, and then Daventry signalled for cigars. Mr Rippon found himself puffing a huge Havana torpedo.

'I must say, this has been most pleasant,' he said, his face slightly flushed with good living.

'My dear Mr Rippon, that's the idea,' said Daventry truthfully. 'I am so glad you've enjoyed it.'

Mr Rippon blew out some heady Bolivar fumes.

'I think I may have something quite juicy for you soon,' he

confided, lowering his voice. 'I'll be in touch with Pettifer.'

'Oh really?' remarked Daventry.

'You're very much in demand with my clients,' continued Mr Rippon. 'I think some of them say a little prayer at night that you won't start accepting prosecution briefs.'

He laughed a little throatily. Daventry ordered another Napoleon. He felt the moment had come.

'I wonder if you could do a little thing for me, Mr Rippon,' he said.

'Anything, anything.' Mr Rippon was warm, contented.

'I'd like you to brief me on behalf of a client.'

Mr Rippon stared at him.

'What client?'

'A Miss Howard.'

Mr Rippon's brown furrowed. 'Howard? Miss Howard. I don't think I . . . '

'No,' interrupted Daventry. 'You don't know her.'

Mr Rippon sipped the brandy, but his eyes were surprisingly alert.

'What is the case?'

'She would like me to represent her in an application to a judge in chambers.'

Mr Rippon waited.

'To set aside a subpoena,' added Daventry.

'She'd better come and see me,' said Mr Rippon.

'Well,' said Daventry, 'as it so happens, I have all the facts. She's already consulted me. Quite unofficial, you understand.'

'Oh yes?'

'But I feel that as I will act for her, it is time to regularise the position. I should now be formally instructed. So if you could oblige me . . . '

'Hmm,' said Rippon, savouring the delight of being asked to do Daventry a favour. 'Rather unusual, is it not? A member of the bar asking a solicitor to brief him?' He winked. 'Not that I mind, of course. Not among colleagues.'

'It's perfectly correct procedure, I assure you, Mr Rippon,' said Daventry, and for the first time there was a hint of the old formality in his tone. 'As you know, it is no breach of etiquette to advise a personal friend . . . '

Mr Rippon's eyes narrowed. 'The lady is a personal friend, then?' Daventry regarded him stonily. 'Not that that is my business, of course. Perhaps I should know what this subpoena is all about?'

'It is a witness summons for her to give evidence at an American court martial.'

'Oh really? A British national?' Mr Rippon swallowed some more brandy. 'What is the case?'

'An officer is being tried for adultery,' said Daventry almost reluctantly.

Mr Rippon exposed yellowing teeth in a wolfish smile.

'Goodness me! If our courts could try people for adultery, I'd have to treble my practice. What a lark.'

'Anyway, she doesn't want to give evidence,' said Daventry.

'Naturally not,' nodded Mr Rippon as if he knew everything. 'Well, I'll get in touch with Pettifer . . . '

'No,' said Daventry. 'I will not require that.'

'Oh.'

'But I assure you that you will not be out of pocket, Mr Rippon.'

'The lady has means?'

'All your costs will be met,' Daventry assured him.

'Well, then . . . ' Mr Rippon hastily gulped down the remainder of the brandy.

'Good,' said Daventry. 'That's settled then. You have formally instructed me.'

'Yes.' Mr Rippon inclined his head. 'On behalf of Miss . . . Oh yes, Miss Howard.'

'And I accept your instructions,' said Daventry. 'And I am now acting on her behalf.'

He signalled the waiter for the bill.

'I would like to meet the lady,' said Mr Rippon.

'Perhaps there'll be an opportunity,' replied Daventry carelessly, and regretfully Mr Rippon started to feel shut out again.

'Does Pettifer know about our . . . er . . . arrangement, Mr Daventry?'

'He will,' said Daventry. 'He will.'

Friday, July 7, 1961 – LONDON

'I don't understand what this is about,' protested Serena Howard, staring from one to the other.

'It's at the request of the American authorities,' explained the shorter of the two Special Branch men.

'The American authorities . . . '

'Well,' he went on, with just the hint of a sneer, 'You've had a GI staying here quite a lot, haven't you, miss?'

She flared up.

'I have a friend, yes,' she retorted. 'He's an American officer. What's that got to do with you?'

'We've been asked to search your flat at the request of their authorities. Since you're a British national, it has to be done by us,' stated the short one, as if that answered everything.

In the corner of the room, remarkably inconspicuous for a man of his bulk, stood Unterberg. Despite his size, he had a knack of merging with his surroundings.

She moved towards the phone.

'I want to call my . . . my lawyer,' said Serena.

The taller Special Branch man was there before her.

'Certainly, miss,' he said, 'but not right now. We only want to look around, it won't take long.'

'Have you got the right . . . '

'Yes, miss. We have a warrant.'

She sat down, pale faced.

Unterberg sat down opposite her, uninvited.

'It's nothing to do with you at all,' he confided, leaning forward almost conspiratorially. 'I'm sorry you're being inconvenienced. All we're interested in is Captain Tower.'

'Who are you?' demanded Serena. The shock was beginning

146

to wear off a little.

'My name is Unterberg.'

'Well, Mr Unterberg, I am not going to answer any questions. I want you people out of here. I . . . ' She paused. 'Do I make myself clear?'

Out of the corner of her eye, she saw the taller policeman pulling out books and shaking them, opening sideboard doors and drawers.

'Tell him to keep his bloody hands off my things,' she shouted, half rising.

The short one sighed. 'We *do* have a search warrant.'

'You're the bastards who've been plaguing me, sneaking after me, following me,' she burst out.

'I'm sorry,' said the short one, 'I don't know what you're talking about.'

Unterberg said nothing. His smile was very faint.

The short one waved a hand at the Mexican masks.

'Do you smoke?' he enquired, almost casually.

'You're all crazy,' cried Serena, her hand nervously ruffling through her blonde hair. 'Do I smoke? What's my private life got to do with you? What do you care?'

Unterberg did his confidential act again.

'These are British police officers, Serena,' he said in a low voice. 'I guess they're interested to know if Captain Tower brought you any class VI liquor. Or PX goods. That's an offence, possessing our duty-free stuff if you're a British national. So of course is smoking marijuana . . . '

Her eyes widened.

'My god,' she said. 'You're trying to frame me. You're going to plant something on me . . . '

The short one drew himself up to his inconsiderable height. It did not make him look much taller.

'Now look here, Miss Howard,' he began in an official voice, 'that's a very serious charge to make but I will overlook it. The purpose of our visit is to see whether Captain Tower left anything on your premises which might . . . might be a breach of security. Now let me ask you, did Captain Tower, to your knowledge, give you anything classified? Papers, notebooks, photos, documents? Did he ask you to keep anything for him?'

She just shook her head.

'You're sure? You won't be in any trouble, I promise you. If he gave you anything you shouldn't have we just want it, that's all.'

'No,' she said quietly. 'He did not.'

'I don't have to tell you that Captain Tower is facing court martial charges, and it would be an offence for you to withhold evidence . . . '

The taller one had picked up Tower's framed photograph.

'That's him, isn't it?' he asked Unterberg.

'Put that down,' hissed Serena. She rounded on the small one. 'He's not being tried for espionage, damn you.'

She was breathing heavily, furiously.

'Nobody's mentioned espionage,' said Unterberg. 'Why do you?'

'Oh god,' she cried, and clenched her hands until the knuckles were white.

She sat slumped, watching them go about their business, swiftly, expertly, and yet she felt they weren't as completely thorough as they could be. If they were looking for documents, or photographs, they didn't look under the mattress of her bed, or under the carpet; they only casually looked over the luggage in her wardrobe. In her distress, and her indignation, she still found time to wonder why.

All the time, Unterberg sat next to her, not taking his eyes off her.

'I don't know if it's any consolation, Serena,' he said unexpectedly, 'but you're not the only one who is going through this. His wife had a visit from the FBI.'

'His wife?'

'Yes,' he said suavely, 'you know about his wife of course. The lady in New York. Or didn't he mention her?'

'I told you, I'm not saying one word.'

Unterberg included his head. 'Your privilege, Serena.' Then he added: 'At the moment.'

Two hours later they left the flat and all they took with them was the framed photograph of Captain Tower.

HUNTINGON

The moment Verago returned to his room at the George and Dragon he knew someone had searched it. The notepad he had left on his bedside table lay at a different angle. His ballpoint pen which had been on top of it had rolled onto the threadbare carpet.

'Shit,' swore Verago. They had gone through the wardrobe, and the two shirts and underwear in the drawers of the tallboy.

His holdall had been moved, and when he unzipped it, he was sure somebody had gone through it. He hadn't stuffed the three handkerchiefs in like that. The book mark in his law manual had been stuck between the wrong pages.

'Inefficient bastards,' growled Verago. He was almost angrier that they cared so little they hadn't even bothered to put things back as they had found them, than at the intrusion itself.

Verago thumped heavily down the creaking stairs.

He found the landlord sitting in the cubby hole that passed for an office, talking to somebody on the phone.

'Yes,' he was saying, 'beautiful countryside all round. And home cooking. You and your missus will love it here. I'll have your room ready.'

The landlord hung up, and Verago thought what a pity he couldn't warn the couple what they had in store.

'Somebody's been in my room,' complained Verago.

The landlord blinked.

'Who?' he asked bovinely.

'Listen, friend,' said Verago, 'if I knew that I wouldn't be asking you. Did you see anybody go up?'

The landlord belched. He shook his head. 'Anything been taken?' he asked, easing his bulk out of the chair.

'Not that I know.' He stopped. 'Tell me, have any Americans been here? Civilians?'

'You know how close the base is,' he said. 'I don't notice anymore who comes and goes.'

'Has anybody asked for me? Or what room I'm in?'

Even as he asked, Verago knew it was pointless. The OSI wouldn't need to ask. They'd know it all.

'Maybe you made a mistake,' said the landlord. 'Seeing nothing's gone. Maybe it's Ethel. She may have moved something.'

Ethel was the garlic maid.

'Nobody's just moved things. My room's been searched.'

'I can tell you, nobody's had your key while you've been out. I don't see no way they could have got in,' the landlord sniffed. 'Anyway, I'll tell the missus and Joe to keep their eyes open.'

Joe was the handyman, doubling as porter, barman and waiter.

'Thanks,' said Verago.

'By the way,' said the landlord, 'you asked for three eggs this morning.'

'So?'

'I'll have to charge you extra,' said the landlord. 'Set breakfast is two eggs and one rasher.'

'Home from home, isn't it?' grunted Verago.

Two jets roared over the neighbourhood, so low that a lantern hanging from the gabled ceiling shook.

'Ah,' said the landlord. 'They're busy at the base.'

'Yeah.' Verago nodded. 'They're very busy.'

KARLSRUHE

The afternoon Verago's hotel was searched, Helmut Pech had a meeting with his chief of section B1.

Herr Unruh looked tired, thought Pech. The department was, of course, under great pressure, and his boss had evidently been working long hours.

'I have heard from the Americans,' said Herr Unruh. 'He goes on trial on July 25th!'

'Excellent,' said Pech.

'I have always admired Yankee ingenuity,' commented Herr Unruh, who had been a junior Waffen SS staff officer in the war, but whose de-Nazification file had fortuitously gone astray after VE day. 'They are very efficient people. I think they've handled it beautifully.'

'Absolutely,' agreed Pech respectfully.

'However . . . ' Herr Unruh looked at his subordinate across the desk, suddenly gloomy.

'A problem?' ventured Pech.

'The woman, Helga. Just how secure is she in Marienfelde?'

'Very.'

'You appreciate the problem she could present. If she eluded us, if she managed somehow . . . '

'I don't think there's the slightest chance,' insisted Pech. 'If I may say so, camp security is tight. I myself have given special instructions. Somebody always keeps an eye on her . . . '

Herr Unruh put his fingertips together. He was about to deliver a little homily.

'I was taught never to take a chance. I have always followed that principle. In our work, Helmut, we must assume the worst and act as if it could happen any moment. You follow me?'

'Of course,' said Pech, 'but I assure you . . . '

'We are dealing with an unusual problem, and it requires an . . . unusual approach. You understand? Of course you do. Now, we have nothing to worry about with the American. As for that man . . . ' Herr Unruh clicked his finger. 'You know the one I mean . . . '

'Martin,' volunteered Pech, 'Martin Schneider.'

'Yes. Well, somebody did us a favour. He is dead. So we've no more worry on that score. Which leaves us Helga. I think we should make sure that even if, by some bad luck, she

151

managed to, er, to get out and about, she'd be stuck, unable to go anywhere.'

Pech waited.

'And, Helmut, I need not remind you that it must be done legally. We are bound by democratic laws.' The smile was a very thin one. 'We have to observe every dot and comma of the citizen's rights. We must adhere at all times to our constitution.' The smile became broader. 'Indeed, I stress that our organisation is charged with its protection.'

'No question, sir,' said Pech.

'So I suggest we use a purely administrative method.'

Pech liked Herr Unruh. The man really knew how to run his section. Everything could be tape recorded because everything always appeared perfectly legal.

'Have you seen her passport?'

Pech shook his head.

'Or any other of her papers? Birth certificate? Driver's licence?'

'No,' said Pech. 'You know the state she arrived in . . . '

'Of course. No papers. No identification. So in truth you do not know who she really is, do you?' said Unruh and beamed.

'Oh we do,' interrupted Pech, 'we know everything about her. She . . . ' then he stopped. He stared at Unruh.

'My dear Helmut, you are so trusting,' said his boss. 'Sometimes I think much too nice to deal with the kind of people who are our customers. The fact is, isn't it, that we have no proof that Helga Braunschweig is who she says she is. Why, we don't even have evidence that she is German. East or West. Everything is her word.'

'You are trying to say . . . '

'I'm saying, Helmut, that for all we know she might be Russian, Polish, anything.' He laughed. 'She could have been born in Warsaw or Kiev. She could be a very dangerous security risk. And certainly not a German citizen.'

'She has a number.'

'6221. Which we gave her. That's all she has.'

He opened a drawer and pushed a thin file across to Pech.

'This is an administrative order declaring her stateless. It should clip her wings a little, don't you think, even if she tried to leave the nest?'

'Can we do that?' asked Pech, but already his face was full of admiration.

'It is our duty, Helmut. B1 has to sort the wheat from the chaff. The impostors from the genuine article. The phoneys they try to plant on us, the fifth column they send across the zonal boundaries. In the absence of valid documents, we must grade a suspect stateless. No passports. No visa. No travel permits. Stuck in Berlin.'

He could not disguise his pleasure at the idea.

'Perfect, don't you think? A very good way of keeping her in . . . isolation, don't you agree?'

Pech reached for the file.

'Herr Unruh,' he said, 'I will see to it forthwith.'

After Pech had gone, Herr Unruh basked in a glow of self-satisfaction. It was really remarkable how with a clean and final stroke of the pen and the right rubber stamp, he could reduce someone to the status of non-being.

In a way, he was sorry for Helga, of course. The existence of DP was something he wouldn't wish on his worst enemy, and he had nothing at all against the girl.

It just had to be done.

On his desk calendar, Tuesday July 25th had been ringed in red pencil.

Herr Unruh was counting the days to the court martial of Captain Tower.

Saturday, July 8, 1961 – LONDON

The next night, Ivanov called Laurie at 10:50 p.m.

'You are a very popular woman,' he said. 'Every time I

153

phone, you're out.'

'Only sometimes.'

'I would like to see you again, Laurie.' He paused. 'Can it be arranged?'

'What did you have in mind?' she asked.

He laughed, and she could visualise his smile.

'You sound so suspicious. What do you think?'

'No,' said Laurie. 'You tell me.'

'How about going to see a show? Is that innocent enough?'

This time she laughed.

'You free Monday evening?' he went on.

'What's the play?'

'No play,' said Ivanov. 'The Palladium. Second house. I'll meet you there. Eight o'clock. How's that for you?'

'The Palladium,' she said, surprised. 'Alright, I'll be there.'

'Fine.' There was faint music in the background. 'Where are you? Where are you calling from? I can hear "My Fair Lady".'

'Oh, I'm over at Stephen's,' he said. 'Want to come across?'

Oh yes, she thought, you do spend a lot of time with Stephen. But aloud she said: 'No, thanks, Gene, not tonight. I'm too tired.'

'You don't need to get up early for work,' he said, sounding a little mocking. 'Tomorrow's Sunday.'

'I'm just tired. Thank you for calling. See you Monday evening.'

'You bet,' said Ivanov, in his best American, and he hung up.

'That was him?' asked Unterberg, sitting in the armchair opposite her.

Laurie nodded. 'He's taking me to a show Monday.'

'Did he say what he wanted?'

'What do you think?' she said.

Unterberg sat studying her for a moment. Then he asked: 'You know what you're doing, sweetheart?'

'You tell me.'

'Getting away with murder.'

And her smile worried Unterberg for a long time

Sunday, July 9, 1961 – CZECHOSLOVAKIA

O for Oboe exploded 29,000 feet up, eleven miles from Bratislava, at 0415 hours.

Just as the electronics specialist who spotted the tell-tale blip was about to warn the commander, the missile struck the lumbering plane. There wasn't even time to send an emergency signal to Laconbury.

The aircraft disintegrated in a ball of fire, momentarily lighting up the night sky around it. Then it was all over.

For once, ironically, Oboe's crew had been reasonably relaxed. It was their third ferret mission in two weeks, and they were on the return run to the United Kingdom. They were looking forward to breakfast at Laconbury, and seventy-two hours in London.

Nobody had talked about it, but they had started to convince themselves that this latest batch of spy missions had turned into something of a milk run.

As always, Oboe's men knew, the Russians were keeping electronic eyes on them, but perhaps they had got used to Oboe's visits. Maybe the Russians weren't all that worried about nosey intruders over Czechoslovakia and Hungary.

Not that these missions weren't important. General Croxford himself had attended their last two briefings at the base, before take off. He had sat, hunched on a chair, while the intelligence officer had outlined their flight plan, and, as he put it, 'special areas of interest'.

They also knew that the electronic radar pictures they took, and the information the intricate gadgets on board recorded, were always rushed away, as soon as they had landed.

But they'd got used to it, like the SAC bomber crews at Brize and Heyford got used to getting hourly weather reports

155

about their alert targets, and the bomb technicians at Wethersfield and Bentwaters had become unmoved by the loading of nuclear weapons aboard the standby aircraft.

It was all part of the daily routine, although for ferret crews it meant a little more. They, after all, had to fly over enemy territory.

Before the attack, the misshapen, ugly WV-2E had had an uneventful night. A couple of times, the probes had picked up enemy aircraft but that wasn't out of the ordinary. There had been some unusual radio transmissions at one point, which they recorded for analysis back home.

As always Laconbury was monitoring them, even though radio silence was the order of the day. It would have to be something mighty special to start them chattering.

The actual blast that was Oboe's heavenly pyre had been picked up by various monitoring facilities on the other side of the border, and by the time Oboe was due to touch down at Laconbury again, General Croxford already knew what had happened.

When daylight came, a few pieces of wreckage lay scattered over a wide area, among the fields, and in the woods, but that was all that was left of the big spy plane. And its crew.

Czech army lorries soon arrived, and the soldiers cordoned off the area. A couple of hours later two car loads of Soviet air force experts turned up, and every scrap of burnt, twisted metal was carefully examined and then taken away for further scrutiny. The Russians searched hard and long for any piece of electronic equipment, but the explosion had not left much for them to find.

The curious thing was that nobody said a word about the destruction of O for Oboe. The US Air Force did not announce the loss of its plane and crew, and the Russians stayed silent. No communiqué was issued by either side, no hint given to anyone, and no one, East or West, knew it had ever happened.

If there was a cold war going on, at that moment in time it was apparently by mutual agreement that certain things were kept secret. Even things they did to each other.

Monday, July 10, 1961 – LONDON

It was like sitting in a mausoleum, she thought. Outside it was a brilliant July day, the sun blazing down from a cloudless sky, the girls in the Strand wearing their bright summer dresses, the pavements hot and sticky.

But here, in the Law Courts, it was dark and cold. Footsteps echoed in the big gothic marble hall, and people held whispered conversations outside the court rooms, like intruders at a funeral.

Serena Howard sat at the end of one of the interminable mazes of corridors, hands clenched in her lap. A few feet away was a door, and on the handle an usher had hung a card reading, 'In Chambers'. Behind that door Daventry was asking one of Her Majesty's judges of the Queen's Bench to set aside her subpoena.

Momentarily she considered running out of this vast medieval undertaker's palace, into the fresh air, running as fast as she could, anywhere, anyplace, to an airport, getting on a plane, fleeing to some far away country, just to escape from all of this.

'I'm sorry I've been such a time,' came Daventry's voice, and there he stood, looking down at her.

'He . . . he said no?' She tried to keep the tremor out of her voice.

'I explained the situation,' said Daventry, sitting down beside her. He had three law books under his arm, and now put them on the oaken bench. 'His lordship was very understanding.'

'But he won't . . . '

'Look, Serena,' said Daventry, 'he's bound by the law . . . '

'What happened?' She was twisting her silver ring.

'I'm afraid he's declined to set aside the subpoena.'

She simply nodded.

'His point is that under the Visiting Forces Act an allied military tribunal in this country trying one of its own servicemen is entitled and empowered to summon any civilian witness it needs and that he could not really go against that . . . '

'But adultery,' interrupted Serena.

Daventry shrugged. 'He took the point. But he said it is not up to him to pass judgement on another country's laws . . . '

'My flat was searched,' she pleaded. 'Did you tell him that?'

'Serena, they were entitled to do it with a warrant. It was quite legal . . . '

'So,' she said slowly. 'There's nothing else I can do . . . '

'Not at the moment.'

'I have to go to the trial?'

'Yes.'

'God.' She bit her lip.

'What we can try,' said Daventry, 'is to talk them out of it.'

'What?'

'I will attend the court martial with you. I will try and submit that to make you give evidence is . . . well, unreasonable. Unfair. I will ask them not to call you.'

'Can you do that?' she asked.

'I can try,' said Daventry. 'If they'll let me appear before them. I'm an English barrister, you see, and it's an American court. But I'll do my best.'

They made their way into the sunshine outside.

'Serena,' he said suddenly.

'Yes?'

They were standing by the arched entrance to the Law Courts.

'The judge asked a curious question.'

'What?'

'He asked me if I had any reason for thinking this case involved . . . well, security.'

She stared wide eyed. 'Security?'

'He didn't take it any further.'

'I don't understand.'

Daventry looked around.

'You don't think your, er, boyfriend is involved in

158

espionage?' He lowered his voice as he said it.

'John? Of course not.'

For a moment, he thought her voice lacked conviction. Then he felt ashamed for doubting her.

'Judges get ridiculous bees in their bonnets sometimes,' remarked Daventry.

They walked across the zebra crossing to the other side of the road.

Duval did not follow them. Instead he waved down a cab.

'US Embassy,' he said, 'Grosvenor Square.'

KARLSRUHE

The little light glowed on Pech's secure phone, and he picked it up at once. It was the direct connection to the chief's office at B1.

'Pech here.'

'This is Fraulein Scholtz.'

She was Herr Unruh's confidential secretary, and always very formal. She did not believe in first-name departmental relationships.

'Yes, Fraulein Scholtz?' said Pech respectfully. His boss's secretary rated deferential treatment. Pech, as the Berliners say, knew which side his bread was buttered on.

'Has Herr Unruh left yet?' she asked.

'Herr Unruh!' he repeated dumbly.

'Yes,' she said, with a hint of impatience. 'Is he on his way back yet? I have an urgent message for him.'

Pech collected his thoughts.

'I'm sorry, Fraulein Scholtz,' he said at last, 'but I haven't seen him. Are you sure he was coming here?'

'Of course I am sure,' she snapped. 'He was due at your

office at 10 a.m.'

'Nobody told me,' said Pech.

'He wanted to see you personally. It was something important.'

You bet it was, thought Pech. If the boss decided to turn up out of the blue, the ceiling must be caving in. Herr Unruh was a stickler for protocol, and the privileges of rank. He summoned subordinates, he didn't call on them unexpectedly.

'You mean you haven't seen him?' asked Fraulein Scholtz.

'I regret, no. I've been here since 8:20 this morning, and Herr Unruh certainly hasn't been here.'

It was now just after four.

'I don't understand it,' she said. For the first time, her voice was a little uncertain. 'It isn't like him. He told me he would be back by lunch. I can't keep stalling Bonn.'

'Bonn?' echoed Pech, interested.

'Yes, the minister wants him.' In her disarray, Fraulein Scholtz was being more indiscreet than she would normally ever allow herself.

'Oh.' Pech thought for a moment. 'What about Herr Unruh's chauffeur?'

'He drove himself this morning,' said Fraulein Scholtz. The disapproval was clear.

'Have you tried the radio?' Like all B1 cars, Herr Unruh's Mercedes was fitted with two-way short-wave radio.

'Of course,' she snapped. 'I would hardly be calling you if we had made contact.'

Pech decided to be greatly daring.

'Do you happen to know what it was Herr Unruh wanted to discuss?'

'No, Herr Pech. It was obviously urgent, and highly confidential. But Herr Unruh did not enlighten me. In any case,' she added severely, 'it would hardly be up to me to discuss it.'

'No, you're absolutely right. I wonder if he mentioned it to anyone else?' He was so anxious to know that he pressed his luck.

'I have no idea,' she said. 'He did mention that he wanted to talk to the Americans urgently. He had put in a call to Mr Unterberg in London, just before he left to see you.'

'And?' asked Pech eagerly.

'He didn't reach him. Mr Unterberg was not in his office.' She sniffed. 'I only mention it because I know you have been working with Mr Unterberg.'

'I am very grateful, Fraulein Scholtz,' said Pech, and he was.

'Well, you obviously can't help me. I will try elsewhere. If by any chance you hear from Herr Unruh, kindly ask him to contact me at once. You can say that Bonn has called twice.'

'Of course, I will,' said Pech. 'I'm sure he'll be in touch quite soon.'

'Goodbye,' said Fraulein Scholtz coldly, and hung up. The light on the phone went out.

But Pech was wrong. Two hours later, Herr Unruh was found. He was lying slumped in the driver's seat of his Mercedes. It was parked in a layby on the autobahn.

He had a bullet hole in his right temple, and his right hand was still holding a Luger, with one bullet spent.

It was clearly a case of suicide, decided the first detectives to examine him. But then investigators from B1's parent, the Office for the Protection of the Constitution, took over.

And they remembered that Herr Unruh was left handed.

LONDON

The phone started ringing just as Daventry and his wife began eating dinner. Daventry answered it in the hall.

'Sloane 7937,' he said.

There was no one at the other end.

'Hello,' said Daventry, a little irritably.

But there was only silence.

'Who is it?' called Alex from the dining room.

'Who's there?' demanded Daventry, but the silence continued and then, suddenly, there was an abrupt break, and the dialling tone returned.

Daventry slammed down the receiver.

'Bloody idiot,' he said.

'That was short and sweet,' commented Alex when he came into the room.

'Wrong number,' said Daventry. 'But I wish they'd have the courtesy to say so. Rude bastard just hung up.'

'Hmmm,' said Alex.

He looked at her sharply. 'What's that supposed to mean?' It had been an aggravating day, and he had a lot on his mind.

'The phone's been behaving rather strangely recently.'

He frowned.

'In what way?'

'Haven't you noticed?'

'Noticed what?'

'Perhaps I'm imagining it, but I'm sure I've heard some curious noises. Like . . . the odd click.'

'Go on,' said Daventry, tersely.

'This morning, for instance. When you called me from your chambers. A sort of . . . background noise, and that wasn't the first time. I had it last week. During a couple of calls.'

'Did you report it?'

Alex shook her head. 'I just wasn't sure. I mean, the phone's working alright. Sometimes though, there's the odd tinkle. As if it's about to ring. When I pick up the receiver, there's nothing. Just the dialling tone.'

'How long has this been going on?' said Daventry slowly.

'Oh, just a few days. They must be working on the line or something.'

He was silent.

'I think,' he said at last, 'that maybe our phone is being tapped.'

Alex's eyes widened.

'Good god, why on earth? Who by?'

Daventry reached for his wine glass. 'I don't know,' he said.

'At least, I don't think I do.'

'But you've got an idea . . . '

He drank from the wine glass.

'I could be quite wrong,' he said.

Alex was not being put off. 'No, you do know. Who is it? Who could possible be interested in eavesdropping on us?' She was becoming indignant. 'How dare they?'

'It could be a case,' he said, casually. 'Maybe that business with Serena Howard . . . '

'Why, for heaven's sake?'

'Well, she thinks she's been kept under surveillance. She says somebody's been watching her. Over that court martial.'

'That's crazy,' said Alex. 'And why tap *your* phone?'

'I made an application in chambers on her behalf.'

'You didn't tell me.'

'It was just a routine thing. To get her subpoena put aside. So they know I'm involved in her case.'

'*They*?'

'Whitehall,' said Daventry. 'The authorities. You know how it's all hush hush with the Americans. They're security crazy.'

'Give me some wine,' said Alex. He got up, and while he poured it out, she said firmly:

'Well, you must take it up with somebody. It's outrageous. They can't just start listening in on you. What's next, steaming open your mail?'

He sat down again.

'There's not much point in raising a stink,' he said. 'If they are tapping the phone, they'll never admit it. It's all kept very secret.'

'My god, Gerry, this isn't 1984, it's England, it's 1961. It's . . . it's like the Gestapo.' She was irate. 'Go to the Bar Council. Raise hell.'

'Look,' said Daventry, 'leave it to me. It won't go on for long, *if* it's going on at all. We may just be imagining it. One wrong number tonight, a few noises on the line, and we're getting all worked up. Don't worry about it.'

She looked unhappy.

'You're going to represent her at the court martial?'

163

she asked.

'I may do. Yes.'

She nodded. 'And you think our phone's being tapped because of her? It's getting a bit sinister, isn't it?'

'I'll talk to the GPO tomorrow,' he assured her, but inwardly he knew he would not even try, because it was pointless. He had experience of Home Office orders. 'It's probably all a mistake anyway.'

What he didn't tell Alex was that Pettifer had complained about the phones at the chambers. He had said, jokingly, that it almost sounded as if they were being tapped.

LONDON

They came out of the second house at the Palladium, and Ivanov took her by the arm, and steered her through the crowd into Oxford Street.

He had a knack, Laurie discovered, for catching cabs, while others stood around waving in vain. He spirited one up, under the nose of the competition, and they got in.

'Where are we going?' asked Laurie.

'A little place you'll love,' he said. 'It is very intimate.'

And he grinned at her.

He was fun to be with, and so completely un-Russian. At least thought Laurie, unlike the popular conception of the Russian heavy. Dangerous he might be, one of their top men, but his manner was charming, light-hearted. She actually enjoyed his company, and that made it doubly hazardous.

He had picked a small restaurant in Marylebone High Street, where they obviously knew him, and had a table for him in the corner.

'Stephen introduced me to this place,' he explained. 'He

often brings his girls here.'

'His girls?' said Laurie. 'It sounds like a harem.

Ivanov merely smiled.

'I'm sorry about the show,' he said during the meal.

'Why, I enjoyed it.'

'Good,' he said. 'Personally, I didn't think it lived up to its title.'

The show was called 'Let Yourself Go', and the programme described it as a 'revusical'.

'I thought it was very provincial,' he added. 'I shall have to take you to something really exciting, to make up for it.'

'Gene, I've had a very nice evening,' said Laurie.

He poured her some Chianti.

'I'm having a very nice one,' he corrected her.

Then, a little later, he got down to business.

'We can be very useful to each other,' he said. 'Have you thought about it?'

She studied him across her wine glass.

'Are you making me some kind of offer, Gene?'

'You work for the Americans. Out at Ruislip. You know what I do. It seems to me we have mutual interests . . .'

'Are you trying to get me into trouble?' asked Laurie.

'Oh please, my darling, don't be funny. We have the same rules, don't we. For instance, they must always be told if we meet anyone from the other side. Isn't that so? If you, who work for the Americans, come out with me, who work for the Soviet government, it can only mean two things . . .' He paused, and there was a twinkle in his eye. 'Either you have fallen madly in love with me and don't care, or they know all about it and you have your uncle's blessing.'

'My uncle?'

'Uncle Sam. A cunning gentleman.'

The espresso coffee came, and they waited until the waiter left the table.

'Is that why you asked me out?' she said at last.

To her surprise, he took out a little piece of paper and slipped it under the saucer of her coffee cup.

She took it. It was folded in two, and when she opened it, one

165

line was written in ink:

'I find you most desirable.'

Laurie read it, and then suddenly glanced round the restaurant.

'Are you looking for somebody?' Ivanov asked.

'Yes, a man with a camera.'

'Please,' he said, 'I don't understand.'

'It would be a useful photo for you to have would it not? An Air Force secretary receiving a piece of paper from a Soviet diplomat in a discreet little restaurant,' said Laurie coolly.

He appeared shocked.

'Laurie, my beautiful, how can you believe I would stoop to something so low. Look around, if you're so suspicious. Where is your man with the camera? I am very upset.'

She nearly laughed at the schoolboyish sulk he put on.

'You see, I am really very shy,' said Ivanov earnestly, and now she did not attempt to disguise the smile. 'I wanted to tell you that, but I did not know if I would have the courage. So I wrote the note, to give to you at the right moment.'

'And this is the right moment?' murmured Laurie.

He sighed.

'The two things are separate. In our official capacities, we can establish a useful line of communication. These days it is very important that there is direct contact through all kinds of channels, in our mutual interest. You and I, we can be a link between our people.'

'I think you got the wrong party,' said Laurie. 'You need somebody pretty high-powered.'

'And I think you're just the right party,' retorted Ivanov quietly.

'I'm just a secretary.'

'Of course,' he said smoothly.

'You're crazy, Gene, you know that.'

'Humour me,' he said. Then he reached across the blue tablecloth and took her hand. 'So much for the official business. But I mean what the note says. I desire you very much.'

Laurie withdrew her hand slowly.

'I am sure you know your reputation, Captain Ivanov,' she said lightly. 'Why don't we leave it at that?'

He wasn't put out.

'For the moment, why not?' he shrugged. 'We will meet again, and then we will see. I think tonight is the start of a beautiful relationship. I am very excited.'

'Business and pleasure?'

'That is up to you, Laurie. But I think we should both be very grateful to Stephen. After all, if it wasn't for his party, we might never have met.'

'Yes,' said Laurie, 'wasn't that a coincidence.'

He didn't even blink.

'I hope you'll come to the next one he gives,' said Ivanov. 'You might have some fun. Something unexpected always happens at Stephen's parties.'

He signalled for the bill.

'Now what would you like to do, Laurie? A little jazz at Ronnie Scott's maybe? A night club?' He paused. 'A drink at my place perhaps?'

'The next stop is over there,' said Laurie, nodding at the door marked 'Ladies'.

She was lucky. In the powder room was a phone box. She put in her two pennies, dialled and pushed the button.

She came out of the cloak room, with fresh lipstick, and a whiff of the perfume Verago liked so much around her.

'Why don't we listen to a little jazz?' she said.

Ivanov smiled.

She never mentioned the phone call she had just made.

Tuesday, July 11, 1961 – LONDON

Twice Verago pushed the bell marked 'Howard' but nothing

happened. The front door next to the Marxist bookshop remained closed.

He knew from the OSI reports that Serena Howard lived on the first floor, over the bookshop, and he stepped back, looking upwards to see if he could spot anyone in. But no activity was visible.

Verago stood undecided in Charlotte Street. He liked the neighbourhood. First appearances pleased him. The Greek restaurants were a tempting sight. Verago's ancestry was dormant in all but his taste buds, and he would go far for a good moussaka, or a well-done steftilha. But nationalism aside, even the Turkish restaurant looked like a place Laurie might like. He made a mental note to get to know this part of London better.

He had been hanging around now for about ten minutes, wondering why he had taken it for granted that the Howard girl would be in. The surveillance reports described her as a part-time model, and he realised he didn't really know much about her. But he had assumed, for some reason or other, that she might be at home if he showed up.

Verago looked at his watch, chewing his lip. Then he made up his mind. He went into the bookshop.

A serious-looking girl with glasses and no make up was just hanging up a poster declaring 'No US Bases'. It didn't surprise Verago. He had seen Mao in the window, and the array of Marxist literature.

He wasn't in uniform, but he looked American. He felt slightly embarrassed.

'Excuse me,' said Verago.

'Yeah?' The girl was just climbing on to some steps to get the poster in position. She wore shapeless trousers.

'Do you know Miss Howard? The lady who lives upstairs?' asked Verago.

'Ron,' yelled the girl. Her nose was shiny. Hanging the poster was also giving her trouble.

The man who appeared from behind a bookshelf had shoulder-length hair, wore denims, and sprouted three badges. One said 'No H Bomb', another 'Workers Solidarity', and the third 'Yanks Out'. 'Yanks Out' was a big, round badge, and Verago was very conscious of it.

'What is it?' asked Ron, shuffling forward.

'Bloke asking about upstairs,' said the girl.

Ron regarded him balefully.

'What do you want?'

'Is the lady usually in during the day? Do you know if she'll be back soon?'

Ron sniffed with disdain.

'Yank, are you?' he asked.

'When would be the best time to find Miss Howard in?' asked Verago.

'What do you want her for?' enquired Ron.

Fuck community relations, thought Verago.

'None of your business, buddy,' he said. 'You want to help or not?'

'Not particularly, mate,' said Ron and grinned. One of his front teeth, noted Verago with satisfaction, was black.

'Thanks a lot.'

'Pleasure,' said Ron sarcastically.

Verago turned his back, walking out past the glowering images of La Passionara, Che Guevara, Lenin, and thought he'd like to buy a couple of posters and stick them in Jensen's office.

But instead, he stepped into the street just as a cab drew up. He immediately recognised the girl who paid off the driver. The OSI photographs had been very good.

'Miss Howard,' said Verago.

She turned, startled. She was carrying some shopping, but when she heard his accent, and saw him, her eyes opened wide. He didn't know if it was surprise – or fear.

'Who are you?'

'I'm Captain Tower's counsel,' he said, sensing her hostility. 'I would like to talk to you.'

'Are you from the Air Force?' she demanded suspiciously.

'I'm an Army lawyer,' he said, and threw in for good measure: 'I'm nothing to do with the Air Force. My job is to defend Captain Tower.'

She put down the shopping bag on the pavement.

'I'm sorry,' she said. 'I don't want anything to do with the Americans.'

Ron had come to the door of the shop and was watching with interest.

'Listen, Miss Howard,' said Verago. 'I'm sure we're on the same side. You can help me a lot. But we can't talk on the sidewalk. Can I come up to your apartment?'

He bent down and picked up her shopping, and smiled.

'Please,' he added.

She hesitated.

'I won't keep you long,' he assured her.

She got out her keys, unlocked the door, and led the way upstairs into the flat.

'Sit down,' she said coldly, as he placed the shopping on a table.

'What do you want with me?' she enquired tersely.

'I'd like to ask you a few questions,' replied Verago. 'I think they're going to call you as a witness, and we ought to get a few things straight.'

She sat down opposite him, perching on the edge of the sofa.

'What is your name?'

'Captain Verago.'

'You say you are defending John?'

'I'm trying to.'

'What exactly do you want to know?' she asked without warmth. Her enmity came across to him in waves.

'Did you know that you and he were being watched? That you were under surveillance when you were together?'

'I know now.' She was bitter, hard.

'Have you any idea when it began?'

'No.'

'Have you any idea why they were watching you?'

'Yes, Captain Verago,' said Serena acidly. 'Because in your armed services it is apparently a crime for a man and a woman to have a relationship.'

He cleared his throat. 'Er . . . not exactly like that.' She glowered at him. 'Look, believe me, I hate this kind of case as

170

much as you do. My sole object is to get him off as lightly as possible.'

'I see,' she said. It was so unforthcoming it disconcerted him. He tried again. 'Have you any idea what his job was?'

'No.'

'Did he ever talk about his trips? What he did? Berlin?'

'I think you'd better leave, Captain Verago,' she said.

He remained seated. 'I haven't even started yet, Miss Howard,' he said gently.

'I'm sorry,' she said. 'If you want to know anything else, talk to my lawyer. Mr Gerald Daventry, of Lincoln's Inn.'

'You don't seem to understand,' protested Verago. 'I'm working against time. There's a lot I . . . '

'No,' she said. 'I don't want to discuss it. Goodbye.'

Slowly he got to his feet.

'I wish you'd listen, Miss Howard,' he said. 'Captain Tower isn't exactly helping me, and now you . . . '

'Goodbye, Captain Verago,' she said again.

She watched him from the landing as he walked down the stairs and let himself out of the door.

In the street, he took out his little memo pad and noted Daventry's name and address. Then he got a cab.

Ron, leaning against the door of the bookshop, watched him until the cab turned into Percy Street.

CHOBHAM

Joe Pryor stretched his long legs and settled his lanky frame more comfortably into the deck chair. He closed his eyes, and relaxed.

He was sitting on the lawn of Welk's house, half shaded by a big elm tree. The only irritation was the buzzing of an insect,

171

and once or twice he opened his eyes to see if the enemy was in sight. But the wasp was more interested in raiding the flowers.

It was an impressive, mock Tudor style residence with a large garden, rose bushes, flower beds and a little fountain with a thin trickle of water. Sometimes Pryor wondered how Welk could afford it, and the Daimler in the garage, on his civil service salary. Air Force information officers were hardly overpaid.

But right now he couldn't care less. The warm July sun, the fragrance of the garden, the summer stillness were much too pleasant to worry about Welk's bank balance.

That was Pryor's trouble. He was too lazy. Working for *Stars and Stripes* was a cosy niche. The paper had a huge circulation, from Norway to Turkey, and was read by virtually every American serviceman and dependant in Europe. But it never carried an editorial, and all controversy was taboo. What can you expect, Pryor sometimes told himself wrily, from a newspaper edited by a colonel.

The barbecue started to sizzle and Pryor half opened an eye. Welk, a blue striped apron tied round him, was broiling the steaks.

On his way down to Chobham, Pryor tried to work out why Welk had actually invited him for dinner. They saw a lot of each other, but not socially. He didn't really like Welk, but the man was the Air Force mouthpiece at headquarters in South Ruislip, and Pryor played along.

'Come and get it,' called Welk, just as Pryor started to doze off again.

Jennifer, Welk's English wife, had set the table on the portico that overlooked the lawn.

Pryor shambled over. He lived a bachelor existence, and any meal eaten outside a restaurant was an attractive proposition.

'I've put you here, Joe,' said Jennifer, indicating his chair. 'You don't mind eating strictly al fresco, do you?'

It was a typical English remark. The table was well laid, with side plates, napkins, wine glasses, and even a vase of flowers. Jennifer, though she had been married to Welk for more than four years, had never stopped being strictly suburban London.

172

It was remarkable how she didn't seem to have assimilated any American touches.

'I think I missed my vocation,' said Welk, when they sat down. 'I should have been a short-order cook. Maybe I'll quit when we go home, and open a diner.'

'Oh, Jack,' protested Jennifer. Even as a joke, she felt it was in bad taste.

Pryor was enjoying his Air Force commissary steak, twice the size of anything he could buy in England. The charcoal flavour brought back memories of beach parties at San Diego.

Then Welk spoiled it.

'Al is coming round later,' he announced. 'Just for a drink.'

'That's nice,' lied Pryor. Al was Major Longman, the Air Force chief of information at South Ruislip. He was Welk's boss, a time server. His ambition was to go to the Directorate of Information at the Pentagon, and he intended his UK tour to be the stepping stone.

'He couldn't come for dinner, because he's over at the general's,' explained Welk. His tone indicated that, to an extent, the kudos of being in the general's favour extended to himself, because the general's guest was coming straight to his house.

Pryor couldn't resist it. 'I hear the general's wife is a lousy cook,' he said.

Welk looked pained and Jennifer hastily intervened: 'Some more wine, Joe?'

After the meal, they returned to the deck chairs on the lawn and had coffee. One thing Pryor did have to admit, Jennifer had learnt to make decent coffee.

'Well,' said Welk contentedly, 'this is the life, eh?' He glanced round the lawn. 'I guess I must have been a feudal baron in another existence. You want some French brandy? The real stuff?'

Jennifer got up at once. 'I'll get it,' she said and went into the house.

This was as good a moment as any, decided Pryor.

'You heard anything about a court martial at Laconbury, Jack?' he asked casually.

Welk took a long drink of coffee. Then he put the cup down.
'Can't say I have.'

'Some officer being tried. For adultery.'

Welk frowned. 'Who says that?'

'Oh, just scuttlebutt,' said Pryor.

'Haven't heard a thing,' replied Welk. 'Anyway, what's your interest? *Stripes* would never run a thing like that.'

'I like to know what's going,' said Pryor. Almost defiantly, he added: 'It *is* my job.'

'Joe, you don't want to bother yourself with scandal stories.' Airily, he added: 'Anyway, you know latrine rumours. Nobody told me about any guy being tried for hanky panky. And we get to know it all. Believe me, buddy.'

'You checked with Colonel Kincaid?'

'Don't have to check,' said Welk curtly. 'We get the SJA's list of trials every week.'

Jennifer appeared with a tray. On it were balloon glasses, and two very expensive bottles of antique brandy.

Welk poured them all triples.

'Salut,' he toasted.

'You got good stuff here,' said Pryor, the Armagnac warming him.

A man appeared at the other end of the lawn, and waved. He came towards them.

'Hi, fellows,' said Major Longman. 'And how is the gorgeous Jennifer?'

He kissed her. Then he saw the brandy.

'Guess I'm just in time,' he said amiably. 'Start pouring, Jack.'

Welk stood up.

'Al, can I just have a quick word?' he asked.

Longman looked surprised. 'Sure,' he said. 'Now?'

'Yeah. Let's go in the house.'

Longman winked at Pryor. 'Secrets, secrets, all day long,' he laughed. 'Don't drink all the brandy.'

They walked across the lawn and disappeared in the house.

'Oh dear, Jack never stops working,' sighed Jennifer. 'Sometimes I hate his job.'

174

'Yes,' said Pryor thoughtfully.

'More coffee, Joe?'

He nodded, and she poured him another cup.

'Have you had your leave yet?' she asked. 'We're thinking of going to Garmisch.'

She was making hostess talk.

Welk and the major emerged from the house and began coming towards them. Whatever Welk had to discuss so urgently evidently hadn't taken long.

'So, where's that drink?' asked Major Longman.

Welk gave him a triple and topped up Pryor's glass.

The major took a deep swig.

'What's all this crap, Joe?' he asked.

'Come again?'

'Laconbury. What are you after?'

Jennifer rose. 'I'll clear up in the kitchen,' she excused herself.

'I'll come and help you, honey,' said Welk following her.

'I'm not after anything, Major,' said Pryor. 'I just asked Jack if he knew anything about a court martial. What's so strange about that?'

'That's not the kind of news your paper wants,' declared Longman. 'Don't waste your time on it. Besides, who says there's any court martial?'

Pryor shrugged. 'Just thought I'd ask.'

'And Jack told you. We know nothing about it. I'll give you some advice for free though. Do some positive stories, Joe. Sports, lots of sports. Travel features, so the guys know where to spend their leave. Hobbies. That kind of stuff.'

The major took another sip of brandy and then leant forward confidentially.

'A word to the wise, Joe. You got a good berth here. Nobody bothers you. You're doing a fine job, and we all like you. I'd hate to see you recalled to Darmstadt and put on the rewrite desk. I'm sure you wouldn't like it either.' He smiled. 'Would you?'

'I got the message,' said Pryor, and hated himself for playing along.

'Good,' said the major. 'As I told the general, we're all one big happy team over here. Let's keep it that way.'

The sun concealed itself behind some clouds. Suddenly, it had definitely got much colder, decided Pryor.

NEW YORK CITY

Lou Conn returned to his law office on the nineteenth floor of the black skyscraper at the corner of Sixth Avenue and 52nd Street from lunch to find an unexpected message.

'You had a call from England,' said the note his secretary had left on his desk. 'It was a man called Verago. He said he'd call back.'

In his office he sat down, looking at the piece of paper in his hand.

Tony Verago! It was like turning the clock back. Back to their days in law school, and the big plans they had to form a partnership. It had never worked out, and they had gone their separate ways, but they remained good friends. The kind of friends who didn't see each other for years, but immediately took up where they had left off when they met again.

The last he had heard of Verago was that he was an Army lawyer, somewhere in Germany. He looked at the note again. What was he doing calling from England? It must be something important. Even urgent, if Verago was going to call back.

He wondered how Kathy was. He liked Verago's wife. She had gone to Germany with him, but he couldn't quite see the ebullient, bubbling Kathy, a fun-loving, madcap of a girl, settling into the staid routine of being an Army wife, living in dependent housing, holding bridge parties, spending an afternoon a week on Red Cross work.

Maybe she and Tony, he figured, being stationed in Europe

176

took advantage of travelling a lot. Rome, Paris, Vienna; Kathy would like that and even on a captain's pay, they'd be able to afford to.

The phone buzzed, and Conn picked it up.

'Your call from England,' said the switchboard girl.

He recognised the voice immediately.

'Lou,' said Verago, 'how are you?'

It was a good, clear line. Verago sounded very close.

'Tony, for heaven's sake, what a surprise,' called out Conn. He was genuinely delighted. 'What are you doing in England? How's Kathy?'

There was a silence. It seemed a very long silence. Then came Verago's voice, strangely subdued.

'I'm sorry. I never told you, did I? Kathy and I were divorced last year.'

'Oh I'm sorry.'

'It was for the best, believe me. Anyway, listen, Lou, the reason I called you is I need a favour,' said Verago, and his tone made it clear that Kathy as a topic of conversation was over. 'Can you help me out?'

'Sure,' agreed Lou.

'I got myself a court martial over here, and it's a bitch. The guy I'm trying to defend committed adultery. I need the wife to say it was all over between them, it doesn't matter to her, she doesn't feel sore. Could you fix it for me?'

'Fix it?' asked Conn. Sometimes Verago was difficult to keep up with. Just like the old days.

'She lives on your side. West 30th Street. No. 1 Apartment 6D.'

Almost automatically, Conn jotted it down. It came of long habit.

'Could you be a pal, go and see her, get her affidavit the way I've suggested, and find out if she's willing to come to England to testify for him?'

'Is that all?' enquired Conn drily.

'That's it, Lou. I really appreciate it.'

'You might tell me her name,' said Conn.

'Mrs Marion Tower. Her husband is a Captain John Tower. He's with the Air Force over here. They're trying to shaft him,

Lou. But if you can get her to say the right things, maybe I can do something . . . '

Trust Verago. He made it sound so simple. Just get her to say the right things.

'I'll try, Tony,' said Conn. 'But what makes you think she'll play?'

'Don't see why not,' came Verago's voice. 'They've not made it together since '57 or '58. She doesn't hate him. I think she'll play along. You tell her it's the only thing that will keep him out of Leavenworth.'

Verago heard Conn's intake of breath.

'It's that serious?' said Conn. 'Just because he's been playing around.'

'It's that serious, Lou. They got the rope ready for him.'

'OK,' said Conn. 'You picked a hell of a time, I'm up to here in work, but OK. I'll try . . . '

He could sense Verago's relief.

'You got no idea how I appreciate this, Lou. If there's anything I can do this end . . . '

Conn smiled. 'I'll let you know,' he said. 'Send me some fish and chips.'

'You got it,' laughed Verago. 'Here. This is where you can reach me.'

Conn made more notes.

'You'll hear,' he promised.

The last thing Verago said was:

'Lou, I hope it works out with her. It's the guy's only chance. Without her, I'm sunk. I got nothing. You're my only hope.'

After he hung up, Conn sat reflectively for a little while. He had a feeling that there was a great deal Verago hadn't told him.

After dinner, Mr Justice Daventry led his son to the library, leaving Alex and Lady Daventry to themselves in the drawing-room.

The seventy-four-year-old judge, twenty years a member of the High Court, was a firm believer that the kind of things men discussed were of no interest to women, who didn't understand them anway.

Indeed, Sir Frederick had never made any secret in his courts that, simply because a woman passed certain exams, put on a gown, and wore a wig, that didn't automatically make her a barrister. Not a proper one.

'Cigar?' offered the judge, opening the big oak humidor.

'Thanks,' said Daventry.

He sat down in one of the two leather armchairs by the fireplace. Although it was July, a fire was burning in the hearth. The old judge felt cold very easily.

'Well, my boy, how is life treating you?' asked his father, from the armchair opposite. Daventry might be a successful and distinguished counsel in his late thirties, but his father tended to address him like a schoolboy just up for the summer vac.

'Alright,' replied Daventry. 'Everything's fine.'

'You look tired,' grunted the judge. Old he might be, but he was still very alert.

Daventry shrugged. 'I've got a lot of work on.'

Sir Frederick exhaled some Havana smoke. 'The right kind of work, I trust?'

'What do you mean, dad?'

The judge cleared his throat, as if he were about to give a ruling.

'I saw Finnemore at the club the other day. He tells me that your application for silk looks like being favourably received. Despite your youth.'

'Well, that's good to hear.'

The judge raised a hand slightly. 'But it's not in the bag, Gerry. You must never forget that, in a manner of speaking, you're on probation at this time. Getting silk is a high honour,

179

it's not only recognition of your legal prowess, it confirms your impeccable standing in the profession.'

'I know that.' Daventry was trying to work out what the old boy was getting at.

'I am sure you do,' the judge went on, darting a keen look at him, 'but there are times when it needs restating. You mustn't put a foot wrong. Not at this time.'

'I don't intend to,' said Daventry, a little uneasily.

'Good,' said the judge.

'You're trying to tell me something, aren't you?'

'I've read you my little homily.' His thin lips smiled. 'Here endeth the first lesson.'

'No, dad,' pressed Daventry. 'You've got a reason for mentioning it.'

The judge sniffed, the way he did when a barrister started arguing the law with him in court.

'I have a reason for everything I say,' said Sir Frederick. 'I have seen, in my time, a few ambitious advocates fall at the last fence. I don't want it to happen to you.'

Daventry had to laugh at his solemnity.

'Don't worry, dad, I don't intend to get drunk in Piccadilly, or run away with the Lord Mayor's wife . . . '

'Don't be stupid,' snapped the judge. He was irritated. 'I simply want to emphasise that, for example, the kind of cases you appear in might well be taken into consideration. There's nothing wrong with defending villains, but some cases . . . '

'Such as?'

The judge waved his cigar.

'Borderline. You know what I mean.'

'Is there something you've heard? That worries you?'

'Of course not,' said the judge. 'But . . . '

'Yes?'

'Are you involved in some stupid proceedings in some American case?'

'I tried to get a witness summons set aside. What of it?'

The judge peered at him.

'I should think it's hardly likely to advance your career.'

'Who told you about it?' said Daventry quietly.

'Never mind that,' said the judge. 'The point is that I don't see why you should get mixed up in some sordid little American court martial. Leave it to the Americans. I'm surprised your clerk let you take the brief. Normally Pettifer's judgement is sound. Very sound.'

'It's got nothing to do with Pettifer.' He put his cigar in the marble ashtray. 'Somebody been getting at you, dad.'

'Of course not. But ours is a small world, Gerald. One hears things. And, as I said, people are keeping tabs on you.'

'I'm sure,' remarked Daventry bitterly.

The judge stood up.

'I think it's time we joined the ladies,' he announced, leading the way to the door. Then he turned, and looked straight into Daventry's eyes.

'All I'm saying, my boy, is to think twice. Affairs of state, security, diplomatic considerations, all kinds of things like that can come our way. It behoves the wise man to step warily. Or if I may put it more bluntly, in the modern style, mind your own business.'

The judge was renowned for his sharp, succinct summings up. And Daventry was left wondering where the next threat would come from.

WEDNESDAY, July 12, 1961 – LONDON

'Dear comrade,' said the assistant stage manager of the Leningrad State Kirov Ballet Company, clasping the hand of Yevgenni Ivanov.

Ivanov rose with a smile when Grigorovich entered the Monmouth Street coffee shop. But his cordiality was tinged with just the right degree of respect, seeing that Grigorovich was a senior member of Glavnoye Razvedyvatelnoya Upravleniye, the Chief Intelligence Directorate.

Grigorovich, whose passport gave him another name, and his department found the Kirov's tour of the West exceedingly useful. He had suddenly been appointed assistant stage manager on the eve of the company's departure, and as a mere face in the ensemble, could travel England and the United States to see certain things for himself without raising the slightest suspicion.

The Operations Department had decided before he left Moscow that Ivanov would be his only direct contact while the Kirov appeared at Covent Garden. They had further instructed that such meetings as they did have should be in out-of-the-way places and after ensuring that neither of them had been followed.

'Are you enjoying your stay?' asked Ivanov as they were served with their coffee.

'Tremendously,' replied Grigorovich. 'You should see the audiences. Every seat sold, and the enthusiasm! Who said the English are cold blooded?'

He pulled out an envelope.

'Here,' he said, offering it to Ivanov. 'I know the embassy has its quota, but I thought perhaps you would like a couple of extra tickets. For the gala programme. I gather they're worth their weight in gold.'

'How kind of you, Sergei,' said Ivanov, allowing himself great informality because they both liked each other, despite Grigorovich's seniority. 'And I have a little present for you.'

He also handed over an envelope. Inside was a roll of 35mm film which, when it was developed, would provide the Russians with their first really good photographs of the new American nuclear submarine base just established in Holy Loch.

'Thank you,' said Grigorovich. 'I will treasure it.'

He spooned sugar into his espresso, and stirred it.

'How is the other matter?' he asked.

'You are up to date?'

Grigorovich nodded. 'Your reports have been a model of clarity and conciseness, as always. No, I meant in the last few days.' He smiled apologetically. 'My communications at this moment are a little convoluted.'

182

'The court martial is set,' said Ivanov.

'Have you heard any more about it?'

'I hear things all the time.'

'And?'

'I don't think there will be any problems.'

'Sometimes I wonder . . . '

'What is it?' asked Ivanov, concerned. He respected Grigorovich, and his judgement. If he was uneasy . . .

'Maybe you can explain. You know these people so much better than I do. You fit in. But I have been asking myself, why is it that if they are so anxious to put this man out of circulation, they don't get rid of him? Would it not be so much simpler? You understand me?'

'Perfectly,' said Ivanov. 'But you see that is the difference. It is their system. We can deal with people. We can . . . remove them. It's very difficult for them.'

Grigorovich frowned. 'But why? They are authority. They are government. Surely they have every power. If an individual threatens us, we eliminate him. For the good of all. They can do the same.'

'They prefer doing it legally. Because of public opinion,' explained Ivanov. 'Public opinion, or democracy as it's known in the West,' he smiled, 'can ask questions, demand explanations, perhaps bring down governments. It's like a sleeping giant, quite harmless, but once aroused . . . '

The man from the Kirov ballet shook his head incredulously, then looked at his watch.

'Very well,' he said. 'You clearly understand our friends and their reasoning. I'm delighted you're posted here.'

He got up and Ivanov immediately stood up too.

'Thank you,' said Grigorovich. 'The coffee is very good here.'

He left first. Ivanov stayed behind, and took his time paying the bill. It was several minutes before he wandered out into Monmouth Street. He strolled round the corner, into Shaftesbury Avenue, glancing into several shop windows to see if he was being followed and finally hailed a taxi.

Grigorovich really is a nice man, he reflected as he settled back in the cab. He wondered if it was true that he was the one who had been responsible for having a GRU man executed recently. He must have got on the wrong side of him, Ivanov decided. That was a mistake he would not make.

LACONBURY

Breakfast was a time when Verago liked to be alone. It wasn't until he'd had his third cup of coffee that he felt fully equipped to face the day.

When he saw Jensen approach, carrying his tray, breakfast was already spoiled. And when the man sat down, uninvited, at his table, breakfast was ruined.

Jensen nodded to him briefly.

'You heard who's going to be prosecuting?' he asked happily.

'Surprise me,' said Verago.

'Colonel Apollo,' announced Jensen triumphantly, and shovelled a fork full of scrambled eggs into his mouth.

'Never heard of him,' grunted Verago. He was fascinated by a piece of egg stuck on Jensen's chin.

'Lieutenant-Colonel Dean Apollo. Sharpest trial counsel in the command,' he said with his mouth full.

Verago drank some coffee.

'You sound very happy about it, Cyrus,' he growled.

'He's the one guy you won't be able to push around,' remarked Jensen pointedly. 'He knows the book backwards.'

Verago buttered a second piece of toast. It was a sign of his aggravation. For his waistline's sake, he limited himself to one piece at breakfast, but when he got annoyed, his good intentions slipped.

'Aren't you forgetting something?'

'What?' asked Jensen, slurping his coffee.

'Which team you're on? You're supposed to be helping the defence. Remember?'

Jensen nodded. The piece of egg was still stuck to his chin. Verago hoped it would dry there and stick all day.

'Trouble with you, counsellor, is that you got no feeling for this outfit. We're a community here and you don't even belong to the Air Force,' complained Jensen. 'I hope you don't mind my plain speaking,' he added, almost as an afterthought.

'No, go ahead. Makes a nice change.'

'I think Captain Tower was crazy to ask for you. The whole thing could have been over like that.' He snapped his fingers. 'It hurts, this kind of scandal, and we don't need it. You shouldn't be on this case because it doesn't matter to you how many people get hurt, how much unpleasantness there is, what harm will be done or even what's at stake.'

'What is at stake?' asked Verago quietly.

'I don't doubt you're a good lawyer, but I tell you you're wasting your time,' went on Jensen, ignoring Verago's question. 'Our client is guilty as charged and you should leave it to the Air Force to let us look after our own.'

'That, counsellor,' said Verago, pushing back his chair and standing up, 'is exactly what I'm afraid of.'

'Captain Verago!'

It was a command, peremptory, angry, sharp. It said stop, stay where you are, not another step.

Verago had just been about to enter the PX when he heard it. He turned and saw General Croxford.

The general was sitting in a gleaming red open-topped sports car, a spotless MG.

'Over here, Captain,' ordered Croxford.

The general was wearing civilian clothes, a tweed jacket, an open-necked shirt. Attached to the breast pocket of the shirt was a bleeper. Wherever he went, he was never out of touch. Propped up on the seat beside him was a bag of golf clubs.

'Shift those,' commanded Croxford when Verago came over. 'And get in.'

Verago moved the bulky bag and squeezed into the seat beside the general. He was uncomfortable, sharing the tight space with the golf clubs.

Croxford accelerated, and the MG shot across the base. At the main gate, he slowed down, and the APs snapped to attention like an imperial guard. Croxford acknowledged their salute, and then turned on to the highway.

He drove the car at high speed, ignoring Verago. Apart from the bleeper, a two-way radio was fitted to the MG's dashboard. A lone red light indicated it was switched on, and from a loud-speaker near the steering wheel came the crackling of atmospherics.

'How are you getting on, Captain?' asked the general suddenly.

'Sir?'

'Are you getting a lot of flak thrown at you?'

You should know, thought Verago. You've been throwing some of it.

'Nothing I can't cope with, sir,' he said.

Croxford grunted. He kept his gaze on the road in front of him.

'I guess you think we're a pretty hostile bunch. We must seem a little inhospitable at times.'

'At times, yes, sir.'

The general nodded.

'I don't like this whole business. I don't mind telling you I'd be very happy to see the back of you, your client and the whole shebang.'

'I'm sure of that.'

'Let me tell you something, Captain, just between us. Don't make snap judgements. There's more than one side to any story. Sometimes the good guys wear black hats too.'

The car was going faster, and the wind beat against Verago's face.

'General, ' said Verago, 'I'm simply over here to do a job. But if you think there's something I should know . . . '

Croxford turned his head and glared at him. Then he stepped on the accelerator once more, and the car speeded up. They had

186

left the perimeter of the base well behind now, and Verago wondered just how fast the general would go. Speed limits didn't seem to concern him. And there wasn't another car in sight.

'Don't make out you're a dumb son of a bitch, because you're not,' said Croxford. 'You ever considered that sometimes things have to be done for the good of everybody? Things nobody likes doing?'

'Such as?' Verago looked grim.

The car swerved, Croxford glanced at him and swore:

'Jesus Christ, Captain, don't play the innocent with me. You are a member of the Judge Advocate General's Corps, an Army officer, on active service, and we are at war.'

'Sir?'

'In war, you have to sacrifice people for the general good. It's not a cold war, Verago, that's newspaper talk. It's hot. Men are getting killed, killed in action. On missions from this base. My men.'

'I know, sir,' said Verago quietly. 'But what's that got to do with adultery?'

'I'm not talking about . . . ' began Croxford and then stopped. 'My mistake. I thought you got the point.'

They swung violently round a corner, the tyres screaming.

'General, you haven't answered my question,' pressed Verago.

'You're getting mighty close to insubordination, Captain.'

'I thought this was between us,' replied Verago.

'The trouble with you, Verago, is that you're really not a military man at all. You're a civilian in uniform. You'll never understand what sometimes has to be done in the line of duty. I'm sorry for you.'

Verago flushed.

He started to say something but, without warning, the general stopped the car. He braked so sharply Verago was nearly thrown against the windscreen. Croxford didn't apologise.

'You said you didn't play golf, as I remember,' he remarked instead. 'Pity, I'm just going to play a couple of rounds. I'd have enjoyed testing your handicap, but there's no point, is there? You might as well bail out here.'

'General,' Verago protested, quite mildly, 'I haven't got transportation.'

'Well,' smiled Croxford, 'it's only five or six miles back to the base.' He sniffed the July air. 'I'm sure you'll enjoy a little exercise. It's good for the soul.'

Slowly Verago climbed out of the MG.

'Have a pleasant walk, Captain,' said Croxford, and with a rich roar of its engine, the superpowered MG raced off.

But the expression on the general's face stayed with Verago a long time. And he was to remember it when he knew much more.

RIGA

The man with the shaven head had not touched his breakfast. It stood on the tray, next to his bed; a plate of congealing semolina, coffee, actually a substitute made from acorns, three lumps of sugar, fifteen grams of butter, and two thick slices of black bread.

Daylight penetrated into the small, cell-like room, but he could not see out, for the window had been painted over in white.

The man lay on the bed, staring at the ceiling. He hadn't shaved for a couple of days, and there was a stubble on his chin. That, the shaven skull and the shapeless green pyjamas he wore, gave him an emaciated, haggard look.

A key turned in the lock of the door, and a woman in a white coat entered, followed by a tall man in Soviet uniform. He stood aside as the woman approached the bed, smiling.

'And how do we feel today?' she asked cheerfully, in English.

The shaven-headed man did not even blink. His eyes

continued to gaze into nothingness.

Dr Helena Narkowska, of the Serbsky Central Scientific Research Institute of Psychiatry, was not disconcerted. In her specialist duties for the KGB, she frequently had unco-operative patients.

'You are very naughty,' she chided the man on the bed, nodding at the uneaten breakfast. 'You need nourishment. Don't you like it?' A thought struck her. 'Maybe you would prefer some American cereals?'

The man said nothing.

The officer drew her to one side.

'Is he shamming?' he asked in a low voice.

'I don't believe so.'

'But you're not sure?'

'Major, all I can tell you is that, physically, he has fully recovered. Naturally the mental consequences of such an experience . . . Who knows!'

Major Alexis Fokin frowned. The detailed interrogation of this prisoner was long overdue. The High Command had a lot of questions for him.

'Let me try,' he said.

Fokin drew up a chair next to the bed, and sat down.

'Listen to me, my friend,' he began, also in English. 'You are now perfectly fit, and it's time we had a little talk.'

The man continued to stare at the ceiling.

'You're just being obstructive,' went on Fokin. 'You understand perfectly well what I'm saying to you.'

Dr Narkowska touched his arm.

'If it is amnesia . . .'

'It's an act,' Fokin cut her short. 'He wants to play dumb.'

He took a cardboard-tubed cigarette from a packet, lit it and sat thoughtfully smoking for a moment. The doctor watched him nervously. Fokin had a formidable reputation for breaking people.

But when the major spoke, his tone was gentle.

'You have been well treated, haven't you?'

The man lay motionless.

'You've been given the best of medical care. When we picked

you up, I wouldn't have given you five kopecs for your chances, and look at you now, strong, healthy. But it can only go so far,' continued Fokin. 'Now it's your turn to do something for us. We want a lot of answers from you. Technical answers.'

Dr Narkowska looked away.

'Damn it,' cried Fokin, reaching forward and grabbing a pair of dogtags hanging from a chain round the man's neck. 'You know who you are and where you are.' He jangled the dog tags in front of the man's face. 'You are Captain Matt Kingston, electronics specialist, based at Laconbury in England, and your RB47H was shot down by us on a spy mission over the Baltic. There were six of you. We gave back a couple of the dead ones, but we picked you up half frozen and we have looked after you well. There is nothing wrong with you. Stop play-acting.'

'Please, Major,' intervened Dr Narkowska. 'Don't pressurise him too much. It could . . . '

Fokin turned on her.

'Until now he's been your patient, doctor. Now I have taken over. Understand?'

There was no reaction from the man on the bed.

Fokin stood up.

'Alright, Captain, have it your way. But I warn you that things will get more uncomfortable. Perhaps you need a stricter regime to make you talk. And remember, you are officially dead, so nobody cares a damn what happens to you. Don't think General Croxford is going to come to your rescue . . . '

He peered at the man, wondering if casually slipping in his commander's name would have any effect. But Kingston continued to stare blankly into space.

'Think about it.' Fokin turned to Dr Narkowska. 'I've finished, doctor. For the time being,' he added, the menace implicit.

They left the room, and she locked the door.

'What happens to him now?' she asked.

'He's going to have a change of scenery,' replied the major, and his smile made her feel cold.

Thursday, July 13, 1961 – LACONBURY

Pryor drove down to Laconbury, half wondering why he was bothering. Maybe it was to regain a little pride. They were starting to take him for granted. The way Major Longman had warned him off the court martial had rankled, and made him face a question he had long tried not to ask himself; just what kind of newsman had he become.

His Defense Department ID card, one of the privileges of being the military's tame journalist, got him on the base without difficulty, and as soon as he had parked his maroon car, also supplied by the military, he went to see Ryan in the wing information office.

Ryan, a freckle-faced lieutenant, had one mission: to keep Laconbury out of the news. He had acquired the knack of seemingly helping Press people all the way, while making sure, behind their backs, that they got nowhere. When things became tough, he referred them to Ruislip, and Major Longman.

He received Pryor genially.

'Hi, old buddy,' he greeted him, 'what brings you to this neck of the woods?'

Pryor's unexpected arrival didn't worry him.

Stars and Stripes could be relied on to toe the line.

'You know me,' said Pryor, dumping his lanky frame in a chair, 'always looking for the Pulitzer Prize.'

'You won't find it here, man.' On his wall, Ryan had a framed photograph of General Croxford, and a replica wing's emblem. He also favoured slogan stickers: 'You Needn't be Crazy to Work Here, But It Helps', was the latest one. It showed visitors that he was One of the Boys.

'Tea?' he asked Pryor. Among his ancillary duties, he was in charge of Laconbury's community relations, and had decided it was fitting to offer callers in his office tea instead of coffee.

'No, thanks.' Then Pryor took the plunge. 'What about this court martial, Phil?'

'Eh?'

'The guy who's charged with adultery.'

Ryan's eyes widened in innocent surprise.

'In this outfit?'

'That's right. What can you tell me about it?'

'First I heard of it, old buddy.'

'He's an officer,' said Pryor.

'Where did you hear all this?'

Pryor smiled thinly. 'Maybe a little bird told me.'

Ryan picked up the phone, and dialled the outer office. 'Do we know anything about a court martial, Sergeant?' he asked his clerk. He listened, and then hung up. 'You're out of luck. Nobody knows a thing about it.'

'Quit bullshitting,' said Pryor crisply.

Ryan began to study him warily. Something had needled the guy. He wasn't his usual amiable, complacent self.

'Have you asked headquarters? The major? Welk?'

'I'm asking you,' said Pryor, and began to feel like a reporter.

It was time to be One of the Boys, decided Ryan.

'Look, Joe, this is a big outfit. You got any idea how many men we have here? I don't know everything that goes on. Things happen, and nobody tells me. I'm in the same position as you, old buddy. Really I am,' he said earnestly.

'You're the base information officer,' retorted Pryor. 'You can ask. Why don't you start asking, Phil?'

Not since the day a correspondent from *The New York Times* had come by and begun asking awkward questions about the wing's mission, and was it true that the U2 flew from Laconbury, and had the Russians shot down one of their planes, had Ryan experienced this kind of thing.

'Ask who, Joe? I'm just a peon.'

'How about the legal office, for a start? They should know.'

Headquarters would soon deal with this guy, reflected Ryan.

192

As soon as he had gone, he would get on the hot line to Ruislip, and they'd set things in motion. Meantime, he said to himself, make it look like you're co-operating.

He picked up the phone again, and asked for an extension. A voice answered.

'Lieutenant Jensen,' said Ryan, 'I'd appreciate your co-operation. I have a man here from *Stars and Stripes* who's asking about some court martial. Do you think you could deal with him? Gee, I'd sure appreciate that.'

He put the receiver down, and smiled at Pryor, his sunny, Californian surf rider smile.

'Jensen is our legal eagle, Joe. He's a real square shooter, too. You'll like him. If there's any trials pending, he'll tell you.'

Pryor was taken slightly aback. It seemed to be getting too easy.

'He's waiting for you at the officers' club,' added Ryan. 'He'll give you a straight deal. Just ask him what you want to know.'

Pryor slowly untwined his lanky frame.

'Thanks,' he said a little awkwardly. Maybe he'd got Ryan all wrong.

Ryan rose from behind his desk, and put his arm round Pryor's shoulder as he led him to the door.

'You come and see me any time, old buddy,' he beamed. 'It gets kind of stuffy in here, and it's nice to see a friendly face. And remember, Joe, you're always welcome. We got no secrets from you.'

Then, as soon as Pryor had left, he called General Croxford.

FRANKFURT

'To me, he is a soldier who had died on the field of battle,' said

193

Pech solemnly. 'Like your airmen shot down over Czechoslovakia, or the Baltic.'

'Er, yes,' agreed Unterberg, a little reluctantly.

He had arrived in Frankfurt to confer with Pech after Herr Unruh's demise.

'Of course, coming at this time, with so much at stake, it is rather worrying,' added Pech. 'But the machine is running so smoothly that I don't see anything can go wrong.'

'It had better not,' said Unterberg irritably. He had flown in at short notice, and had had little sleep the previous night.

'Even such a sad occasion has its compensations,' ruminated Pech. 'It has brought you over, Clyde, and you know how much I like to see you.'

'Yeah.'

'But nevertheless, it is a tragedy. Such men are hard to replace.'

'Who takes over B1?' asked Unterberg. There were a few things he wanted to get settled.

Pech spread his hands. 'Ask Bonn. I have no idea. I just do my job. Marienfelde keeps me busy. The refugees. The border crossings. Internal security.'

'Will you?'

'Oh no, Clyde, I am a field man. I go out and do things. I leave others to give the orders.'

He smiled deprecatingly.

'Don't blame you.'

'How long are you staying?' asked Pech.

'Just for the day. I'm taking the last plane back.'

Pech nodded. 'They need you in London, I'm sure.' He stood up. 'Come, it's time for lunch.'

He took Unterberg to a seafood restaurant. Fishing nets were draped round the walls, and huge lobsters decorated the counter that ran the length of the dining room.

'I couldn't even try and compete with the fantastic roast beef you gave me in London,' said Pech. 'So I thought we'd eat fish.'

As was ritual, the important things were left to the end. Over coffee, Unterberg asked.

'How's the investigation going?'

'The minister is keeping it to himself. Not that they seem to have much.'

'What do you think?' enquired Unterberg quietly.

'Inexplicable. That's the only word, Clyde. Why should he do it? A nervous breakdown maybe? Overwork? I don't understand it.'

Unterberg's eyes narrowed.

'Helmut, you don't buy that suicide theory, surely? A left-handed man doesn't shoot himself in the right temple with his right hand.'

Pech's eyes were slits. 'Maybe not,' he said thoughtfully. 'But who'd murder him?' He paused. 'Who'd want to?'

'Who'd need to?' asked Unterberg. He absent mindedly toyed with the salt shaker. 'We heard something big had come up.' Now he moved the pepper pot like a chess piece. 'Maybe somebody had to move fast.'

In the nearby Kiserstrasse, a two-tone police horn sounded. After all this time in Europe, it still made Unterberg nostalgic for American sirens.

'Herr Unruh was a most loyal man,' said Pech stiffly. 'If you're suggesting . . . '

'I'm suggesting nothing,' murmured Unterberg. 'I'm trying to figure it out, that's all.'

'Go back to London and relax,' said Pech. 'Make sure your Air Force captain is safely locked away, and leave the rest to us. Herr Unruh's sad death does not affect anything.'

'How's Helga?'

'She . . . ' Pech stopped. 'How should she be?'

'Still in your good care?'

'Of course.'

'OK,' said Unterberg. 'I'll get off your back. They'll be glad to know there's no panic over here.'

They parted outside the Intercontinental, on the banks of the Main.

'Take care of yourself,' were Unterberg's final words. 'We don't want anything to happen to you too, Helmut.'

'Don't worry,' laughed Pech. 'Why should it?'

195

But on his way to his car, he looked back twice to see if anyone was following him.

LACONBURY

In the lobby of the officers' club, the wives were having a whist drive, but the bar was empty except for a trio of pilots. They wore flight suits, with the Cyclops emblem of the wing stitched to their chests. They didn't even glance up when Pryor entered.

'I'm looking for Lieutenant Jensen,' said Pryor to the barman.

The man shook his head. 'Haven't seen him today.'

'Give me a Schlitz,' said Pryor. That was one of the things that he loved about the job, that he could get real American beer, properly iced, on a base, anywhere in Europe.

He was having his second one when Jensen finally arrived.

'Gee, I'm sorry I kept you,' he said. 'Long-distance call.'

It hadn't been at all. But Jensen wasn't about to tell him that he had received certain specific instructions following Ryan's warning call to General Croxford.

'Want a beer?' offered Pryor.

'I can do with it,' said Jensen. He drank deep. 'Let's sit down.'

They walked over to a table, far away from the pilots.

I don't like this man, decided Pryor. He tended to classify people like animals and insects. This one was a slug.

'You want to know about the trial?' asked Jensen. His directness surprised Pryor.

'So there *is* a trial?'

'Sure there is.'

'Man, you'd never believe it,' said Pryor. 'You're the first guy who talks straight. The PR shop at Third throws flak in my face, and your information man here . . .

'Phil Ryan's a good guy,' said Jensen. 'Listen, Pryor, can we talk off the record?'

Pryor hesitated.

'It's the only way,' insisted Jensen. 'Otherwise it's got to be hello and goodbye. I'm sorry.'

Pryor tried to get his long legs under the table into a more comfortable position.

'Why the hell all the mystery? There are guys being court-martialled all over Europe every day? What's so special about this one?' he growled.

Two more officers came in, and went up to the bar. Jensen waited until they had found a seat in an alcove with their drinks before he answered.

'All I can tell you is that an officer is going to face trial under articles 133 and 134.'

'Catch alls,' said Pryor contemptuously. He had been round the military a long time.

Jensen shrugged. 'They cover adultery.'

'And the brass make all that fuss for that?' Pryor shook his head. 'I don't believe it.' He signalled over the barman. 'Another two beers,' he called out.

Jensen eyed him pensively. It was a shrewd piece of acting, strictly by the orders. It intended to convey that he was about to take a big decision. He was about to trust Pryor.

'You're right of course,' he said, after the new round had come. 'You've been around this man's Air Force long enough. You guessed it. They're trying to keep this whole thing under wraps.'

'Why?'

'A good reason.'

They were taking him for granted again. They assumed again that they could lift a little finger, and he'd jump.

'Now wait,' said Pryor. 'That's for me to judge. My job is to get the news.'

'OK,' said Jensen. 'I'll tell you. But remember the deal. Off the record.'

'Alright.'

'This thing is messy. It can have repercussions. NATO. All kinds of nasty repercussions. It's very sensitive . . .'

'A guy screwing a dame?' sneered Pryor. 'Come on, NATO couldn't care a shit.'

'This outfit is a hot potato,' said Jensen earnestly. 'We got a mission here we can't talk about. It's a fine outfit, doing a hell of a job. But we got problems. Community relations. Aircraft noise. Those ban the bomb idiots. We have to walk softly. We don't like to attract attention to ourselves. And we don't want to wash our dirty linen in public. That's why we don't want a word printed.'

You're earning your pay, thought Pryor.

'What's so dirty about this case?'

Jensen lowered his voice. 'It's a real bitch. This guy's been shacking up with an English girl. Cheating on his wife. Can't you see the headlines? "Yank at secret base commits adultery with local girl".'

'That's a bad headline,' said Pryor, needling him.

'Listen, you get the point. We don't want this outfit dragged into the mud, we don't want scandal stories about our wing.'

'Does it involve security?' asked Pryor.

'What do you mean?'

'Is there something classified about it? The way all you guys are flapping about you think the guy had the bomb in his bedroom.'

Jensen's laugh was nervous.

'For pete's sake, I told you what it's about. And why we don't want it reported. You don't want to feed Commie propaganda, do you? No sir, we don't need that.'

'You can't censor it,' said Pryor defiantly. 'No matter how embarrassing a story is. It's public property.'

Jensen smiled.

'Have another beer,' he suggested. Then he saw the Army officer come in. A captain, somewhat untidy, with JAG insignia. Jensen looked at his watch. 'Oh, hell,' he gasped, 'I forgot it was so late.'

'I'm in no hurry,' drawled Pryor. The officer seemed to have a curious effect on Jensen. 'What's the Army doing on an air base?'

'Come on,' pressed Jensen hurriedly. 'I'll take you to your car.'

'Where's the fire?' asked Pryor amiably. 'Why don't we have that beer?'

The Army officer came over.

'Well, counsellor,' he said to Jensen, 'aren't you going to introduce me to your friend?'

Jensen, decided Pryor, is not a slug. Now he looks like a trapped stoat.

'Mr Pryor is a reporter from *Stars and Stripes,'* said the stoat uneasily.

'*Stripes*, eh?' The captain nodded. 'Glad to meet you, Mr Pryor. My name is Verago. I'm a great fan of your comics page. What hot story brings you to Laconbury?'

'I was just asking about you. Didn't expect Army round here,' said Pryor. He peered at the crossed sword and pen on Verago's lapels. 'You're a lawyer, aren't you? Anything to do with the court martial?'

Verago beamed.

'My friend, maybe we ought to have a long talk. Don't you agree, counsellor?'

Jensen's mouth suddenly felt dry. He wondered how he would explain this to the general.

KARLSRUHE

The new man had high cheek bones, thin lips, and a gold tooth. Herr Stamm was Unruh's successor, and Pech's new boss.

Pech didn't know much about Stamm. There were rumours that he was one of Gehlen's bunch, and that he had been closely linked with the Americans. Pech would dearly have liked to know where Bonn had dug him up from. When there was little gossip about a man, it was always a dangerous sign.

'Sit down, Pech,' invited Herr Stamm.

'Thank you, sir,' said Pech, respectfully.

For a disconcerting moment, Herr Stamm studied him. It was like being X-rayed, and Pech, despite himself, shifted uneasily.

'As you know, I have taken over the department,' began Herr Stamm. 'My predecessor will, of course, be sadly missed, and I regret having to come here under such tragic circumstances.'

Pech mutely agreed. What could he say to that? Best to keep silent.

'I have been fully briefed and I am conversant with all current activities,' went on Herr Stamm. 'And of course with what you're doing.'

Pech nodded. He felt strangely nervous.

'I have decided that you are to carry on, and that B1 will continue its operation,' announced Herr Stamm.

Pech relaxed. Just a little.

'Thank you, sir,' he said.

'They trust you, and therefore I trust you,' said Herr Stamm. 'What you are doing is of the most delicate nature, and the implications of what is involved I . . . well, I'm sure I don't have to spell it out.'

'Indeed not,' said Pech. He was beginning to feel secure.

'You seem to have established a good working relationship with our allied counterparts. Both the Americans and the British appear satisfied that you can be relied on at this, er, extremely delicate moment in time.'

'I'm glad to hear that, sir,' said Pech. All was safe.

'You're aware that it is best, under the circumstances, that as little as possible should be on paper.'

'Of course.'

'B1 is off the record, so to speak, and I don't want your section to forget it.'

'I only report verbally. That is how it was with Herr Unruh,' said Pech piously, 'and that is how it will be with you, Herr Stamm. Only verbally. Only you and me.'

'Good.'

Well, that was it, thought Pech. Once again he had landed on his feet.

'And the less you tell me, the better,' added Herr Stamm. 'About the girl, or anything. Only what I need to know, you understand? The fewer that know anything about it, the better.'

'Do you think, sir, I should go to the court martial?' asked Pech.

'In England? Certainly not. It's a domestic matter for them. It has absolutely nothing to do with us. You follow?'

'Perfectly.'

Now that he felt more at ease, Pech glanced round the room. It was Unruh's old office, but there were subtle changes. A signed photograph of Adenauer had appeared on the wall. A curious ornament on his desk, a bullet mounted upright on a slab of marble. Absurdly, Pech wondered if it was a bullet they had dug out of Stamm sometime. And there was Berlin's coat of arms on the wall. The bear, his claws raised.

'One other thing,' said Herr Stamm, interrupting Pech's observations.

'Yes?'

'The investigation into Herr Unruh's death has come up with nothing,' said Herr Stamm, and Pech's heart beat a little faster. 'I find it very unsatisfactory, and I intend to pursue the matter from our end. Is there anything you can think of? Some clue, some explanation?'

'I'm afraid not,' apologised Pech. 'I have thought about it, of course. It was a terrible shock, and when the investigation said it was . . . murder, well, I was stunned. And yet, I was relieved . . .'

'Relieved?' snapped Herr Stamm. The gimlet eyes were X-raying him again. 'What do you mean?'

'Well,' said Pech boldly, 'at least he was the victim of an assailant. I would have been most perturbed to think that Herr Unruh, a man who knew so many secrets, who had such a sensitive job, who knew all about B1, should have found it necessary to commit suicide. I would have worried about what it was that made him do it. When people in our work commit suicide . . . '

'You see it as reassuring that somebody found it necessary to murder him instead?' asked Herr Stamm coldly.

'At least it does not raise any personal question marks.'

'That's all, Pech. Carry on.'

'Thank you, sir,' said Pech diffidently. 'If I come up with anything, about Herr Unruh I mean, I will of course let you know immediately.'

'I am sure you will.'

Pech closed the door with a feeling of relief. What really intrigued him was the bullet on the slab of marble.

SOUTH RUISLIP

As Pech left his new chief's office, over in England, Ivanov called Laurie.

It didn't worry him that he phoned her at South Ruislip, and that the call went through the Third Air Force headquarters switchboard. The operator heard the pennies drop into the slot, and he announced himself as 'Gene'. He was calling from a phone booth, safe, secure, untraceable.

'You are coming to the ballet with me tonight,' he announced when he was put through to Laurie and without further preliminaries. 'The Kirov at Covent Garden. I happen to have two tickets.'

'You shouldn't have gone to all that trouble,' said Laurie. Kincaid's door was ajar, and the colonel was behind his desk, seemingly engrossed in a file he was reading.

'No trouble.' She could almost sense the grin. 'A friend gave them to me.'

In the phone booth, Ivanov smiled. The thought of describing Sergei Grigorovich as a friend had its amusing aspects.

'Well,' said Laurie, 'I'm sorry. I can't. Not tonight.'

Verago had called her, and they were meeting that evening.

'You have a date?' Ivanov didn't attempt to disguise his disappointment.

'I'm seeing a friend.'

'My dear Laurie, if it is a woman friend, it is a shocking waste. And if it is a man friend, I am madly jealous,' he said, but his tone was light. 'So either way you should change your plans.'

'Not possible,' said Laurie.

'It *is* a man then.'

'I'm sure you can find somebody else to take.'

Ivanov studied the mini parked on the other side of Mount Street, across from the phone booth. He hadn't noticed it before, but idly, almost automatically, he wondered if it had been following him. Not that it bothered him. He enjoyed running the other side off its feet.

'Can't you?' added Laurie.

'Listen,' said Ivanov. 'I hear people are paying a fortune for Kirov tickets. I shall utilise the capitalist system. If I can't take you, I will sell them on the black market for the highest sum I can get.'

Laurie giggled. 'Won't your friend mind?'

'He won't know,' said Ivanov. 'Tell me, who is this date?'

'None of your business,' she replied coldly.

'If it is Captain Verago, you should introduce us,' Ivanov said, coolly casual.

At the other end, Laurie froze.

'Are you there?' he demanded.

'Yes.' Her mind was racing.

'Captain Verago sounds a very interesting man. I'm sure we'd get on.'

'I have to hang up,' said Laurie. 'Call me sometime.'

'Of course,' said Ivanov. 'As a matter of fact, we must all get together. The three of us.' He could hear her intake of breath. 'Perhaps a little party. Leave it to me. Au revoir.'

And he rang off.

He left the phone booth, and started strolling towards South Audley Street, whistling gently. The mini didn't follow. Pity, he thought. He would have enjoyed leading them a little chase.

Half an hour later, he kept his promise. He found two disconsolate American 'tourists hanging around the Covent Garden box office, vainly trying to get seats for that night's performance of the Kirov.

Ivanov sold them his two tickets for £100. He acted the part of a black market scalper well, and went straight to Dunhill's to buy himself a box of capitalist cigars.

If he knew, Grigorovich would report him to the inspectorate, he was sure, and that made it all the more enjoyable.

After all, it wasn't the only thing about Ivanov Central didn't know.

LONDON

In bed, Laurie could be passionate, forward, unpredictable, and yet completely feminine. The first time they had made love, Verago had been carried away by her vehement desire, and then amazed by her gentleness afterwards. She was fierce and loving, lustful and soft.

In most things, Laurie was full of contradictions, and it fascinated Verago. There was nothing shy about her, but she was very modest. She never flaunted her body, but in his arms, naked, she could be utterly abandoned.

She sat up in bed, the sheet drawn up over her breasts, smoking a cigarette. She glowed, and it made him happy that she too had enjoyed it so much.

'Some places I know, they could lock us up now,' said Verago contentedly.

Laurie's eyebrows shot up.

'Be warned, kid. It's illegal to fuck in a dozen states, and as for shacking up, that's a crime all over the country.'

'Such as?' Laurie was amused.

'Florida, Massachusetts, Georgia, Wisconsin, oh, lots,' said Verago. 'Even Washington, DC. You name it.'

She turned towards him, and to his pleasure, the sheet slipped.

'Sometimes you talk crap, Tony Verago,' she declared. 'You know that?'

'It's on the statute books,' he protested.

'Oh come on,' said Laurie, 'you trying to tell me everytime somebody screws somebody in Washington they get put in the slammer?'

'Of course not. But they can, if they get caught. If somebody makes something of it . . .'

Laurie stubbed out her cigarette.

'Well,' she said, 'since we're going to jail we might as well make it worth while.'

Half an hour later the phone rang. Dozily, Laurie reached for it.

'Hallo?' she said. The bedside alarm clock pointed at just after midnight.

She listened for a moment, frowned slightly.

'It's for you,' she said, puzzled. 'New York.'

She handed him the receiver, and he sat up.

'Yes?' he said.

'Tony,' came Lou Conn's voice. 'It's me. Glad I caught you.'

Laurie was watching his face. He gave her a quick nod, but his attention was on the call.

'What's the news, Lou?' he asked.

There was a short pause. Then:

'Bad, Tony. I'm sorry.'

'She won't play?'

'She's dead,' said Lou, 3,000 miles away.

Verago felt cold. 'Dead? Mrs Tower?'

Laurie's eyes widened.

'What do you mean? What's happened?'

'I called her apartment, but I couldn't get any reply,' said Lou. 'So I went round, and it was all closed up. The janitor told me. She took an overdose of pills. Two days ago. She was dead when he found her.'

Verago sat very still.

'Tony, are you there?'

'Yes.'

'I'm sorry. I guess that shoots a hole in your case.'

'Are you sure it's . . . it's suicide?' asked Verago.

'No question,' said Lou in New York. 'I checked with the police. I saw the autopsy report. She just swallowed a bottle full of barbiturates. She had been drinking too. She was a lush, Tony. That's all there is to it.'

'Jesus,' said Verago.

'Maybe separation hit her harder than you thought. Maybe the news about the court martial . . . '

'But how the hell did she know?' asked Verago quickly.

'The FBI had been round,' said Lou. 'They also questioned the janitor. Getting background information. For the military. I guess they told her.'

'The FBI,' repeated Verago, more to himself. Laurie lit another cigarette.

'Did you say something?' asked Lou.

'No,' said Verago. 'Did you find out anything else?'

'Nothing. I figure none of this helps you. I'm sorry. I guess it will make things tougher now. They'll use the wife's death, won't they?'

'You bet.'

'Well,' said Lou. 'If I can do anything this end . . . let me know. Anytime.'

'I will, Lou,' replied Verago. 'And listen, friend, thanks for trying. I appreciate it.'

'I wish it could have done some good,' said Lou. 'So long, Tony.'

Slowly Verago put the phone down.

He looked at Laurie. 'I hope you didn't mind,' he said absent-mindedly. 'I gave him your number. In case I was here . . . '

He lapsed into silence.

'Tower's wife. She's dead,' he said at last.

Laurie nodded. 'So I gathered.'

'There goes my mitigation.'

'But will the trial go on, if she's dead?' asked Laurie.

'Sure. It doesn't alter anything. She was alive when he committed adultery. In fact, it makes things worse. Morally, he's going to be tried for murder.'

'But that's . . . that's nonsense. Didn't she kill herself?'

'That's exactly it,' said Verago. 'Nobody's going to say it, but in that court room, it'll be his fault. He abandoned his wife, committed adultery, and drove her to suicide. It's a gift.'

He lay back on the bed and stared up at the ceiling.

'How the hell do you defend a guy for moral murder?' he asked.

Laurie offered him a cigarette but he shook his head.

'Didn't he say something about the FBI?'

'Oh yes,' said Verago with a little grim smile. 'They're in on the act too. I guess suddenly adultery's become a federal crime.'

Friday, July 14, 1961 – LONDON

Pryor located the man he was looking for in the third pub he tried. He had made the rounds of Fleet Street watering holes because he knew that there, somewhere, at this time of day, he'd find Dawkins.

He finally struck lucky in the Mucky Duck, the irreverent alias of the White Swan. Dawkins was propping up the bar, tie a little askew, eyelids heavy, speech a trifle thick. But it was deceptive. One call from the news desk of the *Sketch,* and he would be alert. The alcoholic haze that often surrounded him could be very misleading.

'Slumming today?' he greeted Pryor jovially. He winked at the barmaid. 'He's a Yank, but he means well.'

Pryor didn't resent it. He knew Dawkins's style. He was one of the few Fleet Street types with whom he had made friends.

'What's your poison?' enquired Dawkins.

'Guinness,'

Dawkins nodded approvingly. 'There's hope for you yet.' He raised his glass. 'Cheers.'

Now that he had found his man, Pryor hesitated. What he was about to do was disloyal. If they found out . . .

'You want a good story, Peter?' he asked.

The bloodshot eyes turned on him.

'What story's that?'

Pryor edged him towards a corner, away from any possible eavesdroppers.

'They're trying to hush it up,' said Pryor, adding a bit of bait.

'Who is?'

'The military.'

Dawkins did not react. Instead, he called to the barmaid: 'Same again, love.' Then he focused on Pryor. 'What are you on about?'

'You heard of an air base called Laconbury?'

Dawkins burped. 'You got so many bloody air bases in this country I can't keep up with them. What about it?'

'They're going to court-martial an officer there,' said Pryor, and instinctively reddened. Now there was no turning back.

'Oh yes?' Dawkins didn't appear in the slightest interested. 'What's he done? Flogged PX booze on the black market?' He laughed.

His pint had arrived, and he took a deep drink.

'Adultery.'

'Eh?'

'It's a court martial offence in the American military.'

The newsman's mind clicked into action.

'Is she English? The bird, I mean?'

'I think so,' said Pryor.

208

Dawkins inclined his head. 'Not a bad yarn,' he conceded grudgingly.

'It's all yours.'

Dawkins regarded him reflectively.

'Why?' he asked finally.

'Because I can't use it. The military won't let me. The paper wouldn't print it.'

'You're joking.' Dawkins was genuinely taken aback. 'I know it's a funny paper, but . . . '

'It's not a *news* paper,' said Pryor bitterly. It was his declaration of independence. He had burst the strait jacket. Leaking the story was his assertion of rebellion.

Dawkins extricated a piece of paper from his pocket, and took out a pencil.

'When is this court martial?'

'Soon,' said Pryor. 'I don't know the exact date, but soon.'

'Who can tell me more about it?'

'Why don't you call the Air Force? At Ruislip? Say you've heard a rumour . . . '

Pryor relished the thought. Welk would turn pale when he got the call from Fleet Street. Major Longman would blow his top. He'd give a lot to be there the moment the shit hit the fan.

'Will they tell me?' asked Dawkins.

Pryor drained his glass. 'They got to be careful with you. It's not like *Stripes*. They haven't got you at the end of a string. Just push them.'

'You don't mind?' enquired Dawkins, a little anxiously. 'I don't want to land you in the cart.'

'As long as you keep stumm about how you heard, I'm OK. You can always say you picked up a rumour, can't you. In a pub.' He smiled. 'It's true, isn't it?'

They had another round. Dawkins paid again. This would certainly go on expenses.

'Much appreciate it, Joe,' he said. 'Really do.'

'I met his lawyer,' said Pryor, 'that's strictly between you and me.'

Dawkins didn't believe in such conventions. For him, anything he heard was fair game. But what he said was:

'Sure.'

'The lawyer's come over from Germany. A sharp guy. I think he'd welcome a story. The rest of 'em are all walking on eggs. I don't know what the hell's going on – maybe it's because the base . . . '

He stopped.

Dawkins was very alert now.

'Yes? What about the base?'

'Well, don't say I told you, but I've heard it said the U2 flies from there.'

Dawkins's eyes widened. 'Jesus, that's a hell of a story. "Secret" stuff, great.'

'That's off the record.' Pryor went through the motions. 'Only for your guidance. But it sounds sexy, eh?'

'Fabulous.' Dawkins couldn't believe his luck. A scoop like this, handed to him on a plate. So much for the know alls who said you could never find a real story in a pub. He drained his beer glass.

'I got to go. Where can I reach you?'

'Don't,' said Pryor. 'Don't call me. Don't phone, don't get in touch, nothing.'

Already he was having regrets.

'If they link me with this . . . '

Dawkins picked up his change. 'I understand, don't worry.' He held out his hand. 'I'm most grateful, mate, I really am.'

Pryor shook it. 'Make the most of it, Peter. It's too good to be buried.'

'Watch the front page,' called out Dawkins, and then he disappeared through the curtained door.

Pryor ordered himself another drink. A double scotch this time. He wondered if this is what a man felt like who had started the count down on an H-bomb.

'The chaplain told me,' said Tower unemotionally.

He looks more stooped, thought Verago, older, like a man with a load.

They were walking in the open yard of the confinement facility, within the wire fence. The APs watched them.

'I'm sorry about it,' said Verago. The Air Force had lost no time notifying Tower. He wondered who contacted them. The FBI.

'It's a lousy way to go,' commented Tower. 'All alone.'

'How long had you been married?'

'Since Korea.'

Ten years. And four of them apart.

'Do you want to talk about it?' asked Verago gently.

'Nothing to talk about,' said Tower. 'It didn't work out. Pity it had to end like this, though. Trouble is she never could face reality . . . '

'Is that why there was no divorce?'

'Does it matter now?' asked Tower.

They strolled in silence, a hundred feet one way, a hundred feet the other way. The grass was neat, tidy, cut just right, like the hair of the APs, like the pattern of the wire fence.

'You can ask to attend the funeral,' said Verago.

'What for?' Tower looked away. 'Won't help her one way or the other. It's all over for her.'

'That's up to you,' said Verago coldly.

'Don't sound so goddamn disapproving, counsellor.' Tower had turned on him fiercely, anger on his face. 'I don't need you to make moral judgements. It's my affair, and I got to live with it. That's the end of it. Hell, what do you know how it feels?'

Verago said nothing.

Tower calmed down.

'I'm sorry,' he said. 'It's not your fault. This whole goddamn thing is getting me down. I want to get it over. One way or the other.'

'Sure, I understand.'

'It hasn't helped the case any either, has it?'

'No,' said Verago.

'It won't be easy now to use your mitigation argument, not after this?'

'Well,' said Verago, 'it might not be the smartest thing to do.'

Tower stopped in his tracks. He faced Verago.

'Just for the record, between you and me, I don't believe I'm the reason she did it. She was neurotic, sick. She really was. It could have happened any time. Too much booze, too many pills. I'm not trying to justify anything, but honestly, I don't think for one moment . . . hell, I knew her. I wasn't even surprised.'

'I believe you,' said Verago. 'But it's not me we've got to convince. In a way, it makes it worse. The court might feel you abandoned your wife just when you should have helped her.'

'So what have we got left?'

'I don't know,' said Verago. Then he saw Tower's expression.

'But don't worry, John,' he added, 'I'll think of something. The game hasn't even started.'

He hoped he sounded confident.

The trouble was, he reflected, that all the cards seemed to be marked.

And the guy who appeared to be cheating most of all was his own client.

LONDON

Daventry hailed a cab in Lowndes Square.

'Lincoln's Inn,' he instructed the driver, as he got in and settled back, his briefcase on the seat next to him. It wasn't until they had passed Hyde Park Corner that he realised the cab, instead of going straight along Piccadilly, had turned up Park Lane, towards the Dorchester.

Daventry frowned. It didn't seem the most direct route, but he had learned of old not to argue with London cabbies. They passed the hotel, and in Deanery Street the taxi stopped at the traffic lights.

Suddenly the door was flung open and two men got in. One sat beside Daventry and the other opposite on the tip-up seat.

Daventry was too astounded to say anything at first. The driver took no notice at all. The lights turned green and the cab accelerated across South Audley Street, into Hill Street.

'What the hell do you think you're doing?' gasped Daventry, leaning forward and rapping on the driver's glass partition. 'Stop,' he ordered. 'Driver, stop this cab.'

'It's alright, Mr Daventry,' said the man opposite. 'Nothing to get worried about.'

Daventry gaped at him, then made a dive for the cab door. But the man next to him leant forward and blocked him.

The cab drove on, turning corners, making a twisting, confusing journey around the maze of Mayfair back streets.

'I said stop!' Daventry shouted again.

But the cab just turned another corner. Daventry looked out frantically, hoping to see a policeman, anybody he could yell to, but he knew the men would stop him.

'What do you want?' he demanded.

'We're almost there, Mr Daventry,' said the man opposite soothingly.

The taxi came to a halt half way down a mews. They were near Berkeley Square, Daventry felt sure, but he couldn't pinpoint exactly where. It was a quiet, secluded mews, with dignified, impressive front doors. A shining Bentley was parked in front of one of them.

'Here we are,' announced the man facing him. He opened the door and was the first to get out of the cab.

'This way, sir,' he indicated, respectfully.

'I'm not getting out,' declared Daventry firmly. 'I don't know what you want, but I'm not . . .'

213

'Please, Mr Daventry,' pressed the man.

He wasn't being menacing, but spoke with the authority of a person who knows they are in control of things.

'I'm going to call the police, you know,' said Daventry.

'Yes sir,' said the man.

Reluctantly, Daventry got out, followed by the other man. The cab drove off immediately. Nobody had paid the fare.

One of the men pressed a bell on the ornate front door, which had a brass knocker in the shape of a lion's head.

The door was opened by a third man who could have been a twin brother of the others. They all wore business suits and dull ties. They had the same short haircuts and expressionless faces.

'Good afternoon, sir,' he said.

Daventry was ushered into the richly carpeted entrance hall. It reminded him of a wealthy Harley Street doctor's consulting rooms. He half expected to be shown into a waiting room, with copies of *Punch* and *The Tatler* neatly laid out on a polished table.

Instead, he was escorted along the hall, to a small lift. Only one of them went in with him. He pressed the second floor button. There were only five. One basement and four floors.

I can find this place again, thought Daventry, I swear I can. If I have to take Mayfair apart, I'll trace where this is. And then he realised they weren't really trying to conceal anything from him. It was as if they didn't care if he identified the address.

The lift stopped and the gates slid open automatically.

'The first door on the left,' said the man politely and stood aside for Daventry. 'If you like, I'll take that until you leave.'

He held out his hand for Daventry's briefcase.

'No,' said Daventry curtly.

The man went back into the lift and Daventry heard it purr its way down below again.

He stood, hesitant. The corridor was like the entrance hall, richly carpeted with a couple of oil paintings on the wall.

Then the first door on the left opened.

'My dear Gerald, how good to see you again,' said the man who greeted him smiling.

'Good god!' exclaimed Daventry. 'Brian!'

'Come in, old son,' invited Grierson.

The pretence that this was an aristocratic town house in the heart of Mayfair stopped once he stepped inside. It was an office, comfortable, modern, but utilitarian. A plain desk, a couple of leather armchairs, a telephone, a globe on a side table. *The Financial Times* lay on the desk.

'What a way for two school chums to meet up again, eh?' smiled Grierson. 'I was often going to call you and suggest a little reunion, but you know how it is.'

'I think you owe me one hell of an explanation,' said Daventry grimly.

'Of course. Sit down.'

Daventry sat in one of the armchairs. Grierson, as if to emphasise their respective positions, sat behind his desk.

He doesn't look all that different, thought Daventry. He carries his years well. He was wearing the old school tie. He even had the school colours on his cufflinks.

'You've done very well for yourself, Gerry, haven't you? Quite the legal luminary. Following in the old man's footsteps, eh? Future Lord Chief, maybe? Congratulations, old son.'

Daventry was aware of how silent the house was. He might be alone with Grierson in a tomb. No clock ticked, no typewriters clattered, no telephones rang. There wasn't even the sound of traffic.

'What exactly is this place?' asked Daventry.

'It belongs to you, old son.'

'Eh?'

'Well, you're a taxpayer, aren't you?'

'This . . . is a government office?'

Grierson's smile was twisted. 'Sort of.'

'And you?'

'A civil servant. Sort of.'

'A civil servant who goes about abducting people,' remarked Daventry acidly.

'Not abducting people,' chuckled Grierson. 'It's all rather boring, actually. Hush-hush, that sort of rubbish.'

'MI5?'

Grierson looked pained. 'Something like that. The point is I had a bit of a shock the other day. Saw your name in a file. A yellow file. Not nice, yellow.'

'What do you mean?'

'Nothing to get too steamed up about. But I don't like to see old chums on the list.'

'List?'

'So I thought I'd have a word with you. On the QT. Strictly between us. For old time's sake.'

'What exactly are you trying to tell me?' asked Daventry.

'Well,' began Grierson, 'you're getting yourself involved in some silly stuff. You know, with the Americans. That stupid court martial business. Our lot would be much happier if you kept your nose out. Sorry to be so blunt, old son. Official secrets and all that. You need it like a headcold on your wedding night. By the way, how is dear Alex?'

'Have you been tapping my phone?'

'Let me explain,' said Grierson earnestly, 'you're in no trouble at all, at the moment, Gerry. It's all under control and you don't want to get caught up in it. Believe me, it's a friend you're talking to. Drop the whole thing. Forget about it. I imagine you've got enough on your plate.'

'And if I don't drop it?'

'There'll be repercussions, old boy,' sighed Grierson. 'Who needs repercussions?'

'I'm not sure I shouldn't take this to the Bar Council,' said Daventry. 'Right to the top.'

Grierson nodded. 'You can, Gerry. But I wouldn't.'

'Repercussions?'

'Precisely.'

'You've been watching me, haven't you. Shadowing me? Even that cab . . . wasn't a cab. Things could happen, is that what you're telling me?'

'Don't know what you're on about,' said Grierson. 'But I think we understand each other. And we've never been stupid, have we? Of course not .'

Daventry was white faced when he rode down in the lift accompanied by one of the men in drab suits. Outside the house, in the mews, another taxi was waiting.

'Anywhere you like, guv,' said the driver cheerfully. 'It's on the firm.'

And Daventry knew that there was only one way out.

LONDON

Clutching a bouquet of flowers a blushing schoolgirl had thrust into his arms, Yuri Gagarin waved to the crowd in Earl's Court Road, smiling his boyish smile.

'Tovarish!' shouted an unlikely, elderly lady, her eyes shining.

They were actually cheering him and Ivanov, standing inconspicuously in the crowd with Deriabin, could not help smiling too.

It was a master stroke, he felt, sending Gagarin over to London, driving him around like a movie star, parading him at receptions. If the Queen walked down the street, she couldn't draw bigger crowds.

'A few Gagarins and the embassy could pack up,' he observed. 'They would conquer this island all by themselves.'

Deriabin grunted. He wondered how the crowd would feel if they knew that ten days previously Nikita Khruschchev had informed the British ambassador in Moscow that it would only take eight nuclear bombs to wipe Britain off the face of the earth.

'Let's walk back,' he said.

'No, I'm enjoying this,' said Ivanov.

'You'd think it was the British who'd sent up Sputnik,' remarked Deriabin, a little sourly.

'Absolutely,' nodded Ivanov cheerfully. 'They have the most amazing knack for self delusion. I find it very useful.'

He slapped Deriabin on the back.

'Cheer up, my friend, let us enjoy the luxury of being popular. It makes our lives that much easier.'

But Deriabin looked sour. Typical GRU, thought Ivanov. Boring. Musty, like those plushy Victorian rooms at the embassy in Kensington Palace Gardens.

A roar went up as Gagarin bent down and kissed a pretty little blonde chastely on the cheek, as befitted a Red Air Force officer.

'The man's a born showman,' stated Ivanov, nodding approvingly.

They were cashing in on it too, and Ivanov had played no small part in setting up the hectic agenda for the Gagarin circus. A reception by Prime Minister Harold Macmillan, a lunch with Queen Elizabeth at Buckingham Palace, plenty of patting little children on the head, and the workers hadn't been forgotten. The Gagarin smile had been precisely programmed.

'Incidentally,' said Deriabin unexpectedly, 'congratulations.'

Ivanov glanced at him startled.

'I have heard from the Director,' continued Deriabin. 'Central is very pleased indeed with your snapshots.'

That was the Holy Loch roll of film he had passed on to Grigorovich.

'Thank you,' said Ivanov, surprised. It was most unusual for Deriabin, the taciturn, humourless GRU colonel, to even mention covert activities outside the sanctum of the referentura, even obliquely. It was high praise.

Standing twenty feet away, behind a fat woman with a pram, Unterberg wished he could lip read. It was unusual to see Ivanov and Deriabin together, strolling in the sunshine.

'How's your social life these days?' asked Deriabin as they started to move away.

'She is well,' replied Ivanov and smiled.

Rippon's manner was sharp and to the point.

'I want your man to do a little job for me,' he said highhandedly. 'It's an abortionist, and I'd like him to put on a good show at her committal. Try and knock it out there and then.'

Pettifer blinked in disbelief and held the phone away from his ear momentarily, as if he couldn't believe what he was hearing. The puffed-up presumption of the man, demanding Daventry's services as if his master were an office boy at Rippon's beck and call.

'It's not really our kind of case,' replied Pettifer frostily. He also felt like adding, not their kind of money. It simply wasn't worth Daventry's while to drag himself to some suburban magistrates court to represent some back alley abortionist.

'Oh, I'm sure it can be arranged,' said Rippon. 'Tell the old man it's a favour for me.'

It was incredible. Pettifer couldn't understand what had happened. Usually, Rippon fawned and scraped to secure Daventry for one of his dubious clients, pleading with Pettifer, oozing obsequiousness. And suddenly, here he was, loftily commanding his presence, and most amazing of all, calling his master 'old man'.

'Look here,' said Pettifer firmly. 'Mr Daventry is not available.' The man really had to be put in his place. 'I couldn't possibly ask him.'

Normally, Rippon would immediately have cringed. But not this time.

'Don't give me that, Petti,' argued Rippon. Pettifer gasped: no one dared call him 'Petti'. 'Just ask Daventry. Tell him who it is. I think you'll find he'll want to oblige.'

And he put the phone down.

Pettifer took a little time to recover his equilibrium. Rippon, he finally decided, was suffering from delusions of grandeur. And, as far as Pettifer was concerned, he had accepted the last brief from the man. True, he had been a steady, lucrative source of income, but this was too high a price to pay. Plenty of other solicitors wanted Daventry for their clients. They didn't need this stuck-up jackanapes.

Pettifer knocked on Daventry's door.

'May I see you for a moment, sir?' he enquired, with his usual diffidence.

'What is it?' asked Daventry.

Pettifer had noticed that these last few days he seemed to have been under a great strain. Too well mannered to take it out on his clerk, Daventry had nonetheless been irritable, anxious.

'Sorry to bother you,' began Pettifer, 'but I think we must do something about Mr Rippon.'

Daventry's eyes narrowed.

'The man's become quite insufferable,' went on Pettifer and Daventry was startled to hear him refer to a solicitor in such terms. 'I have just had him on the phone, wanting you for a case. But instead of offering the brief, he practically demanded that you take it. Quite an unsuitable brief, I fear, but he virtually ordered you to take it.'

'What did you say?' asked Daventry. He had taken off his reading glasses and was playing with them abstractedly.

'Well, sir,' said Pettifer, bristling, 'he was quite improper. He had the temerity to suggest that when I told you it came from him, you'd want to "oblige" him. Those were his actual words, sir. "Oblige him".'

'I see,' said Daventry.

'I don't think we can have a relationship with him on that basis, do you sir? The man sounded as if you were under some sort of . . . ' Pettifer searched for the word ' . . . some sort of obligation to him. Utterly absurd and improper.'

Daventry pushed the spectacles aside. 'Maybe I am,' he said quietly.

Pettifer stood dumbfounded. Nothing seemed to be right today. Now he wasn't even hearing properly.

'I think it's possible Mr Rippon believes he could make trouble for me,' explained Daventry.

'How?' gasped Pettifer, when he'd found his voice.

'I . . . Never mind, it doesn't matter.'

'One of our cases, sir?' ventured Pettifer, still white with shock.

'Not really,' said Daventry, a little awkwardly. 'Nothing in these chambers. At least, no brief you obtained for me. Don't worry about it.'

'Perhaps you'd better tell me,' suggested Pettifer softly. 'In case I could . . .'

'No,' smiled Daventry appreciatively. Pettifer's loyalty was sterling. 'It doesn't involve you. I made the mistake of thinking Mr Rippon could be used to formalise a little, er, informality. Don't worry about it,' he repeated. 'I'm going to talk to him personally. I don't think he will presume on us again . . .'

'Can he make trouble?' asked Pettifer. What he meant was have you offended the rules of the profession? Can he report you to the Bar Council?

'I don't think he will,' replied Daventry, grimly.

Pettifer was still anxious.

'What will you tell him?'

'To go to hell,' said Daventry.

Pettifer took courage.

'Is it the business of the American court martial?' he asked.

For a moment, Daventry was going to demand him to tell him what he knew. But Pettifer interrupted him:

'Perhaps you should take advice, sir?'

Even in his depressed mood, it struck Daventry as comic, his clerk advising him to consult a lawyer. He wondered which silk Pettifer had in mind to enter the lists on his behalf.

'No, I don't think that'll be necessary,' he smiled. 'I believe I know how to deal with it.'

In his mind he had already made his decision, and Pettifer left the room, wondering rather uneasily, why Daventry looked so grave.

Dawkins waited until McDuff, the news editor, was off the phone.

'I think I'll go up to Laconbury,' he announced.

'What for?' asked McDuff irritably. The Sophia Loren exclusive had fallen through, so had a non-story of newly divorced Vivien Leigh and Laurence Olivier getting reconciled, and all together the schedule looked a mess.

'The Yank who's committed adultery, remember?' Dawkins reminded him, and added, for good measure, 'the story I brought in.'

'Oh,' said McDuff. '*That*.' His tone was not encouraging.

'I'm having problems with it,' said Dawkins. 'I tried the American Air Force, and no joy.'

'You mean, they deny it?'

'No,' said Dawkins. 'I tried Ruislip five times, and nobody knows anything, I tried the base, and they say only Ruislip can talk. I tried the American Embassy and they say only the Air Force can talk, and the Ministry of Defence says it's nothing to do with them, it's an American Air Force matter.'

'That's all you got?' asked McDuff ominously. He loathed reporters who detailed at length how and why they couldn't get a story.

'Let me try the base,' suggested Dawkins again.

'What the hell will that do?' demanded McDuff. 'You won't even get on it. You know what these bloody American bases are like.'

'I got contacts,' urged Dawkins, slightly desperately. He really did want the story, and a trip to Laconbury would do wonders for that week's expense sheet.

'Balls,' said McDuff, unfeelingly.

It was turning out tougher than Dawkins had anticipated.

'It's a good yarn, Mac,' he argued. 'Adultery with an English girl. She might be a looker. Come on, it's worth a try.'

'No,' said McDuff.

Dawkins couldn't understand it.

'Why not?' he asked. 'I've got nothing else on. We've got it exclusive. It'll make a good front page.'

'Sorry,' said McDuff, and reached for a pile of wire service copy the boy had just dumped on his desk.

'Oh for Chrissake,' said Dawkins. 'I got this hot tip straight from the horse's mouth. Why the hell not?'

'This is why,' said McDuff, and unlocked a drawer in his desk. He took out a thin folder, and extricated a sheet of paper. 'D-notice. Here.'

The paper was headed 'Private and Confidential', and it instructed all media that the 'forthcoming court martial of a USAF officer at RAF Laconbury is not to be publicised in the national interest as the case involved the security of the United Kingdom and its allies.'

Dawkins read it twice. Then he said:

'Ignore it.'

'I don't propose to go to jail. Neither does the editor. Read the whole thing. They've invoked the Official Secrets Act.'

'But it's only a fucking adultery case,' protested Dawkins.

'I don't know what it is,' said McDuff, 'but we've been having enough bloody trouble with security and it's simply not worth it to stick out our necks for this one. We've also had some unofficial guidance on it,' he added, lowering his voice.

'Guidance?'

'MOD have dropped the hint that any pre-trial story could be interpreted as contempt of court since the court martial will be held on UK soil, and that the case itself will be heard in camera, so there's nothing we could report anyway.'

'Christ,' said Dawkins. 'And you're just going to play along?'

McDuff looked at his notepad.

'I want you to nip along to the Windmill,' he said. 'They got a new stripper there, and we've had a tip that she's the daughter of the Bishop of Wallasey.' His craggy face split into what he considered to be a jovial smile. 'Take one of the photo boys. Maybe she wears a dog collar instead of a G-string.'

'But what about Laconbury?'

'Forget it,' said McDuff. 'It's dead. I've just killed it '

Wednesday, July 19, 1961 – LONDON

'Glad to meet you, counsellor,' said Verago.

'Do come in,' invited Daventry, holding open the door to his office.

Pettifer stood, poker faced, his disapproval under tight control. This American had been badgering him for days and then arrived, unannounced, at the chambers. When he was firmly told Daventry was out at lunch, he had simply declared that he'd wait.

'I'm sure Mr Daventry will want to see me,' he'd said, and that aggravated Pettifer even more. 'And I intend to see him.'

'Could you tell me your business, sir?'

'I'm defence counsel in the Tower case,' explained Verago, and Pettifer bristled. He was praying for the day he'd hear the last of that American court martial.

'Sit down,' said Daventry.

'I apologise for not making an appointment, counsellor,' said Verago. 'But I have tried and since I'm not based in London...'

Daventry looked at the card in his hand.

' "Captain Anthony C. Verago, Staff Judge Advocate's Corps, United States Army". You're a legal officer, I take it?'

Daventry's tone was somewhat sceptical.

'Yes sir,' replied Verago. 'At least, I passed law school.'

He was hot, and Daventry looked remarkably cool and relaxed. He was out of his element, whereas Daventry was very much at home in these musty, funereal chambers with the antiquated furniture and dusty law books. There were piles of old briefs lying around, neatly tied with red tape and a couple of faded prints on the wall of legal luminaries, long since dead.

'You see, counsellor . . . ' began Verago, but Daventry

interrupted him.

'We are not counsellors in this country, we are simply barristers,' he said gently, like an understanding teacher correcting a not very bright student. 'I am plain "mister".'

'I'm sorry. I don't know much about English lawyers,' said Verago, nettled at himself for apologising to this cold eel of a man sitting opposite him.

'We're quite human, I assure you,' smiled Daventry rather drily.

Verago's tweed jacket and slacks contrasted sharply with Daventry's dark, formal suit. Daventry couldn't recall when somebody in a sports jacket had last entered his chambers. And a lawyer at that.

Verago took the bit between his teeth.

'You know of course about this court martial at Laconbury, Mr Daventry, and I think you'll agree it's in our mutual interest to get together. We're absolutely on the same side.'

'Is that so?'

'Sure. After all, I want to get my man off as lightly as I can and I'm sure you want to do the same for your girl.'

'My girl?' Daventry appeared totally detached.

'Miss Howard tells me you're representing her. I've been to see her and . . . '

'I'm afraid, Captain Verago, you have been misinformed,' said Daventry.

Verago sat very still.

'Pardon me?'

'I have decided it would be best if Miss Howard had other representation, if she needs any at all,' said Daventry precisely.

'You mean you're off the case?' gasped Verago.

'Yes.'

'Does Miss Howard know that? She told me . . . '

'I will be telling her,' stated Daventry, glancing away. He wished this damn man didn't look so accusingly at him. 'It is unfortunate that you went to see the lady without speaking to me first. I could have put you in the picture. I am convinced that my decision is in no way detrimental to the interests of Miss Howard.'

'Okay,' Verago nodded. 'But I have a question?'

Daventry raised his eyebrows. 'Yes?'

'Why?'

'I don't follow you, Captain Verago.'

'What's the story? Why are you quitting? Is it something to do with the case? Have you found out something I should know? Hell, I'm defending this guy, and now his girl friend's lawyer pulls out. I think I'm entitled to know the reason.'

He didn't like Daventry's thin smile. Even less his answer.

'I don't need to give any explanation,' said Daventry, his voice hard. 'Nevertheless, I will assure you that it has nothing to do with your client.'

Verago looked him straight in the eyes.

'Have you been pressurised, Mr Daventry? Has somebody been getting at you?'

'That, sir, is a highly improper question,' responded Daventry.

Verago stood up.

'Listen, counsellor or whatever you call yourself, when people tell me I'm being improper, I know I'm on the right track. And when lawyers tell me that, I know I've struck pay dirt. Come on, let's show 'em. Let's get together. Let's you and me compare notes, and see what we're up against . . .'

Daventry also rose.

'There are no notes to compare,' he said. 'Miss Howard asked me to get the witness summons set aside. I tried and I failed. There's nothing more I can do. I'm sure that when it comes to the trial, you will be in a much better position to protect her rights than I would be.'

'That might get awkward.'

'In what way?'

'Because I'm not sure that she's the innocent party in this.'

Daventry straightened his waistcoat. 'That's for you to decide.'

'So, you're washing your hands of the whole thing.'

'I'm sorry . . .'

Verago grunted.

'Can I get you a cup of tea . . . Or perhaps coffee? Instant,

I'm afraid,' offered Daventry.

'I got to get going,' said Verago.

Daventry opened the door for him.

'If there's anything else I can do for you, of course . .'

'I think you've done enough, counsellor,' replied Verago, his eyes glinting. 'I guess you've got your own priorities. I hope they pay you well.'

After he'd left, Daventry sat at his desk, staring straight ahead. He would have given a lot to avoid that encounter.

And now he felt, as that American would probably have put it, a complete heel.

Thursday, July 20, 1961 – SEREBRYANY BOR

The stocky, squat man with the piercing blue eyes studied his appearance in the long mirror.

Ivan Koniev, Marshal of the Soviet Union, was wearing his gold-braided walking-out uniform for the first time in twelve months. It felt good to be back in harness.

He surveyed himself as critically as if he was a new recruit about to go on parade, and he was satisfied.

Both sides of his chest were covered with all his decorations. He had special affection for one of them, the American Legion of Merit, presented to him in the war by Omar Bradley. Not many Red Army Marshals could boast of having been decorated by the United States. He still warmly remembered the day he had received the medal; what had made it so memorable was that he had also acquired Bradley's jeep, in exchange for his white charger.

But of all his medals and decorations, the one closest to his heart was the simple one with the black and yellow ribbon which millions of veterans wore: the one that commemorated Victory over Germany.

Sergeant Vasilly, his batman, came up with the clothes brush, and whisked some invisible speck off the marshal's sleeve. Vasilly had been brushing invisible specks off Koniev's uniform for twenty years, through many campaigns and on many battlefields.

'Will I pass?' asked Koniev jovially.

'Of course, Comrade Marshal,' replied Vasilly proudly, still examining his master from the top of his round, Ukrainian peasant head to the tip of his brilliantly polished shoes. 'As always.'

Koniev nodded. It was important that he should look right. Outside his dacha, the black staff car with the big red ensign was already waiting to take him to Moscow, and his meeting with Nikita Khrushchev at the Kremlin. There he would be told what it was all about.

Koniev had handed over his command in June 1960, and for the past thirteen months had lived a life of leisure. Of course a Marshal of the Soviet Union never retired, and he was only sixty-two, but it had looked like the end of his military life.

Now they needed him. Urgently. Something was about to happen and Koniev, the former Commander in Chief of the Warsaw Treaty Forces, was the only man to handle it.

'Does the Marshal have any idea where we might be going?' enquired Vasilly, delicately.

'Bored, are you, old soldier?' asked Koniev.

'Rural life can be dull,' said Vasilly. On his chest too there were campaign decorations. Only three rows of medal ribbons, but they told enough.

'We will soon know,' said Koniev. 'Do you wish to come with me?'

Vasilly looked stricken at the very question.

'The Marshal knows . . . ' he stuttered.

'Very well,' said Koniev. 'I merely wondered how your wife would feel. You are officially retired.'

Vasilly stroked his flowing moustache.

'As long as the Marshal is in uniform . . . ' he began.

Koniev clicked his fingers.

'Cap.'

Vasily handed him his peaked cap with the gold cockade of oak leaves.

'Gloves.'

Vasily passed them over. This was better. This was like old times.

'I imagine I won't be in Moscow very long,' said Koniev. 'You will be hearing.'

Vasily came to attention.

'At your service, Comrade Marshal.'

A warrant officer was standing ready by the staff car, and as soon as Koniev came out, he saluted and opened the car door.

A warrant officer for a driver, thought Koniev, the trappings of a Commander in Chief.

He got into the car and settled back. He noticed it was equipped with a two-way radio telephone. Yes, he was back on active service alright.

DARMSTADT

Pryor's reception in Darmstadt was as cool as the telex message ordering him over from London.

'Here comes the bad boy,' said Haynes, on the copy desk when he entered the *Stars and Stripes* newsroom. Haynes had never liked Pryor, and his glee was undisguised.

Barnhart, the red-haired photographer, who had often worked on assignments with him, seemed anxious not to catch his eye.

And the rest of the crew sat at their desks, apparently engrossed in the wire service copy they were editing. The prodigal son wasn't coming home.

'Where's the old man?' asked Pryor.

'In his office, and can't wait to see you,' said Haynes, his bad teeth showing.

As usual, there was a lot of noise, teleprinters chattering, phones ringing, typewriters being thumped by two finger non typists, but Pryor knew that, as he walked across to the colonel's inner sanctum, behind his back every eye was following him.

Colonel Steinmetz, *Stripes'* editor, regarded him gloomily.

'Close the door, Joe,' he said, and started filling his pipe. It was a well known signal. When Steinmetz didn't quite know how to handle something, he gave himself breathing space by ramming tobacco into the bowl of his pipe.

'Sit down,' invited the colonel. He wasn't alone. A big, burly man sat in the other visitor's chair.

'This is Mr Unterberg,' said the colonel, and puffed his unlit pipe.

'Unterberg gave Pryor a friendly nod.

'Hi,' he said, but the colonel made no attempt to explain who he was, or the reason for his presence.

'If you're busy, I'll come back,' said Pryor.

'No need,' said the colonel. 'As a matter of fact, we were just talking about you.'

There was a knock on the door, and one of the rewrite men stuck his head in.

'Not now,' snapped the colonel. 'I'm tied up for five minutes.'

So, thought Pryor. Five minutes. That's all they have allocated.

'I don't know what I'm supposed to be doing here,' said Pryor. 'The TWX just said come quickly, most urgent.'

'Yes,' said Steinmetz. 'I wanted to see you . . .'

He struck a match, and lit the pipe. The smoke swirled in front of his face, and that seemed to fortify his courage.

'You're being reassigned, Joe.'

'When?'

'As of now.'

Unterberg was studying the big map on the wall. It showed the circulation area of *Stripes'* European editions, from Norway to Turkey.

'My UK tour isn't over yet,' said Pryor. 'I got another eighteen months. I'm not due to leave until December 1962, and anyway, I thought I'd ask for an extension. I like the London bureau.'

'Well,' said the colonel, a little awkwardly, 'we're making some changes.'

Pryor crossed his long legs. As soon as he had received the telex, he knew this was coming. That didn't make it any more pleasant.

'What's my new assignment?' he enquired, warily.

The colonel blew out more smoke.

'Wheelus,' he said.

'Libya?' gasped Pryor. 'Jesus Christ. Permanently?'

'You're taking over the bureau,' said the colonel. 'It'll be a challenge.'

'What bureau?' demanded Pryor. 'Flies and desert and camels.'

'Wheelus is a very important SAC installation,' said the colonel earnestly. 'It's a key base. We need a good man there.'

'The climate is very good,' interjected Unterberg mildly. 'Much better than England. No rain. No fog. More like California.'

Pryor ignored him. 'I don't w nt to go, Colonel,' he said. 'I'm sorry. I like it where I am. Wheelus is an asshole. You might as well send me to Iceland. It's a dead end. I don't even see why we need a man there.'

The colonel puffed his pipe.

'Well,' he said at last, 'that's the way it is, Joe.'

'Why?' asked Pryor. 'Why does my UK tour get cut short, and you want me in the boondocks? Why, all of a sudden?'

Steinmetz took his pipe out of his mouth.

'I'm running a newspaper, Joe,' he said, as if he was editor in chief of *The New York Times*. 'I'm giving the military a service. I have to make these decisions. In the military, we go where we are ordered.'

'I'm a civilian,' said Pryor mutinously.

'You're an employee of the Department of the Army, Mr

231

Pryor,' said the colonel. 'That makes you part of the military.'

I can quit of course, thought Pryor. I can throw up the tax privileges, my PX card, the free travel, and the security, and start tramping around small-town newspapers in godforsaken places, trying to get a job . . .

'I've been offered a job on the Rome *Daily American*,' announced Pryor.

'Then why don't you take it, Mr Pryor?' suggested Unterberg.

Pryor rounded on him. 'What the hell's it got to do with you?' He turned to the colonel. 'Who's this guy anyway? Why is he sitting in on this?'

But Steinmetz ignored his question.

'I suggest you take the assignment, Joe,' he urged. 'Don't sacrifice all you've worked for. We got a good life on *Stripes*. Security, pension, travel, we see the world, we bring a touch of home to our boys. It's worth something.'

Pryor's rebellion, which had begun so recently, started to fizzle out, and he knew he would hate himself later. There was just one final glimmer.

'I still want to know why?' he asked. 'You don't reassign guys like this. At twenty-four hours notice. Jesus, I've got a lease in London – '

'We'll take care of that,' said the colonel.

' – and I want to know why I'm going to get buried. London's a choice assignment. Haven't I done good work?'

'You have, Joe,' said the colonel sincerely. 'But you need a change.'

'Why?' repeated Pryor.

Then he noticed Unterberg looking at him, and he knew everything.

That drink with Dawkins in the Fleet Street pub had been a very expensive one.

'I don't think, I honestly don't think I can be much more use to you anyway. The defending officer is well able to take care of things. You've met him already, haven't you? Captain Verago?'

'Yes,' said Serena dully.

Daventry had asked her round to his chambers to break the news. He had rehearsed what he was going to say like an actor making sure of his lines.

She was being quite stoic about it, she didn't even seem surprised.

'And I don't believe it would help to have an English barrister at an American court martial. They might not take kindly to it, and that wouldn't help you either.'

'Please,' she said, 'you don't need to explain. I'm very grateful for all the trouble you've already taken.'

She gave him an empty smile and started to gather her handbag together.

Daventry hoped his nagging feeling of guilt didn't show. He had considered telling her his reasons. About the pressures, and the hints, and the warnings. That he couldn't be a martyr for a cause that wasn't even his. That he had too much to lose, that he was on the threshold of becoming part of the legal establishment and that he couldn't afford, by this one ridiculous involvement, to throw it all away.

But, on reflection, he had said none of it.

'If you like, I can still give you the name of a couple of solicitors . . . to hold your hand,' went on Daventry. 'If you pick one, I can have a word with him. It'll be no problem.'

'No thank you,' said Serena. 'Well, I don't suppose there's anything else we need discuss?' she added coolly.

Daventry got up and escorted her towards the door.

'You will go next week?'

'You mean, will I be a good girl, and report as ordered to the court martial?'

'You mustn't ignore the subpoena,' said Daventry, a little

awkwardly. 'Don't put yourself in contempt.'

'I'll see,' she said, her hand on the door handle. 'But in any case,' she continued, a thin smile on her lips, 'I won't be causing you any more problems, Mr Daventry.'

Then she walked out of his office, closing the door behind her.

Daventry felt as if she had slapped his face.

Friday, July 21, 1961 – KARLSRUHE

Herr Stamm was looking for something, there was no doubt about that, decided Fraulein Scholtz. The question was what he was after, and why he wouldn't tell her.

The new boss played his cards close to his chest, as she'd discovered soon after he'd taken over. She often found him in his office before she arrived, at eight in the morning, and he was frequently still working when she left in the evening.

And he asked for all sorts of files and dossiers, and sometimes even went into the archives and the general registry office to look for them himself.

Fraulein Scholtz had the clearance to take them back after he had finished with them, but Herr Stamm always returned them personally. It was almost as if he didn't want her to know what he had been looking at.

At first, she had been highly offended. She wondered if he didn't trust her. After Herr Unruh's unfortunate demise, a cloud had hung over B1, and everyone in the department felt slightly uneasy. But after she got to know Herr Stamm a little better, she sensed he wasn't really suspicious about her; it was more that he liked to keep his thoughts and his activities as secret as possible – even from his own confidential secretary.

Then a curious thing happened. Herr Stamm came into

her room.

'Tell me,' he said, 'do we have anything else about Martin Schneider?'

'Martin Schneider?' she repeated, puzzled. She prided herself on having an index-file mind, with instant recall, but momentarily she drew a blank.

'The man who was shot. He had come across from East Berlin. The double agent. Herr Pech was the field officer.'

'Ah,' said Fraulein Scholtz remembering now. 'We have the case file downstairs.'

'I have seen it.' Herr Stamm didn't seem impressed. 'That is why I asked, do you know if there is anything else?'

'Whatever we have will be correctly filed and in his dossier,' pointed out Fraulein Scholtz primly.

'I see.'

'Would you like me to ask Herr Pech if . . . '

'No thank you,' replied Herr Stamm, somewhat hastily, she thought. 'That won't be necessary.'

'Is there anything specific you are looking for?' she asked.

'No, it's alright. By the way, when Dr Berger arrives, please show him straight in.'

And he returned to his office.

In all the years Fraulein Scholtz had worked in B1, faithfully serving the various department heads, she had never been kept in the dark like this. Dr Berger for instance. Who was he?

Herr Stamm had made the appointment privately. Then he had simply entered it in the diary without explanation. It was very galling, not to be taken into his confidence.

Actually, there was nothing mysterious about Dr Berger. He was a scientist from the Bundeskriminalamt in Wiesbaden, where he was the head of the federal crime lab. Herr Stamm didn't particularly want to advertise that he had asked for his services.

'Well?' asked Herr Stamm when his visitor had settled in the chair under the Adenauer portrait.

Dr Berger brought a thin file out of his case.

'It's all in here,' he said.

'Perhaps you could explain it to me in layman's language,

said Herr Stamm. 'I am not very scientifically minded, I regret to say.'

'It is quite simple,' began Dr Berger. 'The man Martin Schneider was killed by a bullet from a PI 9mm pistol. Fired at reasonably close range.'

'And . . .'

'Your predecessor, Herr Unruh, was also killed by a P1 9mm. Fired from close range.'

'Ah.'

'I gather that an attempt was made to convey the impression that Herr Unruh had shot himself, but subsequent investigation showed he had actually been murdered.'

'Something like that,' murmured Herr Stamm.

'We tested the gun that was found in his hand. It was a useful exercise.'

'That's why I brought you into it, Dr Berger,' said Herr Stamm. 'I thought it might prove interesting.'

'Here,' said Dr Berger and put a photograph in front of him. 'Bullet A killed Martin Schneider, Bullet B killed Herr Unruh. Both are 9mm calibre.'

'And both were fired from the same gun?'

'Exactly,' said Dr Berger and for the first time he smiled. 'A completely positive test.'

'So if, for argument's sake, it was Herr Unruh's gun, it would suggest that he killed Schneider and that he then shot himself with it later? But if in fact he was murdered, it merely suggests that the murderer killed first Schneider, and then Herr Unruh with the same weapon?'

'It would seem so, would it not?'

'Hmm,' mused Herr Stamm.

'I have one question,' said Dr Berger. 'As we have the pistol in our possession, you can surely trace if it was Herr Unruh's own gun?'

'My dear doctor,' said Herr Stamm, a little patronisingly, 'people in our department don't necessarily register their guns. Sometimes it is best not to be too official about such things . . . Let us simply say, B1 has weapons available.'

'Well, that's as far as I can help you,' announced Dr Berger.

'I'd like to get back as soon as it's convenient . . . '

'Of course.' He buzzed Fraulein Scholtz. 'Get Dr Berger transportation please. To Wiesbaden.'

'Yes sir,' said Fraulein Scholtz, and slammed down the receiver.

In Stamm's office, Dr Berger snapped shut his briefcase.

'It's none of my business,' he said chattily, 'but it sounds intriguing. This . . . Martin Schneider and Herr Unruh. Didn't I hear somewhere that Schneider was a double agent, an Ulbricht man? Working with an American contact in Berlin?'

Herr Stamm was most courteous.

'You're absolutely right, doctor,' he said politely, 'it isn't actually any of your business.'

LONDON

Verago cashed a cheque at the Columbia Club, and as he passed the reception desk, he saw his name chalked on the message board.

'I'm Captain Verago,' he told the girl.

She gave him a sealed envelope. Inside was a short note:

'Let's meet for a drink. Grosvenor House, today, 6 p.m.'

It was signed 'Dean Apollo'.

He had wondered when he would meet the prosecutor, but this was not the way he had imagined it. He read the note again. Lieutenant Colonel Apollo certainly seemed to know his movements. He was evidently aware Verago was in London, that he might stop by the Columbia Club, that he would be free at 6 p.m.

Verago went back to the desk.

'Do you have a Lieutenant-Colonel Apollo staying here?' he asked.

The girl checked her list, then shook her head.

'Is he due?' she enquired.

'I don't know,' said Verago, and left her puzzled.

It was now 5.30. The note had been finely timed. If he hadn't shown up, he wouldn't have got it in time. The man took a lot for granted.

When he entered the lobby of Grosvenor House, Verago looked round the lounge. He could see no Air Force Officer. He checked his watch, two minutes past six.

A man in an armchair by the window got up. He wore a blue blazer and a sports shirt. He came towards Verago, holding out his hand. He was smiling, not only with his mouth, but his eyes too.

'Tony Verago, glad to meet you,' he announced without hesitation.

Verago shook his hand. The man's grip was firm.

'Colonel Apollo?' he said, intrigued that this man knew him on sight, despite Verago not wearing uniform and them never having met before.

'Cut the colonel crap, Tony,' said Apollo.

'Sir?'

'I said forget the rank bullshit. We're not in court. We're just two lawyers who want to get to know each other. So come and sit down and have a drink with me.'

He guided Verago to the armchair next to his.

'What's it going to be?'

'Scotch and soda,' said Verago.

Apollo gave the order while Verago sat back, studying him. He was youngish for a non-rated light colonel, prematurely grey. He was sun-tanned, and Verago wondered how he managed that in England. His eyes were intense, penetrating.

'I hear you've been making yourself very unpopular,' remarked Apollo.

'I have?'

'You know it.' He gave Verago a hard look. 'Don't you care about your career? Your commission?'

So that's it, thought Verago. The fatherly talk would be upcoming. Shades of Colonel Ochs and the rest of the bunch.

'What career?' asked Verago, offering Apollo a cigarette.

He shook his head.

'Let's see. You've had thirty-eight general courts, and about a hundred specials during your tour in Germany, mostly defending. You lost the majority of them.'

'But I won a few,' Verago reminded him, snapping shut his lighter.

'Sure: you haven't done badly,' agreed Apollo. 'Considering that ninety per cent of all military trials result in guilty findings, you scored a few points.'

The drinks arrived.

'Put them on my room,' Apollo told the waiter. 'I'm staying here,' he explained to Verago. 'Places like the Columbia Club suffocate me. You can't spit without hitting brass. I can take so much, but I like my own fresh air, even if it costs me.'

'It's okay if you can afford it,' remarked Verago.

'Let's talk about Tuesday. Do you think you're going to score any points?'

'I don't think we should . . .'

'Why are you doing it?' Apollo interrupted. 'Why are you sticking your neck out?'

'I look on it as doing my job.'

'Don't we all,' sighed Apollo. He looked Verago straight in the eye. 'I have a feeling, Tony, that you're a man after my own heart.'

Here comes another ploy, thought Verago. The 'we're all boys together' routine.

'Colonel,' began Verago. 'Please save your time. I know the song sheet by heart.'

For a moment Apollo regarded him stonily. Then he grinned, and the grin turned into laughter.

'I didn't know guys like you still existed,' he chuckled. 'You restore my faith, Tony. After all the time servers and all the survivors who keep this military justice machine creaking, you're like a shot in the arm. There's hope for us yet.'

Then the bonhomie faded.

'Pity we're on opposite sides on this one. I wish you had something to get your teeth into . . .'

'Maybe I have.'

'No,' said Apollo. 'I know what you're thinking, and I'm telling you it's got nothing to do with it. The only question is whether the man is guilty of the charge and specification. Anything else is irrelevant, immaterial and inadmissible. And you know it.'

'We'll see,' said Verago.

'By the way . . .'

'Yes?'

'Have you ever considered you may be on the wrong side?'

'How's that?' asked Verago, warily.

'That the baddies might be the goodies?'

'You know,' Verago said thoughtfully, 'somebody else said that to me.'

'Maybe he was right too,' Apollo shrugged. 'Maybe there are a few, a very, very few occasions when the end does justify the means. Just thought I'd mention it.'

'You're quoting Karl Marx.'

'I'd quote the devil if the point he made was applicable,' snapped Apollo. Then he smiled at Verago.

'Tony, let's get drunk tonight. Let's go, you and me, and tie a large number on. Somewhere disreputable, where no officers and gentlemen should be seen dead. What do you say?'

Verago was tempted, very tempted.

'I'll have to take a raincheck,' he said instead. 'I can't tonight. But any other time . . .'

'Sure I understand,' nodded Apollo. 'Have a good time and enjoy it. Whatever they'd like to do with you, they can't charge you with adultery.'

Verago did not smile.

'Why did you want to see me?'

'To save us all time.' Apollo paused. 'Your case has fallen apart. You hoped your client's estrangement could be the big get out. Mitigation for having an affair. Well, she's dead and that puts the skids under you. Frankly, her suicide will alienate the whole court. So what have you got left? You know the answer. A big, fat nothing.'

'You're telling me to stop fighting City Hall, are you?'

'Well, what other choice have you got?'

Verago stood up.

'Thanks for the drink,' he said. 'See you in court.'

'You bet.'

He sat and watched Verago cross the lobby and leave the hotel. He seemed amused.

Outside, in Park Lane, Verago felt irritated.

The trouble was the man had hit it on the head. And he knew it.

LONDON

Laurie was high. He hadn't seen her like this before. They had got drunk together, they had shared hangovers, but this was different. It wasn't alcohol. Her eyes were bright, her lipstick a little smudged, her voice a shade too loud. Her blouse had four buttons, and three of them were undone. He had seen her naked, but found this half glimpse of the cleavage of her breasts tantalising, disconcertingly erotic.

'You want to do something tonight?' Verago asked, trying to gauge her mood.

'Like what?' she asked, her eyes almost flashing. It came like a challenge. What can you come up with? The thought seemed to amuse her. 'I can guess what you want to do.'

'I'd like to have dinner,' said Verago. 'Let's go eat.'

'How romantic,' mocked Laurie. 'You really know how to sweep a girl off her feet. "I'd like dinner, let's go eat". How could I resist such a tempting invitation?'

'What's the matter, Laurie?' he asked her quietly.

'Nothing's the matter. What should be the matter?' She picked nervously at a loose thread in her slacks. 'I'm sorry,' she sighed. 'Perhaps we should have a little talk.'

'Talk about what?'

'Us,' she replied, not looking at him. 'What's going to happen to us?'

He took off his jacket and hung it across the back of a chair. The windows were open, but he felt hot, uncomfortable.

'Well?'

'One of the things I like about you is that you don't ask questions,' said Verago.

'You mean, I just asked one too many.'

'Maybe.'

She nodded, as if that's what she had expected.

'Would you like a drink?' she offered.

'Please.'

She got up, and poured him a scotch, dropping in the ice cubes, one by one.

'It can't go on like this, you know that?' she said, her back still to him.

'Why? Why can't it?' he asked, low.

'Because it can't,' she said swinging round. She handed him his drink.

'I don't see . . . '

'Oh, for Christ's sake, Tony, stop kidding yourself. You won't even be in England soon. It'll be finished. You'll be stuck back in Germany . . . '

'I can still get over here. Weekends. Furloughs. I can take my leave . . . '

She laughed. It was a forced, strident laugh, so unlike her.

'A forty-eight-hours screw every three months?' The tone of her voice was bitter, her eyes steely. 'If that's your idea of a relationship, you can save yourself the trouble. There must be plenty of frauleins on the spot . . . '

'You know that's not what it's about,' he interrupted.

He stood up, white faced, and went over to her. He took hold of her shoulders and his face was close to hers. Those strange eyes glittered.

'What's the matter, Laurie?' he asked again. 'You're stoned out of your mind. What's got into you?'

'Nothing,' she whispered, and there were tears in her eyes.

242

Suddenly she clung to him. 'I don't want to lose you ' she mumbled, her head against his chest. He could feel the wetness of her tears through his shirt.

'But you're not going to,' he comforted her. 'I'm sticking around, don't worry. You're not rid of me so easily, sweetheart.'

He held her close. Her body felt soft, vulnerable, defenceless.

'It's alright, Laurie,' he soothed. 'Everything's alright. We got each other, no matter what . . . '

She looked up, her face tear-streaked, and nodded.

'You got a hanky?' she asked.

He gave her his and she broke away, wiping her eyes. She caught a glimpse of herself in the mirror by the shelves.

'Jesus, I look a sight,' she muttered, and it was the Laurie he knew. She turned to him. 'I'm sorry, Tony. You must need this like a hole in the head.'

'Sit down,' he said, 'and tell me what's bothering you.'

She came over. 'I like you, Tony,' she said, resting her head on his shoulder. 'I like you lots. Trouble is, I think I need you. When you're stuck out at that damn base, when I don't see you, I miss you . . . '

'I'm sure you've got other company to pass the time,' he said, and nearly bit his tongue off for sounding so unfeeling and insensitive.

She gazed at him gravely.

'I have,' she agreed. 'But it isn't you.'

'I'm sorry,' he began. 'I didn't mean to . . . '

She took his hand. 'You know what we should do? Stop apologising to each other. The next guy who says "I'm sorry" gets ten demerits. OK?'

'OK,' concurred Verago. It had been a long time since he had been so fond of a woman. Not, an inner voice added, that you've ever known such a woman before.

'You still want to eat?' she murmured.

'It can keep,' he smiled and undid the fourth button.

They went into the bedroom and after that, when the light was out, there was very little conversation. But they didn't need words to say what they meant to each other.

Outside, in Sloane Avenue, the black Chrysler was back. The two men in it sat silently, watching the apartment block, and making a note when the light was switched off in her room.

It wasn't H-hour yet, but the count-down had begun.

Monday, July 24, 1961 – LACONBURY

'You will be gratified to know that the Senate has resolved sixty-six to nothing to ask the Air Force to confer appropriate posthumous decorations on the crewmen, and that the Secretary of the Air Force has sent condolences to their families . . . '

Brigadier-General Croxford slowly put down the letter that arrived from the Pentagon. It was the final epitaph for O for O for Oboe.

In a way, they were lucky. They were allowed some official recognition. Croxford thought of the others from the wing whose deaths remained as secret as their final missions.

If security had allowed a memorial to be put up for the lost ferrets at Laconbury, already there would be one hundred and eight names on it.

Twenty-six aircraft to date had been shot down over or near Communist territory. Men from Laconbury and sister bases had died over the Black Sea, the Baltic, Hungary, Czechoslovakia, the Adriatic, Armenia, the Ukraine, the Arctic Circle . . .

One hundred and eight of them. So far.

Croxford sighed.

For him, it was not a cold war.

And Laconbury was not at peace . . .

The general picked up another piece of paper from his desk. It was a typewritten list of names, the officers who had been selected to form next day's court martial of Captain John Tower.

He didn't envy them their job. But he knew they would fulfil their oath.

They had, after all, been very carefully picked.

Tuesday, July 25, 1961 – LACONBURY

It was the same dream again.

He was standing in the buffet of the bahnhof wearing civilian clothes with Martin Schneider who was eating a bratwurst, dripping it into the mustard on the cardboard plate.

'It's too dangerous. Don't go back,' he pleaded. 'Stay on this side.'

'You know that's not possible,' Martin replied. 'I have to be there.' He was unshaven and looked tired. 'Somebody has to keep an eye on things.'

'There are others . . . '

'Who can we trust any more?' asked Martin. He slapped him on the back. 'Come on, Johann, don't look so worried.'

'Not Johann.'

'Sorry,' apologised Martin, slightly mocking. 'I forget sometimes.'

He resented Martin's apparent carelessness and looked round cautiously. But nobody seemed to be listening and Martin was amused by his uneasiness.

'I have played the game so long now that it has become second nature,' Martin reassured him. 'But I don't take chances, I promise you. Not when it matters.'

He nodded, but without conviction. For as long as they had worked together, Martin's coolness had baffled him. It was as if, sometimes, he didn't appear to care . . .

'My friend, I intend to come out of this alive,' Martin added, almost reading his thoughts. 'When it's all over, I shall take a good long vacation.'

He finished the bratwurst.

'And never eat in railway stations again.'

'Martin,' he said.

'Yes?'

'If it gets too hot . . .'

'Don't worry, I have it engraved on my heart. I have the two phone numbers and I know the address. If I'm in trouble, I take the S-bahn into the West sector, and ten minutes later I'm safe and snug in our little hideaway.'

'Good. And don't talk to anybody, except Pech.'

Martin burped. 'Sorry, the sausage. No, of course not. You or Pech.' He paused. 'One thing. You'll look after Helga. You'll make sure she's alright?'

'You have my word.'

'You know what they'll do to her if they get hold of her?'

'Martin, I promise you. We owe it to her after all.'

'You do,' said Martin gravely. 'You do indeed.'

There was a pause, then he said: 'I may have to be out of Berlin for a little while, Martin.'

'Oh?'

'You can imagine I have many things to do.'

Martin understood. 'Of course,' he nodded. 'I wish you good luck.'

He gave a thin smile. 'Thanks, I'll need it.'

For a moment they looked at each other silently. Then he went on quietly:

'Thank you for everything. I won't forget you.' He held out his hand. 'Bon chance.'

Martin grasped his hand, and pressed it firmly.

'Auf wiedersehen. In every sense of the word.'

'I'll always have the souvenir,' he smiled, touching his scar.

Martin dug into his pocket, and came out with a lighter.

'Here, this is a better souvenir. Keep it. I'm sorry it's so cheap but it's Russian,' he said wrily. 'Anyway, it works. I must leave now. Ciao,' and he was gone.

The last he saw of Martin Schneider was his back disappearing through the swing doors of the railway buffet.

The last he saw of Martin . . .

Tower woke up with a start. He sat up in the dark. He was sweating. The replay of his last meeting with Schneider had been so vivid that for a moment he wasn't sure whether it had just happened, or was merely a dream.

The nightmare.

Tower reached for the light switch. The lamp's illumination brought him back to reality. The drab, austere quarters that had become his world. The ceiling, the walls at which he had stared so often he knew every crack, every piece of flaking paint.

His watch said 3.40 a.m.

Beside the lamp were his cigarettes and next to them the lighter. Martin Schneider's lighter. He took out a cigarette and put it in his mouth. He picked up the lighter, stared at it, then lit his cigarette with it. He held his thumb on it and gazed thoughtfully at the flame before extinguishing it. He put the lighter down.

Soon it would be morning and his court martial would begin.

He shivered. He was afraid. He was afraid of what was about to happen to him.

Suddenly he realised he had to see Verago. He had to tell him everything before the curtain went up.

LONDON

The oblong piece of paper lay on the table like an overdue bill waiting to be paid. And today the deadline for the settlement had arrived.

In a way, she was almost relieved the time had come. By the end of the day, maybe, at last, she'd be rid of the whole, ghastly ordeal.

Serena Howard absent-mindedly fingered the silver ring she

always wore. It had become a nervous habit, and now, suddenly, she was aware of it. Her mind went back to the evening John Tower had given it to her. She remembered him pulling a little box out of his pocket and saying:

'Hope you like it.'

It fitted her finger perfectly.

'You shouldn't have,' she'd said.

'I think it suits you.'

The little box the ring had come in had a jeweller's name embossed on it. 'Heinrich Mueller.' And the address: 'Reinhold strasse 73, Steglitz, Berlin.'

'Is that where you got it, Berlin?' she'd asked a little surprised.

'Yes,' he'd replied. 'Souvenir.' But that had been all.

'It's very unusual,' she'd observed, studying the curious ornamental face.

'You do like it, don't you?'

'Of course,' she'd said, and meant it. 'Thank you.'

That had been only a few months before, but now it seemed like years ago.

The ring of the door bell startled her.

When she opened the door, she was faced by a man with dark wavy hair. She knew he was American before he said a word. Everything about him confirmed it, his haircut, his tie, his shirt.

'You all set, Miss Howard?' he asked pleasantly.

She stared at him.

'I've come to fetch you,' he explained smoothly. 'It's a hell of a trek to the base, so we thought we'd lay on transportation for you. Are you ready?'

'Transportation?'

'To the trial. I got a car downstairs. We should make it in a couple of hours.'

'Who are you?' she asked at last.

'Oh, I'm sorry,' he smiled apologetically. 'I should have introduced myself. My name's Duval.'

LACONBURY

The trial wasn't due to start for two hours, but the court room was ready.

Seven vacant chairs stood behind a long, raised table, notepads neatly laid out in front of each place.

Facing them, the witness stand, the law officer's desk, the tables for the prosecutor and defence.

Verago entered the empty room and slowly walked up to the long, raised table. He stood and stared at the unoccupied chairs.

He was in his Army uniform, and for once he looked smart, the trousers pressed, shoes polished. Everything about him was crisp, except his face. He looked tired, for he had been up most of the night. He had freshly shaved, and showered, but that hadn't removed the shadows under his eyes.

He paced down the aisle of the court room, almost as if he was measuring it. Then he turned and faced the seven chairs. The unwavering eye of the cyclops emblem stared back at him from the wing coat of arms on the wall over the long table.

He walked over to the lone chair that represented the witness stand, to the right of the table, and sat on it.

Verago, always so conscious of the smell of a place, sniffed the all-pervading odour of polish. The wooden floor of the court room shone. So did the tables and the chairs.

The door of the court room opened and a staff sergeant came in, carrying a tray with four carafes of water, and some glasses. He stopped when he saw Verago on the witness chair.

'Oh, excuse me, sir,' he said.

'You go ahead, Sergeant.'

The sergeant put the carafes down on the two lawyers' tables, with the glasses.

'You're early, sir,' he remarked. 'Court isn't due to convene until 9 a.m.'

'I know,' said Verago. It was only just after seven.

'Going to be a nice day, sir,' observed the sergeant conversationally. The sun was coming in through the windows, strong and bright.

'You think so?' He screwed up his eyes. Damn it, he wished he had had more sleep. 'Sergeant, you think you could rustle up a cup of coffee? Hot. Black.'

'Sure thing,' said the sergeant, and disappeared through the swing doors.

Behind the wooden barrier, there were sixteen chairs, in two rows of four on each side of the aisle. The public section. For justice to be seen to be done. Verago wondered just who would occupy them today.

The sergeant came back with a mug of steaming coffee.

'Thanks,' said Verago gratefully, and took a much-needed drink.

The sergeant was curious. He was a clerk in the wing's legal office. He didn't often see Army lawyers.

'Is this your first Air Force trial?' he enquired.

'Could be my last too,' said Verago, with a tight little smile. He took another sip of coffee. 'You get many courts here?'

'It's a pretty gung ho outfit,' said the sergeant enigmatically.

'How about adultery? Had one of those?'

'No, sir,' said the sergeant, and for some reason he seemed to think it funny. 'How about the Army?'

Involuntarily, Verago yawned. He was paying for his sleepless night.

'I guess I'd better get on with things,' said the sergeant diplomatically. His tone indicated, man, you'd better get some shut eye before it starts. Maybe there was even a touch of contempt. Some lawyer. Can't even stay awake before the case. Glad you're not defending me, buddy.

'Carry on, Sergeant,' said Verago, and closed his eyes.

But he was not asleep when Lieutenant-Colonel Apollo quietly came in, carrying an attaché case.

'Good morning, Tony,' said Apollo cheerfully. 'Can't wait

for it to begin?'

'Just looking round, sir.'

This time Apollo did not suggest he drop the rank formalities.

Apollo put his attaché case down on the prosecution table, by the wall.

'How long are you going to keep us, counsellor?' he asked jovially. 'When will you let us get out of here?'

Verago slowly got off the witness chair. He came over.

'I've been up half the night, Colonel,' he said. 'With my client.'

'Oh yes?'

'He asked to see me at four o'clock this morning.'

'That's really tough,' said Apollo, sympathetically. 'Couldn't it wait?'

'No, it couldn't,' replied Verago, and he was very much awake. 'And that's why I want to see you, Colonel. I want you to stop this case.'

Apollo nodded, as if Verago had made a most reasonable request.

But what he said was: 'You know that's impossible.'

'And you know why I am asking,' said Verago. 'Captain Tower has told me everything.'

Apollo opened his case, and took out some law books, a pad, and a couple of exercise books. He spread them out on the table.

'Tony, all I know is that we have a man accused of a violation, and he's going to be tried for it. Anything else is irrelevant.'

'The hell it is,' said Verago.

Apollo looked at his watch.

'Guess we'll find out who's right at nine. Come and have breakfast?'

But Verago had already gone.

Lieutenant Jensen was rushing along the corridor like a man who's about to miss a train as Verago came through the swing doors.

Jensen skidded to a stop.

'There you are,' he puffed. 'Jesus, you realise what the time is?'

'Yes.'

'Well, Christ almighty, hadn't we better have a strategy session?'

'I don't see why.'

Jensen was trying hard to control himself. He was clenching and unclenching his pudgy hands.

'You've been avoiding me, haven't you, Captain Verago?'

'What makes you think that, Cyrus?'

'I hear you spent half the night with Tower. Couldn't be bothered to get hold of me, could you? Want to do it all behind my back?'

'Lieutenant,' said Verago, 'do we have to discuss all this right here?'

Two office doors in the corridor stood open. People could hear them. An officer was standing by the entrance to the washroom, listening, fascinated. Not often did two legal eagles have a stand-up row like this in public.

They found an empty office, and Jensen slammed the door.

'Now,' he said, facing Verago, who sat down on the edge of a table. 'I know you don't like me, and frankly, Captain, I can't wait for you to get back to Germany. But meantime, let's get this trial over, OK?'

'There won't be any trial,' said Verago quietly.

'Why not?'

'You leave that to me.' He saw the flush on Jensen's face. 'Frankly, it's best you don't know. I don't want you to be a party to anything you don't believe in.'

'I –'

'Forget it,' said Verago.

'I'm going to report this to Colonel Kincaid. I think the Army may be interested too . . . '

'You can report to the devil for all I care,' said Verago. He got off the desk. 'Just sit with me in court, and keep stumm. That way you won't get burnt.'

But Jensen didn't move.

'What precisely did Tower tell you?' he asked softly.

'Everything,' said Verago. 'Excuse me.'

'You're making a big mistake,' exclaimed Jensen. 'You can't beat the government. You know that. Don't you care? Don't you care about your career? Don't you realise what's at stake?'

'Sure,' said Verago. 'That's why.'

He pushed past Jensen, and in the corridor outside he saw Unterberg heading for the court room.

And he suddenly wondered if this time it would all blow up in his face.

For after what Tower had told him, he knew that they could not let him get away with it.

KALININGRAD

The sounds had become the important things in Captain Kingston's life now. The slamming of iron doors, the turning of keys, footsteps echoing on the stone floor outside, these were the big moments of the day.

He sat on his bunk, holding his shaven head in his hands, eyes closed, trying to work out yet again where he was. The sounds of his closed world did not reveal much.

The days after he had been picked off a life raft by a Russian motor torpedo boat in the Baltic remained a blank. Then the room with the overpainted windows in the hospital. How long was he there? Days, weeks? He did not remember.

On the day he was finally shifted from the hospital, the woman doctor gave him an injection. He did not recall much of the subsequent journey. They had exchanged his pyjamas for a shapeless prison uniform but, curiously enough, they had allowed him to keep his fur-lined flying boots.

Again he tried to figure out where this place might be. Deep inside Russia? Or was he still on the Baltic coast somewhere? In Poland? East Germany? He could find no clue. He didn't even have a chance to see the sun or the stars, so there was no way to plot a geographical direction.

One thing he did know for sure. Officially, he was dead. Since he no longer officially existed, he could not hope to be returned to the West. Major Fokin had made that point very clear. He often wondered how the Pentagon had worded the telegram they had sent to his wife after the RB47H went down.

He had lost count of the sessions he had had with Fokin. Keeping up the pretence of amnesia, now that his memory had returned, was proving an almost intolerable ordeal. Fokin was a shrewd and clever interrogator and Kingston didn't know how much longer he could continue the charade. He knew Fokin didn't believe his mind was a blank but, so far, he hadn't been able to crack Kingston.

'You're a good actor, Captain,' Fokin complimented him. 'You should have had a career in Hollywood. Like Gary Cooper.'

The major laughed at his own joke. Kingston didn't smile.

Fokin's face clouded over. 'At least Gary Cooper says "Yep" and "Nope". You don't say a word. You don't realise how stupid you are being. We know everything anyway. We know about the missions from Laconbury. What you are after. We know everything . . . '

Kingston knew it was a trap. Fokin was goading him to react. To say, 'then you don't need me to tell you anything,' to betray that he was alert.

Patiently, Fokin kept asking the same questions.

'Tell me about the APR-14 intercept receiver. Is there a new model? Have they fitted the modified APR-8B panoramic adapter yet? Are they going to change the ALA-5 pulse analyser?'

He concentrated on the ferret equipment Kingston operated, and he knew it very well.

'I hear that the high fidelity of the tape recorders you use to capture our radar signals leave something to be desired,' Fokin would say conversationally. 'Frankly, our boys are having the same trouble.'

But Kingston just stared at him dumbly.

One of the reasons Fokin had a high reputation as an intelligence interrogator was his indefatigable perseverance. But Kingston was beginning to wear it down.

'Have you heard of Vorkuta, my friend?' he asked Kingston one day. 'It's located just above the Arctic circle. It is a coal mine. A prison coal mine. Not a nice place. Very cold.' He paused. 'I would hate you to spend the rest of your days there.'

Kingston's worst fear was that he would go crazy. Since he talked to nobody, he mouthed words to himself in the dark. He was good at mathematics and physics, and he tried to solve problems in his mind. They had provided him with a pad and pencil, probably in the hope that his doodles would give them an insight into his mind, so he kept the pages blank.

Then Fokin brought him a book. A slim volume in English. It was *Alice in Wonderland.*

'Perhaps it will revive childhood memories,' remarked Fokin.

But he was only interested in other memories. Next day he asked again about U-2 flights from Laconbury.

'I can understand why you are keeping silent,' he said. 'You have some very important information in here.' He tapped his own forehead. 'Your people were very anxious that none of you should fall into our hands. They even sent a submarine to try and find you. Sorry it missed you.'

Fokin sighed.

'The sad thing is that your buddies did perish. I imagine ferret crews have very close bonds. Almost like a family? Sorry they didn't survive. But at least, you're lucky.'

For a moment their eyes met. Fokin leant forward. He knew he'd touched a raw nerve and hoped that that would make Kingston open up. But he just turned his face away and stared at the wall.

'Never mind, Captain,' said Fokin. 'You will talk, believe me.'

And soon after, at two o'clock in the morning, Kingston began another journey.

LACONBURY

The three captains, two majors, and the lieutenant-colonel sat alternatively to the right and left of the president, according to their rank and seniority.

It was the president, a full colonel, whom Verago studied closely. Colonel Henry Voigt was a formidable looking man, erect as a ramrod, unsmiling, sharp grey eyes unblinking. He wore two sets of wings, the silver ones of an Air Force command pilot on his left breast, and a pair of RAF wings on the right side.

His medal ribbons were as formidable as the man. They included the colours of the European Theatre in World War Two, the Pacific war and Korea. On each were rows of battle stars. He had won the Distinguished Flying Cross, the Silver Star, many Air Medals, and a cluster of Purple Hearts. The French had decorated him, and the British had given him their DFC.

The other six officers looked hand-picked too, all flyers, all veterans of the service, all men who had served their country round the globe.

The law officer sat down at his desk, and nodded briefly to the seven officers of the court. Then, like a priest about to quote from the Bible, he opened the maroon law manual in front of him, straightened the notepad, and the neat row of specially sharpened pencils he had laid out. He glanced round the court room, focusing briefly on Tower. He avoided looking at Verago.

Tower sat at the defence table, next to Verago, staring straight ahead.

'How do you feel?' whispered Verago to him.

Tower shrugged.

'Let me do all the talking,' said Verago. 'Remember what I told you. Leave it to me.'

Tower nodded. He was pale.

Jensen leant back in his chair, on Verago's right, edging a little sideways, like a man in a restaurant who's been made to join a table he doesn't really want to sit at.

'You take notes,' Verago instructed him. 'Every damn word.'

'That's what the reporter is for, Tony,' scowled Jensen. 'I'm not –'

'I want my own record, and you take it,' hissed Verago. The ugly look he gave Jensen curtailed further argument.

Verago felt the seven officers of the court watching his every move. Surrounded by blue Air Force uniforms, his Army olive picked him out as a stranger in their midst. He tried to tell himself that he was imagining the waves of hostility that kept sweeping towards him.

There was a movement at the back, and Verago looked over his shoulder. General Croxford had sat down in the spectators section. Next to him were Colonel Kincaid – and Laurie.

She had not mentioned that she would be coming. It was like a sudden betrayal. He caught her eye, and she nodded briefly, distantly.

'The court will come to order,' growled Colonel Voigt.

Keep your head clear, Verago kept telling himself. Think only of what you are about to do. But he kept thinking of Laurie, sitting five feet behind him, yet like a stranger.

Apollo was on his feet, resplendent in beautifully cut, custom-made uniform.

'The convening authority has directed that these proceedings shall take place in private, and that the record shall remain secret,' he announced, almost casually.

Tower gave a little smile, but Verago jumped up, suddenly wide awake.

'We object,' he cried. 'We very much object. Maybe trial counsel can tell us just what makes alleged adultery a military secret.'

'Sir,' said Apollo without heat, 'there is nothing for Captain Verago to object to. It's not a decision of this court. It's a direct instruction from the convening authority. As for military secrets, I remind Captain Verago that the regulations provide for courts martial to be closed for security or "other good reasons". I guess the command has "other good reasons".'

'No point arguing about it,' sighed the law officer. Major Collins was going to cut it short. 'We are all subject to superior orders.'

'Court's closed,' commanded the president.

'In that case, what are General Croxford, Colonel Kincaid and that lady doing here?' demanded Verago.

Jensen tugged at his sleeve. 'You crazy?' he whispered urgently.

'They're all cleared for classified information,' interjected Apollo smoothly. 'There is no objection . . . '

'What classified information?' Verago faced him. 'Just what is so secret that we're going to hear . . . '

'Just one moment,' said Major Collins, and brought out his throat lozenges. He opened the tin, and popped one in his mouth. 'Defence counsel has a point. I think all those not needed here right now better leave the room.'

He looked sad as he said it.

At the back, Croxford stood up. He let Laurie go first, then he and Kincaid followed her through the swing doors.

'Let the record show there are no strangers present,' intoned the trial counsel.

But Verago hardly heard him. He was wondering why Laurie smiled the way she had as she left.

Like the proverbial cat that has swallowed the canary.

258

LONDON

'How was your weekend in the country?' asked Deriabin sourly.

'I had a very nice dip in the swimming pool,' replied Ivanov. He didn't add that the little house guest who joined him, a pretty red-haired model, didn't wear anything.

'I am glad you had an enjoyable time,' sniffed Deriabin, slitting open the pile of sealed envelopes that had arrived for him in the diplomatic bag, 'but that is hardly the point of the exercise, is it? I sometimes wonder if your friend Stephen is nothing but a glorified pimp. Don't let that world seduce you, my friend.'

'There were some interesting people there too,' said Ivanov hastily.

'Ah.' Deriabin put down the envelope he had just picked up. 'Anyone I should know about?'

'I will put it all in my report,' said Ivanov.

'Please hurry it up. Moscow is waiting. The time table is well advanced. By the way, did you know Marshal Koniev has been recalled?'

'No.' Ivanov wasn't quite sure how to react. He decided to play safe. 'He was a great soldier.'

'He is a great soldier,' said Deriabin. 'I was on his staff, when he captured Berlin.'

'I had no idea.'

'Yes, I stood beside him when we hoisted the red flag over the Chancellery. I shall never forget it. It was a moment of pride a man can have only once in his life.' He paused, clearly enjoying the memory. 'And his recall to command this special operation is a wise and logical decision.'

He took out a big handkerchief and blew his nose. 'I can't seem to shake off this damn cold,' he said, stuffing the handkerchief back in his pocket. 'Now, do me the report on your aristocratic weekend in the swimming pool. Oh, and what about the American?'

'The court martial started this morning.'

'Good.'

'If all goes well, it'll be over in twenty-four hours.'

Deriabin frowned.

'What do you mean, if all goes well? What can't go well?'

Ivanov wished he had kept quiet. Deriabin was a terrier. Once he had a rat in his teeth, he kept shaking.

'It's this Army lawyer defending him,' Ivanov reluctantly explained. 'A man called Verago. He could make a little trouble.'

Deriabin bared his teeth.

'Then don't let him, Captain,' he smiled. 'I am sure there are ways and means. Everyone relies on you.'

'I will keep an eye on it,' promised Ivanov. He must really remember not to tell Deriabin too much. 'I'll get on with the report now.'

'Oh, by the way,' said Deriabin when he reached the door, as if he had had an amusing afterthought. 'That little swim in the pool? Were you all alone?'

Ivanov thought quickly. One never knew what the GRU was aware of. Better be safe.

'Well, actually, there was a very pretty little nymph splashing around.'

'Did you sleep with her?'

'No, Colonel,' replied Ivanov truthfully. 'Not so far. At the moment she is more interested in a British cabinet minister.'

One after the other, the seven court members raised their right hand.

How often have I heard those words intoned, thought Verago. How often have I seen them stand ramrod stiff, as the trial counsel led them through the ritual.

'. . . faithfully and impartially try, according to the evidence, your conscience, and the laws and regulations . . . '

Beside him, Tower stood straight, watching each officer in turn as he swore the oath. And Jensen, on the other side, was stiffly at attention, like a man on parade.

'So help you God.'

'I do,' they swore.

Then it was the lawyers' turn, first Apollo himself facing the president with raised hand, and then Verago.

Colonel Voigt cleared his throat.

'The court is now convened,' he announced.

Apollo glanced across at Verago. He seemed to expect some kind of move, but Verago just sat, doodling on his pad.

'The accused, Captain John Tower, is charged with conduct which undermines the good order and discipline of the armed forces, and behaviour which is totally unbecoming an officer,' began Apollo. 'The specifications allege adultery, and by that I mean sexual misconduct with a woman not his wife. We will prove that on various occasions in London and elsewhere, Captain Tower has engaged in sexual intercourse with this woman, although a married man . . . '

The seven officers' heads had swung round and they were all gazing at Tower as if he was an exhibit.

'. . . and at these places sexual intimacy took place . . . '

Christ almighty, thought Verago, how many more times is he going to say it. Sexual misconduct. Sexual intercourse. Sexual intimacy.

'. . . the prosecution will produce documentary evidence, hotel registry entries, receipted bills, photographs, surveillance reports, and we will of course call the lady in question to testify of her relationship with the accused . . . '

Tower tensed, and Verago laid a hand on his arm.

'Take it easy,' he whispered, 'leave it to me.'

He hadn't seen Serena Howard, but he guessed they had her somewhere on the base. Well under wraps until they chose to parade her in court.

'We believe we will demonstrate that Captain Tower's conduct dishonoured and disgraced him as an individual, as a married man, and seriously compromised his standing and mission as an officer in the United States Air Force . . . '

Apollo sat down. This time he avoided Verago's eyes.

Jensen leant over. 'Well, Tony, I guess that about sums it up, wouldn't you say.'

'Don't they even ask me if I plead guilty or not?' asked Tower.

'Not yet, not yet,' retorted Verago. He was concentrating on Colonel Voigt. An interesting man, he thought.

And as if on cue, Colonel Voigt growled:

'Does the accused desire to challenge any member of the court?'

Slowly Verago got to his feet.

'Well, sir, the defence would like to avail itself of the right to do a little voir dire questioning,' he said genially.

He could see, out of the corner of his eye, Apollo looking attentive.

'Go ahead, Captain Verago,' said Major Collins.

Verago picked up a clip board on his desk. Attached to it was a list of names, the roster of the court.

'Thank you,' he said politely. He walked up to the row of court members and stopped at the first one.

'You're Captain Wallace, sir? 20th Tactical Fighter Wing at Wethersfield?'

The man regarded him stonily.

'Yes.'

'Don't worry about this, Captain, it's quite routine,' purred Verago. 'Are you married, sir?'

'Why yes,' said Captain Wallace.

Apollo started to rise, but he was too late to stop Verago.

'Well, now . . . ' began Verago, his tone mild. 'Tell us, Captain Wallace, have you ever committed adultery?'

TRANSCRIPT OF
GENERAL COURT MARTIAL PROCEEDINGS
US v TOWER
RAF STATION LACONBURY

TRIAL COUNSEL:	Objection. Irrelevant. Immaterial.
DEFENSE COUNSEL:	I wouldn't say that. In fact, I would suggest . . .
LAW OFFICER:	Now just hold it. Will counsel approach. (OUT OF HEARING OF THE COURT)
LAW OFFICER:	Now, Captain Verago, is this line necessary?
DEFENSE COUNSEL:	Sir, if my client was charged with shoplifting, would it not be highly material and relevant if one established that the jury trying him had itself indulged in larceny?
LAW OFFICER:	But you're not asking if they have committed a crime, you're questioning them about their private conduct, their morals.
DEFENSE COUNSEL:	Precisely. The very thing Captain Tower is on trial for. His morals.
LAW OFFICER:	Well, counsellor? What does the prosecution say?
TRIAL COUNSEL:	I don't blame my friend for clutching at straws. Maybe I'd do the same in

	his shoes. But I do not think this matter touches the basic competency of the court members. This court is not a confessional. It's a good try by Captain Verago but it won't wash.
DEFENSE COUNSEL:	I hope you rule against me, Major Collins. I hope you forbid me to continue this line of questioning. That'll do fine for appeal purposes. Nothing would make me happier than to be prevented from exercising my rights. It'll look great on the record.
LAW OFFICER:	You're not helping the court.
DEFENSE COUNSEL:	I didn't come here to be helpful.
LAW OFFICER:	You insist on asking the question?
DEFENSE COUNSEL:	Yes, sir.
LAW OFFICER:	I wish you wouldn't. It's . . . it's very embarrassing. But I guess, well, I like to allow the defense every latitude. (IN THE HEARING OF THE COURT)
LAW OFFICER:	Objection overruled. Counsel may proceed.
DEFENSE COUNSEL:	Thank you. Would the reporter read the last question?
REPORTER:	'Tell us, Captain Wallace, have you ever committed adultery?'
DEFENSE COUNSEL:	Well? Have you?
CAPTAIN WALLACE:	No, sir.
DEFENSE COUNSEL:	Thank you. How about you, Captain O'Neal?
CAPTAIN O'NEAL:	I'm not married, sir.
DEFENSE COUNSEL:	In that case, I guess I have no further question for you. Now, Major Bunyan. Are you married?
MAJOR BUNYAN:	Definitely, sir. Very happily, with three children.

DEFENSE COUNSEL:	I'm glad to hear it. Nevertheless, and you'll excuse why I have to ask you, we are all only human –
TRIAL COUNSEL:	Objection.
DEFENSE COUNSEL:	I withdraw. We'll concede that apparently the prosecution does not believe everyone is human. So I'll ask you, Major, have you ever had an extra-marital affair?
TRIAL COUNSEL:	Objection. He is asking the witness to incriminate himself.
DEFENSE COUNSEL:	He seems to assume the major has something incriminating to say. Colonel Apollo should have more confidence.
LAW OFFICER:	Ask the question.
DEFENSE COUNSEL:	Have you ever committed adultery?
MAJOR BUNYAN:	Of course not.
DEFENSE COUNSEL:	Colonel Voigt, how long have you been in the service?
COLONEL VOIGT:	Nineteen years. Twenty next October.
DEFENSE COUNSEL:	And I can see you have had a very distinguished career. Very distinguished indeed, to judge by the ribbons on your chest. And you have served in many parts of the world?
COLONEL VOIGT:	I have seen action.
DEFENSE COUNSEL:	In Europe, during the war?
COLONEL VOIGT:	England. North Africa. Italy. I was in the Eighth Air Force. And with the Ninth.
DEFENSE COUNSEL:	And after VE-day?
COLONEL VOIGT:	The Pacific. Japan.
DEFENSE COUNSEL:	Korea?
COLONEL VOIGT:	Yes, sir.
DEFENSE COUNSEL:	And are you married, sir?
COLONEL VOIGT:	Since 1942. I married before I went overseas.

DEFENSE COUNSEL:	Now, sir, this is a voir dire examination. Voir dire means to speak the truth. And you are of course on oath.
COLONEL VOIGT:	I am aware of it. And you certainly don't have to remind me, Captain Virgo.
DEFENSE COUNSEL:	Verago, sir. Of course not. And you swear that in all those years, in all those places, on your own, cut off from home, at all times, you never –
COLONEL VOIGT:	I consider it insulting to be asked such a question.
DEFENSE COUNSEL:	I'm sorry about that. I don't enjoy it much myself. Nevertheless, you assure me that in wartime England, in London, in the black out, alone, in Italy, in the bright lights of Tokyo, you never once found yourself in a relationship . . .
COLONEL VOIGT:	I don't fornicate. I have never committed adultery. Satisfied?
DEFENSE COUNSEL:	That's all I wanted to know, Colonel. How about you, Lieutenant-Colonel Hargreaves?
LT-COL HARGREAVES:	No. Of course not.
DEFENCE COUNSEL:	Major Correy?
MAJOR CORREY:	No. Never.
DEFENSE COUNSEL:	Captain Wilkins?
CAPT WILKINS:	No.
DEFENSE COUNSEL:	Thank you, gentlemen. I have no further questions at this point.
LAW OFFICER:	Alright, Captain Verago. You've asked what you wanted and you've had the answers. Do you now wish to challenge any member of this court?
DEFENSE COUNSEL:	Not . . . yet.

266

LAW OFFICER:	Not yet? What do you mean?
DEFENSE COUNSEL:	At this point, I request that these proceedings be recessed. Because we have a lot of digging to do.
PRESIDENT:	What do you mean, recessed. We haven't even started yet?
LAW OFFICER:	Just a moment, Colonel. What digging?
DEFENSE COUNSEL:	Checking up.
LAW OFFICER:	You had adequate time to prepare your case, Captain Verago.
DEFENSE COUNSEL:	I hadn't had these replies.
PRESIDENT:	Do I understand that counsel intends to investigate the private lives of the members of this court? I don't know how you do things in the Army, but by God, in the Air Force we don't –
LAW OFFICER:	Please, Colonel.
DEFENSE COUNSEL:	I ask for a fourteen-day recess.
LAW OFFICER:	Counsel, we want to get on.
TRIAL COUNSEL:	This is a phoney stunt, sir. How can Captain Verago probe the morals of seven officers who in the last twenty years have served all over the world? Assuming there's anything to probe? What are you going to do? Travel around, checking a million hotel registers? It's . . . it's insulting.
DEFENSE COUNSEL:	That's what you did to Captain Tower. But I repeat, sir, if you refuse to allow us the time we need, it's clear grounds for appeal. Again, I almost wish you would.
TRIAL COUNSEL:	You're not trying to blackmail the court, are you, Tony.
DEFENSE COUNSEL:	Who? Me?
LAW OFFICER:	Alright. I'll give you one week. Seven days. And listen, Captain Verago, I

267

DEFENSE COUNSEL: So do I.

LACONBURY

She honked twice. Her car was standing by the gatehouse, at the entrance of the base, and she was sitting behind the wheel, waiting for him.

Verago walked across to her. She had lowered the window on her side, watching him. The almond-shaped eyes were hidden behind dark glasses.

'Going somewhere?' asked Laurie.

'I'm waiting for a cab. Going to London.'

'Jump in. I'll take you.'

An AP came over.

'Your cab's here, sir,' he said, pointing at a battered old Austin that had pulled up by the perimeter fence.

'Pay it off,' said Laurie. 'I'm going your way.'

He found the dark glasses disconcerting. They concealed too much.

'Well?' she challenged.

'OK,' he said.

The cab driver wasn't pleased.

'That'll be a quid. Minimum charge.' His hopes of a lucrative trip had been dashed. 'You lost me a good job.'

Verago gave him his pound, then got in beside Laurie. The Volkswagen had a Third Air Force decal on the windscreen, admitting it to all US military installations.

'I want to get off at the pub,' said Verago. 'Pack a few things.'

'Taking a trip?'

'Yeah.'

When they reached the little Norman church, by the village green, she took the right turning without him having to direct her. She seemed to know the exact way to the George and Dragon.

'You know you're in the shit,' remarked Laurie suddenly. 'Right up to here. Kincaid's reporting you to the Army. He's going to ask Colonel Ochs to discipline you. For abusing your position.'

Verago looked out of the window.

'What were you doing in court?'

'The boss wanted to come. So I tagged along. Until you kicked us out.'

'You could have told me you'd be there.'

Her lips tightened. 'I don't have to tell you everything, Tony.'

He inclined his head, as if agreeing.

'What in particular makes them so mad?' he asked mildly.

She smiled coldly. 'What do you think? You're embarrassing them. Playing games. They don't like it.'

He wished she didn't have those dark glasses shielding her. 'I'm not playing games, Laurie. And I don't think they are either.'

She pulled up outside the inn, and turned off the engine.

'So. What happens now?'

'My client has to sweat it out some more.'

'I didn't see the girl,' said Laurie.

'I guess they're keeping her on ice. But they'll have her there when the trial resumes.'

He opened the door, and started to get out of the car.

'I'll wait for you,' she said.

'No,' said Verago, 'come on in.'

LACONBURY

Serena Howard sat in a waiting room near the chaplain's

office, mostly staring at the wall. They had given her some magazines to read, but she hadn't been interested in them. Twice a white-capped AP brought her cups of coffee and a doughnut.

She smoked a lot, and when Duval came in, the ashtray was piled with cigarette ends.

'They won't need you today,' he announced. 'I'll take you back to London.'

The colour came back to her face. 'You mean, it's all over?'

'Trial's been recessed for a week.'

'Why?' she asked. 'Why the delay?'

'Defence needs more time. Ready?'

'I want to see him,' she said. 'I want to see Captain Tower.'

He waited until the noise of a jet on the flight line abated. Then he said:

'You're here for the prosecution, lady. You're our witness. You follow?'

'It's personal,' she pleaded.

'Sorry,' said Duval. 'Why don't you wait until it's all over?'

'No,' she insisted. 'Now.'

'Anyway,' said Duval, 'Captain Tower doesn't want to see you.'

'I don't believe that,' she snapped. 'I don't think anybody's even asked him.'

'I'm sorry,' said Duval again.

In the staff car, on the way back to London, she asked:

'I'll still have to testify?'

'You bet.' He gave her a quick glance, 'But it'll be over quick, you'll see.'

She asked one more question, later:

'Did . . . did he know I was on the base?'

'He wasn't even interested,' said Duval, and kept his eyes on the road straight ahead.

After that, Serena said nothing more.

Laurie looked up at the stained ceiling.

'Not the Ritz, is it?'

The bed still hadn't been made, and a pair of socks was lying on the worn carpet where Verago had dropped them.

'Take off those glasses,' he said.

She faced him and then, slowly, deliberately, she removed them. The violet eyes regarded him quizzically.

'Well?'

He kissed her long and hard. After a moment, she yielded, her body becoming soft, pressing herself against him. Her mouth was open and met his, and he felt a surge of desire and excitement and urgency.

Then they were on the bed. He unzipped the back of her dress, and started to remove her bra with eager, greedy hands when she stopped him

'No,' she said. 'The door.'

He got off the bed, walked to the door, and turned the key from the inside.

And when he turned back, she was lying on the bed, naked, and welcoming.

She smiled at him, a little mockingly.

'You always make love in Class A uniform?' she taunted.

Then he realised that in his eagerness for her, he had not even started to undress. Hurriedly he stripped, while she stretched out in front of him languidly, increasing his passion as she displayed her body.

And yet, even as everything gave way to his desire for her, a curious voice at the back of his head reminded him how, even at this moment, she was so in control that she remembered a detail like locking the door.

But then, he descended on her and as they embraced each other, and their bodies intertwined, he would, at that moment, have betrayed the universe to possess her.

It was joyful, sensual, pagan lovemaking. They relished in the strength of their bodies, and the energy lust gave them. Yet

271

despite the intensity of their desire, they took their time for as long as they could, to draw the utmost pleasure and delight out of their naked intimacy.

Later, they lay, her head on his chest, and she almost purred:

'You're good, very good.'

It jarred slightly, like the time in her apartment when he'd found the razor and the shaving cream. Good, by whose standards? Who had provided the criterion by which she judged him?

'I'm glad you're pleased,' he murmured.

She turned her head to look up at him.

'And you?'

'Very nice. I enjoyed it.' He thought he was a bastard to put it like that, as if he was commenting on a gourmet meal in a four-star restaurant.

She lay sprawled, relaxed.

'You were very tense,' she commented. 'Like you had something on your mind.'

'Was I?'

'Is it the case?'

'Maybe.'

'Or . . .'

He took her in his arms, and kissed her.

'Your trouble is, Miss Czeslaw, you ask too many questions.'

She asked for a cigarette and he gave her one and lit it for her.

'Wasn't there anybody else?' she persisted. 'Before we met . . .'

'I thought we had an agreement,' he said. 'No questions.'

'Of course. I was just curious.'

'You mean, my wife? What went wrong?'

'If you don't want to talk about it,' she began, and he interrupted her.

'I don't. OK?'

'Sure,' said Laurie. She stubbed out the cigarette in the ghastly 'Souvenir from Lowestoft' ashtray beside the bed. 'So let's not talk.'

And this time she set the pace of the lovemaking, directing him where she wanted to be pleasured, guiding him around her

272

body, and then, when he was aroused again, yielding to him as he took her.

Half an hour later there was a knock on the door.

They sat up, staring at each other.

'What is it?' Verago called out.

The voice of the garlic maid came through the door.

'I want to do the room.'

'I'm busy,' shouted Verago. 'Come back in a couple of hours.'

They heard her shuffling away, and then he and Laurie looked at each other, and started laughing.

'Hell, I *am* busy,' said Verago.

Laurie looked up and addressed the ceiling.

'I wonder when you last saw it in the middle of the day,' she called out and they both laughed again.

They got up, and began dressing.

'By the way,' said Laurie, as she fastened her dress. 'You said you were going on a trip. Where?'

Verago straightened up from the case he had pulled out from under the bed to pack.

'Oh, didn't I tell you?' He hesitated just for a moment. Then he said:

'Berlin.'

Wednesday, July 26, 1961 – LONDON

For the second time, Daventry scanned *The Times,* the paper spread out in front of him, his eyes moving up and down every column, on every page. Except the sports section and the advertisements.

Across the breakfast table, Alex watched him.

'What are you looking for?' she asked.

'Pass me *The Telegraph,*' he replied, abstractly.

Without a word, he studied the front page, and then skimmed the inside, not reading any of the stories, but searching all the headlines, screening every item, whether it was a page lead, or a tiny news in brief paragraph. Finally he threw the paper aside.

'Nothing,' he said. 'Not a line.'

'About what?'

He took a piece of toast, and scraped some butter across it. Then he said:

'Serena Howard's case. The court martial.'

'Should there be?'

'It began yesterday. I can't understand it. I was sure it'd get into the papers.'

He put the piece of toast down.

'Maybe,' said Alex, 'they don't want anything published.'

He stared across the table at her. 'They?'

Alex poured herself some more tea.

'I should think it's very likely, don't you,' she remarked.

'I don't see why . . . '

'Oh come, Gerry.' She could be very practical. 'All that fuss. You know they desperately wanted to hush it up. They're probably holding it in camera. There have been a few at the Old Bailey like that, after all.'

'Only security cases. Official Secrets Act.'

'Well?' said Alex quietly. 'Isn't that what your school chum said it is?'

He was still turning the pages of *The Daily Telegraph,* but finally gave up.

'I was sure Fleet Street would find out,' he muttered.

Alex got up, and came over to his side of the table. She put a hand on his shoulder.

'Gerry, do me a favour,' she said. 'Stop having a guilt complex. You did the only thing that made sense. You're well out of it.'

'Am I?' he asked quietly. 'You think I really am?'

'What do you mean?'

'Remember that yellow file Grierson talked about? *My*

yellow file. I wonder what's happened to it . . . '

'Oh, I'm sure that's all torn up.'

But she didn't sound very convinced.

LONDON

In his check Harris tweed jacket, roll-top sweater and brown corduroys, Ivanov fitted into the clientele of the Spaniards. He was drinking beer, a lager, because it gave him time to stand and watch people. There was nothing unusual about a beer drinker lingering over his pint.

He had been watching, in particular, the two girls having a snack in the corner. They were chatting animatedly, and occasionally one of them burst out laughing at something her friend said. There was a close intimacy in their gossiping. Men, decided Ivanov. They were discussing men.

They were both blondes, slim, leggy blondes, and Ivanov thought of Stephen. They'd do well in his set up. He could just see them at one of his parties. Being introduced as models. Or actresses. It didn't really matter, they'd go down in a big way.

He was half inclined to try his luck. Walk over and sit down at their table. Make some excuse. Get into conversation. They could be fun.

But not today. He had come to Hampstead on official business. There wasn't time for pleasure. Regretfully, he finally drank up his beer, and left the inn. The two girls hadn't even noticed the interest they had aroused.

Ivanov walked around on the Heath for half an hour. He strolled slowly, enjoying the clear air here, high up above London. He seemed to walk aimlessly, but he knew exactly where he was going.

He came to Kenwood, entered the grounds of the Iveagh

Bequest through a gate in the railings, and turned left, following a path along the edge of the woods at the back of St Columba's Hospital.

Then he came to the tree. There were a lot of trees around, elders, yew, white poplar, chestnuts, pine, fir. And there was an oak tree, centuries old, a great, solid individual, a chieftain among his tribe.

Ivanov walked on a little, and then, abruptly, turned back and retraced his steps. He went back to the ancient tree.

He stopped, and lit a cigarette. Then, almost casually, he reached into a cavity inside the big, weather-beaten trunk. His fingers felt inside it, and grasped the matchbox.

He took it, and put it in his pocket.

Ivanov didn't approve of this kind of dubok. A dubok, in the parlance of the organisation, was a clandestine hiding place. Ivanov regarded the system as old fashioned, just as he did the department's obsession for cover names. Intermediaries were always 'cut outs', the KGB the 'neighbour', the local Communist party a 'corporation', a legal front for an illegal activity a 'roof', a passport a 'shoe'.

And a secret collecting point, like a tree on Hampstead Heath, a 'dubok'.

It was risky, felt Ivanov. The opposition also knew a thing or two. But there were times when the only safe link with a special contact had to be this way.

Ivanov continued to walk along the path until it led to Hampstead Lane. There he hailed a passing taxi.

'Tottenham Court Road,' he ordered.

'Whereabouts?' asked the driver.

'Drop me at the Dominion.'

He sat back in the cab, and, when it pulled up for a red light, he took out the matchbox, and slid it open.

Inside was a tiny piece of paper, neatly rolled up.

He unfolded it. One word was written on it in neat, legible letters:

'Windrush'.

The traffic lights changed, and the cab drove on. But Ivanov still sat, the piece of paper in his hand.

Then, under his breath, he swore in Russian.

He took his lighter, and burnt the paper. It was very thin paper, flared·up for a second, and then disintegrated into nothing.

The taxi stopped outside the cinema. Ivanov didn't even acknowledge the driver's thanks for the generous tip he gave him. He was not in a good mood.

He went down the steps into the subway, to the row of phone boxes inside the station. He put in two pennies, dialled a number and, when it answered, pressed button A.

'Laurie?' he said. 'I think you and I had better have a little talk.'

It sounded rather like an order.

Thursday, July 27, 1961 – WEST BERLIN

'Oh, you want the agentensumpf, eh?' said the cab driver with the peaked cap.

'The what?' Verago spoke German quite well, but this was a new one on him.

'Marienfelde. The spy swamp.' The cab driver laughed at his own wit. 'That's where they keep the ones they can't trust. It's crawling with them.'

'Really?' said Verago.

'It's a long way out,' pointed out the cabby. 'Wouldn't you like a tour of the sights instead?'

'No.'

'OK,' said the driver resignedly.

He drove Verago through the suburbs, past the cheap housing estates, the drab warehouses, the long rows of allotments and garden plots where many Berliners grew their vegetables.

'You with the army in Berlin?'

'Just visiting,' said Verago.

They came to the Monastery of the Good Shepherd and then the cab, a creaky Mercedes, stopped at the main entrance of the camp.

'There you are,' said the driver. 'Marienfelde. Gateway to the free world.'

Verago got out.

'You want me to wait?' offered the cabby hopefully. 'Not many taxis round here.'

'No thanks,' said Verago, and paid him off.

The guard at the gate directed him to the administrative offices.

'Building C,' he said.

He didn't ask about his business. The Army uniform was a good passport.

'Thanks,' said Verago.

The place reminded him of an army barracks. The barbed-wire fences, the anonymous brick-built barracks, neatly laid out in rows.

He came to building C and entered.

'Yes, Captain,' enquired the girl at the reception desk.

'I want to see Fraulein Braunschweig,' said Verago, 'Helga Braunschweig.'

WEST BERLIN

Pech came forward, his hand outstretched, a welcoming smile on his face.

'Captain Verago,' he cried. 'You've just won a bet for me.'

He held open his office door.

'Come in, make yourself at home. Not that it's much

of a place.'

'You are . . . '

'Oh, I'm sorry, I thought you knew. Pech. B1. Documentation. That sort of thing.' He gave a little bow. 'Please sit down.'

'You were expecting me?' enquired Verago cautiously, sitting down on the chair Pech indicated.

'But of course. That was the bet I had with myself. Sooner or later, I was sure, Captain Tower's lawyer would show up here. And you have.'

'But why did you think that?'

'Instinct,' beamed Pech. 'I know something of this case.'

'You do?' Verago's eyebrows shot up. It was becoming too easy. And he always worried about people who were too helpful.

Pech unscrewed a thermos flask. From a drawer he produced two plastic beakers.

'Coffee?'

'Please.'

Pech poured out the black liquid. It looked lukewarm – and it was. He pulled a face when he tasted his.

'Sorry about that,' he apologised. He put the beaker down on his desk. 'You want to see the woman of course.'

'Right,' said Verago. 'Fraulein Braunschweig. Helga Braunschweig. I want to ask her some questions.'

'So do I,' said Pech grimly.

'What does that mean?'

'It means, Captain Verago, that our little lady has pulled a fast one on us. She's gone.'

'Gone where?'

'Back into the East zone.'

Verago stared in disbelief. 'They've kidnapped her?'

'No, no, no, of course not. She walked out. Marienfelde is not a prison. People come here of their own free will. And they can leave to return home. She obviously changed her mind, and decided to do just that.' He waved a hand airily. 'The zonal boundary is only a few metres away. It's not difficult.'

'You believe that?' Verago demanded.

Pech shrugged. 'My job is to deal in facts. American intelligence brought her over. She had something big to tell them, apparently. So your Captain Tower and a double agent he was working with said.'

'Martin Schneider?'

'Correct. They smuggled her across. B1 had doubts about her. So we've kept her here until we could sort it out.'

'Now she's disappeared, Martin Schneider is dead, and Captain Tower in the hoosegaw.'

'Yes, very distressing,' said Pech.

'Did you interrogate her at all?'

'Helga? She was very uncooperative. She refused to be debriefed by us. She would only talk to Captain Tower and he . . . ' Pech smiled drily, '. . . was not, shall we say, available. She wouldn't talk to us because she apparently had a bee in her bonnet that we had been infiltrated. By the SSD.'

'The Staats Sicherheits Dienst? The East German Gestapo?'

Pech looked pleasantly surprised. 'Oh, you know, Captain Verago?'

'Yes,' said Verago. 'I know.'

'It's nonsense, of course.'

'Of course.' He nodded his agreement. 'But don't you find it curious that this woman who defects at great risk with some apparently vital information and is so terrified she won't even talk to West German security in case there's a leak suddenly decides to return to the other side?'

'Not only curious,' said Pech, 'but extremely significant. There's a simple explanation, isn't there?'

Verago wondered about this man. How many people he had hooked and played like a fisherman until he had landed them in his net, how many intrigues he had masterminded, how many betrayals . . .

But aloud he said: 'What simple explanation, Herr Pech?'

Pech put his fingertips together, leant back in his chair, and beamed at Verago.

'I'm sure you're there already, Captain. The explanation seems to be that Helga Braunschweig was a plant, foisted on us by the other side. When she saw that my people weren't fooled, she decided to get out. Before it was too late . . .

He sighed.

'I'm sorry this can't be of much help to you or your client.'

'On the contrary,' said Verago, cheerfully. 'Do you have any records about her?'

'Of course,' said Pech primly. He got up and went to a wall safe. He spun the dial, standing so that Verago's view was obscured and the combination would remain a secret. There was a click, and he opened the safe door. He took out a folder, and returned to his desk.

'6221,' he said.

'Eh?'

'Her number. Everybody here gets a number. To protect their identity. We do take precautions, you know. That's her.' He pushed a photo across that he had taken from the folder.

It was a striking face, thought Verago. Distinctive. Big eyes. A determined mouth. The lips slightly curved as if she couldn't resist a faint, rather mocking smile at the camera.

'What's her job?' he asked, still looking at the face. 'What does she do?'

'She's bright, there's no denying it,' said Pech. 'Speaks English quite well, and French. Smattering of Russian. Does 190 words a minute shorthand. I could do with a secretary like that.'

'That doesn't sound very remarkable.'

'Please, Captain, you're missing the point. She is a secretary. In fact, she was one of the secretaries in Walter Ulbricht's personal office.'

LONDON

On the second floor of the mews house near Berkeley Square,

the leggy blonde reported to Grierson.

'He entered the Spaniards about 1:15,' she said, reading from a little notepad with a tasteful crocodile leather cover. 'He stood by the bar, and had a lager.'

'By himself?'

'Yes sir.'

'Did anyone approach him?'

'No.'

'You sure he didn't talk to anybody?'

'Definitely not, sir.'

Grierson grunted. The full surveillance Whitehall had ordered on Ivanov was proving troublesome. Sometimes it was difficult to keep tabs on him; when, for instance, he went on his aristocratic weekends in feudal Berkshire, and disappeared behind the high walls of a lordly estate. On other occasions, it wasn't so difficult, but the results were always negative.

Like his little excursion to Hampstead Heath.

'Were you on your own?' asked Grierson.

'No sir. Miss Shepherd was with me.'

'So nothing happened in the pub?'

'Nothing unusual.'

'And then?'

'He finished his drink, and went for a walk.'

'Go on.'

'Well,' said the blonde, a little awkwardly. 'It was rather difficult to follow him.'

'Why?' demanded Grierson coldly.

'He strolled around, and then went into a rather secluded part of Kenwood. He would have noticed anybody shadowing him.'

'You lost him?'

But the blonde was an expert at her job, and she resented that.

'It just became difficult. Miss Shepherd and I split up. I played a little hide and seek. Kept myself concealed behind trees.'

'I hope he didn't see you,' remarked Grierson.

The blonde smiled.

'No way.'

'What happened next?'

The blonde glanced at her notepad.

'Well, he came to a big tree . . . I . . . think he took something out of it. I couldn't see too well from where I was hiding, but it looked to me . . . '

Grierson leant forward, interested.

'What do you mean, took something out of it?'

'From a sort of hole in the tree trunk.'

'Ah.' For the first time, Grierson seemed to be satisfied.

'Then he walked away, and picked up a cab in Hampstead Lane.'

Grierson glanced down at the typed report in front of him.

'Yes, I have the rest. After you handed over to Kirby.'

The blonde hesitated. Grierson nodded encouragingly.

'Something else, Susan?'

'Well, yes sir,' she said. 'There was this other man. A big fellow. He was in the pub too and I had a feeling he was watching Ivanov as well. Bulky sort of chap, but he had the knack of making himself inconspicuous. You know, like a pro.'

'I know. Go on.'

'He left the pub when Ivanov did. And Jenny thought she saw him once. In Kenwood.'

Grierson's eyes never left her face.

'You mean, he was following Ivanov too. What a jolly little convoy. Did this chap see you?'

'Oh no, sir,' said the blonde, scandalised at the suggestion. 'But he was good. We didn't see him again. But Jenny spotted him in Hampstead Lane. He was still on Ivanov's tail. He looked . . . sort of American. You can tell 'em, can't you?'

'Oh indeed,' sighed Grierson.

'Are the Yanks in on this?' she enquired.

He opened a folder containing a sheaf of typewritten pages. Pinned to the top of them was a photograph.

'Was this the man?' asked Grierson, not answering her question. 'The man who followed Ivanov?'

The blonde looked at the photograph of Unterberg.

'Yes sir,' she said firmly. 'That was him. No question.'

Grierson covered up the photo again with a screening sheet.

'Susan,' he said, 'you deserve a bottle of champers.'

WEST BERLIN

Like a man who hasn't seen one of his dearest friends for a long time, Pech appeared reluctant to part company.

Four hours later, they were still together, sitting in the corner of a smoky establishment in Zehlendorf. The Rote Fuchs was a small drinking dive in a back street, and Pech drove there from Marienfelde.

He seemed more relaxed once they were away from the barracks and barbed wire fences of the sprawling refugee camp.

'You're not in a rush, are you?' he asked Verago.

You're keeping tabs on me, thought Verago. You want to know what I'll do next, where I go. The joke is, I wish I knew.

'This is a good place,' confided Pech over the third schnapps. 'A kneipe. A real kneipe. Not a bar. Not a club. Not a pub. In Berlin, you got to go to a kneipe.'

'And what's so special about it?' asked Verago.

'My friend, just smell. Look around you. The atmosphere. That's what's different. Here a man can do serious drinking, uninterrupted by the world. Like we should do. Like this.'

He knocked back the schnapps.

He signalled the burly man with the apron who was sweeping the floor with a broom.

'Noch zwei,' he ordered.

He was slightly red-faced, and a single rivulet of sweat ran down the side of his neck. But the eyes were alert. As alert as ever.

'Helga was quite a catch, wasn't she?' said Verago suddenly.

Pech blinked. 'Catch? Why catch?'

284

'Well, Walter Ulbricht's secretaries don't defect every day.'

The schnapps came, and Pech raised his glass.

'Prosit.' He smacked his lips. 'Excellent.' But he could see Verago was waiting for him to reply. 'Ah, yes, I see what you mean. But of course she was not the only secretary. She worked in his office. *One* of the secretaries . . . '

'Nevertheless, she must know a hell of a lot.'

'So?'

'You just let her stew in Marienfelde? With 3,000 other refugees. I should have thought she'd get very special treatment. A VIP hide out. Away from Berlin . . . '

Pech reached over and slapped his back.

'Good, very good. I should have thought so too. God knows how their minds work.'

Verago sipped his brandy. 'Whose minds?'

'In Berlin, the left hand doesn't know what the right is doing. Do you know how many intelligence agencies operate in this city? In the three Western sectors alone? Thirty-three, my friend. And I don't count the freelances?' He laughed. Perhaps it was a little too loud. The schnapps was having its effect. 'Sometimes, I think there is one spy here for every two citizens. And we have two million people in the Western sector. That's funny, isn't it?'

'Have another one,' invited Verago, and nodded to the burly man.

'If you want to make me tipsy, you'll find me very happy to accommodate you,' said Pech.

'I was thinking,' ruminated Verago slowly. 'Supposing . . . supposing Helga came across with something really big. That's why she was smuggled over. That's why Tower and the other guy risked their necks to bring her out. Well, supposing they didn't want to know.'

Pech held up his glass against the lamp on the table, and peered into it.

'Who didn't want to know?'

'Our people. Your people. Supposing she told them something they didn't want to hear.'

'Verago, why don't you go back to England, finish your little court martial and take a long leave?'

Pech's eyes looked straight into his.

'In fact, why don't you go to that phone in the corner, call Tempelhof and reserve your seat on the next plane to London?'

The man with the apron came over.

'Are you Herr Pech?' he asked.

'I might be,' said Pech, warily.

'There's a call for you,' said the man.

Pech looked across to the pay phone.

'I didn't hear it ring.'

'In the office,' said the man, surly.

He pointed at a staircase leading down into the basement.

'Down there, first door on the right.'

Pech stood up, and followed him.

'Don't go away,' he said to Verago.

The bar was half empty. At a table by the entrance sat a woman who kept looking across at Verago. Her face was in the shadows. He wondered whether she was interested in him, or just curious about an American Army officer in this joint. Her companion had his back to Verago, and he wore Italian-made shoes. Fancy shoes with trimmings.

Pech came up the staircase.

'The department,' he explained, as he sat down again. 'How the hell they tracked me down I don't know.'

'Anything urgent?' asked Verago.

Pech appeared lost in thought for a moment. Then he caught on. 'Oh no, just routine. Some bloody duty officer wanted to check something. They can't leave a man alone. Where's my drink?'

The surly man brought another two schnapps. He ticked the beer mat. There was a formidable array of pencil ticks already on it.

'We're both still too sober, but the night is young,' said Pech. He paused. Then he asked:

'You're serious, aren't you?'

'What about ?'

'Getting hold of the Braunschweig girl.'

'Of course,' said Verago.

Pech looked round the room. Then he leant forward and

286

lowered his voice.

'Listen,' he said. 'I don't know where she is except it's in the East sector. I don't know how you could find her. But if you insist on being a fool and want to break your neck, that's your problem. I can give you an address.'

Despite the lamp on the table, there was a shadow across Pech's face. Verago wished he could see it more clearly.

'What address?'

'Her parents. Here.'

He took out a little pad, tore off a page and wrote an address on it. 99b Kolwitzstrasse.

'Take it,' said Pech. 'It's in the Russian sector.'

'Why are you doing this?' asked Verago, putting the paper in his wallet.

'To get rid of you, Captain Verago.'

And Pech wasn't smiling.

Friday, July 28, 1961 – THE CELL

The pretence had stopped. There was no longer any suggestion that he was in hospital, being given special treatment. This was a cell, a prison cell.

And it was in a big prison, of that Captain Kingston was sure. He could hear doors clanging, and the echo of boots on stone floors.

His cell had a tiny window, with three bars and wire mesh between them. The door was heavy steel, and there was a peep hole through which a guard peered from time to time.

From the ceiling hung a bulb that was never switched off. At night he tried to shield his eyes from the yellow glare.

But he didn't know where he was. They had given him some kind of shot that confused everything: he was pretty sure there had been a helicopter flight, and a car drive in the dark. But he couldn't actually remember arriving here.

The place was different, but Major Fokin was still around.

'I'm sorry they've brought you here,' he said as if he had nothing to do with it. 'I'm afraid that's the result of not co-operating. You haven't answered a single question after all this time. You may think that's heroic, but there are those who consider it dumb insolence. And dumb insolence, Captain, is a military offence in the service, as I'm sure you know.'

He walked round the cell.

'Pretty bleak, isn't it? And I'm afraid the diet won't be very appetising. Prison food never is.'

The copy of *Alice in Wonderland* lay on the bunk.

'Oh good,' said Fokin, 'they let you take it with you. Have you finished it?'

Kingston stared at the wall. It was damp. Outside, the July air was warm, but in here everything was dank and moist.

'Pity is your people don't even know how resolute you are, Captain,' went on Fokin. 'All this wasted effort. I know General Croxford would be very proud of you, but the joke is he doesn't even realise you're still alive. You've been written off, and you might as well make things easier for yourself. No? Ah well.'

He rapped on the door, for the turnkey to open it.

'Just think of this. You may force us to put you on trial. After all you are a spy. You intruded into our air space on a spy flight. You know what happens to spies.'

There was a rattle of keys, and the door swung open. A grey-uniformed guard stood waiting for Fokin to come out.

'I'll leave you *Alice,*' added Fokin. 'It's a book worth reading and . . . ' he glanced up at the eternal light, '. . . you've got plenty of opportunity. It's a wise book too, Captain. Chapter 3, for example. "I'll be judge, I'll be jury, I'll try the whole cause and condemn you to death." '

The door slammed, and the foot steps gradually died away.

And in the cell, Captain Kingston cried.

EAST BERLIN

So this is what it feels like to put your head in the noose, thought Verago as he entered the S-bahnhof at the Zoo station.

He was in civilian clothes. For what he had to do, it was better not to wear uniform. As an allied serviceman it would be easier to get through the checkpoint, but once he was in East Berlin the American officer's uniform would stick out like a blazing torch.

No, he was going to be Tony Verago, US tourist. He had his civilian passport, and it described him as 'attorney'. Which, after all, was fair enough. He wondered about carrying his military ID card; if they found it, there could be complications. On the other hand, with luck, he wouldn't be searched; he decided to take the risk.

The train came into the station, and Verago took a window seat. His fellow passengers were a drab lot. Was it his imagination, or did they all avoid each other's eyes? But one or two did furtively steal a look at him; his clothes were American. He looked too smart, too prosperous to be one of them.

Twenty minutes later, they arrived at the Friederichstrasse stop. Now there was no turning back. He had crossed the line.

He got off the train, and started walking towards the exit steps, trying to look confident. But almost at once a green uniformed Vopo, a carbine strapped to his shoulder, stepped into his path.

'You,' he said unceremoniously, 'papers.'

'American tourist,' smiled Verago. He waved his green passport. He tried to work out why he had been stopped. The other passengers were shuffling along the platform. Then he attempted to reassure himself: of course, I stand out. It's the way I look. But he wasn't totally convinced.

'Over there,' ordered the Vopo, pointing. 'Passport control.'

People were lining up in a long queue, all the passengers from the train. They knew the routine. He joined them. It was a slow, agonising wait. The line moved forward at snail's pace.

Two men were sitting at a table, in front of a shack. The shack had a little opening, like a box office in a theatre. Nearby hovered three Vopos, with the customary carbines.

One of the men at the table had a pince nez clipped on his nose, like the one Ulbricht sported on all his photographs. Clearly pince nez were fashionable in the east sector.

Pince nez held out his hand.

'Passport,' he demanded.

He opened it, studied it, turning every page slowly, then handed it to his colleague, who repeated the process, then passed the passport through the window of the shack.

'I want that back,' said Verago.

'Foreign passports have to be checked,' said pince nez. Verago didn't expect the next question.

'How much money have you got with you?'

'Eighty marks,' said Verago, 'and 200 dollars. In US currency.'

'Show me.'

He took the money and counted it.

'Is that all? You have no other currency?'

'None.'

'It is a serious criminal offence to import or export smuggled currency or to engage in financial speculation in the German Democratic Republic,' said pince nez pretentiously, handing him back the money.

'I understand.'

'Why are you visiting East Berlin?'

'Pleasure,' said Verago. 'Pure pleasure. Also . . . '

'Yes?' demanded the second man sharply.

'I much admire Brecht. I want to visit the Berliner Ensemble. Your theatre is very famous.'

Pince nez frowned.

'You are an American tourist?'

'Correct.'

290

'And how long do you intend to stay?'

'Twenty-four hours.'

'Where are you staying in West Berlin?'

'At the Hilton.'

'You're alone?'

Verago took a chance. 'I hear there are some very attractive girls in East Berlin.'

It was a mistake. Pince nez drew in his breath audibly. 'I must warn you that hooliganism is severely punished. Nor do we allow immorality. Is that clear?'

'Absolutely.'

The two men exchanged looks. Then the second one said: 'You're an attorney?'

'Yes.'

'Perhaps you will have the opportunity to study our justice at first hand.' He laughed. 'I am sure you will be welcome at a sitting of the People's Court. It might open your eyes.'

'I don't know if I'll have the time,' said Verago mildly. He was beginning to feel the strain.

A hand suddenly appeared in the opening in the shack, holding his passport. Pince nez took the document.

'Very well,' he said. He started filling in a card. 'V...e...r...a...g...o. An unsual name. It does not sound American.'

'My folks came from Greece . . . way back.'

'Ach so,' said pince nez agreeably. 'I forgot. There are no pure Americans.'

He finished filling in the card, and stamped it. Then he stapled it to the passport.

'You have a tourist visa for twenty-four hours. Do not lose it. You must show this when you leave, or you cannot depart.'

'Thank you,' said Verago. He turned to go.

'I hope the Berliner Ensemble is not booked out,' the second man called out. 'It would be a pity to have come for nothing.'

Verago left the station. He didn't once look back.

He knew what they had done with his passport in the shack. They had photographed it. Every single page.

291

EAST BERLIN

He had the feeling he was being followed, but every time he turned round to glance back, he could see nothing to confirm it.

He was surprised how strangely deserted the streets were and, sixteen years after VE day, the many scars of wartime still around him. Shell holes still pock-marked the sides of some buildings. There were ugly gaps in rows of crumbling houses, like cavities caused by rotten teeth.

The grimness of the place was a shock after the bustle and prosperity of the Western sector. An even greater shock were the first Russians he saw, two soldiers walking on the other side of the road. Verago had not seen Russian troops face to face before, and he had to stop himself staring at them. They strode past without a second look at him.

He found a cab at last, and asked to be taken to Kolwitz strasse. It was only a short ride, and when the driver stopped outside the block of flats, Verago told him to wait.

It was a four-floored apartment house, and like so much in East Berlin, it looked down at heel. There were eight flats, and each had its own buzzer at the front door.

He pressed the one that said 'Braunschweig'. Nothing happened.

He pressed the bell again, and stood waiting. Flat C was on the second floor, but the front entrance of the building remained shut, and there was no sound from the call-down system.

He tried a third time, and then saw a man's face peering at him blankly through the window of the ground-floor apartment next to the front door.

The railings prevented Verago getting near the window, but

he signalled to the man, mouthing: 'Can you let me in?'

The face suddenly disappeared, and then, almost to his surprise, the front door opened, and the man stood there. He wore carpet slippers and needed a shave. He was elderly, and regarded Verago with undisguised hostility.

'What do you want?' he demanded.

'Braunschweig,' said Verago. 'Flat C.'

'Not here.' He made to shut the door.

Verago put his foot in the way. 'When will they be back?'

'I didn't say they're out, I said they're not here,' growled the man. He scratched his unshaven chin as if it itched.

'What do you mean, not here?'

'Don't you understand German?' said the man rudely. 'I've told you. They're not here. They've gone. Departed.'

Verago felt his stomach tightening.

'Since when?'

'I don't know,' said the man sullenly. 'Who are you?'

He had shapeless trousers, and they were held up by a belt that had makeshift holes punched into it. Maybe the man had lost weight.

'I'm a friend,' said Verago vaguely.

'Foreigner, eh?'

'Who are you?' asked Verago.

'The caretaker.' He tried to close the door again, but Verago wouldn't shift his foot.

'Look here,' said Verago, 'they can't have disappeared into thin air. When did they go? Have you got their new address? Did they tell you anything? It's important.'

'Nothing to do with me,' said the man, 'and if you've got so many questions, you'd better go to the authorities. I don't want anything to do with foreigners . . .'

He said it quite loudly, as if he wanted the world to hear.

'Especially not Americans,' he added for good measure. 'Now let go of my door . . .'

'Just a moment . . .'

'I tell you for the last time, the Braunschweigs have gone and you won't see them here again. The flat's already been let.'

It was hopeless. Verago stepped back, and the man

slammed the front door in his face.

Verago stared up at the windows of the flats as if they would yield a clue, but there was no sign of life beyond the dirty windows and their soiled curtains.

He wondered why the man had made the crack about Americans. Sure, Verago looked like a foreigner. His clothes were too good. His German was accented. But why take him to be an American? He could have been an Englishman, or even a Russian. Was his nationality that obvious?

Half an hour in East Berlin, and he had reached a dead end.

Damn it, I'm not beaten yet, he said to himself, even if it sounded a little bit like whistling in the dark.

He turned back to find the cab.

It had gone.

LONDON

The motor torpedo boat raced across the water, skimming the waves, straight at the yacht with the bright yellow sails. Then, as collision seemed inevitable, it suddenly altered course, and veered round in a big circle, making for the schoolboy standing at the edge of the Round Pond who was operating the craft's radio controls.

Ivanov sighed.

'I wish I'd had toys like that when I was his age,' he said. He held out his bag of bread to Laurie. 'Here, you want some more?'

She took some crusts, broke them up, and flung them towards the ducks. But a sea gull swooped down and stole most of it as it fell.

'You always come here feeding the ducks?' she asked. Sometimes, he surprised her.

'But, of course,' he replied, mockingly. 'I am a Communist. I share my last crust with the under-privileged.'

'They look pretty well fed to me,' she observed.

'It's all in the eyes of the beholder. Sometimes things are not what they seem.' He looked her in the eyes. 'Are they, Laurie?'

She studiously followed the course of the little torpedo boat.

'There,' said Ivanov. He emptied the last of the crumbs on the ground, screwed up the paper bag, and tossed it aside.

'Hey!' exclaimed Laurie. 'That's against the law. No litter.'

He took her arm. 'You keep forgetting. I have diplomatic immunity.' It amused him. 'Absolute immunity. So I can get away with all sorts of things . . . '

'I know,' she nodded. 'But I wouldn't push it, Gene.'

They were walking between the trees towards the big bronze statue of the muscular man riding the huge horse.

'I am surprised about your friend,' he remarked suddenly.

'What friend?'

He shook his head almost pityingly. 'Please, Laurie, it's not playtime. What other friend can there be?'

A slight breeze blew some hair into her eyes. She brushed it away. 'I have lots of friends, you'd be amazed.'

'I thought Captain Verago was a smart man,' he went on, as if she hadn't made any comment. 'Instead, he seems to have . . . well, if one wanted to be melodramatic one could say a death wish.'

She shivered slightly, but it wasn't the cold. The July afternoon air was soft and balmy.

'I don't . . . '

'He's sticking his nose into things he doesn't understand . . . '

She looked at him defiantly. 'But perhaps he does, have you ever thought of that?'

They came to a bench, and he nodded at it.

'Let's sit down.'

For a moment he said nothing. She gazed back at the Round Pond and the outline of Kensington Palace in the distance with unseeing eyes.

'You know what I'm talking about,' he said at last. 'We all do, because we're all in this together. Your Captain Verago is a fool if he hasn't worked that out yet. How can he take on everybody? Your people, my people, the Germans? Doesn't he realise that this is a game without frontiers and without sides?'

She was still staring straight ahead.

'Why are you telling me this?'

He shrugged. 'I think you're quite fond of the guy, and if somebody could get to him, before it's too late . . . '

She turned to him. 'You're talking to the wrong person, Gene. There's nothing I can do.'

But he put his head closer to hers. 'Laurie, you can pass the word. Everybody wants to see this Tower business dealt with. What do any of us gain from it? But if he goes on tipping the balance, meddling unnecessarily . . . ' He spread his hands helplessly. 'My people won't sit by. There's too much at stake.'

A woman walked by with a Pekingese and a Shitzu terrier. The Pekingese tottered along sedately, like a dignified elderly functionary, but the Shitzu darted all over the place. It rushed up to Ivanov and sniffed his shoes. He leant forward and stroked the dog.

'What exactly have you heard about the Tower trial?' asked Laurie.

'Come along, Sanki!' came the woman's command from where she stood some yards away and Ivanov watched the Shitzu run towards her.

'Nothing officially,' he said. 'But I know they're worried about the way it's gone so far. And when my people get worried, they do drastic things.'

Laurie stood up.

'I'm cold,' she said.

'I'm sorry,' said Ivanov, and he sounded sincere. 'I had to tell you. After all, what are friends for?'

EAST BERLIN

Verago sat in the café, feeling like a fly snared in an invisible web. He knew he was caught when the cab had gone; not even in East Berlin did taxi drivers take off without being paid.

He walked into the café, and sat down to take stock. It was in a small side street, near Kolwitzstrasse, and had seen better days. There were four tables. On the wall hung a rack of newspapers for patrons to borrow; but the only paper displayed were three copies of *Neues Deutschland,* the official organ of the East German Communist Party. By the toilet, whether by accident or design, hung a portrait of goatee-bearded Walter Ulbricht.

Verago ordered a beer and the Czech-brewed Pilsner tasted good. The place smelt of boiled cabbage, and needed redecorating. A radio faintly played brass band music. At one of the tables sat a man, noisily slurping the contents of a big bowl of lentil soup.

Only one person came in, a red-haired girl. She wore thick lisle stockings, and limped slightly.

'Hello, Trudi,' called out the woman behind the counter, 'how's tricks?'

'Shitty,' snapped the redhead, and sat down by herself. She gave Verago a cursory look.

He was thinking he had three days. That was all. The court martial resumed on Tuesday. Here was the key to it, somewhere, and he had to get to it before returning to England. To Laurie. To . . . He sighed. At this moment, England, Laconbury, the whole circus, seemed as remote as a distant planet. So did the chance of finding what he needed to throw a spanner in the works.

The redhead got up, and came over.

'It is OK to sit down?' she asked in English.

He hesitated, and then shrugged.

'Sank you,' she said. Her accent was atrocious. And close up, she looked thin and undernourished. Her make up was grotesque, a red slash that passed for lipstick on her mouth, and

297

heavy eye shadow that made her look tired, and badly in need of a good night's sleep.

'You are a Yankee?'

Jesus, and he had kidded himself that if he didn't wear uniform he wouldn't be so conspicuous.

'My boy friend is a Zhee I,' she continued without waiting for him. 'He will take me to Texas. He is an MP.'

'Oh yes?'

'I go to the West to see him at weekends,' she added. 'You buy me a drink?'

He felt sorry for her. Her blouse had a button missing, and she was clutching a cheap, plastic handbag. A thread was running in her worn wool skirt.

'What would you like?' asked Verago. She didn't need a drink, he figured, but something to eat.

'Schnapps,' she said and smiled. 'You join me?'

'One schnapps,' Verago called to the woman behind the counter.

She pouted. 'Only one?'

'I have to go in a minute.'

The brandy came, and she raised her glass.

'To America, chin chin.'

'Where did you learn English?'

'I pick it up,' she said, and coughed. 'From boy friends. Zhee Is.'

Verago wondered what kind of GI had taught her to say 'chin chin'. He began to rise.

'Wait,' she said. She had taken a crumpled handkerchief from her purse and was dabbing her mouth. 'You sell me some dollars?'

So, thought Verago. That's it. A set up. The man with the pince nez crossed his mind. 'It is a serious offence to speculate . . . currency . . . ' That's what they want. An excuse.

'I'm sorry, fraulein,' he said, rather formally, and in a loud voice. 'I only have a little money, and I need that.'

'Not fraulein, please,' she said. 'I am Trudi. And I give you a good price. A very good price.'

'I'm sure.' Now he was on his feet. 'Thank you very much,

Trudi. Some other time.' He signalled to pay.

'Please sit down.'

It was her tone that made him look at her again.

'It is important,' she added, in a low voice.

He glanced round the café. The man was still eating his soup.

'Please,' said Trudi, her tired eyes pleading.

Slowly Verago sat down again. The woman came over with the bill.

'Noch ein bier, bitte,' said Verago, 'und ein schnapps.'

'Sank you,' said the redhead.

Careful, thought Verago. Be very careful what you say from now on.

'What is so important, Trudi?' His voice was soft.

'You have been asking questions. About the Braunschweigs.'

He tensed. 'How do you know?'

'I know,' she said, rather sadly.

The drinks came. Verago took a sip of his beer, looking at her across the rim of the glass.

'How?' he repeated.

'Do you want to know about Helga or don't you?' she demanded with a touch of impatience.

'I want to know who you are.'

'Go to hell,' she almost spat at him. She had finished her first schnapps, and now took a big gulp of the second one. Again she coughed. She got up.

'Goodbye,' she said curtly, and began to walk back to her table.

'Just a moment.'

She paused. 'Yes?'

'What about Helga?'

'You want to find her?'

You're a damn fool, said Verago to himself. But he risked it.

'Maybe.'

The girl turned her head, to make sure nobody was listening. Then she whispered:

'She's at Reinhof's.'

'Where?'

'Reinhof's. Liebermann Platz 43. On the ground floor.'

He started to say something, and she put a hand on his arm. Two of her fingernails were broken.

'You must go now.'

'Now wait a second . . . ' began Verago.

The door of the café opened and a man with cropped hair and rimless glasses came in.

'Please,' hissed Trudi. 'Go. Not a word. Just go.'

Verago threw ten marks on the table, and walked out.

He wondered if this was how a fish felt when it swallowed the bait.

EAST BERLIN

It was an undertaker's shop. 'Reinhof' read the sign, and underneath 'Leichenbestatter.'

Verago didn't know the German word for mortician, but he knew what leichen were. Bodies. Corpses. Cadavers.

And the shop window made the message clear. It was a simple display. Just a marble urn.

He stood across the road, in the Liebermann Platz, and he thought this is where I should get off. Back to the Friederich-strasse, jump aboard the first S-train, and half an hour later order a triple scotch in the Golden City bar of the Hilton. That would be the wise thing to do.

Because of course Trudi was a set up. Maybe the idea had been to frame him. To lure him into doing some illegal currency deal. Or get him shacked up with a prostitute. Then they could charge him with almost anything; black-marketing, immorality, you name it.

But they obviously had prepared for all contingencies. And when he didn't play the game, they had this joker up their sleeve. An address for Helga.

And yet . . .

Why an undertaker? Why not an ordinary address, some faceless building? And supposing Trudi wasn't one of them? Supposing somebody had sent her to help him find Helga?

No, you're a goddamn fool, Verago, his caution kept saying, get out of this while you can. He stood in a doorway, took out a pack of cigarettes and lit one. He saw a man at the nearby bus stop stare at him. He must have seen the cigarette pack. Lucky Strikes. From the PX. Nobody smokes Lucky Strikes in East Berlin . . .

He turned his back on the man. Coming down the street were half a dozen youths in shabby trench coats, heavy boots, and peaked cloth caps. They were laughing loudly, and suddenly Verago felt fear. He didn't want them to see him. It was a grey, drab neighbourhood, and they were like a pack of scavenging wolves. Or was he getting paranoid?

He melted into the doorway, and the group went past, guffawing and laughing among themselves. They didn't even look at him.

Jesus Christ, Verago, you've come this far, and you're not going to chicken out. What the hell can they do to you anyway? Kick you out of the People's paradise? Deport you from East Berlin? OK, let Colonel Ochs have his field day, and accuse you of causing an international incident. They've got your card marked anyway, might as well give them something good to burst their blood vessels.

He crossed the road, and put his hand on the handle of the undertaker's door. For a moment, he hesitated. Then he walked in.

Inside was a small office with a table and two chairs. Dark velvet draperies divided it off. There was a faint, sickening-sweet smell of incense, and, very softly, organ music. Funereal muzak, thought Verago with distaste.

The curtains parted, and a thin, weedy man appeared.

'I . . . ' began Verago, and stopped. He didn't quite know how to put it.

But the man smiled sympathetically, gave a slight bow and asked softly:

'Braunschweig?'

The cloying aroma of the place began to make Verago feel slightly sick. He swallowed, and nodded.

'Fraulein Helga . . . '

'Of course,' said the man with deepest understanding. He went to the table, and opened a leather bound book lying on it. He pushed it towards Verago and held out a pen.

'Please,' he invited.

It was like a visitors' book, with signatures on each page. Verago paused momentarily, then bent down and signed.

The man gently slid the book back towards himself and glanced at the signature.

'Ah, Herr Verago,' he said softly, as if the name explained everything.

He straightened up and held one of the velvet curtains open for Verago.

'This way, please.' His tone was compassion itself.

This is crazy, thought Verago. But he went through the gap in the curtain. The thin mournful man did not follow him.

Verago found himself in a small, dark chapel. Four enormous white candles stood in tall holders at each corner of a bier. On the bier was an open coffin. And in the coffin a body.

Verago stepped closer. It was a woman, and despite the gloom the light from the four big candles was enough to illuminate the face. He recognised it. He had last seen it as a photograph in Pech's office.

The dead woman in the coffin, looking peaceful and contented, was Helga Braunschweig.

Verago stood stiff, dazed. He stared at the face like a hypnotised man. He took another step forward, and then stopped.

Suddenly, he felt faint and dizzy. The whole room began spinning and it seemed to him that the soft organ music had grown louder, the sweet syrupy smell more suffocating.

He heard the velvet curtains rustle, glimpsed a man with cropped hair and rimless glasses. He experienced a moment of panicky fear. Then Verago felt sudden great pain and knew no more.

KARLSRUHE

Only one lamp was burning in the office. Herr Stamm sat at his desk, and with two fingers slowly typed the report that only the minister was to see.

It was after 10 o'clock at night, and the offices along the corridor were silent. Herr Stamm had locked his door. And there was only one sheet of paper in the typewriter; there could be no copy of what he had to say.

He had headed it 'Sehr Geheim', and it was indeed most secret. So secret, in fact, that he could not dictate it to anyone.

What he had to say would not make him popular. And he realised, in view of what he already knew, that it could even put his own life in danger.

But Herr Stamm was good at his job, and loyal. Bonn had to know that treason was in the air.

Already he had typed the list of names:

Colonel Karl Otto von Hingeldey, of the Bundeswehr general staff;

Heinz Felfe, former Abwehr officer, and now a civil service member of the BND, the Bundesnachrichten Dienst, the special intelligence bureau in Bonn;

Peter Fuhrman,, a senior controller in MAD, the Militaerische Abschirmdienst, the Bundeswehr security service.

Three esteemed men, experienced intelligence officers, entrusted with the most delicate state secrets, and privy, as part of their duties, to the most highly classified NATO documents.

And each one of them a Soviet agent.

Herr Stamm sat back, and looked at what he had awkwardly typed so far.

He sighed. Bonn's whole intelligence network, all its various special agencies, the very heart of security and espionage, had been penetrated.

The light from the lamp fell on the secret file that contained the background on General Edgar Feuchtinger. The man who had recruited the ring. The man who inadvertently had led Herr Stamm onto the trail . . .

He didn't have to make a special report on the general. He was dead. Herr Stamm allowed himself a cold smile. People died rather conveniently in Berlin.

He looked at his watch. He felt tired, and he wanted to get home before midnight. But he wasn't finished yet.

He had to add one more name to the list of traitors.

EAST BERLIN

'Stop play acting,' ordered an unfriendly voice in accented English.

Verago opened his eyes, but shut them again as the glare from a white light stabbed into his eyeballs. His head was thudding, and he felt sick.

'Look at me,' commanded the voice.

He tried again, and squinted, trying to escape the harshness of the light. He was handcuffed, sitting on a chair in a room with whitewashed brick walls. At a desk opposite, a fat man contemplated him. The man was bald, but for a single piece of hair, like a string of spaghetti, which was pasted across his shiny pink head.

Verago licked his lips.

'Where am I?' he asked.

The man laughed. 'Don't you know? I'm surprised. You're under arrest.'

Gradually Verago became conscious that not only his head

ched. His body hurt. As if somebody had kicked him; he
wondered if they actually had. He couldn't remember it.

'Arrest? What . . . what for?'

'Espionage, of course,' said the fat man. 'My name is
Schultz. Sicherheits Dienst. SDD. You understand?' He held up
an object. Verago tried to focus on it. It was his wallet.

'You recognise this?'

Verago nodded. The handcuffs were biting into his skin.

'Could you loosen these, please. They're cutting my
wrists . . . '

Schultz was holding something else he had taken out of the
wallet.

'And this? You recognise this?'

He thrust it in front of Verago.

'It's my ID card. My Army identification.'

The man threw it on the desk and jumped up.

'So!' he exclaimed, 'you admit. That is very sensible of you. I
think we'll get on.'

The light was still bothering Verago. He tried to look away.

'I don't know what this is about, but I want the American
authorities notified. And I want to know what I am doing here.'

With surprising agility for a fat man, Schultz swung himself
on top of his desk, and sat on it facing Verago.

'You are in no position to want anything. You are in deep
trouble. You are here illegally. As a spy. You – '

'You're crazy,' cut in Verago. He felt awful, but his
indignation was taking over. 'I have a visa. I . . . '

Schultz leant over and picked up Verago's passport lying next
to his blotter.

'Oh yes,' he said, 'you have a visa alright. Obtained by fraud.
You did not tell anybody you were an American officer. You
said you were a civilian. A tourist. You deliberately deceived the
customs and immigration. Why are you running around in
civilian clothes and not in uniform? Why did you call yourself a
lawyer? Why didn't you cross at the official border post used by
allied military personnel? Why smuggle yourself into our
country?'

Schultz took a deep breath. Before Verago could say

305

anything, he rambled on:

'I will tell you. You are on a special mission. A spy mission. Or maybe sabotage. Unfortunately for you, we have caught you redhanded . . .'

He nodded with satisfaction. He brushed his head with his right hand, to make sure the string of spaghetti was still stuck in place.

'Your mission was doomed from the start, of course. You spies don't realise we are always ready for you.'

'You know you're talking nonsense,' said Verago quietly. Maybe he could try reasoning with the fat man. 'I just came across for twenty-four hours, as a visitor. I am a lawyer. I'm here privately, not on duty. I came to see the sights . . .'

'Oh sure,' agreed Schultz sarcastically. He swung his legs joyfully. 'In time you will tell us everything. What were you doing there anyway?'

'Where?' asked Verago.

'The place we found you.'

'Oh, the funeral parlour . . .'

Schultz's eyes widened. 'Funeral parlour? What funeral parlour. I warn you not to play the fool. No, the bomb site where we found you. In the Krollstrasse.'

Verago's head was splitting. 'I don't understand. I was in the mortician . . .'

'You're wasting your time. You had a struggle with a man on a bombed site. You were seen. The police came. The man had run off, and you were lying unconscious on the ground. By a wall. He must have hit you. Who was the man? Why did you fight?'

'There wasn't any fight, there wasn't any bomb site,' said Verago.

'But we have a witness.' Schultz raised his hand. 'Please. Don't take my word for anything.'

He got down from the desk and went to the door. He opened it and shouted to somebody outside:

'Bring him in.'

He turned to Verago. 'Why do you insist on telling lies? You know the truth will out. This is an old American saying, is it not? Anyway, I will prove it to you.'

There was a knock on the door.

'Come in,' shouted Schultz.

A man entered. He had cropped hair and rimless glasses.

'Is that him?' asked Schultz.

The man studied Verago. The bright light shone on his glasses, they reflected the glare.

'Yes,' he said.

'Tell me again,' ordered Schultz.

'I was walking along the Krollstrasse. I saw two men struggling. On the bomb site. By the demolished cinema. You know the one?'

Schultz nodded impatiently. 'Yes, yes, go on.'

'It looked nasty. A robbery perhaps. This was one of the men. I recognise his foreign clothes. I ran for the police. But when the Vopos arrived, the other man had gone and this one was lying on the ground, unconscious.'

'Well,' said Schultz to Verago, 'what do you say to that?'

'It never happened,' replied Verago.

Schultz sniffed his distaste. 'And you will tell me that you of course have never seen this man before?'

'No. I have, as a matter of fact.'

The man with the rimless glasses turned his head towards him. His face was expressionless.

'Ach so! How surprising,' Schultz smirked. 'And where was that?'

'In a café,' said Verago.

'What were you doing there?'

'Drin'.ing a schnapps.'

'Really.'

Schultz scratched his chin. Then he asked the cropped-hair man:

'Did you see this American spy in a café?'

'No.'

'Sure?'

'Positive.'

Schultz spread out his hands like a man who gives up.

'There you are, Captain Verago, I do not understand your

little game, but it's not very successful, is it? This man is just an innocent passer-by. Obviously he never saw you before.'

Interesting, thought Verago. They don't want to know about the café. Or Trudi. They don't want to ask me any questions about anything there.

He shrugged.

Schultz nodded to the man.

'You may go, with the thanks of the authorities.'

'Happy to do my duty,' said the man.

It was a nice little command performance, thought Verago, as the man shut the door.

'Well,' said Schultz sitting down behind his desk. 'I don't know what you were doing to get knocked about by a stranger.' He leered suddenly. 'Maybe you don't like girls? Maybe you prefer young men and made a very improper advance to this individual? Is that why he beat you up?'

Verago smiled coldly. 'Are you enjoying yourself, Schultz? Or do you judge everybody by your own standards?'

Schultz tightened his lips. 'That's not the way to get rid of your little bracelets,' he warned.

He opened a desk drawer and took out a pencil. It had a very sharp point, and he felt it with his thumb. It seemed to satisfy him. Then, from another drawer, he took some foolscap sheets of paper and placed them neatly in front of him.

'Now, then,' he said, 'you have a clear choice. You can now make a voluntary statement, a full confession about your mission, what your objective is, who your superiors are, your contacts here, who's working with you, the lot. If you do that, I promise you everything will be quite pleasant, and we can part the best of friends. How's that?'

'Very considerate.'

Schultz's eyes narrowed. 'Or you can go to a little place where everybody is eventually persuaded to tell the truth. I am sure they'd be delighted to welcome you at Hohenschoen-hausen.'

'Hohen – what?'

'Hohenschoenhausen,' repeated Schultz with relish. 'A little SSD holiday establishment. After all, you said you want to see

308

the sights of East Berlin, and that's a sight you'll long remember.' He laughed. 'Well, which is it to be?'

He sat poised, the pencil hovering ready to write.

'I want to talk to the American liaison mission,' said Verago.

Schultz shook his head. 'You are very badly informed. Your authorities do not have relations with us. You are on your own. Perhaps you should persuade Washington to recognise us. Sooner or later, they'll have to. Unfortunately it'll be too late for you.'

He waited, but Verago stayed silent. Eventually he sighed, and put down the pencil.

'I'm sorry,' he said. 'I'll arrange for transport.'

He put the paper back in the drawer. He was a methodical man.

'In a way, Captain Verago, you're very privileged. Not many tourists get to see the inside of Hohenschoenhausen. The trouble is, even fewer ever come out again.'

Then he stood up and called the escort.

Saturday, July 29, 1961 – EAST BERLIN

The little convoy raced through the streets of East Berlin at high speed, two Vopo motor cycle outriders leading the way, and a jeep-load of Vopos, cradling submachine guns, bringing up the rear. They had priority, and at road junctions and traffic lights, police waved them through, imperiously holding up everybody until they had passed.

They were escorting a windowless, all-steel, grey truck with no insignia, and only a couple of small ventilation slits. It was like a self-contained bank vault on wheels carrying high value cargo. The handcuffed man sitting inside, between two expressionless guards, had no idea where he was being driven.

He couldn't see the propaganda maxims painted on bullet scarred walls, the banners hanging from windows, the red streamers flying from long poles, all with slogans. Dictums like 'Socialism Is Triumphing, We Are Stronger', 'A Strong German Democratic Republic Ensures Peace', 'The Working Masses Will Conquer'.

Nor did he see the hoardings with the gigantic portraits of the man with the pince nez and Vandyke beard, 'Spitzbart', Walter Ulbricht.

But he heard the klaxons of the motor cycles, and he could feel the pain of his handcuffs. The guards sitting either side of him studiously avoided looking at him, but their hands hovered near their guns.

He knew that he was rated an important prisoner. Not that that was any consolation. They had taken away his passport and his Army AGO card. He had no identification. No papers to prove who he was.

With a shock, Tony Verago suddenly realised that he had ceased to exist.

HOHENSCHOENHAUSEN

Utter darkness enveloped him, suffocated him. Even when his eyes adjusted, he still could hardly see anything.

It was so pitch black that he stumbled around, holding out his manacled hands, trying to grope his way about, to find the walls, to get some idea of the size of the . . .

The what? The room? The cell? The dungeon?

Was this the place Schultz had talked of? Hohenschoenhausen. The SSD prison. Reserved for the use of the State Security Service of the German Democratic Republic.

He had heard sharp commands when the convoy finally had

310

halted. Then one of the guards had blindfolded him and unseeing, stumbling, he had been half guided, half pushed across a courtyard, taken, so he thought, into a building, along various corridors, up a staircase, along another passage, and then an iron door had clanged shut behind him. After a time, a guard had entered, taken off his blindfold, and left again. It made no difference to his eyes. The darkness was impenetrable. Not even a slit of light under the door, a glimmer through a crack in the wall.

And it was silent. Terribly silent. No voices, no footsteps. This cage was sound proof.

They're trying disorientation, thought Verago, desperately attempting to make his brain reason and concentrate.

They want me to lose all sense of time and direction. And, Christ, they're succeeding.

Already time had started to become meaningless. He tried to retrack his movements. The Braunschweig apartment block. The café. The funeral parlour. Schultz. Now this. How long had he been in East Berlin? A day? Two days? Was it morning, was it night?

Without warning, suddenly he was standing in light. From the high ceiling, a powerful bulb shone down on him. It hurt, and he closed his eyes, tight.

He heard the door being unlocked and, squinting, Verago saw a man enter. He wore civilian clothes but had military bearing. The door was shut behind him.

'Sit down over there,' instructed Major Fokin.

Verago looked round. For the first time he took in the geography of the cell. It was very bare. A bunk and a three-legged stool. That was all.

Gingerly Verago sat down on the stool.

'I understand you've been very unco-operative so far,' said Fokin, quite pleasantly, 'but I'm sure you've been thinking it over, and we'll get on famously.'

He spoke excellent British English.

Verago held out his hands.

'Take these off,' he said. 'Please. They hurt.'

'Certainly,' said Fokin. He seemed to have come prepared

for the request. He pulled out a key, and unlocked the handcuffs. Verago's wrists were so numb that he didn't even feel relief. He started rubbing his left wrist with his right hand. That one, especially, had been sheer agony.

'Don't worry,' said Fokin, 'it'll pass.'

'Who are you?' asked Verago thickly. His mouth felt awful. More than anything, he wanted to clean his teeth.

'My name is Fokin, and I'm here to establish some facts about you so we can get this whole thing cleared up.'

'Oh yes?'

'My advice is for you to be perfectly frank, Captain Verago. You can start by telling me which agency you work for.'

'Agency?' echoed Verago.

'Agency. Organisation. Service. Which is it? CIA? The Counter Intelligence Corps, CIC? Army Security? The OSI? The NSA? The JIC?'

Involuntarily, Verago yawned. 'I'm sorry,' he said, 'I'm tired. Really bushed.'

'Of course you are,' Fokin sympathised. 'But you must tell me. Which organisation?'

'I'm a lawyer,' said Verago dully.

Fokin nodded. 'I know. Judge Advocate's Corps. Your boss is Colonel Ochs. You've been in England with the Air Force. Laconbury. Brigadier-General Croxford is the commander. It's an excellent cover. Just out of the ordinary enough to make it believable. But your real mission? Here in Berlin? That's what I want to know.'

'The Geneva convention – '

'– does not apply to intelligence officers who enter foreign countries as tourists in disguise.'

'Some disguise,' remarked Verago bitterly. He glanced down at his clothes, shapeless, stained.

'I can see you are tired,' said Fokin, and his sudden consideration baffled Verago. 'Think things over. You have plenty of time before the real interrogation.'

The real interrogation. He just slipped it in, but it startled Verago.

'I have to be back in England,' he explained. 'I am defending

312

a man in a court martial, and the trial resumes on . . . '

'My dear Captain Verago, forget it,' said Fokin.

WEST BERLIN

'I'm a friend of Captain Verago's,' said the lean, angular man. He had never met Verago in his life, but lying came to him quite naturally.

'Oh yes?' The duty manager at the Berlin Hilton wore his fixed public relations smile. He was Swiss and humourless, but he was always polite, except to people whose credit cards weren't sanctioned.

'He's asked me to collect his luggage and pay the bill,' said the lean man.

'Just a moment,' the duty manager excused himself politely. He disappeared into one of the administrative offices, behind the reception desk. The lean man stood in the lobby, unconcerned.

When the duty manager reappeared, his smile was a little forced.

'You say you are a friend of Captain Verago's?'

'Yes.'

'Well, he checked in on Wednesday and said he wanted a single room for several days. We haven't seen him since.'

The duty manager strongly disapproved of this kind of irregularity.

'That's right,' nodded the lean man. 'He's been called away.'

'Without telling us?' It was clearly a gross breach of good manners in a hotelier's book.

'It happens,' said the lean man.

The duty manager had the bill in his hand.

'Of course we will expect him to pay in full. We held the room.'

The man took the bill, and glanced at it.

'That'll be fine,' he said. 'You take dollars?'

'Of course.' The smile was a little warmer.

'Maybe we could go up to his room, and get his things,' suggested the man.

They took the lift up to the eighth floor, and the duty manager unlocked the door of the room. Verago had scarcely used it. There were a few toilet things in the bathroom, but his suitcase still contained his shirts and underwear.

In the wardrobe hung his uniform.

'I'll just pack it,' said the lean man, taking it off the hanger. He gathered the toilet things, and also put them in Verago's case. Then he quickly, expertly glanced round the room. It was a trained look, which took in everything.

'That's about it, I guess,' said the lean man.

Downstairs he went to the cashier's cage, and paid the bill in full. He carefully put the receipt in his wallet.

'Captain Verago should have let us know,' said the duty manager.

'Yes, he should have,' agreed the man.

'It would have saved him some money.'

'I appreciate your co-operation, sir,' said the man.

'Well,' smiled the duty manager, 'we try to be helpful.'

Just as well, thought the man. The less we have to get official the better.

'You sure your friend won't need the room again?' the duty manager added.

'No,' said the man, 'I think you can take that as definite. He won't need the room again.'

As he carried Verago's case out of the hotel, he wondered what it was all about. He was a CIC agent, but the Army Counter Intelligence Corps sometimes didn't tell its own men everything.

Some hours later, Verago's cell door was unlocked, and two armed guards beckoned to him. They wore East German uniforms, but they weren't Vopos. Theirs was the grey of the death-strip guards, the Grepos.

'Come with us,' commanded the taller one.

Verago got to his feet wearily, and followed them. Another series of corridors, passage ways and staircases, and then he found himself in the open. They crossed a big courtyard and for the first time Verago saw the ten-foot walls that surrounded the confines of Hohenschoenhausen. Surmounting them, at strategic points were guard towers, with searchlights and machine guns.

He thought of all the stockades and military detention centres he had visited in the line of duty. It was an unpleasant realisation that here, for the first time, he wasn't a visitor. Nobody would wave him out of the main gate. These machine guns were there to mow him down if he made a false move.

'Keep going,' ordered the taller Grepo.

They led him into another cell block, where the small windows not only had bars, but were covered with fine wire mesh. Inside, doors were unlocked and he was marched down another long corridor, their footsteps echoing on the stone floor.

At last they stopped, outside a cell door with the number 183.

'In here,' said the taller Grepo, unlocking the door. As soon as Verago stepped inside, it was slammed shut again, with a thunderous clang.

He stood, adapting to the yellowish lighting. A gaunt man, with shaven head, and a shapeless uniform was already on one of the two bunks. He sat, his chin sunk on his chest, his cheek bones prominent in his emaciated face.

Verago walked over to the other bunk, and sat down on it.

He studied the other man, who hadn't even bothered to look up. Poor bastard, he thought, they've put him through it alright. And then he froze. Round the man's neck was a thin chain. And hanging from the chain were two dogtags. Military dogtags. US identity discs.

He sat staring, mesmerised by the dogtags. He couldn't believe it.

'Are you a Yank?' Verago called over.

Slowly the man raised his head, and his sunken, shadowed eyes looked at Verago.

'Are you American?' asked Verago urgently.

As if he had to think it over first, the man nodded.

Verago went over and sat on the bunk next to the man. He held out his hand, but the man just looked at him.

'What the hell are you doing here?' said Verago.

The man said nothing.

'Excuse me,' said Verago, and reached over for the dogtags. He read them quickly.

'Kingston? Matt Kingston? Air Force? Is that you? Are you an Air Force officer?'

Again, very slowly, the man nodded, his eyes never leaving Verago's face.

'Well, say something, for chrissake,' demanded Verago. Then he controlled himself. 'I'm sorry, fella, I'm Captain Verago. Tony Verago. United States Army.' The man didn't react. Verago pulled out his own dogtags from under his shirt. 'Look.'

The man's hand shot out and grabbed the dogtags and stared at them.

'My home's New York,' said Verago. 'Where are you from?'

The man let Verago's dogtags drop.

'You're American?' he said at last. His voice low.

'What's your outfit?' asked Verago. 'How did you get in here?'

Kingston stared at him sceptically.

'What did Rhett say to Scarlett?' he asked suddenly.

'Eh?' Verago gaped at him.

'If you're American, you know what Rhett said to her. Every American does.'

The guy's crazy, thought Verago. Then he remembered. 'I don't give a damn.'

For the first time, there was a flicker in Kingston's eyes.

'You're from New York?'

'That's right.'

'What's the name of the toy store at the corner of Fifth and E. 57th?'

'What the hell is this, quiz time?' snapped Verago.

'You tell me the name and I'll believe you're from New York,' said Kingston.

'Schwartz.'

The man suddenly appeared interested.

'What's your outfit?'

'I'm a lawyer. Judge Advocate's Department. Where's your base?'

Again the hesitation. Then Kingston said:

'England. Laconbury.'

'Oh my god,' said Verago and momentarily he thought he had gone insane.

'What's the matter?'

'That's where I'm from. I'm at Laconbury. On TDY.'

The gaunt man shrank back as if he was suddenly frightened.

'You're a goddamn stool pigeon, aren't you,' he hissed viciously. 'They've planted you, haven't they. Go and fuck yourself, you bastard . . .'

'Hey, wait a minute . . .'

Kingston laughed, a slightly demented sound.

'You go tell Fokin, he's got to think of something better than this crap.'

'Don't be a fool,' said Verago angrily.

The man calmed down.

'Who's the commander?' he said.

'Croxford. Brigadier-General Croxford.'

'That proves nothing,' said Kingston. 'Fokin knows that too.

But if you're from Laconbury, you tell me what the general does in his free time. Every minute of his free time.'

'How the hell do I know?'

'I knew it,' said Kingston. 'You're a stoolie. Fokin doesn't know that either, so you don't . . .'

'Wait a second,' interrupted Verago. 'Golf. He plays golf. He's crazy about golf.'

Kingston scratched himself. Then he frowned. 'Well, maybe you're . . . maybe you're what you say. Just don't ask me too many questions, that's all.'

'Like how come you're here?'

'Oh, that's no secret. They shot me down. In the Baltic. On a ferret run. I'm dead, you see. Missing presumed dead. And you?'

'I'm just missing, I guess,' replied Verago. 'Not presumed dead. Not yet, I hope.' He looked around the cell. 'What happens here anyway?'

'You'll find out,' said Kingston.

They heard the sound of the door being unlocked from outside and a guard entered carrying two battered tin plates covered with a brown mixture looking like thin glutinous mud, and two tin mugs containing watered-down coffee made from acorns.

Verago regarded his food with distaste, and tried hard to ignore the obnoxious aroma.

Kingston laughed. 'It won't kill you,' he said, hungrily shovelling the muck into his mouth with a plastic spoon. 'You'll get to appreciate it.'

'What is it?' asked Verago, fighting back the nausea.

'If it's got lumps in it it's called goulash. If it's only liquid, it's just plain slime.'

For the first time Verago noticed the state of Kingston's hands. They had blood-encrusted cuts and slits all over them.

'Matt, what's happened to your hands?'

'Occupational therapy. The socialist democratic kind.'

'What do you mean?'

'Spanish Riders,' said Kingston bitterly. 'You'll get to know.'

'I don't understand.'

318

'They're working overtime in here on a special project. Getting the Spanish Riders ready.'

'I still don't get it.'

Kingston had already finished his plate. He put it down. Verago understood why he appeared so undernourished. If this was the main meal . . .

'Spanish Riders,' explained Kingston patiently, 'are sawhorse street barriers. Like the kind of things they put up in New York streets on St Patrick's Day. To cordon off an area. Get it?'

'No. Not really.'

'They got all the inmates in here working overtime preparing them . . . '

'How do you mean, preparing . . . '

'Wrapping barbed wire round them. Spikes and garlands. So you get cut to ribbons if you try to climb over them. That's how . . . '

He held up his scarred hands.

'I started bleeding too much, so they've given me a break. I'll be back at it soon. They need everybody, they're in such a rush. Truckloads of barriers come in every hour, and huge rolls of barbed wire. We do the rest.' He grinned. 'Our contribution to the workers' paradise. Building barbed-wire barricades.'

He looked at Verago's hands.

'Don't worry if the spikes stick into you. They draw blood, but they don't come through the other side. Guess it'll make a change from reading law books, eh?'

The door was flung open, and Verago thought they had come for the plates and mugs. He wondered what they'd do to him, because he hadn't touched any of the stuff.

But instead a guard appeared.

'You,' he said to Verago. 'Come with me. Interrogation.'

Kingston, on his bunk, grimaced. It made his skull look like a grisly death mask.

'Good luck, buddy. Keep your cool. Fokin can get real mean.'

But it wasn't Fokin who faced Verago in the interrogation room.

HOHENSCHOENHAUSEN

Helmut Pech's East German Volksarmee uniform was custom made, and fitted him to perfection. His shoulder tabs were those of a major, and he had a medal ribbon on his chest that Verago didn't recognise.

Pech started laughing. 'You should see your expression, you really should.'

'You . . . *here.*'

'Of course. Where I belong.' He took Verago's elbow and guided him to a chair, like a host. 'Sit down and get used to it.'

'You're SSD?' It wasn't so much a question, as an awful recognition.

'Correct. Or as you so neatly put it once, the East German Gestapo. That was very unkind.'

'My god!' murmured Verago. 'You of all people . . . B1. Bonn's counter intelligence. Working for *them.*'

'Not working for them,' corrected Pech with amusement. 'One of them. All along. There's a big difference.'

He sat down and regarded Verago silently. Then he said:

'Oh please, don't look so baffled. It's quite simple. Haven't you got used to the fact that nothing is what it seems these days? Old enemies are new friends. Friends turn into foes. Traitors become patriots. One man's cowardice is another man's bravery. It just depends on where you're standing.'

'And you? What are you?'

'The same package I've always been, but in new wrapping.' Pech liked that. 'Quite clever that, don't you agree, Tony? You don't mind me calling you Tony?'

'No, Major, I don't mind.' Verago's tone was icy.

320

Pech picked up a paper knife and started playing with it. It was a long, thin dagger with a vicious pointed blade. An inscription was engraved along the blade, but Verago couldn't read it from where he sat.

'It's a pity it had to end like this,' remarked Pech. 'I was doing a very useful job, even if I say so myself. I kept my nose very clean.' He frowned. 'Maybe I made a mistake shooting Martin Schneider, but . . . '

'You killed him?'

'Of course. He betrayed us. He passed Helga over to your people, to your agent, or should I say your client.' He gave a thin smile. 'Anyway, one can't let that sort of thing go unpunished, can one? Unfortunately, my late boss . . . you have heard of Herr Unruh?'

Verago shook his head.

'Well, Herr Unruh was a better spy catcher than I gave him credit for. He began to put two and two together.' Pech sighed. 'So . . . It gets like a gambling debt. You incur one to pay another. Of course, I tried to make it look like suicide, but Stamm . . . '

'Stamm?'

'My new boss. He started digging a little too deeply. It was time for me to depart. So here I am. You see how simple it is?'

The man fascinated Verago. He was like a creature in the reptile house whose one single bite meant death.

There was a knock on the door.

'Herein,' called out Pech, and a Grepo entered carrying a tray with a bottle in an ice bucket, and two glasses on it.

Pech indicated a place on his desk, and the man put the tray down, clicked his heels, and left.

'It's not the greatest,' apologised Pech, pouring some wine and pushing a glass over to Verago. Then he filled his own glass. 'This place doesn't have a good cellar.' He grinned. 'At least, not that kind of cellar. But Piesporter is always quite acceptable, don't you think? Prosit.'

Deep inside, Verago wanted to make some gesture, like throwing the wine in his face. But he had a craving for it suddenly, a great desire to taste alcohol, to feel it warming him.

He took the glass and drank, all the while hating himself for drinking with a traitor. That's something to be proud of, there's real defiance for you, he thought.

'Oh don't look so disapproving,' chided Pech. 'It's not that bad a vintage.'

'It's not the wine that's bad,' growled Verago.

'You should look on this as a little celebration,' said Pech. 'I know you're no spy. These idiots over here, they're like Pavlov's dogs. They've got spying mania. Any foreigner is suspicious. If he's American, and an Army man in civilian clothes, he must be a spy. It's lucky you weren't wearing dark glasses. A dummkopf like Schultz would have had you shot right away.'

'And that's exactly what you set up, isn't it?' broke in Verago.

'If you want to tilt at windmills, don't blame me for setting up a few for you,' smiled Pech. He poured some more wine. 'Tell me, what did you hope to achieve anyway? If poor Helga was still around, and you mananged to get hold of her, what good would that have done you?'

Verago looked away. 'I don't know,' he said slowly. 'I'm not sure. I wanted to bring her back to England. To produce her in court. To have her testify . . .'

'What exactly?'

Now Verago faced him. 'To say on oath the thing she told my client that's so explosive he has to be gagged. By his own people.'

Pech scraped back his chair. He went to the window and looked out. Even here the window was barred. But there was no wire mesh.

'You don't understand, do you?' he said, his back to Verago. 'You don't understand that you're up against us all. That hasn't sunk in yet, has it? It's us and the Americans, and the Russians, and the French and the British, all agreed on one thing, that nobody's going to prevent . . . August 13th.'

'Is that when it happens? August 13th?' asked Verago quietly.

Pech came back to his desk and sat down once more.

'Now then,' he said, as if they hadn't had any conversation so far. 'I'm sure you want to get out of here. Frankly, you should never have been brought to this place. As I told you, they overreact. Right now, they're like dogs on heat.'

Charming, thought Verago. A delightful way of describing your colleagues. But August 13th kept on hammering at the back of his mind.

'You haven't actually been ill treated, have you?' went on Pech, anxiously. 'Nobody's touched you, have they?'

'If you mean, have I been made to cut up my hands winding barbed wire round hundreds of street barricades . . . no.'

'Good.' Pech seemed relieved. 'I have given orders that you're not to be put in the workshops.'

'These wooden barriers, they have to be ready for August 13th, don't they?'

Pech stared at him. He clutched his paper knife, and the knuckled showed white. Then he relaxed.

'I'm going to order your release, Tony. I want you out of Berlin, out of the DDR, out of Germany. Understand?'

Something worried Verago. Like a caution light that was blinking. But he replied: 'Thank god for that. I have to be back in the UK on Tuesday. I've only got a couple of days. Just let me out of here and I'll catch the next train to the West sector.'

Pech tried to pour some more wine, but the bottle was empty.

'Damn, a dead man, as you say. What a pity.' He slammed the empty bottle back in the ice bucket. 'Tony, I'm afraid it's not as simple as that. It's got to be done, as you say in the American services, through channels.'

'Like the way I was tricked and knocked out and kidnapped, through channels? Is that it?'

'Properly. It's got to be neat and tidy. I have, as we put it, a stempel mentality. I like the right rubber stamp on the correct document. You have to be handed back formally and officially. I can't just let you wander back by yourself. Supposing questions are asked? Supposing you make allegations? Tricked, did you say, kidnapped? It could be very awkward . . .'

Verago swallowed. 'I'll keep quiet about it.'

'I'm sure,' purred Pech. 'Nevertheless, your handover has to be done correctly.'

'When?'

You leave that to me.' He bent down and from a drawer in his desk, he pulled out some magazines. 'Here, *Look, Life, Time*. To keep you amused.' He laughed suddenly. 'Very appropriate, wouldn't you say? *Look. Life. Time.*'

'I find the German sense of humour very unfunny, East or West,' remarked Verago stonily. 'I just want out, as quickly as possible.'

'Of course, of course,' agreed Pech genially. He took Verago to the door, and slapped him on the back. 'One day soon, you and I will crack a bottle, and we'll laugh about this, believe me.'

He opened the door, and nodded to the Grepo who stood at attention, cradling a machine pistol.

'183,' said Pech. 'See you soon, Tony.'

It was as he marched along the corridors, the guard at his side, that a terrible realisation dawned on Verago.

Pech had told him too much. Far too much for a man who was going to be handed back.

LACONBURY

Tower sat in the interview room in the headquarters building, wondering why the APs had brought him there.

He soon knew when Colonel Kincaid came in, followed by Jensen.

'Relax, Captain,' said Kincaid. 'I'm Third Air Force judge advocate, but this is sort of unofficial.'

'We've had some bad news, John,' interjected Jensen, but he didn't seem unduly depressed.

'You've lost your lawyer,' announced Kincaid.

Tower raised his head, and his tired eyes stared at the colonel

324

with his boyish movie star looks.

'Captain Verago went to Berlin, and I'm sorry to say he strayed into the East zone. He's missing.'

'Missing?'

'Yes, Captain. We've no idea what's happened to him or where he is. I guess you could say he's missing.'

'I see,' said Tower slowly.

Jensen leant forward.

'The point is, John, he can't be here for the resumed trial. I doubt if we'll get him back for months. They're holding him.'

Tower stared at him.

'How do you know that?' he asked quietly.

It was Kincaid who replied. 'It's an educated guess, Captain. We've been in touch with the Army in Berlin. CIC's found out he boarded a train into East Berlin, and after that he disappeared. He didn't go officially, he wasn't in uniform, so if they're holding him, it complicates things. He's got no status.'

'You know why he went to Berlin, John?' enquired Jensen silkily.

Tower resisted the temptation to laugh.

'Oh come on, you know and I know,' he began, but Kincaid interrupted:

'No, Captain, I know nothing officially. And I don't want to. As far as I'm concerned, Captain Verago's unfortunate absence has nothing to do with your case.'

'And anything in Berlin is immaterial and irrelevant to the court,' added Jensen. 'You sent him on a wild-goose chase, John.'

Tower started to say something, and then shut his mouth. After a while, he asked:

'What about the trial?'

'That's why we're here, Captain,' said Kincaid. 'I suggest we carry on, with Lieutenant Jensen handling your defence. You could request a delay, even fresh counsel, drag out the whole thing, but I really don't think that's in your interest . . . '

Jensen lowered his voice.

'Listen, the colonel's come here specially with a proposition Haven't you, sir?'

He was a model acolyte.

'Well?' said Tower.

Kincaid gave him a frank, honest beam. He was very good at it.

'We all want to get this business over as painlessly as possible, don't we, Captain? If you go along with my suggestion, I think it's pretty likely things will go easy for you.'

'How easy?'

'Well, I think Lieutenant Jensen can fill you in.'

'You let me handle things,' explained Jensen earnestly, right on cue, 'and it'll become a formality. You plead guilty, you'll get your knuckles rapped, maybe a little confinement, but I can promise you it'll be favourably reviewed. You'll be a free man in no time. They'll wipe it all out. In due course.'

'Turn Captain Verago's absence to your advantage, Captain,' urged Kincaid. 'Start all over again. It's only a suggestion of course,' he added hastily, 'I'm not trying to influence you. You have to decide. But I think you'll find my advice is pretty sound. Yes sir.'

'It stinks,' said Tower.

Kincaid's expression didn't change.

'I never heard that,' he said. 'But what can you lose? The way you're going, you're asking for the book to be thrown at you. The other way, you might be home for Christmas.'

'The point is,' said Tower, 'it's all served its purpose, hasn't it? Soon it won't matter if I'm around to shoot my mouth off . . . '

Jensen glanced nervously at Kincaid, but the colonel was bland.

'I don't know what you're talking about, Captain. I just want to make it painless for you,' he said.

'Pain, Colonel?' Tower lips twisted. 'Don't worry about that. It stopped hurting a long time ago.'

The cell was empty when Verago returned. He expected the guard to slam the door behind him, but instead he escorted him inside. He stood and regarded Verago thoughtfully, his fingers playing nervously with the strap of his machine pistol.

For a moment, Verago was frightened. A crazy thought crossed his mind that this was how they were going to do it. Here. Now. In this cell. A sudden burst from the gun, and his body filled with bullets. They could always say that he tried to escape. It would make an adequate explanation, if anyone wanted to know.

But who was there to ask questions anyway?

'You want something?' asked Verago, hoping he didn't show his fear.

The trooper stood rock still. Verago realised he had spoken in English. So he asked in German:

'Where is Captain Kingston?'

The soldier shook his head. He had blonde eyebrows, freckles and very blue eyes.

He pointed at Verago's watch.

'Bitte,' he said.

It took a moment to sink in. Then Verago said incredulously: 'You want my watch?'

The soldier nodded.

'Ja, bitte, ihre Uhr.'

And very gently he raised the barrel of his gun so that it pointed straight at the pit of Verago's stomach.

It didn't jell. Something was wrong. The Grepos were too disciplined, too military to steal from prisoners. Verago felt certain of that. These were not ragged mercenaries who looted, but professional soldiers.

And yet . . .

Verago shrugged. He slipped the watch off his wrist, and handed it to the man.

'Danke schoen,' said the Grepo respectfully, and clicked his heels. He put the watch in his pocket, and as he did so, Verago noticed the man was already wearing a wrist watch.

The door slammed, and Verago was left alone.

He went over to his bunk and sat thinking about the incident. Of course! The guard wasn't robbing a prisoner. He had been given orders to take away Verago's watch. They didn't want to make an official thing of it, that was why Pech hadn't asked for it, but they didn't want him to know the time any more.

How long he was alone, Verago didn't work out, but then the door was unlocked, and Kingston limped in. He painfully made his way to his bunk, and lay down on it.

'How was it?' he asked.

Verago shrugged. 'I don't think I'm going to get out of here.'

'Is that what Fokin said?'

'It wasn't Fokin. It was . . . the new Gestapo.'

'Aren't they all.'

'How about you?' asked Verago.

Kingston held up his hands. They were bloodied, and covered with gashes.

'I did my chores.'

He sat up.

'Tony,' he whispered. He patted his bunk. 'Sit here.'

Verago went over. 'I know why they put you in here,' said Kingston, his face an inch away, his voice a hoarse whisper. 'I think the place is bugged. They hope we'll say things . . . '

'I know.'

'So be careful. There's something else.' He spoke in Verago's ear. 'The barbed wire that they're using. It's being supplied by the West.'

Verago looked at him incredulously. Kingston nodded vigorously. 'I saw the delivery labels. On some bales. It's been rushed here from West Germany. They're using so much barbed wire they've run out of it. So the West is sending more.'

'To make street barricades?'

'Christ, man, what the hell do you send barbed wire to East Germany for?'

Verago suddenly felt sick. He kept hearing the echo of Pech's voice: 'Don't you understand . . . ?'

'The Vopos are trying to hide it from us,' went on Kingston

urgently. 'They're going round tearing off the tags . . .

He looked at the bleeding, oozing wounds on his hand.

'Made in Essen,' he said bitterly. 'Courtesy the workers' paradise and Papa Ulbricht. Doesn't make sense, does it?'

Verago took a long time to answer. And then he whispered:

'It's beginning to.'

'Jesus, what's going on?'

Verago put his fingers on his lips.

'Listen,' said Kingston. 'If you get out of here . . . '

'If . . . '

'Will you do something for me? Go and see my wife. We live in a small town you've never heard of in California. Near the Nevada border. Independence. Can you remember that? Mrs Irene Kingston, Independence, California. Tell her . . . that I'm still alive . . . and maybe . . . one day . . . '

He broke off, biting his lip.

'As good as done,' said Verago, and meant it. 'But you got to promise me one thing.'

'What's that?'

'You invite me to dinner when you're back with your wife.'

'That's a date,' said Kingston, and tried to sound confident.

'Independence is a nice name,' murmured Verago thoughtfully.

Then the guards switched the lights off.

Monday, July 31, 1961 – PANKOW

It was going to be a busy day for Walter Ulbricht. At 11 a.m. Marshal Ivan Koniev, the newly arrived commander in chief of the Soviet forces in Germany, was due to call on him, accompanied by Mikhail Pervukhin, the Kremlin's ambassador.

Already the enclave at Pankow was on full alert, the smart,

329

jackbooted guards of Ulbricht's personal Watchtregiment standing at attention, ready to present arms when the marshal's staff car swept into the grounds.

Only one thing so far spoiled the morning, a beautiful sunny day. Ulbricht had just finished reading a report marked 'Geheime Staatssache' – 'Secret State Document'. There were only three copies of the document, and they made unpleasant reading.

To date, reported Leuschner, three and a half million East Germans had defected across the border to the West. Bruno Leuschner, Politburo member for economic planning, was blunt:

'We are bleeding to death.'

And he quoted some of the secret statistics: So many men had fled that eighty per cent of the working force in many factories was female; one citizen in five who was left was too old to work; old-age pensioners and school children, the non-productives, outnumbered the working population by four to three.

'If this goes on,' warned Leuschner, 'the DDR will collapse.'

It was just too damn easy to get out, reflected Ulbricht. As the latest SSD briefing had only told him last week, the 163-kilometre border with the Western sectors of the city was wide open. The eighty-eight crossing points simply couldn't be supervised adequately, and the elevated railway shuttled scores of defectors into the West on every journey.

Ulbricht knew all this, but he hated to be reminded of it. Anyway, it wasn't going on much longer. He glanced at the date ringed in red on his desk calendar, next to the miniature DDR flag. It would all stop on August 13th. That was, after all, why Koniev had been brought out of retirement.

His intercom buzzed.

'General Hoffmann is here, sir,' announced the voice of his aide.

'Good, good.' He sat upright. 'Ask him to enter.'

'They were old comrades, he and the tough, leathery Karl-Heinz Hoffmann, minister of national defence, and the man who shared the big secret of August 13th. One of the few privileged ones.

Hoffmann wore his best parade uniform, just as Ulbricht had put on the dark double-breasted suit he only wore on state occasions. Marshal Koniev was famous for noting these details, and they knew they would be inspected like the steel-helmeted guard of honour outside.

'I see you've polished him,' said Hoffmann drily, nodding at the silver-framed, signed photo of Nikita Khruschev. The frame shone brilliantly.

'It's a valuable frame,' stated Ulbricht, and they both understood each other.

Hoffman sat down, crossing his jackbooted legs.

'By the way, Walter, don't forget, the old man likes his drop of vodka.'

'I have already seen to that,' replied Ulbricht, nettled. 'Refreshments will be served.'

It was a special concession. Ulbricht, a strict teetotaller, refused to have drink in his office, and frowned on people smoking in his presence. Hoffmann missed no opportunity to needle him about it.

'We have half an hour,' said Ulbricht, peering at his watch.

'You haven't, you know,' said Hoffmann. 'I asked you to pencil Major Pech in for this morning. It won't take long.'

'Ah, of course, Major Pech.' Ulbricht nodded. 'It will be a pleasure.'

'He's waiting outside,' said Hoffmann. 'Very punctual, is our Pech.'

Ulbricht switched on his intercom.

'Please send in Major Pech,' he instructed.

Almost immediately, the knock on the door came, and Pech entered. Both men stood up. It was a rare token of appreciation. Pech snapped to attention, and stood rigidly straight.

'At ease,' said Hoffmann, with a wave of his hand.

Ulbricht came forward with outstretched hand.

'Major Pech, my compliments. I have been looking forward to this. I am so sorry it is such a casual occasion, but of course, men in your work appreciate that they do not receive public acclaim, more's the pity.'

He shook Pech's hand, a loose, moist grip, and behind his pince nez, his short-sighted eyes blinked. Ulbricht never felt quite secure in the presence of double agents.

'I am honoured,' said Pech.

Hoffmann cleared his throat. 'On behalf of the armed forces of the German People's Republic, I wish to congratulate you on your marvellous work while *sub rosa.*' He thought it was a neat phrase for treason.

'I have here a little token of our appreciation,' said Ulbricht, picking up a small box. He took out a medal, and pinned it on Pech's uniform.

'I am honoured,' said Pech again.

'It carries with it a small pension,' added Hoffmann, ever practical.

Ulbricht stepped back. 'I am sorry of course that you had to surface,' he added. 'You were very useful over there. But I am sure you will continue the good work on this side.'

'Right now,' intervened Hoffmann, 'the important thing is there must be no leaks. The world must know nothing. Once it's happened, nobody will do anything, but until then . . . I look to you to make sure nothing can, er, embarrass us.' A thought struck him. 'I hear you're holding an American officer. I hope that won't cause any complications.'

'It won't, General,' said Pech. 'I don't think you will hear from him any more.'

'I leave that to you,' said Hoffmann.

Ulbricht glanced at the ornamental clock next to the silken Chinese tapestry hanging on the wall.

'Major, would you excuse us now? I'm sorry to cut this very pleasant meeting so short, but we have a rather important visitor coming.'

Pech sprang to attention, and clicked his heels.

He did it very smartly. It made such a change from the way they did it on the other side.

'How do you feel?' asked the doctor solicitously. Under his white coat, Verago could see the grey Volksarmee uniform.

'I'm OK.'

The doctor shook his head doubtfully.

'Let's take your pulse again.'

The hospital wing of Hohenschoenhausen stood in a building apart, and Verago had been marched there under armed escort and then taken to a cubicle.

'Take your shirt off, please,' requested the doctor who came in. He was grey haired, and had a furrowed brow, like a man who worried a geat deal.

'There's nothing wrong with me,' protested Verago.

'No harm in making sure,' said the doctor.

He jammed the cold stethoscope to Verago's chest.

'Well?'

'Open your mouth,' instructed the doctor and peered inside with a penlight. 'Yes, you've got good teeth. Your American dentists know their job.'

'Doctor, what the hell is this about?' demanded Verago. The entrance to the cubicle was guarded by a soldier with the ever-present machine pistol.

'We just want to make sure you are in tip top condition,' said the doctor. 'You're going back to your friends, aren't you? Well, we don't want to give them a sick man. It would be a bad advertisement for us, wouldn't it?'

'Maybe you ought to give people better food then. Or stop them twisting barbed wire bare handed . . .'

But the doctor shone his penlight into Verago's eyes.

'You've been under a strain, haven't you?'

'You surprised?'

'Sleeping badly?'

Verago snorted.

'I think you need a good rest, a really good rest,' said the doctor.

'You know what I need. To get out of this place.'

333

'Yes,' agreed the doctor. 'It's not a holiday home. But I don't think you've been badly treated. Have you ever been in Moabit?'

'No.'

'Ah, then you would know how unpleasant things can get. I disapprove of places like Moabit.'

'Glad to hear it,' said Verago buttoning up his shirt.

'No,' said the doctor. 'Roll up your sleeve . . . '

He was busying himself over a trolley containing jars and bottles.

'What for?' asked Verago, his uneasiness growing.

The doctor turned round. He was holding a hypodermic syringe.

'Now wait a moment,' cried Verago. 'I'm not . . . '

'Don't be childish,' said the doctor mildly. 'This is only a little injection to relax you. It will give you a good night's sleep . . . '

'In the middle of the day?'

'Hagen!' yelled the doctor. As if on cue, a burly man in a short white jacket entered the cubicle. He had jackboots.

'Just hold this patient's arm for me, will you?' requested the doctor.

Hagen grabbed Verago's right arm and held it in an iron grip.

'I want . . . I want Major Pech,' gasped Verago desperately.

'I am doing this on Major Pech's instructions,' said the doctor. 'He wants you fully fit so that the Americans can't complain about your health. We are not monsters, you know.'

And he jabbed the needle into Verago's arm.

'There,' he said, 'that didn't hurt, did it?'

He nodded to Hagen, and the vice-like grip was taken off. The relief was like the time Fokin removed his handcuffs.

Verago sat still, pale faced.

The doctor laughed, quite sympathetically.

'Relax,' he said. 'You look so worried. You won't feel a thing . . . '

Involuntarily, Verago shuddered. He recollected a transcript he had read. The record of a war crimes trial. He remembered vividly a witness who recalled the words of the doctor in the death clinic. 'You won't feel a thing . . . '

'You people can't get away with this kind of thing, not any more,' croaked Verago. 'Not in 1961. People will look for me. The Army . . . '

'You see, you are suffering from hypertension,' said the doctor. 'I suppose it's only understandable, but your nerves are in a shocking state. You have a good rest now.'

Verago staggered to his feet.

'I want out,' he cried, 'I want out of here, you bastards, I . . . '

Then he folded over, and crashed to the floor.

They stood watching, not even trying to prevent him from falling.

LONDON

Ivanov was late, and Laurie watched the entrance of the lounge at the Westbury anxiously. She hadn't touched the coffee she had ordered, and her fingers twisted nervously round the strap of her shoulder bag.

When he came, a smile crossed his face as soon as he spotted her.

'Forgive me,' he excused himself, sitting down, 'but I find walking down Bond Street most seductive. I love the shops – they could make me change my allegiance, I think. My country for Asprey's . . . '

But she didn't smile, and he reacted to the strain in her eyes.

'Laurie, how selfish of me. You have a problem? A big problem, I think?'

'Tony's in trouble,' she burst out.

The bonhomie faded.

'Yes,' said Ivanov soberly, 'I regret to say Captain Verago is in big trouble.'

'You've got to do something, Gene. You must.'

He called the waiter over.

'I would like something stronger than this. For me and the lady.'

And he pointed to the cold coffee with a gesture of contempt.

'Are you resident, sir?' enquired the waiter.

'No.'

'I'm afraid the bar is only open to residents at this hour.'

Ivanov looked shocked. Then he ordered some tea.

'I have changed my mind,' he confided. 'No way could I give a country that does not serve a drink in the afternoon my allegiance.'

'Please,' appealed Laurie.

'Ah yes. Your Captain Verago. He is a lucky man, for you to care. It is not just official, I take it?'

'I think he's in great danger,' said Laurie. 'He . . . '

She broke off.

'Yes?'

'Can you get him out?' she asked. She was very anxious.

'I personally? Laurie, I am not that important . . . '

'You know who to contact,' she said impatiently.

He shook his head. 'Rumour has it,' he began, carefully picking his words, 'that he is in East German hands. That's unfortunate. Papa Ulbricht is a hard liner, you know. His boys are very humourless . . . '

The waiter brought the tea, and Ivanov poured himself a cup, ignoring the milk jug. He put six lumps of sugar in the cup, and looked sheepish doing it.

'The East Germans will do what your people say. He *is* an American officer. I am sure nobody wants an incident . . . '

'What would Washington do? Break off diplomatic relations with Pankow? Oh come on, Laurie, the US doesn't even have official diplomatic relations with Ulbricht. No, your lot have to do it . . . '

'What?'

'Get him out,' said Ivanov quietly. 'Forgive an atheist for quoting the old saying, ''God helps those who help themselves''.'

'You know that's impossible,' said Laurie quietly.

'Is it?' He raised his eyebrows.

Momentarily her lip quivered. 'Oh god,' she whispered.

But Laurie was not a woman to cry in public. She tossed her head, and said rather defiantly:

'So there's nothing you can do?'

'I didn't say that, but it is difficult,' murmured Ivanov. 'He got himself into this mess, you know. Nobody asked him to. We were all very unhappy about it, weren't we?'

He sipped his tea, and pulled a face. 'Too sweet. I should only have put four in.'

'Alright,' said Laurie. She sounded like a woman who had made up her mind suddenly. 'Thanks anyway.'

'Of course,' said Ivanov silkily, 'I will do my best. Only that I can't make a promise.'

She put a half-crown on her bill.

'Gene, I'm not sure that's good enough,' she smiled coldly.

He rose as she got to her feet.

'By the way,' he asked softly, 'what about the court martial?'

Laurie looked away, avoiding his eyes.

'Oh, the court martial,' she said, 'that's all being taken care of.'

'Well,' he said after a pause, 'in that case perhaps I might be able to do something after all.'

'Like what?'

'Have a word in the right ear,' he said and smiled.

Tuesday, August 1, 1961
TRANSCRIPT OF RESUMED GENERAL
COURT MARTIAL PROCEEDINGS
US v TOWER
RAF STATION LACONBURY

PRESIDENT: The court will come to order.

TRIAL COUNSEL: All parties to the trial who were

	present when the court adjourned are again present in court except Captain Anthony Verago, the individual defense counsel.
PRESIDENT:	Why is Captain Verago not here?
TRIAL COUNSEL:	It is my understanding that Captain Verago is not at present in the United Kingdom.
PRESIDENT:	Why not? Has he been excused?
TRIAL COUNSEL:	I think it's fair to say that Captain Verago is unavoidably detained outside the jurisdiction of the United States, and is not in a position to be able to attend these proceedings.
PRESIDENT:	This is outrageous. I intend to cite Captain Verago for contempt of court.
LAW OFFICER:	Sir, it has not been established that Captain Verago is voluntarily absent.
PRESIDENT:	What does that mean?
TRIAL COUNSEL:	I understand that Captain Verago is missing, and may have fallen into East German hands. He was last seen in West Berlin, and has not been heard of since crossing into the East sector.
PRESIDENT:	And what was he doing there?
LAW OFFICER:	That, sir, is not a matter for this court.
PRESIDENT:	Now wait a moment. Is he AWOL?
TRIAL COUNSEL:	That is not for me to answer . . .
PRESIDENT:	Well, damn it, I intend to have an answer . . .
LAW OFFICER:	Colonel, please. Has the prosecution a statement for the court?
TRIAL COUNSEL:	Yes sir. If you please, in view of the absence of individual defense counsel, I consulted with the appointed

338

	defense counsel, Lieutenant Jensen. He indicated that in the circumstances, to avoid this case remaining unresolved, he is willing to take over the defense, and for the trial to continue. Since it is possible that Captain Verago may not be available for an indefinite time, the prosecution is agreeable . . .
LAW OFFICER:	Does the accused consent?
	THE ACCUSED HESITATED, THEN NODDED.
LAW OFFICER:	Let the record reflect that the accused indicated his agreement. Lieutenant Jensen?
DEFENSE COUNSEL:	Sir, I much regret Captain Verago's failure to show, and so does the accused. I have persuaded the accused that, since Captain Verago may be in Communist hands, it is likely we may not even see him again . . .
LAW OFFICER'	I don't want conjectures, Lieutenant. You say you have made the position clear to the accused?
DEFENSE COUNSEL:	Yes sir. Forcibly. And he wants to get this thing over with. He now sees there's no point delaying matters.
LAW OFFICER:	So the defense is willing to continue?
DEFENSE COUNSEL:	Yes sir.
PRESIDENT:	What I want to know is, is somebody taking disciplinary action against this Captain Verago?
LAW OFFICER:	With respect, sir, that does not concern you or this court.
PRESIDENT:	Damn Army lawyers . . .
LAW OFFICER:	Sir!
PRESIDENT:	Oh, alright.
LAW OFFICER:	Lieutenant Jensen, I want to remind

	you that the accused has the right to ask for a new individual counsel and to request that this case be continued until such time as a fresh defense lawyer is ready . . .
DEFENSE COUNSEL:	Captain Tower doesn't want to know. He says he'll leave it to me. He seems to feel that, er, it doesn't matter any more.
LAW OFFICER:	Is that correct, Captain Tower? (PAUSE). Let the record reflect that the accused nodded.
DEFENSE COUNSEL:	So we're all set, sir.
LAW OFFICER:	Proceed.
PRESIDENT:	Let's get on with it.
TRIAL COUNSEL:	With the consent of the defense, I'll omit the reading of the charges.
DEFENSE COUNSEL:	We agree.
PRESIDENT:	Good.
TRIAL COUNSEL:	Captain Tower, how do you plead?
DEFENSE COUNSEL:	It's alright, Captain Tower, I'll do it for you. To all specifications and charges, the accused pleads guilty.
PRESIDENT:	Captain Tower, by pleading guilty you have admitted every single element of the offense. As a result, you may be sentenced by the court to the maximum punishment authorised. Do you understand?
CAPTAIN TOWER:	Yes sir. You got what you wanted.
PRESIDENT:	Address the court properly. Since you understand what it means, do you persist in your plea of guilty?
CAPTAIN TOWER:	Yes. It'll just save you time, gentlemen, won't it?
PRESIDENT:	Sit down.
LAW OFFICER:	Colonel Apollo, in view of the plea, how long do you think this case will

| | now take? |
| TRIAL COUNSEL: | Not long. Not long at all |

Wednesday, August 2, 1961 –
HOHENSCHOENHAUSEN

'I am sorry about your hands,' said Fokin.

Kingston's head was bowed, and he sat on the bunk, his hands bandaged lumps. His wounds had turned septic.

'We will try to feed you and . . . do all the other things . . . help you as best we can . . . ' continued Fokin, a little awkwardly.

Kingston looked up, and his skeletal, almost cadaverous face was a mask of hatred.

'Barbed wire,' he hissed, and it came out like a curse.

Then he spat at Fokin.

Fokin first flushed, then turned ashen. He raised his hand, a clenched fist, and slowly lowered it again.

'I'm sorry. You should have co-operated. Told us what we wanted to know. Answered a few technical questions. Surely that is too heavy a price?' he asked, indicating the bandaged hands.

Fokin was unhappy. This flyer had not provided the information they had expected. It was a black mark on Fokin's record as a crack interrogator.

'This is probably the last time we will meet, Captain. I regret they have other plans for you now.'

The inflamed eyes bore into him.

'You are a credit to your service, Captain,' continued Fokin, 'and I respect you as one officer respects another. But I am afraid all that will be no consolation to you now when . . . when others take over.'

For once, he felt distinctly uncomfortable.

'Fokin,' said the emaciated man.

'Yes?'

'What has happened to him?'

'Who?' asked Fokin. It was disconcerting to suddenly hear Kingston, after all this time, ask questions.

'The man . . . who was in here . . . with me . . . the Army captain . . . '

'Captain Verago?' Fokin hesitated. 'He . . . ' He paused. Then he came straight out with it. 'You will not be seeing him again, Captain Kingston.'

Hours afterwards when he was sitting in the dark, alone, his hands stumps of agony, the fever beginning, Kingston was still wondering which of them would die first.

He or Verago.

Friday, August 4, 1961 – EAST GERMANY

He couldn't move his arms or his legs. His limbs seemed paralysed. And everything was shaking, the roof, and the walls.

Those were the first moments of conscious awareness. But he wasn't really awake. He tried to focus his eyes, but his vision was blurred. And he felt tired, terribly tired.

He wondered how long he had been unconscious. A long, long time, his instinct told him. Not hours. Days. Nights. Or was he dreaming?

He strained, hard, to move his arms, but something cut into him. He tried to move his head from side to side. That was possible. And it gave him encouragement.

He couldn't understand the shaking, the bumping, and then suddenly he realised he was travelling. It wasn't a ceiling he was looking at, but the roof of a vehicle. These weren't walls, but the sides of a . . . a truck? A van?

And then he understood why he couldn't move arms or legs. He was strapped down. He was strapped to a stretcher, and he was on the move, being driven somewhere.

He was utterly helpless, and whatever they had pumped into him was still in his system. He tried to make his brain work, to control his thoughts, to begin to reason things out . . .

But it was too much for him. He groaned, and then everything became giddy, and suddenly he was plunged into darkness once more.

Wednesday, August 9, 1961 – EAST GERMANY

It was the most comfortable bed Verago had ever known. A soft mattress, a cool sheet, a feather-filled duvet covering him.

He stretched out, luxuriating in the sheer sensual delight.

Then he sat bolt upright. Awareness and bewilderment took over.

He looked round the bedroom, with its thick pile carpet, and big windows. He could even hear birds singing.

He swung his legs off the bed and stood up. He was unsteady on his legs, and utterly confused.

He was wearing pyjamas, and he felt clean, refreshed. Somebody must have washed him. He touched his chin; and shaved him too.

Slowly he tottered to the window and looked out. Below stretched a beautiful garden, with a well-mown lawn as its centrepiece. He could just see rose bushes and a weeping willow tree. An empty deck chair stood invitingly on the lawn.

'My god! You'll catch cold,' said a woman's voice.

He turned round and saw a buxom, rosy-faced woman in the doorway. She had flaxen hair tied in a bun on top and although she beamed at him, her eyes were wary. She was carrying a tray.

'Back into bed with you, at once,' she ordered like a reproving matron. A prison matron, it flashed through his mind.

'Where is this?' asked Verago.

'Into bed,' snapped the woman good naturedly.

He got back in and pulled the duvet up. She dumped the tray on his lap.

'Eat your breakfast,' she said. Suddenly she broke into a bright smile. 'It's nice to see you about again.'

Her bonhomie worried him.

'If you need anything, just ask,' she said, waddling to the door. Then she was gone.

Verago was starving and it was an appetising breakfast. Orange juice. Tinned pears. Two eggs, sunnyside up, just the way he liked them. Crisp strips of bacon, done the American way. A pot of coffee and toast and English marmalade.

He shook his head in disbelief, then he tucked in.

After he'd finished breakfast, he lay back against the pillows, trying to collect his thoughts. But they were a crazy kaleidoscope of memories he couldn't pin down. He had a vague recollection of some endless ride in a truck, being tied down like . . .

Or had that been a nightmare? Had he dreamt it all?

The buxom woman came in without knocking. She had his clothes over her arm.

'Here you are,' she announced, putting them on an armchair. 'They've all been cleaned and pressed.'

She took the tray.

'Now have a bath. It's next door, everything you need, soap and towels. Then get dressed. You haven't got much time, you know.'

'Just a moment,' said Verago. 'What's your name?'

'Maria.'

'Well, Maria, what am I doing here? Who brought me here?'

'Were the eggs alright?' she asked, and shut the door without waiting for Verago's answer.

He had his bath, wallowing in the warm water, soaping

imself like a man trying to wash away the stain of foulness. But e couldn't get rid of his nagging unease.

Then he dressed. His clothes had been beautifully finished. ven the button that he'd lost from his collar had been placed. And when he found his shoes at the end of the bed, ey had been polished to a gleam.

He put on his jacket, and froze. He took out a wallet from e inside pocket. The wallet the man Schultz had waved in his ce. And his passport, and inside that, his Army ID card.

He was perspiring and he felt weak. He sat down in the rmchair and tried to work it out.

The room offered him no clues. An anonymous, flowery allpaper, a print of some old castle on the opposite wall, a edieval map on another. He looked more closely. It was a xteenth-century chart of the Baltic.

The door opened and Pech walked in. He stopped when he w Verago.

'Tony!' he exclaimed delightedly, 'you look great.'

He was wearing a grey suit and saw Verago eyeing it.

'Simpson's,' Pech told him proudly. 'Bought it on a trip to ondon when I was still my alter ego.'

'Where am I?' asked Verago.

'You were quite ill, you know. At one time, I got really orried. You were out like a light. Gave me the shock of my 'e.'

Verago stared at him grimly.

'I asked where am I?'

'Oh,' shrugged Pech, 'a little village. I borrowed a friend's ouse. Let you sleep.' He glanced at his watch. 'We'd better get oing.'

'Where to?'

'Now, where do you think it could be?' smiled Pech, and his es twinkled. 'Home sweet home. I'm going to take you back your people.'

'*You* are handing me over?' Verago couldn't believe it.

'Well, I won't come with you all the way,' said Pech. 'It ight be a little awkward for me, crossing into the West sector. ut I'll wave you goodbye anyway . . . '

345

He suddenly looked concerned.

'Have you got your papers?'

Verago patted his breast pocket. 'Yes.'

'Good. It would be just like those idiots to forget to return them.'

He glanced round the room.

'Sure you haven't forgotten anything?'

'I wasn't exactly overloaded with luggage,' remarked Verago drily.

'Let's go then,' said Pech, holding the door open.

Outside the bedroom was a landing and a richly carpeted staircase leading down to the entrance hall. It was an old house and very ornate. A big tapestry, with an ancient coat of arms, hung on one wall.

'You got aristocratic friends,' observed Verago as they descended.

Pech just smiled.

Before the front door stood a black Mercedes. Pech opened the passenger door like a chauffeur.

'Your carriage awaits, sir,' he announced with mock civility. 'I hope you trust my driving.'

The buxom Marie was nowhere in sight.

'All set?' asked Pech.

Verago nodded.

But he knew it couldn't be just this simple.

'ZUR LETZTEN INSTANZ'

They drove along a country road, past the tall trees of a wood stretching either side, and then into open countryside, dotted with a few farms and a line of telegraph poles.

'I wish there was time to show you Potsdam,' said Pech. 'It'

346

ry impressive.'

A small convoy of six People's Army trucks was ahead of
em, and he followed it for a mile or so. Verago could see steel-
lmeted soldiers in the back of the trucks. Then Pech got
apatient, and sounding his horn, overtook the convoy.

So far they hadn't seen any civilian traffic, or even people.
nly soldiers seemed in evidence.

'Where are we?' asked Verago.

'That was Steinstuecken, over there,' said Pech.

'Where do I cross?'

'Not Checkpoint Charlie,' grinned Pech. 'Something a little
ore discreet, OK?'

'Far from here?'

'Anybody would think you're tired of our hospitality.'

They came to an inn. In Gothic lettering it proclaimed its
ame: 'Zur Letzten Instanz'.

'How appropriate,' said Pech. He saw Verago looking
azzled.

'The Last Resort', he translated. He stopped the car in the
obbled forecourt.

'Let's have, as you say, a quick one,' said Pech. 'A goodbye
ink. For old time's sake.'

Verago followed him into the old inn which they had to
emselves. He didn't feel like a drink. He wanted to cross to
e other side as quickly as possible.

But Pech was in no hurry.

'Your very good health,' he toasted, after the landlord had
ncorked a dust-covered bottle of wine from the cellar. It was a
uperb vintage. Pech knew what to order.

'I'll miss you, Tony,' he said, a little sadly. 'I hate saying
oodbye.'

'Well,' said Verago, 'I'll be glad to get back. I'm sure you
nderstand.'

'You think Tauber is worth all this?'

Verago stared at him. 'Tauber? Who's Tauber?'

'Nobody told you, I suppose. Your Captain Tower. You
now what his real name is? Tauber. Johann Herman Tauber.
hat's what he was born.'

347

He let it sink in, looking pleased at the effect.

'Yes. A German refugee. His parents left early. 1933. Wen
to Delaware, of all places. Changed their name to Tower.'

He sipped some wine, and smacked his lips.

'Excellent stuff, this.'

'I gathered he speaks German like a native,' said Verago.

'Obviously. Perfect for undercover work.' He gave Verago
sharp glance. 'All this is news to you, is it?'

Verago stayed silent.

'In this kind of work, you have to be unemotional,' went o
Pech, twirling the green stem of his wine glass. 'Stay detached

'Like you?'

'Precisely. Tower has the wrong background. His peop
having to flee from Hitler, losing everything, penniless. It
made him too involved.'

Why are you telling me all this, asked an inner voice. Why a
you opening the dossier for me? But aloud he simply said:

'I don't follow. What do you mean, too involved?'

'Of course you know. Berlin is going to be sealed of
Divided in two. Cut in half. Regretfully, people will have to be
separated. A million people will be locked in. It's sad, of cours
but it has to be.' Pech's mouth was firmly set. 'The goo
captain couldn't stomach it.'

Pech poured the last of the wine.

'I'd like another bottle, but I'm driving,' he said ruefull
'The Grepos are very hot on drunken drivers. Worse than th
Vopos.'

'Berlin,' said Verago. 'You were talking about Berlin bein
cut in two . . . '

Pech sighed. 'We have to do it, Tony. Your side recognises
as well. We can't continue to lose the cream of our peopl
Three thousand a day. No country can survive that. And yo
side can't cope with the refugees. Three and a half million s
far. They can't control the flood any more. They're bein
swamped. So we've made a deal. East and West. Berlin must t
divided for the good of all. For once we are allies.'

He smiled. 'Now do you see?'

'A deal . . . ' repeated Verago, almost to himself.

'The stupid cow Helga defected with the secret agreement. She took the minutes of the planning meeting in Pankow. Tower brought her across to the West. Your people told him to forget about it but he wouldn't listen. He said he was going to shout it from the rooftops. Too emotional you see. East and West can't be seen to be making such a deal. He had to be . . . '

'Put out of circulation?' suggested Verago.

'Until it's a fait accompli.'

'That,' said Verago, 'was one of Hitler's favourite expressions.'

'Was it?' Pech's look was cold. He paid the landlord, who took the money respectfully. He had seen Pech's official licence plate.

'Let's go,' said Pech.

As they got into the car, Pech's jacket pulled to one side and Verago caught a quick glimpse of a pistol's butt.

The car continued along the road, passing two observation towers from which grey-clad soldiers watched them through field glasses. They passed a Volkarmee patrol jeep which contrasted with the rural scene of cows grazing near a farm house.

Pech glanced at Verago.

'You're very quiet, my friend,' he said.

'I was thinking.'

'Oh? What about?'

'I was wondering why you told me,' said Verago. 'Why you told me everything.'

Pech accelerated a little.

'Well,' he said, 'for one thing . . . '

'Yes?'

Pech smiled. 'Because it doesn't matter any more.'

And suddenly Verago knew why Pech was packing a gun

DEATH STRIP

A couple of miles further on, Verago became aware of the sound of a helicopter, droning menacingly. He caught a glimpse of it, hovering briefly and then swinging away into the distance. It had a five-pointed red star.

'They like to keep an eye on the border,' said Pech.

It was flat countryside around them now. On the left, row after row of tidy, orderly fields, totally empty. In the distance, Verago could see a wire fence.

Pech pulled up, and cut the engine.

'Well,' he said, 'here we are.'

Verago looked round.

'What do you mean? Where?'

'This is where you cross over,' said Pech.

'I can't see a frontier post. There's no crossing here.' Verago felt fear gnawing in his stomach.

'Can't you see the sign?' asked Pech.

It had a death's head, and German and Russian lettering.

'That says, "Danger",' said Verago slowly.

'Exactly. Get out, please.' The pistol was in Pech's hand, pointing straight at Verago.

'Are . . . are you crazy?'

'I told you. Just discreet.'

The pistol made a little movement. Its meaning was unmistakable.

Slowly Verago climbed out. Pech followed, the pistol never wavering.

'This is the zonal boundary,' said Pech gently. 'Normally of course people don't cross at this point. There's a technical problem. You see, those fields are the death strip.'

Verago's throat was dry. 'So . . . what do I do . . . ?'

'Cross. Just walk across. Quite simple.'

'But that . . . '

'That's right,' smiled Pech. 'You'll walk into a highly sophisticated minefield. With specially planted anti-personnel mines. Half a dozen steps . . . '

'Nobody . . . lives.'

'Correct.' He waved the gun slightly. 'Come along. I thought you were so eager to get to the other side. Start walking.'

'No,' said Verago.

Pech shrugged. 'Please yourself. Then I will just shoot you. In self defence. The other way it looks better of course. Fugitive American killed trying to flee across the death strip. But I don't mind . . .'

Verago stood motionless.

'The walk will do you good,' said Pech and laughed.

The edge of the field was two feet away. It looked so innocent. Just empty farm land, so inviting for a stroll to the other side. . .

'If you're lucky, you'll be half way across before you step on one,' said Pech encouragingly. 'And I won't let you lie in agony, I promise. If it just blows off a leg or two, but doesn't kill you, I'll put you out of your misery. I am quite a good shot from this distance. I feel I owe you that for friendship's sake.'

And then he fired a shot. The bullet kicked up the earth two inches from Verago's feet.

'I mean it,' said Pech. 'You walk or I kill you now.'

Verago looked backwards. He felt the sweat trickle down his neck. He wanted to be sick with fear. And anger. Anger at this murdering bastard.

What is there to lose, he thought. A bullet might be less painful anyway. In Korea, he had had a buddy who took three hours to die in a minefield.

'You're a damn fool, Pech,' he said.

Pech smiled.

'I shall count to five,' he said.

'It's you they're after,' said Verago.

Pech blinked. 'Who's they?'

'Your own people,' said Verago, like a chess player sacrificing his last pieces. 'They don't trust you any more.'

'You're just wasting time,' said Pech, but the second's hesitation wasn't lost on Verago. He made his final move.

'Don't you realise you've been set up?'

'Who by?' said Pech, eyes glinting.

'Your own side,' bluffed Verago.

'How do you know?' hissed Pech.

'That's why I'm here,' said Verago, and wondered if it would do any good.

'You're lying,' snarled Pech.

The pistol wavered, and Verago jumped him. He grabbed Pech's gun arm, and with his knee tried to ram him in the genitals, fear and panic giving him ferocity that he did not know he had in him. Pech struggled violently, and they were locked together, wrestling for the pistol, gasping, teeth bared, fighting savagely, brutally. Pech's left hand scrabbled for his face, the fingers trying to claw at his eyes, and Verago desperately butted him with his knee again, and then he heard the shot.

He was still clinging on to Pech, as the man slowly sank to the ground, his eyes wide open with shock, still clutching the pistol where its bullet had ploughed into him.

Pech lay at his feet, the blood staining his shirt, and Verago did not have to feel his pulse to know he was dead. He was staring at the man with a mixture of relief and horror, and the sudden shock realisation that, for the first time in his life, he had killed a man.

He knelt by the body, breathless from the struggle, hurting, blood on his face, trying to think, and to stop himself shivering with panic.

Then he saw the feet. And he looked up, into the barrel of a Kalashnikov AKM, held by a steel-helmeted soldier with a Mongolian face. Slowly Verago stood up, and although not a word was said, he raised his hands.

The three Red Army soldiers standing beside their jeep didn't have to speak. Their guns, covering Verago, said it all.

Overhead hovered the helicopter with the red star, circling its prey.

LONDON

The car cruising down Du Cane Road came past Hammersmith Hospital and then, as it drew level with the ornate frontage of Wormwood Scrubs prison, slowed down momentarily.

'That's where he is,' said Deriabin, and Ivanov nodded glumly.

'It shouldn't be that difficult,' went on Deriabin, increasing speed again. 'He couldn't be more central, could he? Ten minutes from the embassy. It's almost as if they want us to get him out.'

And he laughed at the thought.

Special instructions had come that morning from Central about the man inside the Scrubs. George Blake, Ex-MI6 resident in West Berlin, had been in there now since May 3, serving his forty-two years sentence for being a double agent.

Moscow wanted him sprung.

'I want you to work on it,' Deriabin told Ivanov. 'I know what a heavy load you already have, and current operations must take precedence. But Blake has to be liberated. After all, we owe it to him.'

'It's going to take a lot of preparation,' said Ivanov. He wasn't overjoyed by the extra assignment. 'It needs time to set up.'

'Of course,' agreed Deriabin. 'But put it high on your list.'

He turned the car round, and drove past the Victorian penitentiary again on their way back to Kensington.

'What about Molodny?' asked Ivanov. Molodny, dark, handsome, with a soft Canadian accent, had been a friend of Ivanov's. Now, better known as George Lonsdale, he was also an enforced guest of Her Majesty, sweating out twenty-five years for espionage.

'Don't fret about the colonel,' Deriabin reassured him. 'That is already in hand. It will be done through diplomatic channels. We will exchange him. But Blake we must break out. The British would never let him go. You understand?'

Ivanov chewed his lip.

Deriabin glanced sideways at him.

'Don't worry,' he said, reading his thoughts. 'The field work will be executed by others. I just want you to do the planning. You have such an ingenious mind, Yevgenni, and I am sure you will come up with a cunning little blueprint.'

Deriabin's praise usually left his subordinates uneasy. Ivanov was no exception.

'Blake is burnt out,' he said, 'is it worth the risk?'

It was a mistake. Deriabin slammed on the brakes, and the car halted suddenly in Holland Park Avenue. He turned to Ivanov.

'I am surprised, comrade. What is the most important thing in our work? Loyalty?'

Ivanov avoided his eyes. A lecture on loyalty from Deriabin was supreme irony.

'Our agents in the field know that, no matter what happens, we will get them out. Never do we allow our people to rot, correct?' Deriabin was in full swing, as if he was lecturing tyro spies. 'They know that even if they are caught, they will never be forgotten. No matter how savage the sentence, how deep the dungeon, how terrible the treatment, they will never serve out their punishment. It is an unbreakable contract. That is why Blake must be got out. So that every other Soviet operative in the world can see we keep our word . . . Clear?'

'Clear,' said Ivanov. 'But my other work?'

Deriabin started the car up again.

'Your other work must come first right now,' he declared. 'That, of course, has supreme priority. The calendar dictates it. But Blake must not be forgotten.'

'Alright,' grunted Ivanov. He was thinking that, with luck, Central might yet send somebody from Moscow to do the Blake job. He had more important things lined up.

'American,' said Verago, keeping his hands high. 'Amerikanski.'

He wished, desperately, he could speak Russian. The soldiers were staring at him with unfriendly eyes.

'I am American,' repeated Verago to the uncomprehending Mongolian. One of the other soldiers came forward and bent over Pech's body. He looked up, and said something.

The others stared at Verago. One of them had a walky talky, and started speaking into it rapidly. His companion kept Verago covered, while the Mongolian began searching him. He found the US passport in the inner pocket of his jacket, and handed it to the walky-talky man.

'Kamerad,' said Verago. He felt a fool, not being able to say anything they could understand. 'Tovarich.'

The Mongolian gestured with his gun, indicating that Verago should move towards the jeep. He stepped forward warily. He didn't want to make a mistake. Their faces were stony, unsmiling, and he sensed one false step would be fatal.

The Mongolian ordered him into the jeep, and climbed in beside him, the gun aimed straight at his stomach. The walky-talky man got behind the wheel, and, with a sudden jerk, the jeep raced off, leaving the third trooper standing by the body.

They drove rapidly along the country road, until, in the distance, a crossroads appeared. Parked beside it were two tanks, their long gun barrels pointing across the fields.

The walky talky lay on the seat beside the driver. Suddenly it began crackling. The driver reached over, picked it up with one hand, and continued driving. He seemed to acknowledge some kind of message, and then put the walky talky down again.

At the crossroads, the Mongolian waved to a couple of soldiers in the turrets of the tanks. The jeep swung right, and drove into a wood, following what seemed to be a makeshift road.

It was bumpy, and Verago held onto the jeep. The Mongolian never took his eyes off him, and his finger on the trigger of the gun made Verago more nervous. He wondered what would happen if they bumped too much, and the finger jerked on the trigger . . .

Suddenly they entered a large clearing. Spread before them was a small military camp, with tents, and a large radio mast jutting from some kind of communications truck. A couple of staff cars and a few jeeps were parked in neat rows, and from somewhere behind the trees came the aroma of cooking. In front of one of the tents two sentries stood stiffly.

The jeep stopped, and the Mongolian prodded Verago to get out. Then he marched him over to the tent with the sentries. He gestured again, and Verago went inside.

It was a makeshift office with a trestle table, and a couple of canvas chairs. There was a battery of field phones, and a big board on a tripod easel. Pinned to the board was a large-scale map, and an officer with a sheet of paper in his hand was just sticking some pins into the map.

He looked round sharply as they entered, and the Mongolian snapped to attention and spoke tersely. As he made his report, the officer looked at Verago. He had a foxy face, and blonde eyelashes. His shoulder boards had a red stripe and two small stars; a lieutenant.

He listened to the Mongolian, and then snapped his fingers. The Mongolian froze.

Foxy Face walked up close to Verago and nodded to him.

'You spion,' he said.

Verago didn't need any Russian to know what that meant.

'I'm American . . . ' began Verago as the Mongolian handed the lieutenant his passport. Foxy Face slowly turned the pages.

'You spion,' he repeated, with firm conviction.

He went over to the field phones, and picked one up, cranking the handle. He spoke crisply in Russian. Then he read from the passport:

'Da. Verago. Anthony Verago. Da. Spion.'

He listened, and nodded. Then he replaced the receiver. He walked to the door of the tent, and shouted something.

Three armed soldiers came into the tent. Two held Verago's arms while the third blindfolded him.

Then they half dragged, half pushed him out of the tent.

What a hell of a way to go, thought Verago, stumbling between his guards. A firing squad in a wood.

The thing that hurt was Pech. The son of a bitch was going to have the last laugh.

BRIESELANG

Still blindfolded, he was shoved into a car. Guards sat on either side of him, and he heard the doors slam.

It was another bumpy ride, and not a word was said. The bandage had been wound tight round his eyes, and increasingly it became uncomfortable.

He lost both sense of time and direction, but it wasn't a long car ride. Then they bundled him out of the car, and into some kind of house. Footsteps resounded on wooden floorboards. He heard the ringing of telephones, and the chatter of typewriters. And there were some sharp commands.

Somebody knocked on a door, and a voice ordered them in. Then the blindfold was taken off.

Verago faced a burly officer sitting behind a desk. He was in his shirtsleeves, but this one had four stars on his shoulder epaulettes; a colonel. The shirt was crisply ironed, and the neat tie held in place by a clip.

But it was the woman who took Verago's attention. She too was in uniform, a beret with a Red Army badge perched on her curly blonde hair. She wore thick horn-rimmed glasses, and Verago wondered if, like the movies, she would look a stunning blonde if she removed them. The heavy spectacles made her look severe.

She was only a lieutenant, but to his surprise it was she who spoke while the colonel just glowered at him.

'I am Lieutenant Borisova,' she said, and her English was excellent. 'I am the interpreter.'

'Thank god there's somebody who speaks English,' said Verago. 'You see . . . '

'This is Colonel Machenko,' she went on, ignoring him. 'You are in a very serious position. You are being held as a spy. And there is also a question of murder.'

She made the murder sound less heinous.

'You got it all wrong,' began Verago. 'I want you to contact the United States authorities and . . . '

But again he was cut off. The colonel said something in Russian, and the blonde nodded.

'Colonel Machenko points out that you will be interrogated in due course by the appropriate authorities, and the less you say until then the better. That is in your own interest. Do you understand?'

She gave him a quick smile, as if to say don't make life difficult.

Verago glanced round the room. He was flanked by two guards. Through the window he could see a courtyard.

'Where am I?' asked Verago.

'This is the field headquarters of . . . ' She stopped herself, and said instead, '. . . a Soviet army formation.'

'Where is Berlin?'

'You're not far away,' she said. 'But you were caught in a restricted zone. It is banned to all. Especially Americans in civilian clothes.'

Again the colonel said something.

'Colonel Machenko wants me to point out that you are in a very serious position. He hopes you realise it. The man you killed was a member of the Democratic People's Republic security organs. You were evidently trying to escape to the West. You understand how grave your situation is?'

'Well,' said Verago, 'tell the colonel I got a good idea, that he'd be smart to get in touch with the American liaison people as fast as he can . . . '

She pursed her lips. She only used faint lipstick, and as far as he could see behind those spectacles, very little mascara.

'Right now, your status is in question,' she remarked. On the colonel's desk lay his passport, and beside it the ID card they had found inside it. 'Your visa expired long ago. You have an American officer's identity card. You are dressed as a civilian. Need I say more?'

'So what do you intend to do right now?' demanded Verago, and the defiance in his tone made her raise her eyebrows slightly.

He heard a commotion outside. Through the window he could see some soldiers running across the courtyard. There was the roar of motor cycles, and he saw three staff cars with an escort sweep into the forecourt. At the same time, the colonel's phone shrilled. He picked it up, and listened, rising to his feet as he heard what was being said.

Outside the door, suddenly, there were sharp commands, and the stamping of feet and rifle butts. He heard the march of boots come nearer. Then the door was flung open.

A short squat man in a magnificent green uniform stood on the threshold. Verago had seen plenty of officers in military finery, but never a man with so much gold braid.

His flashing gold shoulder boards proclaimed his rank to Verago's startled eyes: a Marshal of the Soviet Union. He had a gold belt, gold braid on his sleeves, and his cap, jauntily sitting on his head, was a dazzling display of oak leaves. His chest was covered with decorations.

Everyone in the room except Verago turned into marble at his appearance. Colonel Machenko was strictly at attention behind his desk, the girl lieutenant stood rigidly straight, and the soldiers guarding Verago were frozen stone.

Marshal Koniev nodded to them. He came in, went up to Verago and stood looking at him.

'So,' he said at last in English, 'you are the mysterious American.'

'Captain Verago, sir. United States Army.'

Koniev tilted his head to one side, inspecting Verago.

'Well, Captain Verago, you are a nuisance.' He said it quite amiably. 'I and my staff are far too busy at this moment to be bothered by you, you understand?'

'Sir,' said Verago. 'I'm more than anxious to get out o
your hair.'

Koniev said something in Russian to the colonel who replied
still standing at rigid attention. Koniev nodded.

He turned back to Verago.

'A decision has been made about you,' he announced. 'You
are a very lucky man. No one wants an incident involving a
American this week. Next week, who knows? But this week
no.'

He smiled.

'You understand me?'

'Yes sir,' said Verago, but he wondered if he did.

'I am advised that, all things considered, we would just a
soon be rid of you.' Koniev paused. 'No, don't misunderstand
me. By that I mean, we want to see the back of you. You are no
worth a crisis that could upset everything.'

'I think I ought to explain . . .'

Koniev held up one hand. 'Do not explain anything. It is
better.'

'The dead man . . . he tried . . .'

Koniev shrugged. 'I am not interested. Omar Bradley taugh
me an interesting phrase. Rocking the boat. I do not want you
to rock this boat. I have bigger things to worry about this week.'

He said something sharply to the colonel, who bent down and
opened a cupboard in the desk. Hastily he produced a bottle o
American brandy and four glasses. He poured the brandy.

'A pleasant trip,' toasted Koniev and drank his brandy in one
gulp.

Lieutenant Borisova had taken off her glasses. Verago was
right; it made a lot of difference. He wondered what else she did
beside interpreting. She could certainly drink brandy. She too
made it disappear in one gulp.

The colonel snapped his fingers, and the two soldiers who
were still guarding Verago saluted and stiffly walked out.

'I would invite you for dinner,' said Koniev, 'I enjoy the
company of Americans. I like talking to them.'

He pointed to the ribbon of the US Legion of Merit on his
chest.

'You see, I still wear it. Yes, I'd like to, but unfortunately, I have a big staff meeting. It is after all, as Eisenhower called it, D-day minus three.'

Verago stared at him.

The marshal held out his glass, and Colonel Machenko poured some more brandy. He said something peremptorily in Russian, and the colonel clicked his heels.

'I have arranged for you to be escorted back to your sector,' announced Koniev. 'The colonel will provide a car. You will have no problems. You are a lucky man, Captain. Be grateful for good friends.'

He smiled again, but this time rather enigmatically.

'Thank you, sir,' said Verago slowly.

Koniev's steely blue eyes seemed amused by something. 'I will leave you in good hands. Lieutenant Borisova here will be your escort officer. She will deliver you safely, I am sure.'

'It will be my pleasure,' she said in English.

She hadn't put the glasses back on, and the way she looked, Verago thought, the movie people are right; it can do wonders for a girl.

OBERBAUMBRUECKE

The car was an unmarked civilian one with ordinary licence plates. The driver was a military man, his whole manner betrayed that, but he was in plain clothes.

And Lieutenant Borisova had changed for the journey. No uniform, no spectacles. She was smartly, attractively dressed, and now she was out of uniform, Verago realised what a good figure she had. Her make up too was different, the lipstick a deep red, the mascara artfully used.

'I am sorry it has had to be such a short acquaintance,' she said as they drove through the countryside. 'I would have liked to practise my English with you.'

'I don't think you need to practise, Lieutenant.'

'Sonia,' she said. 'My first name is Sonia.'

She waited expectantly, but Verago did not respond.

'When do we get there?' he asked.

She looked at her watch. 'It has been arranged for 2300 hours.'

'Where?'

'You know the Oberbaumbruecke?'

He shook his head.

'It is a bridge between our zone and your sector. Near the Warschauer strasse. Your friends will be there.'

'Friends?'

'I am sure you will have a reception committee,' she said drily.

'You've been in touch with the Americans?'

'I,' she said, 'have not done anything. That is all a matter for higher authority. But,' she confided, 'I think there is contact.'

She took out a pack of cigarettes. To his amazement, they were Lucky Strikes. She offered him one.

'Where did you get those?' asked Verago.

'I told you,' she said. 'There is contact.'

She held a cigarette lighter in her hand and lit his Lucky.

'May I see that?' he said. He took it from her, turning it over. It was familiar. The same make as the one Tower had. Well, that made sense. Tower's was Russian too, and there wasn't much variety in consumer goods in the Soviet Union. It was probably the standard model of People's Cigarette Lighter.

'Why are you so interested?' she enquired curiously.

'I . . . I know somebody who has one like this.'

'Is he Russian?'

'No, he was given it.'

The car was roomy, and she crossed her legs. She had very good legs. In uniform, she looked efficient, military, practical. But like this . . .

'Tell me,' said Verago, 'where did you learn to speak English so well?'

'We have schools,' she said.

'Your accent is very good.'

'They are good schools.'

They were stopped at a checkpoint, but the driver produced a document which passed them through without the passengers even being scrutinised.

'Do you have a family?' asked the blonde.

'No.'

'Not married?' She was surprised.

'Not now.'

She thought for a moment. Then she said:

'I suppose it is better for people in your work not to be married.'

'What do you mean?'

'It can be difficult when one is an intelligence agent.'

'Listen,' said Verago, 'I am not in intelligence.'

'Of course not,' she said, with a very knowing smile.

'I am an attorney.'

'Sure,' she smiled.

Half an hour later, they entered Berlin.

'It won't be long now,' she said.

The driver in front said something in Russian, and she replied briefly.

'We're right on time,' she said.

Then he saw the bridge, ahead of them. The car stopped.

'You get out by yourself,' she said. 'I will stay in the car. You walk across the bridge. Half way across somebody will meet you. That is the arrangement.'

'Well,' said Verago, 'thanks for everything.'

She held out her hand.

'Here,' she said, 'for you. A souvenir.'

It was the lighter. Verago stared at it.

'Something to remember me by,' she smiled.

'Thanks,' muttered Verago. He put it in his pocket. 'Thanks again.'

He got out of the car, and started walking across the long steel bridge. He didn't look back.

From the other side, a figure came towards him. A man.

Verago was more than half way across before he recognised Unterberg.

'Welcome back,' he said, his hand outstretched. Then he took Verago's arm and led him towards the end of the bridge.

'Don't look so scared, you're safe now,' he exclaimed.

'Yes,' agreed Verago dully. He wished he felt safe. He glanced sideways at Unterberg; the big man was leading him forward purposefully. Ahead was a parked car and two men stood beside it.

Verago stopped. They were three quarters across the bridge. He turned and looked back. The Russian car on the other side had departed.

'Come on,' said Unterberg impatiently, 'let's get out of this.'

The two men beside the car stood silent when they arrived. Unterberg gave them a quick nod, then opened the door of the car.

'Pile in,' he said.

Verago got in. The driver in front reminded him curiously of the Russian driver in the other car. The same straight, erect, military bearing. The same soldierly appearance despite the civilian clothes.

Unterberg eased himself in beside Verago. The two men stood watching as the car moved off. Out of the window, Verago saw one of them raise a walky talky to his mouth.

'Who were they?' asked Verago.

'Friends.' It was final. You don't need to know.

Unterberg glanced at Verago.

'You OK, Tony? You look a little pale.'

'I'm alright,' replied Verago.

'Had a rough time, eh? Well, I guess you asked for it. You're lucky some people care . . .'

Verago opened his mouth to snarl at him. But then he controlled himself.

'What's happened to the trial?'

'It's all over,' said Unterberg. 'Finito. You can relax.'

'What the hell does that mean?'

'What I said. It's finished. He finally pleaded guilty.'

'Fuck!' cursed Verago with feeling. 'What did he get?'

364

'A discharge and six months. He'll be out by Christmas.'

'He's finished,' said Verago. 'Dishonourable discharge. You know what that means?'

'He should care. He wanted out anyway, didn't he?' Unterberg smiled cynically until he noticed Verago's expression. 'Jesus, Tony, what did you expect? You didn't show up in court, no word, no nothing. Of course they carried on.'

'Sure,' remarked Verago bitterly. 'That's what they wanted all along, wasn't it?'

'Oh, for pete's sake,' growled Unterberg. 'Stop bleeding to death.'

Verago turned his head away. He stared out at the Berlin streets, but he had no sense of direction, no idea where he was.

'Where am I going?' he asked at last.

'Take it easy, buddy.' Unterberg popped a stick of chewing gum into his mouth. 'I told you, you're safe now.'

'I . . . I've got to pick my things up from the Hilton. I've got a room there . . .'

'All taken care of,' said Unterberg. His jaws were moving rhythmically. 'And your bill. Cheap trip, eh?'

Verago looked out of the window again.

'You know what's going to happen here, don't you?' he said after a while, still staring out at the passing streets of Berlin.

'Tell me.' Unterberg's voice betrayed nothing.

'A million people, imprisoned behind a wall . . .'

'Really?' said Unterberg, chewing.

Verago looked him full in the face.

'You son of a bitch,' he said.

Thursday, August 10, 1961 – LONDON

The buzzer at the front door of her flat was followed by a sharp rapping sound, as if somebody was also knocking with a coin.

Laurie unlocked the door, but kept the chain on as she cautiously opened it. Through the gap, Ivanov smiled at her.

'My god,' she said, 'do you know what time it is?'

'After midnight, what does it matter?' he cried. 'Does it matter when one brings good news?'

Momentarily she hesitated. Then she pulled out the chain, and opened the door. In the corridor, a couple were standing, waiting for the lift.

She was in her pyjamas, and, almost defensively, she ran a hand through her hair, to tidy it.

'You should have phoned,' said Laurie reproachfully, and shut the door.

'I thought you would want to know right away,' said Ivanov. He walked past her into the living room. 'Tony Verago is safe. You'll soon be hearing from him, I feel.'

He beamed at her, and her relief was such she forgot her confusion at his sudden invasion.

'You sure he's alright?'

'Absolutely in one piece.'

'When did you hear?'

'Tonight.' He was amused by her eagerness. 'Through my people. That's why I came now.'

The colour flooded into her face. 'That calls for a drink,' she said.

He watched her slim figure as she went over and poured them two Armagnacs.

Then she raised her glass. 'Thank you for your help, Gene.'

He took a massive gulp without blinking.

'And now,' he said, 'I would like very much to seduce you.'

She laughed.

'No, I am serious,' he said solemnly. 'I would like nothing better than to come over, pick you up, and carry you to that bed in there. I think I told you once, I find you most desirable.'

It was so stylised she had to smile.

She played it lightly. 'Now, Gene . . . ' she began, but he cut her short.

'Unfortunately, that is not the way it is to be.'

Her violet eyes were suddenly hard.

'What do you mean?'

'I mean,' he said sadly, holding up his glass to the lamp and gazing into the amber liquor, 'that in this world nothing is for nothing. You understand?'

She suddenly understood very well, but all she said, coldly, was 'No.'

'Oh, you do, sweetheart, you do very well. It's not much to ask, is it?'

His mouth was still smiling, but nothing else.

'It is so sad,' he went on reflectively, 'that with you around, duty demands that I console myself with little playmates who don't mean that to me.'

And he snapped his fingers.

'Like Stephen's girls?' she said.

'Targets of opportunity, that's all,' he replied. 'Of no meaning to me.'

'Including the one you share with that British cabinet minister?' said Laurie.

He didn't betray any surprise that she knew.

'Oh, her. She's a good swimmer,' he said. 'No, Laurie, now you and I . . . '

He sighed again.

'It won't be made difficult for you, I promise,' he said encouragingly. 'We will know where you are, and when we need you, we will be in touch, and you can – repay us.'

She crossed her legs.

'Suppose,' she said, 'suppose I say no.'

'That would be very ungrateful,' he replied reproachfully. 'And not practical. After tonight.'

Her fingers tightened round her glass.

'You see, Laurie, what would Washington make of a photo showing you letting me into your apartment in your nightclothes?' The lips were still smiling.

'That's – that's rubbish,' she gasped.

'Not really,' he went on softly. 'That couple outside. Waiting for the elevator. Actually, friends of mine. They took a picture. It will be adequate, I assure you. And how will you explain Ivanov the spy being welcomed by you in that . . . '

He waved a hand airily at her attire. Nervously, she suddenly fastened the top button of her pyjama jacket where he had been looking at her cleavage.

'I am sorry,' he said, quite sincerely. 'But you know it's true. Nothing is for nothing.'

She stood up, and faced him.

'I never want to see you again,' she declared.

He also rose, and bowed rather gently.

'You see, that's what I meant,' he said. 'One sacrifices such beautiful relationships in the line of duty. Of course, we will meet again, and when it's not me, it will be somebody else. The bill will be paid. I know you always honour your debts. You're that kind of woman.'

She took a step forward, and then stopped.

'I'll let myself out,' said Ivanov.

'Just go,' said Laurie tersely.

'I keep thinking what a lucky man Tony Verago is,' he murmured. Then he left the room and she heard the flat door slam.

She stood very straight. She did not go to the window.

Perhaps Ivanov would have had a shock. For Laurie was smiling, a deadly smile. She had been well trained to play the game.

And for her, the real game was only just beginning.

WEST BERLIN

'Have you been to Berlin before?' asked Grierson.

'No,' Serena Howard answered curtly.

'It's an interesting place. Not my cup of tea, but it has its points.'

'Well, I don't suppose I'll be seeing much of it,' she said.

They were being driven in a car that had picked them up at Tempelhof Airport. She was wearing a smart travelling outfit and Grierson had the distinct impression that she kept edging away from him, as if she didn't want there to be any physical contact between them.

'You're lucky, you know,' he said.

'Really?' Her tone was cold.

'Absolutely. Do you know what Section One carries? Fourteen years.'

'Mr Grierson,' began Serena, 'the Official Secrets Act is a matter of supreme indifference to me.'

'It shouldn't be,' he said. He was still holding the folded copy of *The Times* he had picked up at Heathrow when he'd escorted her aboard the plane. He hadn't opened it during the flight. 'After all, that's what you would have been charged with. Section One. The big one.'

Serena smiled thinly.

'Mind you,' went on Grierson chattily, 'I'm glad it's worked out this way. You wouldn't have enjoyed Holloway. Much better that you join your friends.'

'Have you got a cigarette?' she asked, as if his statement didn't even merit a reply.

'Of course.' He held out a packet of Players. She took one, and he lit it for her. 'I don't suppose you'll be smoking many more of these. They don't go in for English cigarettes over there. Their taste runs more to American brands.'

'I'll manage,' said Serena. She was totally in control of herself.

'I'm sure you will,' purred Grierson.

She studiously ignored him and seemed engrossed staring out of the window. But after a while she asked him:

'Is it an exchange?'

'Is what, Miss Howard?'

'Me for somebody else?'

'Well,' said Grierson, 'in a way, perhaps. Not precisely.' He paused. 'You could say it's a way to get rid of an embarrassment. On both sides.'

She exhaled a cloud of smoke almost into his face. It could

have been taken as a studied insult, but Grierson didn't even blink.

'I'm curious,' said Serena. 'When did you first find out about me?'

He hesitated. The driver honked at a taxi that had just cut in.

'Oh,' said Grierson finally, 'quite some time ago.'

'How?'

'Your taste in boyfriends. One boyfriend in particular. We're also interested in girls who pick up American officers on highly classified work.'

Her eyes flashed. 'I didn't pick him up,' she snapped. 'You know very well . . . '

'All I know is that your relationship got rather intimate.'

'And then?'

Grierson looked at her. 'We found out the rest about you. Fancy a girl like you . . . ' He shook his head. 'Who made the first contact? You or . . . them?'

'You're really stupid,' Serena said, studying him as if he was someone beneath her contempt. 'You don't understand about commitment or caring, do you? I wanted to do something. Not just sit back and watch the world get blown up.'

'Oh really?' remarked Grierson drily. 'Touching idealism.'

'Fuck you!' she swore, and it was the first time he'd heard well-bred, Roedean-educated Serana Howard use an expletive.

Even when they had arrested her at her flat in Charlotte Street she had kept her cool. She'd even smiled a little when she'd seen them taking the bookshop downstairs apart, and not finding a thing, of course. But now, on the eve of her being handed over to her friends, there was an edginess about her, a growing tension.

'You still haven't told me who you're getting back for me.'

'It's rather funny,' smiled Grierson. 'Actually, you know him.'

She waited and he could see she was interested.

'You remember Captain Verago? The Army lawyer?'

She nodded, puzzled.

'Well, the Americans are getting him back.' He paused. 'If you ask me,' he continued silkily, 'they're getting a much better

370

bargain than your friends. Personally, Miss Howard, I wouldn't give tuppence for you.'

And at last, he unfolded *The Times* and read it for the rest of he journey.

Saturday, August 12, 1961 – LACONBURY

Three hours previously they had landed at Heathrow, and Unterberg had hustled Verago down the steps of the Viscount and straight into a car which had pulled up on the flight line as the plane taxied to a halt. It was a black, anonymous Chrysler and they were driven straight out of the airport.

Only later did Verago realise he had never cleared customs, never shown his passport.

'I didn't go through immigration,' he pointed out.

'So?' enquired Unterberg.

Which meant that, officially, Verago had never returned to England. The same thing had happened in Berlin when they'd left Tempelhof. There too Unterberg had hurried him through passport control, and no documents had been shown. So, as far as the record was concerned, he had never left Germany.

It worried Verago. Unterberg noticed his expression.

'Sometimes, Tony, it's best not to have too many things on paper,' he said cheerily.

Now they had arrived at Laconbury and the car's headlights picked out a bungalow as it crunched up the gravelled driveway, and stopped.

'There you are,' announced Unterberg, but did not move. Just ring the bell.'

Verago hesitated.

'Go on,' urged Unterberg, from the depths of the car. You're expected.'

Verago got out and slowly walked towards the bungalow. He

pressed the bell in the porch, and heard a glockenspiel sound inside. After a moment, the door opened.

'Come in, Captain Verago,' invited Croxford.

The general was wearing an Eisenhower blouse, and his single star flashed in the hall light.

'This way,' he said.

It was a large parlour, with modern furniture, but it had a utilitarian, assembly-line look about it. The only touches of individuality were a few ornaments, models of airplanes, and a big wooden propeller fixed to one wall.

'Sit down,' said the general. By the couch stood the command phone, which Croxford connected to a jack point in whatever room he was in in the house. He carried it around like a life-support system.

Verago didn't know if it was intentional, but a lamp on the table shone onto his face, making him uncomfortable.

'Tell me about Captain Kingston.'

'He's in bad shape, sir. He needs help.'

Croxford peered at Verago.

'You look as if you've had a rough time yourself.'

'It wasn't exactly a joy ride, sir.'

'But not as rough a time as Captain Kingston's having?'

'General, they've been trying to break him. Make him talk. He just won't give in . . . '

'I've read the OSI report,' said Croxford. 'What you told Unterberg. The way they're treating him. Not pleasant reading.' The general paused. 'He's a fine officer. A very good man.'

Verago thought of the gaunt, haggard wreck he had left behind. The bloody hands . . .

'Sir, we've got to get him out. Somehow. An exchange. Anything. Before it's too late . . . '

He was getting used to the light now. Croxford appeared more careworn.

'If it was possible . . . '

'Why isn't it?' demanded Verago.

He thought he had gone too far. But the general answered slowly: 'Because they've never admitted they've got him. He is presumed dead. And we can't prove otherwise.'

'But I've seen him,' Verago almost shouted. 'That's proof.'

'You?' Croxford's thin smile was chilling. 'You were never over there. That's the deal. That's how you got out. You were never across the border.'

'My passport . . . '

'Will be brand-new, courtesy of the State Department.'

Verago tried to control himself. 'You mean he's going to be left to rot.'

The general sat upright. 'Goddamn you, man, you think it's easy,' he roared, and then he got a grip on himself. 'You're pretty good at making moral judgements, Captain, aren't you? You think I like it, sitting here, knowing one of my men is being tortured?'

Verago swallowed. 'No sir.' He said it very quietly.

'You think it's a big sell-out, don't you?'

Verago was pale.

'Washington doesn't have to justify anything to me, and I don't have to justify anything to you, Captain, you got that? But I'll tell you one thing. Say a prayer every night that you don't have to make these decisions. Believe me.'

The general stood and Verago rose.

'You're very naive, Captain. Don't you realise we're doing a trapeze act, and there isn't a safety net. You talk about deals. Man, we're on a knife edge. Every minute, every hour. Men like Kingston are the price we're paying for this so-called peace, and people don't even know it.'

'There's a lot they don't know, sir,' said Verago boldly. 'Like East and West making a deal to divide Berlin. Like the Russians holding American airmen prisoner secretly. Like . . . '

'You're just about through, Captain,' cut in Croxford. Then the command phone buzzed, and he made a grab for it.

'Yes? OK.' He looked at his watch. 'As of . . . now. Check.'

He put the receiver down. 'We've gone on Bikini Alert,' he announced.

'*Bikini?*'

'Minimal combat readiness. A bikini doesn't cover very much. Only the essentials. Tonight, we're only keeping one eye open.'

'Part of the deal?' suggested Verago bitterly.

'That's all, Captain.'

Verago faced him. 'No sir. I'm going to tell his wife. I'm going to find Mrs Kingston, and tell her what I saw, the state he was in . . .'

'No way,' barked Croxford. 'You're not. That's a direct order. You're going to leave her in peace. Like hundreds of other wives who will never know, because it's . . . better that way.'

'Sir . . .' Verago started to say, and Croxford added:

'But I'll tell you this. Everything you've seen, everything you've heard over there is already known to Washington. The full report. If anything can be done about Kingston . . .'

He held out his hand.

'. . . they'll do it. That's what I wanted you to know.'

It was the first time in his life that Verago had shaken hands with a general. Croxford had a hard grip and it hurt. It hurt a lot.

THE CELL

'I've come to say goodbye,' announced Major Fokin.

Kingston slowly raised his head.

'Here,' said Fokin. He had a carton of 200 American cigarettes under his arm, and put them on the bunk beside Kingston. 'A little farewell present. To remember me by. Don't smoke them all at once.'

'I'm . . . I'm leaving here?' asked Kingston incredulously.

'Yes,' said Fokin.

Kingston's eyes started to swim. He hoped the tears wouldn't come. He didn't want this man to see him cry.

'When am I going?' whispered Kingston. He had a sore on his lip, but all physical aches and hurts didn't matter any more.

'In about half an hour,' replied Fokin.

'You mean, I'm really going home?' gasped Kingston, like man who could not believe his good fortune.

'Well,' began Fokin, and cleared his throat. 'I didn't say at. I said you're leaving here.'

The fear, the cold fear that had become so much a part of his fe took hold of Kingston.

'Not . . . not home,' he repeated, and he knew he would not e able to keep his composure much longer.

'I'm sorry if I misled you,' said Fokin. 'You're going mewhere else, but it isn't home. You see, your government as been asking us about you. They seem to think that instead f drowning in the Baltic, we captured you. A ridiculous atement to make. We have put the record straight, as you say. Ve have officially confirmed that your body has not been iscovered.'

Kingston gave a howl. It was a strangled, final cry of despair, lmost a scream.

Fokin grimaced.

'There is no need for that, my friend,' he chided, rather laintively. 'We have admired your self-discipline. Do not isappoint us now.'

The shaven-headed American sat dazed, rocking to and fro.

'What are you . . . going to do with me?' he finally asked in a w voice.

'I shouldn't really tell you, but we have become good friends, aven't we?' Foking smiled at him encouragingly. 'You are oing to a special camp. Quite far away. Behind the Urals. That why you won't see me again.'

'The . . . the Urals?'

Fokin nodded.

'For how long?' croaked Kingston.

'Let me give you a little advice. Don't think about time any nore. It has lost all meaning for you. You see, as far as the vorld is concerned, you died weeks ago.'

Standing outside the cell, Fokin speculated whether Kingston ould kill himself. He hoped not. One day it might still be seful to have him available.

Sunday, August 13, 1961 – BIKINI ALERT

It became known as 'Das Ding', 'the Thing'.

At 2 a.m., they appeared along the sector boundary from inside the East zone. The Volksarmee armoured cars took up position. The machine guns were set up, pointing at the West.

Then the lorries arrived, and out jumped steel-helmeted soldiers. They lugged the barbed-wire-garlanded Spanish steed into place – the wooden barriers that had, for weeks, been prepared, and wound with wire supplied by the West.

The Vopos stood by with their anti-riot water cannon.

The Grepos had been summoned to action stations two hours previously, and now they were at their posts, all along the boundary, stacking sand bags, erecting obstacles, cutting off access to and from the other side.

The line was ruthlessly drawn. The troopers entered houses ordering families to pack and get out, because the zonal boundary cut through their dining room, or bedroom, or garden. Flats, houses, a graveyard were cut in two. They bricked up the windows of the houses overlooking the Thing and no man's land was established.

The Vopos, fingers on the triggers of their machine guns, had 600 specially coached guard dogs, prowling in 270 'dog alleys', angry, vicious animals, trained to attack at the sound of a whistle.

A few late-night drivers trying to enter East Berlin were waved back. Red lanterns spelt out the message. The frontier was closed.

The last S-bahn train of the night came to a stop. It would not be running again that Sunday. The black-clad East German railroad police stood with fixed bayonets on the east side narding the lines and stations.

And there was not a single Russian to be seen. The troops, the police, the militia who scurried about setting up barricades, manning the observation points, the machine guns, were all East German.

That night a new order came into effect in East Berlin. It was called the Shooting of Line Jumpers Order and decreed that:

'If suspicious persons are in the vicinity of the zonal border, order them first to stop. If they continue in the direction of the border, fire two warning shots in the air. If this measure fails, shoot low to wound. If this fails, shoot to kill.'

Marshal Koniev sat in his operation headquarters, the large-scale mape of Berlin spread out before him, other sectional maps of the boundary on the walls. Every few minutes, the messages came in. Stetlitzerstrasse. Ebertstrasse. Heidelberger-strasse. The barriers had gone up. All according to schedule. Without interference. Without incident. Without anybody on the other side raising a finger.

Koniev sipped his hot lemon tea, and felt satisfied. His information had been correct, absolutely correct. As he had been promised, there would be no problem.

'They've got a Bikini alert on,' joked his intelligence officer, a Ukrainian colonel.

Koniev nodded.

Suddenly the quiet Berlin night was disturbed by harsh automatic chatter. But it wasn't from machine guns. Pneumatic drills were in action, making the holes into which the concrete foundations of the permanent wall were to be sunk.

It was a thorough job, and it had been well planned. 165.7 kilometres of death line, designed to frustrate all attempts to get across. Soon there would be 258 watchtowers, manned by more than 500 sentries with field glasses and guns, and 136 bunkers with machine guns loaded day and night. These men, ready to shoot on sight, became 'Grenzers'. Bordermen. It wasn't what the word meant that made it so nasty. It was the way people started saying it.

'People are beginning to gather on the Western side,'

reported one of Koniev's aides. 'Quite big crowds. There ma
be trouble.'

'There won't be,' replied the Marshal confidently.

And he was right.

Not a single shot was fired the night the longest wall
Europe made one million people prisoners in East Berlin.

The news that Berlin had been cut in two was given to Preside
Kennedy at 11 a.m.

He was week-ending at Hyannis Port, and he did not both
to return to Washington.

Dean Rusk, the Secretary of State, decided he might as we
take time off, and spent the afternoon at a baseball game
Griffith Stadium.

Prime Minister Harold Macmillan felt the best place to
was grouse shooting on the isolated Yorkshire moors.

General de Gaulle disappeared, incommunicado, to h
country estate, and stayed in retreat.

In the State Department operations centre, the contingen
folder for such a Berlin crisis was found to be empty.

And at 6 p.m. that evening, the US Mission in Berlin wa
ordered by Washington not to issue the protest it had planned
make to the Russians about the night's events.

The wall went up, and nobody really seemed very surprised.

It all went so smoothly that next day Nikita Khruschev too
off on his summer vacation.

SONNING

They sat by the Thames, on the terrace of the French Horn
Sonning, and for a long time they were silent.

Laurie had suggested they had dinner at the little Oxfordshi

llage where the swans cruised along the river, and the world
emed far away.

'You know,' said Laurie lazily, 'you still haven't told me
erything.'

'Nor have you.'

'Oh?'

'You work for them, don't you,' but it came out more as a
tement than a question.'

'Who's they?'

Verago smiled rather wearily.

'I don't know any more, but I can guess. The spooks.'

'Well,' said Laurie, 'it doesn't matter, does it? Not really?'

'No. Not really. Not any more.'

He stirred the coffee in the little demi-tasse.

'I've got thirty days leave,' he told her, studiously casual.

'Isn't that nice,' she said. 'So have I.'

Her violet eyes were dancing.

'And after that?' she enquired softly.

'I guess the Army's had enough of me in Europe. They're
assigning me to South East Asia.' One of the swans had
erged from the river and was strutting across the lawn in
ont of them. 'Colonel Ochs says Saigon will be a rest cure for
e.' He glanced across at her. 'What about you?'

'I go where I'm sent,' she said. 'But I can ask.'

'For what?'

'To be assigned to Saigon.'

'Do you want to?' Her answer was very important to him.

'I rather think I do, Tony,' she said slowly.

'I want to kiss you,' he said in a low voice.

'The night's young,' murmured Laurie. 'There's plenty of
ne. I won't run away.'

And they smiled at each other.

On the way back to London, they had the car radio on. The
ws bulletin was full of Berlin, and its fate.

'The bastards,' said Verago.

'Who?' she asked. 'Us or them?'

'Sometimes I wonder. Is there any difference? Ask a
rliner.'

379

She kept her eye on the dark road ahead. Then she said:
'What would you have done? Pressed the button?'
And the question wasn't answered.

On August 26, 1961, Prime Minister Harold Macmilla
remarked about the public outcry following the erection of t
Berlin Wall: *'I think it's all been got up by the Press.'*

And on June 26, 1963, President John F. Kennedy stood
West Berlin and declared: *'As a free man, I take pride in t
words "Ich bin ein Berliner".'*